The Man with Two Arms

The Man with Two Arms

BILLY LOMBARDO

THE OVERLOOK PRESS
New York

*For Jeff Lombardo: You were there from the
first pitch and you stayed the whole game.
This one's for you.*

This edition first published in hardcover in the United States in 2010 by

The Overlook Press, Peter Mayer Publishers, Inc.
141 Wooster Street
New York, NY 10012

Cataloging-in-Publication Data is available from the Library of Congress

Book design and typeformatting by Bernard Schleifer
Manufactured in the United States of America
FIRST EDITION
2 4 6 8 10 9 7 5 3 1
ISBN 978-1-59020-307-1

Be men, or be more than men. Be steady to your purposes and firm as a rock. This ice is not made of such stuff as your hearts may be; it is mutable and cannot withstand you if you say that it shall not. —MARY SHELLEY

Acknowledgments

I will always be grateful to the students, staff, and poetry and fiction faculty of Warren Wilson College's MFA Program for Writers, to the supporters, writers, and editors of *Polyphony H.S.* (the most important literary magazine in the world), and to the following champions, teachers, and friends: Fred Shafer, Anne Calcagno, Debbie Vetter, Trish Flassing, Tamara Fraser, Bob Clevenhagen, C.J. Hribal, David Haynes, Adria Bernardi, Debra Spark, Elizabeth Keegan, Steve Hayward, Mike Mulligan, Tom Hogan, Andy Dziadkowiec, Deanna farinas deLeon, Don Sullivan, Gina Frangello, Dan Fezzuoglio, Butch Whalen, Mike and Melanie O'Neill, Sean Deveney, Michael Pereira, Kate Greathead, Eric Davis, Christine Holloway, Seth Pedicini and Kane Lombardo, Jeff Lombardo, Amy Rita and the staff at *The Forest Park Post*, Veronica Vela, Courtney Federle, Adam Davis, Jeff Windus, Steven Coberly, Gina Frangello, Pamela Mack, Emily Warren, Elizabeth Flock, Robbie Deveney, Jim Joyce, Tom Bower, Aaron Schlechter, Tony Fitzpatrick, Mike Baron, Rachel Hecht, Joe Binder, Linda Buscani, Corrine Serritella, and Stuart Dybek.

First

Several miles west of the exact midpoint between Comiskey Park and Wrigley Field in a town named Forest Park, on a street named Lathrop, in the first floor apartment of a two-story made of lumber and red brick, at eleven o'clock, on the night of May 15, 1984, just fourteen hours before the world's greatest baseball player was born to the world, Henry Granville applied cocoa butter to the mountainous belly of Lori Granville, his very pregnant wife.

A woman named Judy Copeland lived in the flat above the Granvilles. She was 103 years old, and apart from the fact that she controlled the heat, by way of the Honeywell thermostat on her dining-room wall, in both apartments of the stiflingly warm two-flat, Henry had no complaints about the tenant upstairs. She made no noise, and as she was nearly deaf, neither did she complain of it. To offset the heat, Henry, who'd grown accustomed to sleeping on the right side of his wife during their courtship, switched to the left side, next to the window, when they bought the house on Lathrop and inherited Judy Copeland. Even on the coldest of winter nights, when February bit like teeth into the ears of the city, Henry slept with the window open.

Every afternoon Lori Granville checked on Judy and sat with her over tea.

"I'm off to tea with my lady-friend," Lori would say to Henry.

"Give her my regards," Henry would say in reply. "And tell her to turn the heat down, if she doesn't mind," he'd add.

It was Judy who had convinced Lori of the healing properties of cocoa butter. She'd outlived two sons and a daughter, and from the late August day when she learned of Lori's pregnancy, Judy had told her how she'd rubbed cocoa butter on her own belly through each of her pregnancies, and in this way had avoided the "hideous stretch marks" that had "plagued mothers since Eve."

The next time Lori visited her, the old woman asked if Lori had taken her advice regarding the cocoa butter. When Lori said she had meant to pick up a jar of it from the Healing Earth Resource Center in the city, but hadn't, the old woman flashed open her robe in order to show fully naked proof of the balm's healing powers. Lori did not mean to shriek in horror at Judy's sudden and wizened nudity, but she did. She also turned her head and, with her hands, shaded her eyes, which had been pressed shut anyway, but Judy Copeland refused to close her robe until she'd extracted Lori's promise to buy a jar of cocoa butter and begin applying it that very night.

"Okay, okay, okay," Lori promised, laughing through her nose at Judy's naked insistence.

"Excellent," the old woman said, and only then did she close her robe, smoothing it across her thighs as though wrinkles in cloth were a greater breach of propriety than her own bared skin. "Motherhood will provide you with your share of scars," Judy said. "No one needs to *see* them."

That same day, Judy also told Lori that while she was pregnant with Vincent, a doctor, and her oldest child, she read medical books aloud while she rubbed the butter on her belly; she listened to classical music while pregnant with Eloise, who'd become a concert pianist; and she read nothing but great world literature while pregnant with James, her youngest son.

"Did he become a novelist?" Lori asked.

"No," the old woman said. "He's a bit lazy. But he reads like mad and he's quite smart."

All of this Lori mentioned to Henry after having seen Judy Copeland naked. Even as she told Henry, she closed and held her hand over her eyes as if to fight off the thing she had already seen.

"She wouldn't let me leave until I promised to apply it every night for the duration of my pregnancy."

Henry laughed, his fingers twitching as he watched Lori's cocoa-buttered palm move in a slow and deliberate circle around her belly.

Henry had often pondered over the small part husbands played in the pregnancies of their wives, and so, where he felt he could participate more fully in Lori's pregnancy, he did. Between his classes, he phoned her from the high school science lab to ask if she needed anything from the grocery store on his way home. He sent flowers to her at the Oak Park bookstore where she worked part time, or brought them home, made fresh cuts at the bottom of the stems as he'd seen Lori do, filled appropriate vases with tepid water, arranged the flowers, and centered them on the dining room table. He baked bread on Sundays. He bought a throw rug for the kitchen and he took to his wife's clean-as-you-go approach around the house as well, towel-drying the dishes and putting them away immediately after washing them, rather than have them drip lazily on the dish rack. Seeing the cocoa butter as another opportunity to share in Lori's pregnancy, Henry held out his hand to receive the balm.

"Give it here, love," he said. "Let me have a go at it."

And as Henry rubbed his hands together to warm them for his wife's belly, what intrigued him most was this suggestion that Mrs. Copeland had guided the careers of her children by introducing them to medicine and music and literature before they were even born. Henry had heard of this phenomenon, of course—he'd read of it, or had seen it on a TV show—and long had wondered at the truth of it. He reflected on the myriad implications of prenatal education. There was something splendid and hopeful about it, the possibility of giving a child a head start before his first gulp of air.

Judy was old, of course, and whacky enough to bare her 103-year-old breasts to the world, but what if she was on to something? What if you could give shape to a child's future even as it was forming fingers and toes within its mother's womb? And if it were true, how might he shape the future of his own son? Would he pass along his interest in science, or encourage a career in medicine? Music? Art? What else might he give to his son?

What about baseball? Now there was a gift he could give. Baseball was about grace and beauty and character, it was about strength and achievement. It was about competition. It was about fathers and sons, and for the luckiest of mortals it was a way to *play* into adulthood. It was the best use of grass and dirt ever dreamed in the heads of men.

Yes, what about baseball? What would happen if he read baseball books to the child growing inside the mound of Lori's belly? If he watched baseball movies and read baseball articles and watched baseball games in the company of his pregnant wife? If he considered baseball strategies while rubbing cocoa butter on Lori's stomach? Could he somehow pass the gift of baseball to his child?

And on that first night of the cocoa butter—as Lori Granville, beneath the massaging warmth of Henry's fingers, slept the sleep of a child—Henry slowly and quietly swung his feet from the bed and walked to his desk in the unoccupied second bedroom, and ran his fingers along the spines of Lori's books until he found among them the only novel he'd brought to this life with Lori. He tilted it from the shelf and smoothed his hand over the paperback. In the lower right-hand corner, he ran his fingers over the teeth marks that Maude-Lynn, his long-dead cat, had chewed into the cover. He returned to his room then and knelt at the side of the bed, and with his face near Lori's stomach, his fingers moving over his wife in the shape of an infield, he opened the yellowing book to page one and began to whisper to his unborn son.

"Roy Hobbs pawed at the glass . . ."

Henry applied the cocoa butter on every evening of Lori's pregnancy, and if there wasn't a baseball game on television, he read from *The Natural* as he set his fingers to his wife's belly. There were nights that Lori read her magazines quietly while Henry tended to her, and there were nights she listened to him read. Often, Henry would look up from his book and find Lori gazing at him. He would look into the blue of Lori's eyes then and they would seem to sparkle. She would smile.

"You love baseball, don't you?" he would say. "I can see it in your eyes when you look at me that way."

And Lori might smile a tired smile—a mother's smile already—or she might nod and say, "Eh. Baseball's okay."

Many nights Lori would drift into sleep at the sound of her husband's voice, at the touch of his fingers. Sometimes she would speak, sleepily, of the day she had while Henry was teaching his science classes at University High.

And every evening, after Henry bent back a corner of a page to save his place, clicked the tin lid on the glass jar of cocoa butter and twisted it shut, he kissed his wife on the forehead.

"Goodnight, sweet Lorelei," he would say, and even in her sleep it seemed she would smile.

And it was here, several months later, on the night of May 15, 1984, following a line drive homerun off *Wonderboy* that shot into the sky like a star, that Henry prepared to rub cocoa butter on the belly of his pregnant wife for what would be the last time.

Sleepily, Lori arched her back off the bed to free her nightshirt from the weight of her body. Henry slipped it over her stomach, and to warm the dollop of lotion in his palms, passed his hands over a candle he had lighted on his wife's bedside table. Lori's arms were crossed rigidly over her night-shirted breasts. Her feet were flat on the bed and her knees raised. Henry touched one finger to Lori's belly and began to move it in the tiniest of clockwise motions. The small circle started at the hill of her round stomach and as Henry added more fingers to her, the circle opened to include more.

Henry wondered if the child inside of Lori could feel his fingers. He wondered if a fetus made sound.

Lori closed her eyes, and within minutes the tension responsible for the crossing of her arms began to fade, and Henry's hand widened gradually into a greater circle around his wife. As he reached the bottom of her belly, the heels of Lori's feet began to inch away from her along the bed sheet. At the top of the circle, Henry brushed the tips of his fingers against the southern curve of Lori's breasts and the rigid lock of her arms across her chest loosened more. On each return of Henry's hand to the bottom of her belly, Lori's heels moved closer to the foot of the bed, and on each return to the top, Henry slipped his hand further into Lori's nightshirt and whispered his fingers against her breasts more certainly, and the tension in Lori's body diminished until her knees were lowered completely, and her arms had fallen softly to the bed at her sides.

For Henry to hear the gentle, throaty hums escape from Lori's lips was to be paid handsomely in a kind of poetry or song. The sounds were a re-acceptance of a proposal, a first kiss, a wedding, a promise of love and a request for more, and so Henry brought Lori's legs into the ring of his touch, ran his fingernails along the inside of her thighs and slowly they opened to him, and when they did, he knelt between them, and began to circle Lori with both hands. Henry wished for more hands, then. He wanted Lori to feel that his love had many hands, that there was neither beginning nor end to them, that there could be hands on the swell of her belly and on her hips, and hands moving toward her breasts and smoothing across the hem of her panties as well. He wanted hands to brush her hair, and hands to rub her feet, fingers to trace along her legs.

When Henry's fingers were deep beneath Lori's shirt, Lori moaned as though her breasts had been waiting for the fullness of his hands for years. She raised her hips and lifted herself to the possibility that Henry might have another hand available for her there. Henry circled Lori's breasts as she lifted and lowered her hips like a kind of calling. Her hands moved toward her hips then. Her fingers closed around the hem of her underwear and she tugged them downward.

"Take these, Henry," she said, and some of Henry's hands swirled in the eddy he had set into motion above at her breasts, and some of them pressed into the place newly revealed, and some of them pulled gently at the material Lori felt slip down her legs and brush against her toes. Henry undressed and returned to kneel between her legs. Lori began to guide Henry inside of her, then, but barely entering her, Henry put his fingers to where Lori's hands met her wrists and he set them at her side. He held himself there, with his hands on her hips he held himself at the very edge of his wife, and when Lori lifted herself to more of him, he gave himself to her in quantities that were capricious and unpredictable; one offering at a depth nearly imperceptible from the one before, and another that stopped her breath.

They made love. Sweetly, as they always did, and slowly as they sometimes did, and the sounds Lori made as she breathed through her mouth were so like the sounds that emerged between tears that Henry opened his eyes several times to assure himself that she was not crying, or if she *was*, that it was for something other than sadness.

Inside her, Henry pressed and pulled within the rhythms of the murmuring song of her breath, and soon it felt to him as though she were breathing at all only because of him. If he were tall enough to kiss her over the mountain of her belly he would have done so. He would have stood by her side and kissed her, breathed into her mouth—that much life he felt he had, enough life for both of them. All three of them. Several times he began pulling himself from her, slowly and gently, in order kiss her, but so responsible did he feel for her breathing that he returned each time to a greater depth.

And Lori put her hands to the side of her belly, and Henry laid his hands upon hers, while her song moved into her throat, and then into her chest, and her song moved into her stomach and through their almostchild, and into Henry, too, until it reached his own throat and his own eyes, and Lori laced her fingers into Henry's and pulled him deeper until Lori and Henry were both so filled with breath and song and life, that neither could contain it any longer. Henry trembled with all of it, and Lori shuddered and gasped. Her body quaked from her legs to her shoulders.

The shudder, the gasp, the quake that came from Lori turned out to mean a number of things, for within minutes they were on their way, in an easy and quiet rain, to Good Samaritan Hospital.

With the intermittent and rubbery squeakings of the windshield wipers marking time, Henry turned onto the entrance ramp of the

Eisenhower Expressway, wondering if any man in the history of the world had ever made love to his wife so close in time to the birth of their child.

Leaning back in her seat and smoothing her hands on her stomach, Lori looked over her shoulder at the buckle of the seat belt, and then at Henry.

"Be careful, Henry," she said.

Henry angled the rearview mirror until their eyes met in the parallelogram of silvery glass. Lori smiled at him there, her eyes so blue they made him look again.

Were they blue enough, Henry wondered, then, to dominate the brown of his own eyes, given to him by his parents, now gone. What, Henry wondered, of Lori, would he give to his son if the choice were his to make?

For starters she had made a home of nothing. When they were looking to buy a home and first viewed at the two-flat, Henry told Lori he could never live there.

"Don't you think it's kind of dumpy?" he'd said.

"Oh my, no," Lori replied. "You can't see how beautiful it will be, can you?"

So Lori sketched blueprints with colored pencils, drew perfect lines without the aid of a straightedge, she'd shown him precisely how beautiful it would be, and it was. To an empty and ugly place, she'd brought curtains and sheets and tablecloths, she'd wallpapered and painted, and tacked hangings to walls, she brought plates and cups and silverware. She changed the outlet covers and made a home of nothing.

And when she was away—once for a long weekend with her girlfriends from school, and once for a visit back east—the house on Lathrop Street didn't even seem like a home to Henry. It was an apartment when she was away, and nothing seemed right.

If the choice were his to make, Henry would have this be among Lori's gifts to their child.

The driveway to the hospital circled around a flower garden where hundreds of tulips, yellow and red, bloomed in the cones of light from the driveway lampposts.

"Opening Day tulips," Henry said, and Lori, leaning back in the passenger seat, breathing deliberately and massaging circles into her belly, smiled. She knew the story of the tulips.

Henry Granville had only been to one Opening Day baseball game as a child, for it had fallen on the rarest of all afternoons: a Saturday on which his father was not working. Charles Granville had purchased the tickets unexpectedly, and to Henry's breath-stealing delight, and as they'd walked out of the Ramova Grill on their way to the corner to catch a bus to the ballpark, Charles pointed out to his young son that the tulip bulbs in the public flower pots along Halsted Street had chosen, above every other day, that very cold and damp opening day of April to bloom.

"That's a special breed of tulips there, Henry," Charles had said. "Opening Day tulips. They blossom at noon on the first day of the baseball season."

"How do they know it's Opening Day?" young Henry asked.

"One of the great mysteries of the world," Charles said. "They just know it, Henry. They can feel it in the dirt.

Some part of Henry still believed his father. Somehow the tulips felt it in the dirt, the ancient earth inextricably connected to the dirt upon which every baseball game had ever been played, in communication with history itself, with the men of yore who played the game long before Charles Granville had come along. Earth memory.

And it occurred to Henry, as he entered the revolving doors of the hospital, that he would be a father himself when he next saw the driveway tulips. And he wondered at the father he might become.

Henry sat in the chair at Lori's bedside through the night, holding her hand as he faded into patches of sleep, and dreamed in scraps of dreams. In one of them, he sat at the end of a dugout bench next to a dozen babies wearing baseball uniforms, pacifiers pulsating in their mouths as they watched the opposing team of grown men take batting practice on the field.

One dream instant later, he was having a catch with the birthing center nurse, whom he'd woven into his dream. He flinched awake just

as she threw a ball his way, and there was Lori's smiling face, her hair
perfect—she was about to have a baby and her hair was perfect—a
thousand shades of yellow between white and brown, a luminous frame
around the impossible blue of her eyes. Henry pressed his palm over
his own hair, greatly misshapen by the pillow he'd made of his jacket.

Within minutes he drifted off to sleep again, and when he woke
up Lori was watching him and smiling again; he felt as though he'd
been playing baseball while his wife was preparing to give birth.

"You okay, honey?" he said.

"I'm fine, sweetie," she said. "Go back to sleep."

"Oh, I wasn't sleeping," he lied. "Wasn't sleeping at all," and he
drifted again into some inning of another reverie.

The baseball dreams could not be helped. Henry could not rid
himself of thoughts of baseball during the day and dreams of it at
night. He simply couldn't wait for the day he would finally have a
catch with his son—or rather, with his *child*, for the possibility of a
daughter had also occurred to Henry. He hoped to have a catch with
his son whether he turned out to be a boy or a girl. A thousand times
during his wife's pregnancy he'd imagined it.

Lori found him once, standing in the living room with his eyes
closed, throwing an imaginary ball, catching with an imaginary baseball glove, having a catch with an imaginary son. She watched him for
a minute before saying anything.

"What are you doing, Henry?" she finally asked, and at the sound
of her voice, Henry shook himself from his trance.

"What? Oh. Just stretching," he said.

Propped up against pillows in the birthing center, Lori slept a restless sleep, waking twice to pains in her lower abdomen that were
sharp enough to bring tears to her eyes. But for this, the Granvilles'
night in the hospital room passed without event. Aloud, she wondered
if they had come to the hospital too soon. And night became day.

It was just before 1PM when Henry asked the nurse on dayshift if
she wouldn't mind turning on the television so they might watch the

Cubs game. When she had introduced herself to the Granvilles as "Nurse Nan," she kept her eyes closed but raised her eyebrows as if to suggest an insistence on this exact address. She reminded Henry, in fact, of his department chair at U-High, a college classmate of Henry's who had gone on for his doctorate degree, and insisted that his department members called him "Doctor David."

Nurse Nan was a stern and hearty woman with thick ankles, and a blue sweater pulled tight across her chest. She looked at Henry, nodding and shaking her head at once, as though his question wwa final proof of the juvenility of men.

"You're kidding, right?" she said.

Henry looked at the nurse, then at Lori, then back at the nurse.

"Kidding about what?" he said.

Nurse Nan looked at Lori, who only smiled and shrugged, for she had signed on for life with Henry, and baseball came with him.

"I'll get the remote," the nurse grunted, and she pounded her soft-soled shoes out of the room.

Henry looked at the wall clock.

"One o'clock on the button, love," he said, and aloud he considered the major league implications of that point in time; which is to say, that a baseball game would soon be played.

"As we sit here, Lori," he said, "the Chicago Cubs are in the final minutes of preparation before their game against the Pirates."

He slipped his hand from under Lori's and noted the pairings of these teams on the back of a receipt he pulled from his pocket. Someday, he would tell his son what teams were playing baseball on the day he was born; it would be an excellent thing for a boy to know.

And wouldn't it be something, he thought, if these particular pairings turned out to be significant? Like some kind of foreshadowing of events in the life of his son, who would be born this very day? Maybe he would play for the Cubs one day, or the Sox. Wouldn't that be something? Or even the Tigers or Pirates! That would be fine as well.

Henry slipped his hand under his wife's hand again, and imagined a television sportscaster calling his son's name as he walked to the plate. *And here he is, folks. Stepping up to the plate with one out and runners on the corners . . .*

He had only moved his lips to the shape of this silent sentence he had formed in his head, but when he came to the name of the young man who stepped to the plate, he announced, "Danny Granville!" It was an excellent baseball name, strong and definite, like the indisputable answer to a question that had puzzled men for ages.

Lori's eyes had been closed, but she opened them at these words from her husband's mouth and she wrinkled her brow.

"What did you say?"

"Oh, nothing, honey. I was just thinking about the baby," he said.

Lori had loved the name Daniel since she was a child and had heard it spoken by a teacher who read a bible story to Lori and her classmates. *Daniel* spoke of beauty and honor and glory, and if they had a girl . . . why, the name Danielle stood for much the same, and Henry had agreed.

"Did you say *Danny?*" Lori Granville asked. Even though she hated her own given name, *Lorelei,* she'd made it clear to Henry that their child would be called by his or her own formal name—*Daniel* or *Danielle*—not by some shortened version of it.

"Did I?" Henry said.

Nurse Nan returned without the remote control in her hand. She slid a chair to the corner of the room where the television hung from the ceiling, pinched her stiff skirt above her knees and ascended the chair to turn on the game.

"Channel nine," Henry said, and the hearty nurse glared over her shoulder at him. "Please," Henry added, and for his wife's entertainment, he chewed on his fingers in mock trembling at the sternness of Nurse Nan.

It was a sunny afternoon and Henry sat at Lori's side holding her hand, warm and thin and soft. He wondered how other women handled the births of their children. Didn't they scream expletives and curse the days their husbands were born? Wasn't their hair pasted sweatily to their heads? Didn't the veins in their necks bulge blue and struggle angrily for release?

But Lori was a yellow flower with perfect hair, and Henry was the luckiest guy in the world: his child would be born on this day, and there were more than a hundred and forty baseball games left to the summer. And when the pinprick of light sparked in the center of the television, the sunny afternoon, the hope of summer and the bloom and promise of new life, the tumbling and flighty excitement of his love for Lori and all of the rest of it fluttered in his head like so many butterflies in those seconds before a baseball game.

As the first pitch was thrown, Lori's hand rested gently in Henry's, but before the second crossed the plate—she felt another sharp pain in her lower abdomen as the life in her womb began to declare, with great pressure against the walls of its tiny space, that it was ready for the world—Lori clutched Henry's hand, and from that moment, through the next eighteen minutes, though the warmth of her hand remained, the gentle of it abandoned her entirely. As Lori pushed and pulled at the birthing center air through the sibilant filter of her clenched and muscled lips, Henry grimaced at the crush of her slender grip.

But neither the force of her white-boned hold on his hand, nor the baseball game on the television was enough to turn Henry's eyes from the miracle taking place on the birthing center bed.

He would remember this: the dark-haired and shining crown of the baby's head, the tiny arms of new life that seemed to pull its way into the world, the doctor holding a boy in his hands in such a way that the infant, it seemed to Henry, was lifted into the striped shafts of sunlight split into thin bars by the vertical blinds of the birthing center window.

Henry, laughing and crying, wondered if he was speaking, wondering if any words were coming from him, and Lori smiled at Henry as though she were proud of him, and the doctor who held the child was saying something, and the nurse who held surgical scissors in her hands was saying something else, and Henry walked to his wife and he kissed her.

"I love you, Lori." And he laughed and he cried and he told her he loved her again.

"I love you, too, sweetie," Lori said, and she smoothed his hair from his brow. "Cut the cord, Henry," she said. "The doctor is waiting for you to cut the cord."

Henry wiped his eyes, and accepted the surgical scissors from the nurse. When he placed the vee of the tool against the umbilical cord and snipped, it felt as though he were cutting through bread dough.

Lori turned her head and cried.

The nurse attached a plastic clip to the end of the umbilical section that remained, and accepted the baby from the doctor's hands. She swaddled him in a cradle of towels and placed him on a tiny domed bed at Lori's side. Under the warming light of the dome, the baby was squinting and serious, a furrowed brow with puffy slits for eyes. He was wrinkles and shadows, and his wriggling fingers and toes seemed to grapple at something. A word perhaps. He was the tiniest man Henry had ever seen, and he seemed to be searching for some absent thing around which he might wrap his fingers, some missing thing he was at the verge of. It would not have surprised Henry to hear his newborn son speak just then, to hear him declare some profound or poetic thing, if he could wrap his fingers around it.

Behind Henry, the collective cheer of tens of thousands of men, women, and children, rose from the television screen in the corner of the room. Henry held Lori's hand—once again gentle—in his, and glanced over his shoulder at the sound. He turned then, and touched his finger to the open palm of his newborn son, and felt five tiny fingers—thin lines of bone, muscle, and skin—close around his finger, and Henry smiled.

"The Cubs are up by one, Danny Boy," he whispered. "Bottom of the first."

Second

EVEN HENRY GRANVILLE KNEW THAT THE NEXT DAY WAS TOO EARLY to take his son to a Cubs game—even if the sun were out, which it was not, and even if it weren't cold, which it was—for on May 17, 1984, Danny Granville was beginning only his second day of life.

Which is not to say it didn't cross Henry's mind, but he waited as long as he could—two weeks, in fact—before asking Lori if he could take Danny to a game.

"Why don't you take someone from work?" she had said. "Why don't you take Doctor David?"

She didn't look at Henry as she raised this option.

"Because you're not taking Danny," she said. "Period."

Lori held her infant son against her shoulder, and turned away from Henry, heading into the kitchen.

During a nine-game stretch of home games late that May, Henry went to three games by himself. Nothing against Doctor David, but if Danny couldn't come, and Lori couldn't come, Henry would just as soon keep the seat next to him open.

If any of his fellow fans in the field box seats along the third base side asked Henry why he didn't bring anyone with him, he'd tell them he was saving the seat for his son, and the women would moan sweetly, and the men would nod their heads.

Henry watched those games unfold as though he'd left his own heart back at home with Lori and Danny. He kept score with a joyless spirit, his thoughts drifting always toward the great emptiness of the seat next to him.

But Lori wouldn't have it any other way. It was too hot in the sun and too cold in the shade. There was the chance of thrown bats, drunken fans, and the inescapable disruption to Danny's napping schedule. There was also the constant threat of foul balls bulleted into the stands.

"It's a wonder we don't hear about fans being killed at baseball games more often," Lori had said on one occasion of Henry's pleadings. "And idiots who would knock over old ladies to get their paws on a two-dollar souvenir."

"More like eight dollars," Henry had said, and as the words hung in the air between them he wished he could drag them back.

"What?" Lori said.

"Never mind," Henry said.

"No. What did you say?"

"Baseballs are like eight or nine bucks," Henry said. "They're more expensive than you think," and Lori looked at him as though he'd just proved her point.

Still, it was Henry's nature to wake up with a hopeful heart on the mornings of home games. But every time he pleaded with her to allow him Danny's company at Wrigley Field, promising to keep him safe and comfortable, Lori put her foot down in some similar way.

The toughest period for Henry to get through was a week of brilliant weather that mid June carried into Chicago like a new bride. While flowers bloomed, birds chirped, and girls fell in love, the Expos and the Phillies would be in town for seven days of baseball. On the first of those beautiful days, Henry kissed Lori's forehead to wake her up to petition her support.

"Morning, sweetie," he said.

"Let me guess," Lori said as she rubbed the sleep from her eyes. "The Cubs are home today."

"Not only that," Henry said, "But it's simply gorgeous outside."

"He's barely a month old," Lori said.

"He'll be a month old tomorrow," Henry said, and Lori rolled over.

At breakfast that morning, Lori held the Tempo section of the Tribune between them and sipped her coffee. Danny rocked in his mechanical swing at her side, and while Henry stared through the newspaper at her, Lori flipped through pages and reached blindly for her coffee on the table.

Finally, she set the Tribune on her lap and sighed.

"Did I ever tell you of the game my father took me to at Wrigley?" she asked.

Henry shook his head.

"It was June." Lori smoothed the fold in the Tempo section. "The afternoon began with a glorious sun and a cloudless sky, just like this one. But by the bottom of the fourth inning, the clouds had rolled in and a cold front came over the city. My teeth were chattering and my lips were blue, and while I froze, my father insisted on staying until the last pitch of the game."

"Your lips could not have been blue in June," Henry said.

"Henry," she said again. "My lips were blue."

And on went Lori. She'd brought along her winter coat and a blanket on the sound advice of her mother, and still it was so cold she drank eight cups of piping hot chocolate, as much for the warmth of the cup in her hands as for its powers to warm within.

"My lasting memory of the game itself," she said, "is shivering. Shivering and peeing between each inning because of all the hot chocolate."

Henry was certain that Lori's story relied heavily on hyperbole, and he was doubtful that its temporal setting was June. Though it still got chilly in the shade during early summer, it was never enough to make a girl go blue. April could do that, but not June. But there was no arguing against Lori's belief that a baby could freeze to death on a summer day at Wrigley.

Six days in a row Henry approached Lori with a similar kiss on the forehead and a similar report on the weather, and each discussion ended the same way.

"Please. Not yet," Lori would say. "Let's just wait a bit longer, sweetie."

"You used to like baseball," Henry said.

"You know it's not that, Henry," she said.

On the seventh day of that home game stretch, Lori lost her patience with Henry.

"*Please*, Henry," she said. "I shouldn't have to explain this to you every day. It is my responsibility to protect Danny. One would think you would see it as your responsibility as well."

"That's not fair," Henry said.

"Please, Henry. He's an *infant*. Enough of the baseball." Lori turned in her bed to her side and snapped the blanket over her shoulder.

Turned away from Henry, she continued speaking from her cocoon of blankets. "Babies are fragile," she said. "They're not like animals."

If Henry, who taught biology, Primate Behavior and Ecology, and the Social Life of Animals at University High, had said the first thing that came to his mind, he would have told Lori that her statement was so profoundly absurd that he didn't know where to begin his response.

Actually, he might have said, *they are animals*. We are all animals in fact. Members of the highest order of mammals, to be honest. Anthropoid primates. We share 98.5 percent of our DNA with chimpanzees. We are very much animals, he might have said.

What bothered him more than the weakness of Lori's argument, though, was her implication that though Henry might know more about animals than Lori, when it came to *human* babies, Lori was the expert, and Henry should leave such decisions to the experts. Her entire argument presumed the validity of maternal instinct. People used the term so loosely and with such confidence that society had come to believe that women had access to inherent information that allowed them to deal with babies more effectively than men.

Lori rose and walked to the living room while Henry remained silent on the bed.

Henry might have told his wife, in fact, that there was some evidence, in the world *outside* of their little house on Lathrop Street, to suggest a *disconnection* between mothers and their offspring. He might have told her that half of all bird mammal babies died before being weaned. If Lori needed evidence in the human world, there were the Maya who showed little if any emotional attachment to their children, as a matter of course, for at least several weeks after their birth. For millennia, women had been commonly forced to abandon their infants—selection pressure for the emotional detachment. Truth be told, Henry could probably have argued just as sufficiently on the side of *paternal* instinct.

Henry might also have defended himself against her suggestion that he was limited in his knowledge of the human animal. He hadn't studied mammals all his life without making connections to behavior in the human world. He'd learned a thing or two about people.

Henry made the bed before walking out of the bedroom to Lori on the couch. She was looking out the window with her leg crossed away from Henry. She adjusted the pillows at her side—apologetically, Henry thought. As though she were rethinking things.

Lori started to circle her palm over her belly—a habit that must have been hard to break after several months—but stopped immediately as her fingers touched her sundress. During her pregnancy, she had told Henry there were times she felt Danny actually growing inside her. In her seventh month, for three days straight, she'd bumped into the corner of her dresser as she walked into their bedroom, and just as soon as she adjusted to a new spatial relationship with the furniture, her belly had grown just enough to make her bump against it again. At first she laughed at the blunder, but seamlessly then, she cried.

From his end of the couch, Henry looked into Danny's room. The mobile of plastic baseballs moved in slow circles above him, his perfect little body rising and falling with the deeper breath of sleep, his head turned sweetly to the side, his tiny fingers curling around nothing.

At the other end of the sofa, Lori sat with her empty belly. She had nothing to circle her hands around. She had only the skirt of her dress to smooth across her lap, only the sleeve of the couch to adjust. And Henry's once irritated silence became something less certain as he watched Lori soften before him.

Silently he considered the possibility that a current of some larger truth might be rippling sadly beneath Lori's argument.

He sidled close to Lori, reached his arm across her, and Lori leaned her head into Henry's shoulder.

"Sorry, honey," he said. "We can wait a bit."

But between the too cool of June and the too hot of July and August, it seemed there was no weather suitable for an infant and his father at a Cubs game. Countless times, Henry imagined himself at Wrigley Field, keeping score over Danny's back as he slept against Henry's chest, the swirl of Danny's thin hair at the crown of his head, his sweet breath tickling Henry's neck. Sometimes, within the parameters of that reverie, Danny transformed into a young boy, and Henry could see himself handing a box of Cracker Jacks to Danny during the seventh inning stretch.

Henry made the best of the summer. He bought a scorebook from Hildebrand's Sports and sat on the couch in front of the television with Danny, and from that couch he bounced to his feet at the introduction of the National Anthem and sang as heartily as he could without crying, for the National Anthem rarely failed to move Henry Granville to the verge of tears. He sang the song with a fighter's heart, as though the ancient memory of war belonged as much to him as to any man.

And as the days moved on, Henry began to wonder if he hadn't unwittingly passed something of his connection to the anthem to his infant son, for he soon became aware of a difference in Danny's attention to the song, or perhaps to something in the voice of his father as he sang it. He would stop squirming on his blanket and sounds like cooing would emerge from his perfect lips.

Just before a late August home game against the Atlanta Braves, to Henry's great surprise, Danny cried at hearing the National Anthem. As Henry watched the flag on the rooftop of the field ripple in the Wrigley breeze, he felt Danny's eyes upon him, and as the tears puddled in his own eyes, Danny's seemed to puddle as well. There was little sound to this infant weeping, only something like a hum or a moan mumbled through his tiny lips. He touched the tips of his fingers to each other and he barely moved on his blanket.

His eyes awash with tears, his chest filled with a thousand prides—through the red glare of the rockets and the bursting of the bombs, through the dawn's early light, and all of the other proof upon which the flag depended—Henry stood as stiffly as a foot soldier with his hand on the heavy throb of his fatherheart, and when the song ended he wiped his son's eyes, and then his own, and together they watched the game.

Through the summer, from this front row seat on the couch, Danny squirmed on his blanket with his feet in his mouth, and Henry mostly groaned as the Cubs' hovered at .500 baseball. He groaned at base-running errors and missed opportunities, he urged the boys to play to their potential, he questioned line-ups, chewed his fingernails, and argued with the umpires for their inconsistent strike zones and dubious calls, and when the cameras followed the track of a foul ball hit near section 104, Henry would run to the television and tap his fingers to the section closest to his seats. "That's where our tickets are, Danny," he'd say. "Right there. Wait'll you see this place! It's gonna be great!"

Between innings Henry picked Danny up and marveled at the strength of his legs. He tossed him in the air and caught him on the way down. He warmed formula and changed Danny's diapers to Henry's wet and sloppy play-by-play imitation of Harry Caray's voice, which always made Danny laugh.

Henry was happy when the Cubs won and sad when they lost, but Danny was always there at the end of the game, and so the sadness was fleeting.

Danny was four months old on a perfect Saturday morning in mid-September when, after a morning's worth of pleadings, Lori finally allowed Henry to take Danny to his first major league baseball game.

Henry had changed Danny's diaper, fed him, and taken him for a half-hour walk in his stroller so that Lori could sleep in. When he returned she was sitting at the kitchen table with a cup of coffee. Henry took her hand in his and he led her to the front door.

He put one arm across her shoulder and swept the other across the blue-collar landscape to encompass the entire city. "It's crazy beautiful outside," he said. "In all of his life there may never be a better day to take Danny to a Cubs game."

He pulled two tickets for the game from the pocket of his shirt and swung them slowly before her eyes like a hypnotist, and when Lori smiled—softening—Henry quickly turned his argument to the robust health of their son.

"His legs are Sequoias," he said. "And he hasn't sniffled once since the day he was born."

And then Henry, who'd always marveled at the precocity of the ungulates of the Serengeti, likened Danny to the precocial wildebeest, which walked within fifteen minutes of its birth and ran with the pack, chasing the rain within days of its arrival into the world. He returned the tickets to his shirt pocket and pressed Lori's hands against them.

But in the end it was not the spectacular weather that moved Lori to a change of heart. Neither was it hypnotism or logic. Henry Granville's best argument, in fact, was one he never articulated, for it was this that struck Lori as she stood between her son and the man from whom the boy had come: beneath her hand at Henry's chest, beyond the tickets that peaked from the hemmed opening of the pocket of his shirt, was the beating and tender heart of Henry Granville, at once boyish and fatherly. And Lori felt again what she'd felt innumerable times since the day of Danny's birth: that in all of the world—of all the millions and millions of hearts in the world—there were only two that pumped purely with love for a baby named Danny Granville. Her own heart, of course, was one of them. And the other belonged to Henry.

Even so, as she overdressed Danny and packed his commodious baby bag with a great miracle of things, Lori questioned and lectured and warned her husband.

"You will not keep score," she said. And Henry nodded.

"And don't you dare take your eyes off him, Henry. Not for a second."

He would not.

"No Cracker Jacks, either."

"You mean *for Danny?*" he said.

"Yes," Lori said.

"That would be crazy. I share my Cracker Jacks with no one."

"Promise me, Henry."

"I promise," he said.

And Lori stuffed Danny's winter coat into his baby bag, topped it off with an extra bottle, two pacifiers, a rattle toy, and a scarf. She moistened a third pacifier in her own mouth, held it in her hand, kissed Danny twice, and placed the plug in his lips.

Behind Lori, Henry danced a silent victory dance, turned around with his arms in the air and pumped his hands into fists of celebration.

Henry opened the door of the dull gray 1984 Volvo, and set Danny's carrier into the back seat. They rode down Division to Western and turned south toward Addison. When he turned east on Addison, Henry adjusted the rear view mirror to find Danny staring up at him. Henry pointed out the open passenger window.

"Take a good look out there, Danny," he said. "There's no other city like it in the world."

They passed sidewalks lined with rectangles of grass. Tall maple trees stood sentry to the brown brick two-flats behind them. Past Oakley Avenue, where the traffic stopped for more than a minute, the roots of a giant oak—ancient muscles attached to some deeper thing— buckled the sidewalk like a mistake.

Henry turned on Racine, and into an alley to escape the sluggishness of Addison Avenue. Past the first garage, an old woman wearing a hairnet and a black dress held the lid of a garbage drum in one hand and a grease-stained shopping bag in the other. She looked at Henry and then at Danny in the back seat. She held her gaze as they passed.

Behind them, the lid of the drum closed definitely. Two houses down, a grapevine, thick with leaves and fruit, finished a vegetable garden, and beyond it, a garage door was open. Inside, legs splayed from under a wheel-less car resting on cinder blocks. In the middle of the alley a boy faced a netless basketball hoop nailed to a telephone pole. He slapped a basketball in his hands. Another boy—dirty blond hair to his shoulders—sat on a garbage can with his arm in a plaster cast. The rubber heels of his sneakers thumping against the drum. Their teenaged heads swiveled slowly as the Granvilles passed.

Henry parked north of Waveland Avenue, unclicked Danny's carrier from the car seat, and carried him, switching him from one arm to the other until they reached Clark and Addison. There, he unbuckled Danny from his carrier and held him facing the stadium. Before them, Wrigley's red banner boasted like a flag against the green-trimmed white of the stadium.

Past the turnstile, Henry walked with Danny, back in his carrier, to the gravel-throated cry of the scorecard and program salesman.

"First thing you do when you get inside the park, Danny Boy," he said, "is get yourself one of these." He handed a dollar to the man and waved the scorecard at Danny, who quick-blinked his brown eyes and gulped at the breeze from the buckled security of his infant seat.

"Same as at home, but this is official," he said.

Henry held Danny's carrier in his hands before him like a birthday cake, so that Danny might see everything as Henry did. He knew enough about the brain to know that Danny wouldn't remember this day, but he wondered what was happening in his head right now. Could he smell the popcorn and the hotdog steamer? Could he feel the basement cool of these bowels of Wrigley? Could he see through his infant eyes that he was in a place unlike any other he had been? Did he know that these colors, these grays and greens, these blues and whites of Wrigley, were unlike the colors of any other place? Could he feel the shadows and the histories mixed into them? Was it possible, Henry wondered—as the chambered sounds of these basemented voices gave way to the open air of the stadium peppered with the cracks and pops and thuds of batting practice—that a boy was never too young to take in these sounds and colors and smells of baseball and save them until he was capable of shaping them into memory?

Slowly, Henry ascended the steps at the entrance to the field box seats. He held the carrier that held the weight of Danny Granville high above him, like an offering into the square of light that opened into the stadium. He felt the weight of Danny's beefy limbs fidgeting at the air in front of him as though he were trying to grab at the miraculous thing his father had placed before him.

Henry felt an epic charge, warm and chilling at once, surge through him as he raised Danny into the blue and circular sky over Wrigley Field.

"Can you feel that, Danny?" he said, and Henry set the carrier on the cement, unclicked Danny's buckled belt, and held his son in his arms.

"Can you feel that?" he said again. "That's what before a game feels like. That's why we come early," he said, and he laughed.

"This is Wrigley Field, Danny Boy," Henry Granville said to his son. "The most beautiful baseball diamond in the world."

And perhaps Danny saw it just as Henry hoped he would. Perhaps he saw and heard all that Henry did—the silent arcs of baseballs in the air, the clap of them into leather gloves, the easy thuds of grounders through the infield, the shape of the place, its angles and curves, its hard lines and its softnesses against an historic sky that was every bit a part of the park as the field itself, and the rooftops of Waveland and Sheffield beyond the pennants that lined the upper walls of Wrigley, and beyond that the buildings of the neighborhood stacked against each other for support, and beyond that, the city, one of the most significant cities in the world, a city so cramped for space that it invented sky-scrapers, and still, it was a city that thought enough about baseball to give all that beautiful vastness in the center of it to just nine boys—that it thought enough about boys to give them all of this—and it was unlike anything he'd ever seen.

Danny's legs raced emptily in the air, as though he longed to be released in the green and brown and blue and gray of all of it with the men in blue—as though he couldn't understand the point in coming to a park if not to play.

Once he settled Danny's carrier into the stadium seat to his left, Henry filled in the starting line-up for the Cubs on his official score-card, folded it over and did the same for the New York Mets, which is not to say that he planned to break the promise his wife had wrested from him that morning. Henry attended to both the letter and the spirit of his guarantee by enlisting the scoring services of Phil Lorik, who shared season tickets with his twin brother, Ed. Henry explained to the fifty-year-old brothers the promise he had made to his wife that morning, and the Loriks laughed, as though they understood such promises.

As the Loriks—one looking over the other's shoulders—noted the starting pitchers, the umpires, the weather, and the precise time of the first pitch, Henry smiled at the way the brothers seemed to look upon the task with the great weight Henry felt had been given to the day. And for all of Lori's worries, it was possible that no baby was ever more protected at a baseball game than Danny Granville.

The Loriks paid ferocious attention to the game, looking from the batter back to Danny whenever a lefty came to the plate, as if to remind themselves of the angle at which a foul ball might rocket off a wooden bat.

To Danny's right sat two women with their sons seated at row's end. The women also seemed to consider the safety of the baby to their left. One was thin and dark and sunfreckled. The other was pale and short and had dark half-moons under her eyes, and at every swing of the bat they flinched toward protecting Danny.

During the first inning, the freckled woman asked Henry if his wife knew he was at the baseball game with the baby.

"Fair question," Henry said. "It took a great deal of convincing, but she is fully aware."

The women smiled.

"I'll cover him with my body if a ball comes our way," the freck-led one said.

"And I'll cover you both with mine," the other one said, and everyone smiled.

From the end of the row one of the boys leaned toward his mother.

"The ball will never get to you, Mom," the boy said, and without words he simulated in slow motion speed how he would protect the baby from certain disaster. He grimaced in slow-motion exaggeration and leaned across his mother's seat as he imagined catching the bullet of a baseball before it reached Danny.

"Here's me," the other boy said, and he placed his glove on his head and jerked attentively at the imagined crack of a bat. "There would be no time to put my glove on my hand," the boy said, "and I would have no choice but to stop the ball with my bare hands before anyone even knew it was even coming."

Then the boy twisted his face into a silent grimace of pain and everyone laughed.

And how many others, Henry wondered, were aware of the baby sitting in the cradle of a seat in section 104? How many of them vowed privately to see to the safety of that baby, even at the risk of personal security?

How many of these stadium thousands, Henry wondered, wanted to believe—like the uniformed men on the field—that the possibility of imminent glory was present within the bounds of the first and last pitch of every baseball game? That a hero could be born at any moment.

Third

LONG HAD ANIMAL STUDY THRILLED HENRY GRANVILLE. AS A CHILD he watched lions sleep for hours at the Lincoln Park Zoo, took detailed notes on infinitesimal shifts in their movement. Vigilantly he detailed every snarl and sniff of the painted dogs of Africa as they paced nervously along the length of their cages. Through elementary and high school, every class presentation he made—every show-and-tell demonstration, every expository essay and how-to speech, research paper and book review—was a chance for him to study animals. In college he tended to the research animals in the university's forest enclosure, and in graduate school he spent a year studying the social organizations of the dominant mammals of East Africa. He spent two months trailing a family of African elephants and two more on the plains zebra. He observed a band of baboons for three months, and then followed a group of giraffes for several weeks, making night observations under fuller moons.

A future in academia, though, was of no interest to Henry. He'd been warned about the inescapable backstabbing among fawning and parasitic junior academics, the push to publish, and the sycophantic sickness of tenure-seeking faculty. He wanted none of it. He wanted to study animals, to observe them in their natural habitats, and make sense of their place in the world. So he dropped out of graduate school, settling for a master's degree and a classroom lab at University High. And as his son grew through his first spring and summer, Henry denied himself none of the tools of scientific observation he'd honed over a lifetime of animal study.

By the time Danny's first September had come to a close, the most notable of Henry's observations was the strength of his son's legs. They were stronger and sturdier, it seemed to him, than a four month-old baby's legs should be. Regularly, he was pulling himself up with the aid of the couch and the rails of his crib in order to stand. Sometimes he squatted at the plastic bars of the playpen, raising himself and squatting again, as though exercising.

It was the apparent strength of Danny's legs that led Henry to believe his son was ready for the tot-walker he'd received at his baby shower, and while Lori took a nap one early October afternoon, Henry assembled the device on the living room floor. Danny watched with great interest, though he had no idea what his father was doing, nor of what excitement awaited him. As Henry snapped the tray on the walker, the final step in its assembly, Danny was working on an arrangement of a series of stacks of blocks. As he was placing the penultimate block onto the tower he felt the grip of his father's hands in the hollow of his arms, and with a block remaining in each hand he was very quickly whooshed into the air. When he came to a stop, he was standing in full view of his father.

Danny squinted. He looked into one hand and then the other as if to question the *how* of his standing without aid of rail or couch. He looked ahead at Henry as if by some kind of trickery he had managed to hold Danny at the diaper and yet stand some several feet away.

Wildly, Danny flailed his arms in the air and pounded his fists against the tray of his walker in what seemed to Henry an undeniable display of excitement. Danny looked at his feet, which were blocked by the cloth seat of the tot-walker. He hammered his heels against the floor, satisfied with this proof of his invisible feet. He was standing.

Danny looked up at Henry, and flailed his arms and stomped his feet again. When the walker lurched forward he stopped suddenly, expecting, perhaps, to fall. But there was no such falling. He pounded his feet again once more, and urged the walker forward, but if there was a pattern to the stompings that prompted movement, it seemed to escape him.

"Come on, little buddy," Henry said. "Just walk."

Danny laughed again and pounded the floor with his feet.

Henry held his fingers within Danny's reach, and gripping them Danny stepped across the floor and the wheels of the tot-walker rolled toward Henry again, and Danny smiled as though someone had finally addressed his wish for ambulation. When Henry pulled his fingers away, Danny continued moving through the living room and toward the kitchen. And within minutes of its assembly, Danny was rolling through the house, as though he'd been raised in the thing.

"You'll be running around the bases no time," Henry said, and by the time November rolled around, the walker had become Danny's primary mode of transportation.

There was much discussion between Lori and Henry those early days, about the innumerable issues related to raising a child. Though they'd become parents at exactly the same moment, Henry was surprised to learn what an expert on child-rearing Lori had become so suddenly. She hadn't read any more books and articles on parenting than he had, and yet she was convinced of her expertise in this area. Henry wondered if this was an inherent advantage of the mother— perhaps it was a gift a mother was given during the gestation of her child. Perhaps, he reasoned, that by the time Lori had entered the birthing arena, she had already thought of herself as a mother for nine months. It seemed the only explanation for how she was able to correct him with such certainty, when Henry first held Danny in his arms.

"Oh, no, honey," she had said. "Don't hold him like that. *This* is how you hold a baby." She had only just held Danny for the first time herself. "Hold him across your *right* arm. And be sure you support his neck. An infant cannot hold its own head up without support until he's something like three months old."

"What's the record?" Henry said.

"What record?" Lori said.

"The record for the earliest a boy ever held up his own head?"

Another afternoon, Henry was reading on the couch—Lori asleep with her feet on his lap—when the sudden and explosive sound of Danny crying in his playpen reached Henry and he looked at his watch.

"I think he's hungry, sweetie," he whispered.

"What time is it?" Lori whispered sleepily.

"Just after three," Henry said.

Lori tilted her head to better hear the baby's cry.

"No, he's *not* hungry," she said. "He's just *tired*. He hasn't been sleeping well. It's sleep debt. Just put him in the crib."

Henry carried the screaming baby to his crib and secretly gloated at the tears that continued for several minutes. Lori retrieved him and held him against her shoulder, but still the crying continued. Frustrated and tired, she set him back in his crib and closed the nursery door while she busied herself with various and loud housekeeping behaviors. Henry sat on the couch pretending to read while Lori vacuumed around his feet and Danny cried. Finally, Lori bumped Henry's slippered toes with the vacuum cleaner, and shut the machine down.

"*Now* he's hungry," she snapped.

Henry looked at his watch and nodded. It was 3:10.

Lori was quick to dispense advice on burping and spit-ups, on wiping and ear-cleaning, on feeding, nap-time, nail-clipping, and the extraction of mucous, on bathing and rocking and strolling, and on what type of laundry detergent they should use to wash clothes. Henry deferred to Lori on most of these issues, for she held her views with inarguable conviction. He did take the opportunity, though, as Lori helped him fold laundry one afternoon, to joke with her about his preference for how his tee shirts should be folded. Danny, propped up in piles of pillows, cooed happily in the center of the bed, as Lori just finished folding a shirt of Henry's.

"Excuse me, honey," he said. He picked up the tee shirt she had just folded loosely in half.

"What is this?" He displayed it like a waiter with a bottle of wine. "You may be the expert on growing babies, but if it's all the same to you, I'd like my tee shirts folded like this." He spread it backside up on the bed, and smoothed it flat against the bedspread. He spoke as he walked her through the procedure. "Fold the right third over, then fold the left third over so that it meets its counterpart. Then fold the bottom hem to the collar, and *smooth* the wrinkles out flat. Fold it over once more. You see that? Tight. That's how I'd like them folded."

As November came upon them, Henry and Lori discussed any number of issues related to the holidays as well. Though it was not their first Thanksgiving and Christmas together, Danny's arrival in their lives brought an added importance to their holidays, and they both felt it was as good an opportunity as any to take a new look at the traditions that would give shape to their life as a family, that would give shape to Danny's experience in the world. They decided on menus for Thanksgiving and Christmas, both breakfast and dinner, and the times at which these meals would be served. They also considered, over conversations at the dining room table, whether they should buy a real or an artificial tree for Christmas, and when they should put it up. Lori's family had always put up an artificial tree the day after Thanksgiving. Henry's parents had always bought fresh trees and put them up exactly one week before Christmas Day.

"I'm sorry, but I can't wait that long to put up a Christmas tree," she said, and since Henry didn't feel strongly either way, they decided to purchase a very real-looking artificial tree, and put it up the day after Thanksgiving. But despite his concurrence on the Christmas tree issue, as he strung lights to the sound of a John Denver Christmas CD, and Lori decided which ornaments from their separate histories would make the final cut, it felt to Henry as though the shape of their new family traditions was completely in the hands of his wife.

After trimming the tree and putting Danny down for the night, Lori and Henry sat on the couch. The *Sun-Times* was open on Henry's lap. The white lights of the Christmas tree reflected in Lori's eyes as she wet her fingertip and flipped through the pages of a furniture magazine.

Henry picked up the threads of a month-old conversation about what to get Danny for Christmas, a topic to which they turned frequently, and without transition.

"How about a baseball glove?" he said.

"He's barely six months old, Henry."

"Well, that's true, but he'll be older by the time we give him the gift."

Lori raised her eyebrows and nodded her head as she did when sarcasm was imminent.

"Yes, he'll be much older by Christmas," she said. "He'll be ten or eleven by then."

"A month is a world of difference at this age, Lori," he said.

"We should just buy him things he needs," Lori said. "Like clothes. He outgrows everything in a week. He needs a new winter coat already. Or maybe we'll get him a wagon. I saw a great big blue plastic wagon at Target the other day. We can put a stuffed animal or something in it, and wrap it with a ribbon. Anyway, he has no idea it's Christmas."

"What about a big fat plastic bat and ball, then?" Henry said. "You have no idea how much he loves baseball."

"How do you know he loves baseball so much?"

"Oh, my God, Lori. Tomorrow I'll show you. You just say baseball to him and he starts kicking his feet and laughing. I'll show you."

"He can't even walk yet, Henry."

"At the rate he's cruising through the house in his tot thing, he'll be walking by Christmas," Henry said. "Watch."

"Please don't push him, Henry," Lori said.

"It's not a question of pushing him, Lori. What I'm doing is introducing him to something he's going to love."

Lori flipped another page.

"That's what fathers are supposed to do," Henry said, smiling. "That's what we do."

"Please, Henry," she said. "Just. Please."

And though Henry tacitly agreed to put off the gift of the baseball glove until Danny's first birthday—five months away—when he found himself in the company of baseball equipment, he questioned her rationale. And in the days that followed Thanksgiving, Henry Granville struggled significantly to fetter his robust and innumerable longings to buy a baseball mitt for his son. Once a week, while shopping for formula and diapers at K-Mart, Henry drifted along on an unconscious current toward the sports section and daydreamed in the baseball aisle. At the sight of hundreds of gloves and the collective smell of so much leather, he mostly sighed. But sometimes he picked up a stiff glove and began to shape the leather right there.

On the first of December, as Henry returned to the K-Mart once again, he promised himself that he would re-introduce the discussion with his wife. The minute he walked in the door he would ask her to reconsider her thinking on the baseball glove, and he would insist on a better argument from her than the one she had produced on the day of the Christmas tree discussion.

But Henry failed to keep that promise, for on that trip to the Super K, the purchase of Danny's first mitt came upon him like a surprise.

He had entered the K-Mart for baby soap and formula (aisle one), laundry detergent (aisle four), and v-neck tee shirts (aisle fifteen), thinking he had steeled himself against sporting goods (aisle thirteen). On another day it might have worked, but the new display at the end cap of aisle thirteen was entirely devoted to baseball. Six rows of wooden baseball bats lined up like soldiers. Infielders' gloves threaded through steel pins and stacked against each other like spoons, framing the baseball bats in the shape of a perfect diamond. Jerseys, pants, batting gloves, socks, spikes, and sliding shorts were displayed down one side of that aisle, and baseballs, helmets, and more bats and gloves were lined up along the other.

Henry tried to ignore the gloves. He shaded his eyes from the sporting goods and walked two aisles over where he picked out a three-pack of v-neck tee shirts, but on his way back to the front of the store he stopped at the baseball display again.

The first glove Henry set his eyes on was a brown leather Wilson outfielder's mitt that called to him, just at eye-level, from the top of the diamond-shaped frame. Black leather stitches were sewn through it like dotted lines. Henry's fingers twitched at his side.

He stepped toward the glove and pulled it from the steel pin and slipped it onto his left hand. He pulled a shrink-wrapped baseball from a bin in the center of the aisle and popped it in the basket of the glove. He couldn't get a good grip on it, though, so he bit into the seam of the plastic and peeled it free. He held it with a two-seam fastball grip and smiled, snapped it into the glove again. He fielded an imaginary grounder. He leaped at a line drive.

A tall, dark-haired, pimply-faced boy wearing a red vest with a blue "K" outlined in white looked Henry's way as he paused at the end of the aisle. In the boy's presence, Henry looked deeply at the glove and turned it over to look deeply at its backside as well. He pressed his lips together and nodded at the glove to further convince the boy of his serious intentions.

When the boy left, Henry accepted a slow motion, over-the-shoulder throw from an imaginary centerfielder, and tagged out an imaginary runner at third base.

With his hand on the ball in the basket of the glove, then, Henry closed his eyes and tried to imagine having a catch with an older Danny. What would he look like at ten years old? Why was it so hard to imagine such a thing?

And with his eyes pressed shut, while Henry attempted to propel himself into the future in order to see the ten-year-old face of his infant son, what appeared instead on the screen of his imagination was the unmistakably vivid visage and figure of Henry's own father, Charles Granville. The thick stubble of his beard from the middle of his neck to the black half-moons under his eyes was like nightshadow.

Charles Granville died while Henry was in graduate school. He was a quiet and serious man for whom labor was a kind of love, and love, labor. So serious was Charles Granville, in fact, that Henry often wondered if his father had ever been a boy. But when the elder Granville slipped his thick and calloused hands into a baseball glove he became someone else, another man—a laughing, happy man on the verge of the most important pitch of the most important inning of the most important game ever. Winding up slowly for the throw, he would twist his lips into a sneer and stare severely at the imagined batter. He would call up phlegm from deep in his chest and spit it out on the playlot dirt, wipe his mouth on the sleeve of his blue work shirt, and set his glove on the ground before him in order to roll his shirtsleeves above his elbows. He would call attention to his every movement in the drawn-out and trebled voice of Howard Cosell, the only play-by-play announcer he could rely on to honor such moments with the glory they deserved.

And in the baseball aisle of the K-Mart, it seemed as though Charles Granville had never left the world. His eyes still closed, Henry imagined that his father had just thrown him the ball, and he closed the basket of the glove around it and laughed in a way that approached crying, and he prepared to return the throw. He lifted his left leg and reeled back, his index and middle fingers covering two seams of the cowhide-shelled baseball in his hand, and he let it fly with all the pop and promise of the first day of spring training. At the sound of a shelf of Penn tennis balls tumbling and banging to the tiled floor in an explosion of plastic, Henry opened his eyes to find that Charles Granville had disappeared, had been replaced by an annoyed, mystified, pimply-faced boy with a "K" on his vest.

Henry shrugged his shoulders. "Sorry about that," he said, and the boy left.

But sorry was the least of the things Henry felt. He felt as though he'd been given something. A sign. An opportunity to introduce his long dead father to his newly born son. And now, while the spirit of three generations of Granvilles stood together in one aisle, Henry *had* to buy a baseball glove for Danny.

In minutes, he found a right-handed leather Rawlings hidden among the mitts for youths. No bigger than the wide spread of Henry's bare hand, and stitched with dark brown leather strips, it had the weight of a ski mitten and the light brown of a lioness. Henry buried his face in it and pulled as deeply as his lungs would allow—as though the very truths of his father and his son, and even Henry himself, depended upon the smell of the leather in his hands.

And all of it was there. All of the smells he'd remembered from his first whiff of baseball. It smelled like a new car and dirt and country fields, it smelled of boyhood and forest and lemonade, of history and old books, it smelled of horses and ancient wood and damp flour, of dew collected on burlap. And inside the swirl of these things Henry imagined hordes of Europeans aproned above their shirts and vests, ties knotted tightly against their necks, shirts rolled up past their elbows—tanning, stretching, cutting, and sewing leather, poking it with awls to thread the fingers together, and in that moment, if Henry had been forced to choose between the senses of sight and smell, he might have chosen smell.

At home, he keyed the door open slowly, holding the baseball glove behind him at the small of his back. Lori was facing the riser of the couch, asleep in her pajamas, Danny's blue baby blanket tucked around her feet. Her hair spilled gently over the edge of the arm cushion and shone in the December light of the living room window. It had begun to snow. Puffs of it, lacy rose petals, weightless and white, floated windlessly to the ground, disappearing on the sidewalk and sprinkling the still-green grass in flakey brightness.

Lori curled more tightly into herself. She was cold. Henry unfolded a quilt from the top shelf of the closet and spread it over her. From her sleep she sighed and pulled the hem of the blanket to her chin.

In the nursery, Danny lay on his stomach with his face turned to the doorway. His knees tucked under his hips, and his diapered bottom rose puffily in the air. His forehead was pressed against a wooden rail, and his tiny pink lips puckered wetly between the railings. Sometimes Henry was afraid he might bite them, Danny's lips. They were so beautiful.

From the doorway, he looked back at his sleeping wife. She, too, was like a child in her first minutes from sleep. Straight from sleep Lori seemed happiest to see Henry and Danny. As though sleep were a kind of death from which she had managed escape, and seeing her family upon her return was like a tender recollection of them. A reunion after the sweet and tiny missing.

Henry looked into the baby's room and whispered so that no one would hear.

"Wake up, Danny."

He looked to the couch then, and whispered as quietly, "Wake up, Lori."

In the basement, Henry found a box for the baseball glove. He would tell Lori the truth about why he had to buy the glove, and anyway, what was the damage in buying a glove too early? There was nothing wrong with that.

Henry padded the bottom of the box with layers of tissue paper, and atop the tissue he placed the glove, set it there gently—as if it were something else, something that might break if it were hit by a baseball. How perfect it looked sitting on a cloud of white. Henry closed the box and wrapped it with gift paper from Lori's closet. He tied thin white ribbon around it and curled the ribbed side with the edge of a pair scissors. He put the gift on a shelf in the closet, and heard Lori breathe deeply through her nose as she woke from her nap.

Henry walked to the couch and sat at Lori's feet. He smiled at her.

"Hey, sleepyhead."

"Hey," she said, and Henry rubbed her legs through the blanket.

Henry said nothing about the glove until later that night when they finally pulled the bedspread to their waists and propped themselves against the headboard and settled down to their reading. It was eleven o'clock. Lori hardly read a full page before she yawned tearily. She wiped her eyes and began to read again, but set her book on the floor instead and rolled over to face the wall and sleep.

Henry walked to the door and flipped the light switch, set his book on his dresser and returned to bed. In the dark of the bedroom, when the sounds of his returning to bed—the shiftings of limbs, the rustlings of the down comforter—faded to silence, he told her about the glove.

"Lori?"

"Yeah," she said.

"I bought a glove for Danny," he said.

With her head turned to the wall, her silence could have been anything. It could have been indifference or anger or sleep. It could have been.

"Lori?" he said.

"I heard you, Henry."

"Are you mad at me?"

Silence.

"I couldn't help it," Henry said, and while Lori's head was turned toward the wall, Henry told her what he'd meant to earlier, that he'd planned to pass the sports section at K-Mart without incident, that he'd seen the display of baseball equipment, that he'd imagined having a catch with an older Danny, and that the image of his father had come to him instead.

"I know we talked about waiting to buy him a glove, Lori," he said. "I can't explain what happened. It just seemed like the perfect time to do it."

He wasn't certain that Lori had heard a word of it, or if she did, that she understood.

Henry turned from her, and pulled the comforter over his shoulders. They were bookends. He reached behind him and put his hand to her thigh.

"Goodnight," he said.

Lori made a sound that might have been, "Night."

It was still snowing when Henry awoke. Danny sang a wordless song from his crib while Henry opened the closet door and reached for the gift he had wrapped the day before. It was another day.

Lori shifted in the bed behind him. She opened her eyes as Henry nudged her hip to give him room at the edge of the bed. He held the box in his hands.

"You have to see it, honey," he whispered.

"What?" she said.

"This." And Henry pulled at the curled ribbon around the present.

"No no no," Lori said. "Leave it, Henry. Really. Leave it wrapped."

"It's fine," Henry said. "I want you to see it."

Lori sighed and rubbed her forehead while Henry pulled at the white ribbon, and opened the gift slowly, without upsetting the clean lines of the edge of the wrapping. Henry finally pulled the glove from its nest of tissue and held it before Lori.

"Well?" he said. "What do you think?"

Lori shrugged, and Henry went on about the leather and stitching and various other features that made it the perfect glove. Lori looked more at Henry than at the gift in his hands. She breathed deeply and exhaled through her nose. Henry looked up for fear that she was upset, but she only raised her eyebrows and nodded.

Through his demonstration of the glove, Henry noted the stiffness of the leather and decided against immediately rewrapping the gift. It would be difficult enough for Danny's little hands even with a glove of softened kid leather. This was far too stiff for him.

As they sat on the sofa watching *The Tonight Show* later that evening, Henry still held the glove in his hands, still worked the stiffness from the cowhide. He bent the fingers back and forth, considering the hours of his boyhood spent breaking in his gloves in this same way. In the background, the laughter of *The Tonight Show* audience pushed politely, like the heavy breaths of a hundred couples on vacation. When the host finished the monologue and the commercial came on, the glove squeaked like a leather couch in Henry's hands.

Lori looked at Henry and tilted her head to the side. "Are you sure you got that glove for *Danny*?" she said.

Henry stopped working in the leather.

"I'm not playing with it," he said. "There is so much about baseball you have yet to learn," he said. "This is actually very necessary. I'm working it in. I'm softening the leather. I shouldn't have wrapped it in the first place. Trust me, this is a huge favor I'm doing Danny. I'll have it wrapped in plenty of time for Christmas."

And Henry might have kept this promise had Danny not yet discovered the magic of self-propelled motion in his tot-walker.

While Lori was at tea with Judy one Saturday afternoon, Henry sat on the sofa watching television. He pulled the glove from beneath the couch where he'd been storing it, and began working in the stiff leather. When he heard the plastic wheels of the tot-walker cruise over the speed-bump threshold into the dining room, Henry stuck the glove behind his back.

False alarm. Danny rolled toward the dining room table and Henry turned to the television set. Seconds later, though, Danny crashed into the leg of the dinner table, which was enough to tip the vase of flowers over. Danny wheeled away from the sound and Henry jumped to his feet to wipe the watered and flowery mess with the tablecloth before it stained the wood, and when he returned to the living room Danny had the baseball glove in his hands.

Instinctively, Henry reached for it. He had it in the claw of his fingers before stopping himself, for what was the value in taking it from him now? Danny's wild feet stamped sound on the living room floor. Henry wondered if Danny had made the connection between the glove and that afternoon at Wrigley. Did he smell the hundred smells that leather was? Did he see the field of green somehow?

Danny looked up. A swirl of his light brown hair flopped against his forehead like a superhero's curl. His pacifier—a bright blue flat plastic smile with a red loop of a doorknocker swinging from it—pulsed in his lips. Danny grinned and the pacifier fell from his mouth to the tray of his walker. He eyed a leather knot of the glove and brought it to his mouth.

Henry tasted the leather in his own mouth.

"Give it a good taste, Danny Boy," he said.

Every boy deserved that smell. And somewhere deep behind his eyes Henry could smell it, too—not just any smell and not just any leather, but the first smell of baseball leather.

"There you go, little buddy," he said. "It's December the first, nineteen hundred eighty-four, Danny Boy. And you've been given your first baseball glove.

"You're mother's going to be pissed, I'm afraid, but you just let me worry about that."

When he felt that Danny had introduced himself fully to the taste and the smell of the glove, Henry took it from Danny to begin the business of baseball, but Danny screamed.

"Okay, okay, okay," Henry said, and he returned the mitt to Danny's hands. In the basement he found his old glove and a gray, skinless rubber ball and he returned to Danny, who had the thumb of his mitt in his teeth.

"Okay, Danny Boy. This is *my* glove," he said, and he punched the basket again. "That one is yours, okay?" He pointed to Danny's glove. He set his own glove on the white tray of the tot-walker and gently took Danny's glove into his own hands. He held open the space for Danny's left hand. "Put your hand in there, little buddy," he said, and Danny lifted his hand toward the opening of the glove. He worried about Danny's fingers finding their proper spaces in the mitt, and he reflected on the hundreds, or hundreds of thousands, of things a child had to learn in order to make sense of the world. How to put his socks on, how to tie his shoes, blow his own nose, and zip his jacket. He'd have to learn to clean his ears and budget properly, he would need to clip his nails and comb his hair, wipe his own ass, brush his teeth, and Henry worried about all of them.

"Help me out here, Danny," Henry said, and just like that Danny stiffened his fingers and slipped them into the glove. Danny smiled and looked into the empty glove. Henry put his own mitt on and snapped the rubber ball in the basket. He held it open in front of Danny so that he could see how the ball was meant to fit there.

Danny grunted.

Henry removed the ball from the glove and snapped it back again. He kept the ball in the glove and displayed it before Danny again.

Danny's arms stiffened at the elbows, the fist of his free hand tightened, his arms trembled, he stamped his feet. He screamed.

Henry handed Danny the ball and watched him bring it in front of his eyes. He put it in his mouth, then held it above his head in his right hand. Danny lifted his gloved hand in the air above his head. He spun off in his walker and headed for the dining room, his hands high in the air. He sang his happy, wordless song and banged his walker against the doorway to the dining room. He banged his way through the dining room and into the kitchen. He padded his naked feet through the double doors of the pantry, which closed behind him. He was inside the pantry, then, bouncing against the pots that hung from rubber-coated hooks beneath the lowest shelf. Pots and pans clamored against each other like junkyard wind chimes.

Danny rolled through the house with his early Christmas gift firmly on his hand, showing Henry each time he approached him that the ball was still in his glove. He was too excited, Henry thought, for

Danny's first lesson on catching. Today was for burying his face into the loamy and ancient earth of baseball, for filling his mouth with as much of the baseball as he could. A boy needed a day like this, Henry thought.

Still, as right as everything seemed that afternoon, when Lori's keys fumbled against the lock of the door, Henry's heart pounded against his chest, and the second he took the glove from Danny's hands he was sorry he'd done it.

Danny screamed. He raced in his walker toward the sound of his mother's entrance. Henry chased after him with the glove in his hands. Lori entered into the sound of pounding feet and rolling plastic on hardwood floors. Lorie entered into the last sound a young mother wants to hear upon her return home, which is to say, the sound of her screaming child. Lori Granville entered to the sight of Danny, a ball in his hand, his face red and wet with tears, and Henry holding a baseball glove in his hands, saying, "Here, here, here, Danny."

Lori held a paper bag dotted with water stains. Tiny circles of melted snow bubbled on a loaf of bread poking from the bag. Her eyes were a harsh blue against the orange and brown of her plaid coat and hat. Her lips were pressed tightly. Her jawbone twitched. Henry reached for the bag but Lori grunted and backed away from him, staring at the glove. She set the groceries on the floor and removed her jacket, hooking it on the rack in the hallway, and leaned her head to the side to remove her hat. A thousand pricklings of static electricity ticking from her hair. She looked at Henry as though the earth had suddenly turned to ice beneath her feet.

Lori smoothed her hair with her hand, and punched her electric hat into the sleeve of her coat. "I'm glad we talked about his Christmas present," she said.

Fourth

AFTER THANKSGIVING LORI BEGAN SPENDING MORE TIME WITH Judy Copeland in the upstairs apartment. While Henry was with Danny in the basement or at the park and Lori found herself alone, she'd check in on Judy, and even as the centenarian slept Lori would sit with her and wait for her to wake. She prepared Judy's breakfast, lunch, and dinner, and spent on hour with her each afternoon while Judy sipped from a cup of tea so weak it smelled of water.

On December 15th, one day before he turned seven months old, Danny took his first steps. In the morning, Henry had remarked that Danny didn't seem to need the support of his tot-walker anymore, the way he'd been moving around in it lately. Beneath the tray of the walker his legs, thicker by the day, powered him lithely through the house.

After dinner, Lori and Henry were seated at opposite ends of the couch watching *It's a Wonderful Life* without sound, while Danny, shirtless, freshly diapered, and smelling of baby bath, marched between them, holding onto the riser of the sofa.

On the television Jimmy Stewart held Donna Reed and kissed her wildly, his hands all over her face, angry and worried and sad.

"I can't watch this scene," Henry said. "I want there to be less of it." He put his hand within reach of Danny, just in case, and Lori did the same. "There's that scene," he continued, "after the high school dance when he's walking Mary home and he's holding the borrowed football pants at the waist and he's singing that song . . ."

"And dance by the light of the moon," Lori sang, and Henry stopped. He lost track for a moment. He wanted to tell Lori her voice sounded pretty, but he was afraid she wouldn't ever sing again if he called attention to it.

"Yes, and he's just about to kiss her, when Bert or Ernie, whoever the cab driver is pulls up to him and they never get to the kiss. And you're waiting and waiting for the kiss to happen and when it does it's this crazy kiss in Mary's house at the foot of the stairs."

Henry shook his head. "It always surprises me that she lets him kiss her like that."

Henry reached his hand for Danny, who ignored it again as he struggled to make his independent way back to Henry in the deep give of the sofa. Tiny sounds moaned from the back of his throat. His left hand flailed for balance.

"She loves him," Lori said, as though Henry had asked a question to which this was the only possible answer.

"That may be my favorite scene of any movie," she said, and Henry looked at her to see if she meant it. She was looking through the television, it seemed to Henry. She held her hand out for Danny's way back.

Lori turned to Henry. Her hair shined with the lights of the Christmas tree. "It seems like he's ready to go, doesn't it?" she said.

"He's a wildebeest," Henry said. "Have I told you about wildebeests?"

"Yes, you have."

"Highly precocial ungulates. On their feet within fifteen minutes of birth, and running with the pack in a day," he added.

Lori shifted to the edge of the sofa and hooked a lock of hair around her ear. She held onto Danny's fingers with her free hand.

Henry set Danny on the floor at Lori's feet and walked across the living room to kneel at the other end of the rug, positioning himself to receive Danny on the chance that he chose this day to walk. "He's not ready to walk," Lori said.

"*If*," Henry said. "I'm just saying if."

Danny looked back at Lori as if awaiting her response.

"Never mind," Henry said. It was no time to joke about taking

Danny to the park to run the bases.

Lori reached for Danny's hands to steady him, but Danny pulled his hands from hers, when Henry called to him.

"Okay, little buddy," Henry said. "You can do it, Danny. Walk to Daddy."

Lori leaned with Danny's first movement toward Henry, her arms stretching with him as he stepped with his left foot and then his right, his arms at his sides like a baby walking a tight rope. And Danny treaded solidly toward his father, the soft plastic swish of his diaper and the soft pad of his feet the only sounds. Lori's arms trembled in the air behind Danny and stretched toward his hips. Danny took another step—this time surer—and he kept his eyes on his father. Expressionless, Danny moved steadily toward Henry, his arms exploring balance now, not flailing at it, the wooden floor certain and stable beneath him.

It occurred to Henry then, that he and Lori were not alone responsible for the development of their son. There were things like balance and walking that he would learn on his own, really, that could not be taught. There would be teachers and friends from whom he would learn other things. He would come home from school one day with new tricks, new words, and facts about the countries of South America and explorers from the fifteenth century. He'd spit through his teeth one day and sing a new song he'd learned, and at the dinner table would tell Henry and Lori about the symbol Archimedes requested for his tomb. He'd hold a leaf taut in his fingers and make it whistle. He'd teach his father greetings in Spanish.

Danny uttered no sound as he advanced toward his father, no sounds of struggle as he made his way across the living room floor. The papery crinkle of the diaper was all there was.

"If a baby could be cocky," Henry said, "I'd say that was a swagger."

Danny walked cocksure and confident, he looked too small to be walking, and all of it made Henry laugh. Two more steps and Danny began to smile at the growing figure of his father ahead of him.

"Ohmyword, ohmyword," Lori was saying, and it seemed to Henry as though Danny had been secretly walking for days.

"He's a wildebeest," Henry said, and he felt Danny push his arms against his father's victory hug, and turn around, eager for the return trip.

Lori pressed her lips together and put her hand to her mouth as if to keep it from betraying her.

"What's wrong, sweetie?" Henry said, and Danny turned first toward Henry as if for the question, and then to Lori for its answer.

Lori shook her head. She pulled her hand away from her mouth and opened her arms to Danny.

"Come here, baby," she said, and Danny smiled as he stepped carefully toward her, his arms and legs trembling with life. When he reached her she hugged him tightly, and closed her eyes over his shoulder.

Danny struggled against his mother's hold on him. He pushed away from her, and smiled, once released, his body bouncing with the surprise of this unwheeled freedom his legs had found. And Henry, torn only for a second between the miracle of a walking son and the sudden sadness of his wife, followed Danny into the kitchen, from which place came the sound of laughing and clapping. The stomping of feet.

Later, Lori sat against the blond wood of the headboard, a magazine opened against her raised knees. She licked her fingers and turned each page with a snap. Henry lay with his hands folded behind his head, grinning up at the ceiling.

"We should have videotaped him," he said.

Lori turned another page.

"Seven months old," Henry said. "Unbelievable."

Lori pinched another page and snapped it over.

"How old was Marci's kid when she first walked?" Henry said, but Lori did not respond.

"Marci from the bookstore," Henry said.

And Lori said nothing.

"Wasn't she like a year old?"

"I don't know," Lori said.

"I think she was maybe eleven months old," Henry said. "I seem to remember eleven months old. And I remember Rich and Marci making a big deal out of that, didn't they?" Henry said.

Lori pinched and snapped another page.

"You seem mad," Henry said. "Something bothering you?"

"It's not a fucking contest," Lori said, and she closed her magazine, set it on the floor at her bedside, and turned to face the wall. At the looping arc of her tee shirt the muscles in her back knotted.

Henry sat up. "Where did that come from?"

"Just forget it," Lori said.

"Lori."

"I'm fine," she said.

But she was not fine. The first steps of her only son had been taken that night, but she couldn't shake the image of Danny walking across the rug, the swirls of hair at the back of his head, the puff of his diaper, the tiny and perfect muscles of his shoulders as he held out his arms for balance, as he walked across the rug away from her.

Fifth

LORI DID NOT SPEAK FOR TWO DAYS FOLLOWING DANNY'S FIRST steps. Judy Copeland's death, later that week, deepened her gloom. Lori arranged her burial silently, and afterward her funk became a darkness. And in the weeks that followed Lori began to spend some time each day in the abandoned flat upstairs. There was no hurry to prepare it for another tenant, as Judy Copeland had left the Granvilles with what money she had to her name, so Lori emptied it slowly, keeping what furniture she could, and bringing the rest to a homeless shelter in Uptown. When the flat was all but empty, Lori kept a lamp and the old woman's rocking chair in the living room, and it became her quiet place.

Henry encouraged Lori to see someone about her unhappiness. He gave her three articles and a book on depression as well. He'd rushed home from school every day to ease what stress he could from Lori's days with Danny, and countless times he'd asked her what the matter was. But she was fine. She was fine. Each time he asked her she was fine.

"Enough with the questions, Henry," she finally said one day. "Enough with the handouts and the books. Just leave me alone."

She was certain it had nothing to do with postpartum. She remembered Danny's first days as glorious. She remembered his tiny nakedness against her chest. She remembered singing with her cheek against his, she remembered holding his feet against her ears like tiny telephones and laughing. She remembered laughing.

She blamed it on the sun, which hadn't shined it seemed since June. When she was a child she had her easel and paints for the cloudy days, substitutes for the sun.

When Henry walked into the house after his last day of school before Christmas break, Danny greeted him at the front door with his baseball glove stuffed on his throwing hand. A tennis ball wobbled in the basket of the glove. A step behind him, Lori, several days into her dark retreat, dried her hands on a dishtowel and wiped her hair from her eyes.

"He's had that glove on his hand all day," she said, as though the act deserved a punitive response.

Henry touched his fingers to Lori's cheek, kissed her on the lips, told her that he missed her and hated to be away from her for even a minute, and Lori seemed to force a smile.

"I'm going to take a shower," Lori said. "And then I'm going out for a bit."

Henry set his backpack down and mussed Danny's hair.

"Nice try," Henry whispered as he removed the glove from Danny's right hand. "But that's the wrong hand, pal. Left hand glove, right hand ball."

He opened the mitt wide for Danny's left hand.

"Help me out here, sport," he said, and Danny stiffened his fingers and reached toward the glove.

Danny looked into the leather glove for the ball but it was behind his father's back. He smiled when it appeared before him. When Henry placed it into his throwing hand, Danny looked from one to the other hand and smiled again.

"How's that feel, Danny Boy?" Henry said. "Better, huh? What do you say we have a catch, now?"

Henry had been waiting for this exact moment since the first day of the academic year. Two weeks at home with Danny would certainly translate into some baseball progress. Exactly what kind of progress was the question. Henry hoped he could finally move beyond just dropping the tennis ball into Danny's glove, as he'd been doing since he'd given Danny the glove two weeks before.

He took off his coat and directed Danny to stand in front of the sofa so that any errors would land the ball on the couch. He stood just a foot away from Danny then, and held the ball above him.

"Okay, Danny. Squeeze the ball when it hits the glove," he

said, and he dropped the ball into Danny's mitt.

"Atta boy!" Henry said. "Nice catch. *Squeeze* the glove around the ball, like this."

"Again, Danny." Henry dropped the ball. "Squeeze."

"Nice. Again. Squeeze."

Henry stepped backward a foot and threw the ball carefully into Danny's glove.

"Squeeze," he said again. "Atta boy."

Several times he threw the ball into Danny's mitt from the same distance, taking the ball from his glove after each catch and tossing it back again.

Minutes later, Henry took another step back.

"I'm way back here, now, sport," he said. "Look, Danny. Here's the ball."

Danny grinned and Danny grunted.

Henry aimed and tossed the ball to him. It hit the basket of his glove, but rolled up the web and onto the couch.

"You've got to squeeze the glove around the ball, Danny," he said, and several throws later, Danny seemed to get the point.

When Danny had mastered the catch from this distance, Henry moved back two steps.

"Now I'm going way back, Danny," he said. He held the ball in the air and walked slowly back to Danny.

"The ball is going to come across the room into your glove," he said, and he made a whooshing sound with breath and teeth and lips—the sound of wind—as if it might help Danny understand this notion of physics, then placed the ball in Danny's glove. "And when it hits your glove, you've got to squeeze," he said. "Squeeze." Henry put his hands on the outside of Danny's glove and closed the glove around the ball.

Henry backed up again and threw the ball. It hit Danny's glove and rolled to the couch again. Danny recovered it this time, and without warning threw it at his father. It hit the dining room table behind Henry and rolled into the kitchen. Danny opened his mouth wide and made a fist, stomped his feet on the wood floor and screamed.

"Yikes!" Henry said, and Danny laughed. "No problem with throwing, huh?"

A dozen more throws came at this distance, but either the timing of the squeeze was all wrong or Henry's aim was off, and not a single interaction between ball and glove was successful.

Each time he missed, though, Danny recovered the ball and threw it back at his father. Henry prepared for each return throw by crouching and balancing on the balls of his feet like an infielder intent on a grounder. Danny flailed his arms and screamed after every throw.

As Henry continued this same routine of aiming, throwing, and missing Danny's glove, and Danny continued his routine of recovering, grunting, throwing, and screaming, Henry worried that Danny might never learn how to catch a ball.

He seemed okay at throwing, for a baby at least. His form was a little sloppy. His follow-through needed some work, for one. Though he seemed to have a natural inclination to finish his throw across his body, sometimes he followed through on the same side. Easy to correct.

But the inability to catch worried Henry. Danny didn't seem to care if he caught the ball or not. He seemed to catch on to the throwing business, though. And the glove? He could wear the thing all day long if his mother let him. But for the confusion of the proper hand, the glove was never away from Danny for a minute. It was his blanket, his pillow, his teddy bear.

But what if he never learned to catch? How bad would that be? To have a kid who couldn't catch a ball? A kid who reached his hands out and squinted in fear at a ball coming his way. For a moment, it seemed to Henry as though nothing distinguished Danny from any other infant in the world who would grow up not knowing how to catch a ball. Henry's anxiety was burdened by the weight of the complexities of teaching such a seemingly simple task.

Lori passed them several times as she prepared for wherever it was she was going. Henry didn't ask.

When she left, she kissed neither of them goodbye.

"Let's not push him too hard," she said, and locked the door behind her.

"I'm not pushing you too hard, am I, Danny?" he said, and Danny raised his gloved hand.

With only a short break for dinner, Henry and Danny continued to have what was more of a throw than a catch, and as the time passed the scientist within helped mitigate the fatherly worries as Henry reflected on baby athleticism. Each time he threw the ball to his son, Henry observed Danny closely. He watched his eyes and hands and every movement of his body. He observed every motion toward the moving object. He wondered if it was even possible for a child of six months to catch a ball. None of Lori's books on parenting covered having a catch with the baby. Maybe babies weren't capable of this behavior. Was there an age before which no child could properly catch? Were other developmental stages necessary before this thing could be accomplished?

Father worried and son played for nearly two hours, and when Danny began to rub his eyes and fade toward naptime, Henry took his resisting child into his arms, put the tennis ball in his gloved hand to soothe him, and carried him to his crib. There, Henry combed his fingers slowly and warmly over the whispers of Danny's hair, and wondered what softer thing there was in the world. On his own head Henry could feel what Danny felt, the drowsy smoothings of a father's fingers, how the tingle of them stayed for a moment after the fingers had stopped.

In his office, Henry took a legal pad from under a crystal cluster Lori had given him in the early days of their marriage. He had to remind himself, it seemed, that she had happier days. Now it seemed there was nothing to call her away from sadness. She could pass Danny in the hall-way—smiling, arms reaching toward her—without seeing him.

He had done what he could for her. How many times had he asked her to tell him what was wrong? How many times had he scratched her back until she fell asleep? How many times had he told her he loved her? That she was still as pretty as the day they met? How many times had he asked her was she mad at him? Had he done something to anger her? Was there something more he could do?

He had stopped telling Lori what new thing Danny had done, what newness he'd discovered about the world, what new sound he had made, what near word he tried to wrap his lips around. Henry had tip-toed around the house long enough, though. If Lori wanted to live in a shell of sadness without the aid of smile or touch, let her live that way. Henry had a son to raise. Henry had a son to prepare for the world.

He sat at his desk and tapped the eraser of his pencil against the pad. He closed his eyes and tried to imagine himself learning how to catch, but he could not. It was something he felt he'd always known. He'd learned to play baseball just by being a son, by being a boy among other boys. He placed himself in his old backyard—the grass mowed obsessively close to the ground, dense and dark as ivy—and tried to recall learning how to catch, but he could see only a graceful, slow-motion, rhythmic passing of a ball, back and forth between him and the old man. Perhaps learning was something beyond memory. No. He remembered learning how to ride a bicycle, didn't he? He recalled the bike itself, and the day he first rode it without the training wheels. Why couldn't he remember learning how to catch? And if he couldn't remember this, how could he possibly teach it to his son?

Why was it that children could throw with such ease, but not catch? Was it a question of fine motor skills? It required hand-to-eye coordination, which throwing did not. What was it that a child of seven months was capable of?

Henry knew animals. He knew the lemur and fox squirrel and five species of baboons—seven if you counted the drill and mandrill. He knew the African elephant, the plains zebra, the giraffe, the black rhino, the spotted hyena. But how much about the human animal could he infer from his knowledge of the rest of the animal kingdom? In all his years of research and study, of making connections and distinctions between man and the rest of Kingdom Animalia, until that moment Henry had never considered that baseball was perhaps the thing that most separated one from the other. Baseball and nothing more. He laughed and imagined any number of animal species he had studied in his professional life, equipped with baseballs and gloves on a baseball diamond.

Henry tapped his eraser on the legal pad, once for each word of his unspoken sentence. Of-what-was-a-child-of-seven-months-capable?

He could see a ball. This much was fact. But maybe a child could only see a ball when it was *still*—or damn close, anyway. He recalled how Danny looked at the ball in Henry's hand before he threw it, followed by the confusion in his eyes when he locked onto the ball after its journey ended on the couch. Perhaps between Henry's hand and the sofa, the moving ball appeared to Danny as a flash, a shooting star. Perhaps even a slowly tossed ball moved too quickly to be followed by eyes that were only seven months formed. Maybe a ball that moved any faster than a slow roll was lost by Danny's eyes from the start.

If so, it stood to reason that if the muscles of a child's eyes were not developed enough to follow a brief trajectory, how could they possibly anticipate depth and direction when greater distance was factored in? Add to this the strength of hand required to squeeze a leather glove, and it was clear that Danny was not ready.

Was there an earliest age at which a child could perform each of these singular things and put them all together so that he could have a catch? And if there was such an age, what was it?

The front door opened and closed. Henry covered his notepad and met Lori upstairs.

"Hi," he said.

"Hi," she said. "Everything okay?"

"Yeah. Just putting together some notes for next semester."

"I'm going to sleep," Lori said.

In the basement again, Henry uncovered his notes. Lori would do her sit-ups on the bedroom floor, flip through a magazine and fall asleep like a sad angel, but if she had known that Henry was in his office with a legal pad and pencil considering how best to step up Danny's athletic development, she'd have been furious.

Will you please not push him, she'd say. Can't we give him a chance to grow up without your obsessions with baseball and competition? He's a child, Henry. He's just a child.

And what would Henry say to that? That the world was a competitive place and that Henry was not its architect. That it was his responsibility to prepare Danny for success in a competitive world. He could argue for the veracity of survival of the fittest and other such ancient truths according to which the world had been ruled since the beginning of time. But Lori wouldn't understand any of it. It was all an extension of competition in her eyes. And competition, she would add, was mostly responsible for the mess the world was in.

What answer had he against her insistence on a better world?

Still, the question of where Danny stood in relation to the rest of the world's infant athletes was occasion for infinite speculation. The athlete was better prepared for an easier life. Lori was a tough sell when it came to this truth, but it was the truth. It was as simple as that.

Clearly, the sooner a child learned the basic elements of throwing and catching, the better off he'd be. The sooner he would be able to practice them, and the sooner he would be able to perfect them. Were there ways to coach a child to the acceleration of these elements?

"In order to catch the ball you must see the ball," Henry said to no one.

And at the sound of these words breaking into the air, he smiled an inventor's smile, as though in all of ball-sport history Henry Granville was the first human being to come upon the phrase, *keep your eye on the ball*. Maybe those six simple words were the only words Henry needed to focus on in order to teach Danny how to catch.

"In order to catch the ball, you have to see the ball," he said again, and he turned out the light in his office. Tomorrow, the optical attention sessions would begin.

Before Lori awoke the next day, Henry gathered every ball he could uncover in a basement rich with them. Along with a hopper of tennis balls, he found softballs, baseballs, soccer balls, Nerf balls, golf balls, whiffle balls, sponge balls, a basketball, a giant super ball, three rubber balls, a beach ball, and two footballs.

He cleared a playing area in the cluttered basement, and when Lori left for work Henry switched the glove on Danny's hand from his right to his left and carried his properly gloved son into the basement. The plan was to begin the sessions by throwing or rolling each spherical object to Danny, and then noting his ocular grasp of each object, every optical shift and torsal flinch, and then devise a program to accelerate the development of Danny's eyes, so that he would begin to pick the objects up more quickly and to stay with them longer.

That was the plan.

When Danny recovered the first object his father rolled across the floor to him—a skinless rubber ball dried with age, he set it in his glove for little more than a second, smiled, showed his father the captured sphere, and fired it across the room to Henry, who might have caught it had it arrived with an expected pace. It came much faster, though, and Henry's instinct was to duck. It ricocheted off the wall behind Henry and knocked against his head.

"Damn!" Henry said, and Danny laughed.

Henry put his own baseball glove on and rolled a tennis ball to Danny, and laughing, his son recovered it and fired it back to his more prepared father, and it was soon made clear to Henry that the joy of the ball was very clearly in the throwing.

He cleared away the objects he'd spent the morning gathering and brought the hopper of tennis balls to Danny's side, and one by one the young athlete picked the balls out of the hopper, placed them in his glove for a second and threw them at Henry. The optical attention sessions could wait, Henry thought. Today, Danny would have his throw.

On that day and those that followed, between meals, diapers, snacks, naptime stories, baby massages, a winter, and the spring that followed, Danny threw tennis balls at his father in the basement stadium, and Henry recovered them.

Three weeks after Danny's first birthday, on the June evening of his last day of the school year, Henry and Lori took a walk with Danny to the Brown Cow Ice Cream Shoppe on Madison. They'd barely stepped off the front porch when Lori crouched toward

Danny and pointed out the only star in the sky.

"Look, Danny," she said. "Star light, star bright, first star I see tonight. Wish I may, wish I might, wish this wish I wish tonight."

"Are you sure that's how it goes?" Henry said.

"That's the way it goes," Lori said. "I'm sure of it."

When they were just steps from the ice cream shop, Lori pointed to the sky again.

"Look at them now, Danny," she said. The sky was filled with stars, and the moon was a white ball.

"In Africa," Henry said, "the moon casts shadows you wouldn't believe. You could read by the light of it."

Henry and Danny sat at a table outside while Lori waited in line. When she joined them with two single-scoop ice cream cones in her hands she passed them to Henry and returned to the counter for a decaf cappuccino. Through the window, Henry watched her speak with the cashier, a pale, skinny girl whose earrings curled around her left ear like a question mark.

"Two hands, Danny," Henry said. "Nothing sadder in the world than an ice cream cone smashed on the ground."

Danny's hair had just begun to grow, soft wisps of browns and golds looped against his head.

Across the street three girls wearing Nazareth Academy Volleyball jerseys walked out of Byron's Hot Dog Joint and toward the ice cream shop.

Henry licked his cone and peeked at Danny over the hill of ice cream. A chocolate smear circled his mouth like a clown's smile. His hand was clamped around his ice cream and the first knuckle of his index finger poked through the cone. A wet glob dripped over the crotch of his thumb.

Henry steadied Danny's hands in his own and began licking away at the mess of the ice cream cone in an effort to salvage it, and Danny screamed, finally surrendering the ice cream cone to his father as Lori erupted through the door of the Brown Cow.

"What are you doing, Henry?"

"I'm helping him out," he said.

"You're eating his ice cream, Henry."

The girls from Nazareth stared as though waiting for Henry's response.

"I'm cleaning it up," Henry said.

"Give me the cone," Lori said, and Henry handed it to her. She smoothed Danny's hair off his forehead and returned to him his cone.

"When I was a kid I never let my ice cream get messy," Henry said.

"You were an amazing child, Henry," she said, and in the relative quiet that followed this misunderstanding, Henry returned to his own ice cream, licking a slow and spiraling mountain's path around the hill of his cone. Lori, closing her eyes and sighing, stirred a tiny silver spoon of sugar into her cappuccino.

In the mere seconds that comprised this peace, neither Lori nor Henry noticed Danny move toward the street. Neither did they see his pace quicken across the sidewalk. Only when Lori lifted her cup of cappuccino to her lips did she raise her eyes to see Danny step off the curb and into the street.

"Henry! Danny! No!" she screamed, and Henry jumped from his seat, banging the wrought iron chair against the window of the Brown Cow. Lori jolted toward the curb as Danny stepped between two parked cars and toward the traffic of Madison Avenue. She raced off the curb and clamped her hand on Danny's right arm, yanking him above the earth and back to the safety of the curb.

She breathed heavily, strands of loose hair spilled from her ponytail.

In his left hand Danny held a rubber ball he had found against the rear tire of the parked car. He looked down at his ice cream globbed on the curb, screamed again, yanked his arm from his mother's hands, stamped his foot on the fallen dessert, and screamed once more.

And what next unfolded was a scene that Henry would forever recall in slow motion. Customers inside the Brown Cow, at the sound of the chair knocking against the window, stood watching. Passersby, at the sound of a screaming boy and the sight of a heavily breathing mother, hair splayed across her face, stopped to watch the scene. And Danny—screaming, his mouth opened wide, the rubber ball in the two-seam grip of his left hand—reeled back and let the gray orb fly, and it sailed in something like the arc of a rainbow across Madison Avenue, dozens of heads following its trajectory from Danny's left hand over the languid traffic, bouncing onto the sidewalk in front of Byron's, thudded against the window, ricocheted off the edge of a no parking sign, and rolled toward the funeral home before disappearing under a car parked at the curb on the westbound side of the street.

"Holy crap!" Henry said. "Nice throw!" But only when he looked back at Danny, whose left hand still dangled at the end of his follow-through, did Henry realize he had thrown the ball lefty.

He looked at Lori. "Did you see that?" he said.

"He nearly killed himself," Lori said.

"No, Lori," Henry said. "Did you see him throw the ball?"

Lori stared hard at her husband.

"He threw it *lefty,*" Henry said.

Danny's head swiveled between them at the sound of their voices.

"Great, Henry." She picked Danny up and placed him in Henry's arms. "I'm going to get him another ice cream. Should I take Danny with me, or do you think maybe you can handle watching him?"

"He was just getting a ball," Henry said to Lori as she went back to the Brown Cow. The door to the shop closed before Henry completed his thought. "That's what boys do," he said.

And before Lori had returned from the Brown Cow with another ice cream in her hand, Danny had thrown the ball again from the left side.

"He did it again," Henry said to Lori. "We got the ball and he threw it lefty again."

Lori glared at him.

"What?" Henry said.

"How did you not know that by now?" Lori said.

As they walked home Henry was silent. Lori reached for his hand as they approached the corner at Jackson and Circle, and asked him is something was wrong. But what was there to say to her? That he'd failed his son? That despite his scientific background, despite his interest in baseball, despite his interest in preparing Danny properly, Danny's lefthandedness had escaped him? How could he not have seen the signs earlier?

Despite his good intentions, Henry had deprived his son of possibility.

"Henry?" Lori said.

"Yes?" Henry said.

"I asked if something was wrong."

"Nothing," Henry said. "I was just thinking."

On the way home, he observed the way Danny swung his arms, the way he scraped a stick along the mortar between the bricks of the houses, the way he tapped his hand against the parking meters and light posts, as though by watching him closely now—without blinking—for the rest of his life, Henry could make up for the opportunities Danny had missed.

Lori reached for Henry's hand, and held it.

"What's wrong?" she asked.

By the time they reached Lathrop, it was too late for Henry to do the one thing he couldn't wait for: take Danny in the backyard for a re-evaluation. It would have to wait until tomorrow.

In the bathroom, Henry ran hot water over a washcloth until it warmed, and Danny fought against an impromptu bath, blinked his eyes hard and shook his head against it until his father was done. Henry changed Danny's diaper then, and dressed him for the night. Whinnying, Henry horsey-backed Danny to the kitchen where Lori poured white wine into two glasses.

"Have a glass of wine with me on the porch, after Danny's goes down?" she said.

"Absolutely," Henry said.

In his crib, Danny rubbed his eyes with the backs of his hands, and minutes later, was asleep.

When Henry joined his wife on the front porch, she kissed him and handed him a glass of white wine.

"Please let's be sure we drink wine on the porch on evenings like this," Lori said. And it was as if Lori had said so much more. It was as if his she had recalled the perfect day that it was—filled with sunshine and a summer walk. There had been ice cream and wine, they had a son and he was healthy and beautiful, he was safe and sleeping in bed, and it would be a long summer, and they were certain to be wise with how they spent it, and it was even possible that love still ruled the earth. It was as if his wife had said all those things, and Henry wondered if Lori had returned to them. Had something in the night—or in the stars or in the moon, or in Henry's silence on the walk home from the Brown Cow—returned Lori to Danny and Henry? Lori's eyes were soft and Henry thought she might love him still.

He lifted his glass and clinked it to hers.

"Let's," he said.

When Lori finished her glass of wine, she kissed Henry and said she'd be waiting for him in the bedroom.

"I won't be long," Henry said, and while he brushed his teeth, a new wave of regret began its wash over him. What an idiot! How many times had he switched the glove from Danny's right to his left hand? How had the signs escaped him?

He had treated his son no differently than the ignorant, turn-of-the-century parents and teachers who had famously repressed and punished left-handedness throughout history. Henry's father had told him the story of a childhood friend who'd come home from school with welts up and down his arm because his teacher had caught him writing with his left hand, *the hand of the devil.*

Henry, who had shuddered at the story, was capable of the same idiocy some seventy years later. As incapable as he was of observing his own son, what business did he have calling himself a science teacher?

After flossing his teeth, Henry returned to the bedroom. Lori's face was turned toward the wall. Henry listened to her breathing. Until the moment he heard the depth of her breathing, and realized she had fallen asleep, he thought there was a chance they might have made love. And when he peeled back the light cotton spread to find she had not worn pajamas to bed he knew she'd been thinking it, too. But as was often the case when Lori drank wine, she felt sexy while drinking it and sleepy afterward, and the window between the two effects was never open long.

It would have been the perfect thing to take his mind off the greater of the day's failures. He sat up in bed.

His son had thrown a ball lefty tonight. In the quiet and dark of the room he shared with his wife he realized there was too much possibility, too much potential, and too many questions to dwell on this as a failure. This was cause for hope, for despite Henry's unintentional insistence on right-handed throwing, Danny had thrown a ball lefty that very night! It was possible, in fact, that Danny threw that ball across Madison as well as he threw with his right hand.

And what were the measures of handedness? What determined left or right-handedness? With which hand did Danny use his spoon and fork? How did he brush his teeth? Was a child's inclination toward a particular hand something that was decided before he was born or after? Perhaps the human body, during the first two or three or so years of life, made available the *opportunity* for either left or right-handedness.

Was it possible that he actually might have helped Danny by extending the possibility of right-handedness? Henry Granville was well aware of the sensitivity of human development. Maybe there was a window of opportunity for ambidexterity. There were windows for everything! There were windows for creativity and personality and athleticism and musical talent and compassion and altruism, and even genius! Why, there was even a window for gender! The human body was a marvel! Was there a window, then, for ambidexterity? For even-handedness? If Danny's remarkable left-handed throw that night was any evidence, surely Henry had not missed this window. It was still possible for him to direct his son toward perfect and true ambidexterity!

Henry swung his legs over the edge of the bed and stood as though he were about to throw a baseball across the room, with his right hand. He simulated the toss and froze in his follow through—bent over at the waist, right arm at left thigh, balancing on his left leg. Then he repositioned himself on the middle braid of the oval throw rug at the foot of the bed, and transferred the imaginary ball to his left hand, and in the weak light of the bedroom he pretended a left-handed throw, holding his follow-through as he had before. Immediately he followed with another throw from the right side, and another from the left, never lifting his feet from the braided rug that shifted slightly over the tight-grained maple strips of the hardwood floor.

By the filtered glow of the streetlight angling in through the window blinds Henry watched his fluid form in the mirror. Slightly bent at the knees, the bands of his lower quadriceps swelling at the hem of his boxers, simulating throws from side to side, his feet whispering on the rug, Henry moved in something of a dance—a slow, rhythmic thrower's tai chi. Annular and balanced.

He wanted to wake Danny up then, just to be sure it wasn't too late. He wanted to wake him up and put a bucket of balls in front of him just to see what he would do with them. He certainly wouldn't just *stand* there. He was a boy. He wanted to see Danny take one of the balls out of the bucket and throw it across the street with his left hand, just to be sure.

"Tomorrow," Henry whispered. And at the sound of *tomorrow* the thing the word stood for seemed weeks away. And the word hung in the air as Henry finally ended the dance of the switch-pitcher and returned to his bed. It hovered above him inside the yellow balloon of his peaceful sleepiness, and as his eyes closed, he whispered it again.

"Tomorrow," he said, his left hand in the shape of holding a baseball, his right hand in the shape of a glove.

Sixth

BETWEEN HIS FINAL SECONDS OF MORNING SLEEP AND HIS FIRST seconds of clear-headed wakefulness, Henry Granville wondered what day it was, and why the sun was shining. It was Monday and he was late for nothing, for his summer break had begun. Glorious summer! And holy shit, there was this as well: Danny could throw lefty!

Henry would have preferred spending the morning that followed the serendipitous discovery of Danny's ability to throw a ball damn well with his left hand in any number of more sports-related ways. But he awoke to the unfortunate recollection that he'd promised Lori he would paint the living room, and despite this misfortune in timing, the wheels of the promise had been irreversibly set in motion: paint had been purchased, furniture been covered in old bed sheets, carpet protected with plastic, and arrangements had been made for Danny to spend the day with a babysitter while Henry painted and Lori was at the bookstore.

In the car, as he dropped Danny off at the babysitter's house, Henry made a promise to Danny he would never regret.

"I'll pick you up at about five o'clock, little buddy, and then we'll play baseball for the rest of the summer, okay?"

While Henry painted the living room the next day—even as he wrapped his head thoroughly around thoughts of Danny's ambidexterity—there rumbled something. Beneath the surface—beneath his life-long search for meaning and self-fulfillment, his love for teaching and helping young minds realize potential, beneath his desire for order and beauty, his search for knowledge and self-esteem, his desire for belonging and security and health, beneath even his most basic needs—there rumbled something.

He set the aluminum ladder in the corner of the room and climbed to its safety step—the second highest rung—placed the paint can on the shelf of the ladder, and set his first trim line along the highest point of the wall. As he leaned back to assess the line, though, he came close to losing his balance, and nearly tipping over the unsteady ladder. A small glob of paint dolloped on the plastic sheet protecting the floor. Henry breathed deeply, climbed down, and looked long and hard at the single line of trim he had painted.

His arms crossed, his index finger curled between his lips thoughtfully. Henry looked long and hard at this early evidence of his first summer project. Carefully, he removed the can of paint from the ladder shelf and set it on the floor. He sets his hands on the legs of the ladder and tested its stability. Studied the drop of paint. Looked up at his trim line.

"Every shift of the ladder is a cost," he said aloud. Every shift, an expense in time and energy. Every ascent and descent with the can of paint in his hands came with the risk of spillage as well.

He stretched his arms out at his sides and considered the Western Lowland Gorilla. In the crown of his fruit-laden tree the Western Lowland Gorilla had a great advantage over Henry. For starters, it had tremendous wingspan. Its ability to climb and maintain balance distinguished it from man as well, but the ape had an additional advantage: without the expense of moving its feet, the ambidextrous ape could reach an equal distance on either side in order to pluck fruit. Its ambidexterity, in other words, extended its foraging sphere. The ape was a bimodal machine, eating to its heart's content without moving.

The same phenomenon was at work here; painting was a kind of human toiling sphere. Except that Henry didn't use his left hand for the application of the paint. He was a lopsided animal. A crippled ape in a tree.

He shifted the ladder to the opposite side of the room to paint a second trim line as a Western Lowland Gorilla might. He ascended the ladder, painted a trim line to one side with his right hand, and extended the line to the other side with his left, and after measuring the line, determined he'd extended his own foraging sphere—his painting range—by nearly two feet. The trick, of course, was dexterity, and Henry took great care as he continued trimming the high line of the wall with both hands.

When he finished—after saving perhaps three ladder shifts—Henry stood in the center of the dining room and admired his trim line. He filled the roller tray and set to painting the room with an attention he'd never paid before, an attention to bimodal balance. He painted the higher section of wall first, using the roller extension. On the left side of his body he guided the roller with his left hand, and reversed his attention on the right. For the lower section of the walls around the room, he removed the extension and switched the roller from his left hand to his right until the room had received its first coat.

As he stepped back to evaluate his work, Henry rolled his left shoulder in its socket. His shoulder muscles were sore on the left side. He rolled his right arm in its socket. Nothing. Pain on the left side only. And as Henry compared the great strain of one shoulder against the comfort of the other, he wondered about the effects of ambidexterity for a man who, let's say, paid long-term attention to equal-sided behavior. It made sense that such a person would necessarily develop a more balanced physique.

"He would become a more *symmetrical* human being," Henry said aloud. And beneath the surface there was a rumbling.

As Henry applied the second coat according to the theory of the foraging gorilla, he considered what other benefits might come with a lifelong insistence on bimodal balance. He'd read all the major articles on the specialized functions of the hemispheres of the brain. The left —rational and analytic—studied, scrutinized, and organized in linear and sequential fashion, while the right hemisphere—intuitive and holistic—dealt in metaphors, leaped with insight and dreamed. And naturally, since each hemisphere controlled the opposite side of the body, there were theories that held that the development of the weaker side of the body could lead to the development of the weaker hemisphere of the brain.

And then Henry spoke, slowly and deliberately, hesitating between clauses as he massaged his young scientific theory, the pistol of his hand against his chin and lips.

"Could a lifelong insistence—on physical balance—lead to some kind of crossover—of the cerebral hemisphere—giving the practitioner —more equal access—to both hemispheres of his brain? And might this access help him achieve some greater potential?"

And Henry answered in the affirmative, convincing himself, in those few living room hours that the history of human dexterity and the history of hemispheric brain separation were one and the same. At some point, and for some unknown reason, mankind had resigned itself to the superior development of one side of the body, and by doing so, necessarily resigned itself to the inferior development of one full half of its body and brain.

"A misuse of human potential," Henry said aloud.

Henry wondered as well, if it were possible that a lifelong ambidexterity crusade might lead to an extraordinary kind of intelligence, might equip a crusader to solve problems more effectively, might lead a such a person to greater creativity, greater confidence. And who knew what else.

After Henry fulfilled, neatly and efficiently, the promise of painting the living room, he pulled a screwdriver from his bucket of tools, and began to reattach the covers to an electrical outlet in the living room. He transferred the screwdriver to his left hand, and slowly turned the screw to the right. How much had tools to do with the reinforcement of right-handedness? Circular saws were made for righties as well. How ironic. Man develops tools in his struggle toward progress, the tools reinforce the social use of one side, and his dependence on tools keeps him from fuller progress.

He unburied a small rubber mallet from his bucket, and holding it in his left hand, he began to tap, slowly and deliberately, on the tin lid of the paint can. He had been given a gift. The ordinary event of a fallen ice cream cone had led Henry to one of the most important discoveries of his young fatherhood, and now he was on the verge of a watershed moment in the life of his son. He could ignore this discovery and muddle through life like every other ordinary man, with his blinders on and his fingers crossed. Or he could take this hint provided by the universe, and redirect the life of his son on an unstudied hunch.

If he were to simply see to it that every game of exchange for Danny—every handed behavior, every physical interaction with his world—was a symmetric one, he would give Danny a chance to make the most of his gift before the window of ambidexterity was slammed shut on him. What could possibly be the harm in such a thing? There could be no downside. And if there were unknown benefits to a lifelong pursuit of symmetry, together, Henry and Danny would discover them.

Dotted with splatters of paint, Henry stepped outside into the bright light of a brand new day, locked his front door with the key in his left hand, marveled at the right-handed, small-minded engineers who had designed ignitions for right-handed people, and he drove to Hildebrand Sports in order to purchase a left-handed baseball glove for his ambidextrous son. And beneath the surface there was a rumbling.

To observe Henry deliberate over the baseball gloves was to wonder whether the decision involved something far greater than baseball. He walked up and down the glove aisles for an hour and fifteen minutes, soberly assessing the features of a great variety of gloves, before settling on a Wilson A2000 *First Leather* glove.

As he drove home smiling at the opportunity each red light afforded him to work the leather of the new glove in his hands, Henry thought of Lori. How many times had he discussed the purchase of Danny's first baseball glove with her? And now, without discussion, he had purchased a second. If she thought that just having a catch was pushing Danny, what would she think about the symmetry crusade? Would she even know a left-hand glove from a right-hand glove if it slapped her in the head?

It was settled. He wouldn't tell her about this one.

He arrived at the babysitter's house earlier than he'd been expected.

When Danny was buckled tightly in his car seat, Henry lined the rear-view mirror up so that he could see Danny's eyes.

"Guess where we're going, Danny Boy."

In the back seat, Danny's eyes widened.

"We're going to play baseball at the park," he said. "And you're in for one helluva day."

At the park, Henry set a bucket of tennis balls on the infield grass and presented Danny with his new glove.

"Look what I got for you, Danny," he said.

Danny smiled and held his left hand out.

"Not this time," Henry said, reaching for Danny's right hand.

"Help me out, here, sport," he said, and Danny poked the fingers of his right hand into the new glove.

Danny punched his left hand into the glove.

"Bah," Danny said.

Henry dumped the bucket of balls on the grass and Danny raced to them, smiling, while Henry's heart knocked against his chest. Had the throw of the night before really happened? Or was it possible that Henry had imagined the entire thing?

Danny picked up a ball, and set it in the web of his new glove, and babbling incoherent exclamations, threw it into the right field. Henry laughed. Danny picked up another ball and this time didn't touch it to his glove even briefly. He picked it up and threw it without hesitation into centerfield. Smiling, he pickup up another ball and threw it into left field. And one by one he went through the pile of balls, switching between laughing and screaming as though neither behavior was enough to express what it was that he felt in the release of the ball from his fingers, or in the sight of the arc of each yellow orb as it sailed into the outfield grass.

"Giddy up, Danny Boy," Henry laughed, and with each proficient throw from the left side, his parental regret of the night before washed away. It was not too late. It was not too late.

And as the collection of tennis balls turned into a rainbow's arc spread across the outfield, Danny took off his new glove and dropped it to the ground. He picked up another ball with his right hand, and threw it in the outfield. He picked one up with his left hand and did the same.

Danny laughed and screamed. Henry laughed. And like a man who had just returned from a long and prodigal absence, like a man who'd returned with a change of heart, like a recovering squanderer of time Henry watched his son play. He watched as Danny held a tennis ball in each hand, reeled back on the right side and let it fly, then reeled back on the left and let it sail from there.

Among the things buzzing through Henry's mind as he observed Danny, were a coach's thoughts. There was much for the boy to learn. Baseball was a game of infinite intricacies that one could only fully absorb over the course of a lifetime. But as with walking, Danny's early proficiency suggested there were other ways to gain knowledge as well—ways Henry knew very little about. He wondered if Danny might have learned these things before, as if baseball were comprised mostly of lore that Danny had gleaned from some other time, from some other life. For Henry had taught his son nothing about a wind-up, nothing about how to lead with the opposite foot, nothing about the throwing motion necessary for so many sports, from the serve and the overhead smash in tennis, to the throw of a javelin. Henry had taught Danny nothing about following through across the body. And yet here Danny was—all of thirteen months old—winding up, leading with the opposite foot, following through on both sides of his body as if his muscles were being urged from some ancient memory.

Damn! How great would that be if he could talk about these things with Lori? If she had been an athlete it would have been possible. If she'd had a few brothers. Even one. Even if she'd had only one brother, she might understand.

Present, also, among Henry's thoughts, were a father's thoughts; he felt a father's joy at the sound of Danny's laugh, pure and genuine, as he picked up each new ball, and he laughed a father's laugh at Danny's scream, primal and piercing, as he set each ball free.

But Henry Granville was also a scientist, and like a father-scientist, Henry Granville, smiling—lost in some private place between laughter and tears—wondered at the joy on display before him. Was it merely the great happiness of a boy in the presence of sport? A bucket of balls and the freedom in which to throw them? Or was it something else? Did it have something to do with an inherent need for balance? Was it in the nature of man to seek balance? And in its fulfillment was utter joy the only possibility?

As the collection of balls diminished from Danny's sphere of play, Henry walked backward into the outfield to gather them, and from this distance he observed the fluid form of his son. Slightly bent at the knees, the earliest signs of his lower quadriceps just appearing at the hem of his shorts, throwing tennis balls from one side and the other, his tiny feet swiveling tennis shoeprints in the lawn, Danny was smiling with an animal gladness.

"Perfect symmetry," Henry whispered. "Perfect symmetry," and beneath the surface the rumbling grew.

With one eye on Danny, as Henry began replacing the balls in the bucket, he promised not to miss a single instant of Danny's life from that day forward. He would watch him eat, drink, play, work, study, and sleep. He wouldn't even sleep, in fact, nor even blink, if it came at the expense of missing a moment of Danny's life. With a careful eye he would work to help Danny stay within reach of the happiness that only came, perhaps, with perfect balance. He would oversee, whenever possible, each instance of Danny's life that involved the question of handedness. He would set Danny's spoon on the left side of his meals one day, and on the right side the next. He would put Danny's toothbrush in one hand in the morning, and the other hand at night. He would teach him to color and write with both of his hands. Not even the slightest of daily, handed activities would escape Henry's attention to balance in Danny's life.

Later, in his basement office—the vastness of ambidexterity and the operations of the brain swimming through his head—Henry pulled a mechanical pencil from his drawer, and finally addressed the rumbling current of that afternoon ever rising within him. He tore off the top sheet of his legal pad and set his pencil to paper.

Henry wrote a single fact at the top of his legal pad: *Danny could throw a ball with either hand.* And as the rumbling current of that afternoon began to rise within, Henry turned to the world of sport to consider the athletic implications of symmetry. The lead of his pencil scratched on the pad of paper before him.

What added value, in the arena of baseball, came with ambidexterity?

And it was then that the rumbling within finally grew to a point Henry could no longer ignore. He flipped the top sheet of his legal pad, folded it under the cardboard backing and put pencil to paper again.

Switch-pitcher, he wrote, and as he swept his finger across the words, he said them aloud.

"Switch-pitcher."

"What about that?" Henry said aloud. "What about that?"

With the setting of this phrase to paper, the rumblings within him slowly settled. What marvelous possibilities were contained in these two little words!

"What about that?" Henry said aloud. He began scratching notes on his pad.

What about someone who could throw well—really well—from either side?

A pitcher in a major league ball club's starting rotation typically pitched every four days. If he starts on Sunday he doesn't pitch until Thursday.

"But if he were a switch-pitcher," Henry said.

He could start Sunday's game.

"Let's say he gives his legs and torso an extra day to rest."

He could pitch lefty on Wednesday, then pitch righty again on Saturday. That would actually give his right arm six days of rest between right-arm starts. That's two more days rest between arms than a typical major league pitcher gets. And it still gives the other affected areas of his body—his legs and back primarily—three days rest between starts.

"Cubs schedule," Henry said, and he walked into the kitchen for the schedule magnetized on the refrigerator. He turned the kitchen light switch on, and sat at the table upstairs and scratched numbers on the back of an envelope. He computed the number of possible starts for a switch pitcher through a full major league season. Fingers crossed for perfect health, Danny could conceivably start fifty-eight games in one regular season.

"Fifty-eight games," Henry whispered.

Maybe even more if he was in top physical condition and could handle the stress on his legs and back.

If Danny won fifty percent of his starts, he'd have twenty-nine wins for the year. With one win over five hundred, he could be the first thirty-game winner since Denny McLain! And if he had velocity and control—maybe a nice curveball or slider . . .

Of course, he'd have to be good. He'd have to stay in excellent shape, he'd have to be disciplined, he'd have to be a good athlete, Henry thought. And Danny's remarkable precocity as a walking, throwing, and now, running, human being seemed to indicate that was not beyond imagination.

Henry returned to his basement office and pulled a calculator from a drawer of his desk. If Danny won, say sixty-two percent of his games, he'd have. . . . Thirty-six wins! No one had seen those kinds of numbers since Christy Mathewson won thirty-seven in 1908! And if Danny turned out to be as fine a pitcher as there was in the majors, someone who might ordinarily win twenty games a year with one arm, it was not inconceivable that he could break Jack Chesbro's 1904 record of forty one! Not only that, but an equal emphasis on both throwing arms would necessarily lead to strengthening Danny's body in a balanced way. It would lead to greater overall body symmetry, not only in the arms, but also in the shoulders, back, abdomen, and legs.

And so the campaign toward the complete symmetrization of Danny Granville was cemented in Henry's mind as a great and noble pursuit.

Before he left his basement office and returned to his wife upstairs, Henry had a dozen pages filled with the scribbled speculations of a baseball scientist whose son was on the verge of a thing the world had never seen.

When morning came the coffee maker put a sound and smell to hope. Henry opened the curtains of the living room windows, and the sun—a ball of hope at the bottom of the baby blue sky—was almost something to touch.

Danny was asleep in his crib. It would be a day to observe. In the bathroom, he squeezed toothpaste from the tube and while he brushed his teeth he looked in on Danny again. His knees were tucked beneath him as they were at the start of every morning, his cheek pressed against the mattress, his lips in the shape of a baby's wet kiss. It would be a day to assess.

On his return to the bathroom to rinse his mouth, Henry closed the door to his still sleeping wife. She would hardly shift in her bed until noon. She could sleep more than half of every day.

Henry filled his cup with coffee, lightened it with cream, and in the rocking chair in Danny's room, wondered at the dreams of one-year-old boys.

Henry's face was the first thing Danny saw when he opened his eyes to the morning, and minutes later, his little feet tapped against the legs of his highchair. On his tray, Henry spaced twelve Cheerios in a circle. They trembled tinily at the tap of Danny's feet. Henry filled a sippy cup with milk and set it at the top of the circle of Cheerios, and sat in a chair facing him.

In the pinch of his right hand, Danny picked up the one o'clock Cheerio and put it in his mouth. Next went the one at two o'clock and Henry began to wonder if he'd wasted a day's thoughts on ambidexterity.

While Danny had consumed the cheerios at three, four, five, and six o'clock by way of his right hand, Henry wondered again at the measures of handedness. He had set an even number of Cheerios in the shape and spacing of a clock in the center of the tray and Danny had made a right-handed choice. What did he expect? That a perfectly ambidextrous toddler would select one Cheerio with his right hand and the next with his left? Did a boy make *decisions* about what hand to use when it came to the simplest of handed behaviors? Certainly some of life's daily choices were made according to the handedness of the agent. What right-handed person, for example, would brush his hair with his left hand? But of the dozens of things a boy did with his hands in a given day, which could be called actual *choices*? It was not difficult to pick up a single Cheerio with either hand. Did a boy use his hands in such moments without thinking? And did it matter anyway, whether he employed his hands consciously or not? Was it a statement about handedness whether he applied intention or not? And if there were this many questions surrounding the event of breakfast, was it even remotely possible that Henry could help guide the handed choices of Danny's daily life?

And in the space of those first few minutes of that brand new day to which Danny had awakened, Henry knew already that he would drive himself crazy if he deliberated so furiously over every handed decision of Danny's life.

He mussed Danny's hair, and as he hustled into the basement for his legal pad and pencil he began to give rough shape to what would become the symmetry campaign of his only son. He would not attempt to direct every handed movement of Danny's life. He wouldn't be around him every minute of every day. And did it really matter, anyway, if Danny stacked more blocks or turned more pages with his right hand than his left? Did it matter if his first step up every stair was a left-footed choice? It was a right-handed world they lived in. That could not be changed. And Henry would not be able to force perfect balance into every insignificant fine motor behavior of Danny's life. He was not interested in seeing to it that Danny ate six Cheerios with his right hand and six with his left. Nor would it be possible to ensure such a thing over the life of a boy.

When Henry returned to the kitchen the clock of Cheerios was gone. Danny was grunting as he stretched toward the unreachable box of Cheerios lying on its side on the kitchen table. His sippy cup lay next to the upended cereal box, emptied of milk.

What Henry was not able to observe, as he had rushed into the basement for his legal pad and mechanical pencil, was which hand Danny had used to select the Cheerios from seven through twelve o'clock. Neither was he able to observe which hand Danny had used to throw the cup at the box of cereal in a vain attempt to draw it near.

Henry laughed. "Son of a bitch," he said. "Nice throw."

"Bitch," Danny said.

"I mean, *son of a gun*," Henry said. "Don't say *bitch*, Danny."

"Bitch," Danny said, and Henry poured a mound of Cheerios on the tray of the high chair.

No, Henry thought, as he refilled Danny's sippy cup with milk. There would be no lifelong counting of Cheerios. There would be no freaking out over minor deviations from symmetry. If Danny turned every page of every book he'd ever read with the fingers of his right hand, it wouldn't mean a thing against an ambidextrous life. He would foster an environment in which Danny would be given the opportunity to thrive as a symmetrical human being. *That* he could do.

And so the campaign began immediately. Henry would see only to the things that required dexterity. Agility was important. When they went outside for a catch Henry would toss him a lefty glove one day and a righty glove the next. He would teach Danny to bat from both sides of the plate. When Danny starting tending to his own teeth, Henry would put the brush in his right hand in the morning and in his left hand at night. And when Danny started eating with a spoon and fork, Henry would vary the placement of his silverware from day to day. And when he was old enough to help him around the house, he would teach Danny how to screw in light bulbs, swing a hammer, tighten a screw, unlock the door, zipper a jacket, and write out the alphabet with both hands.

And so the campaign began. In the yard, he taught Danny how to dribble, shoot lay-ups and free throws from both sides. He set up empty cans of tennis balls in a pyramid and had Danny knock them down with tennis balls. He taught him how to throw a football with both hands, and how to take a hockey slapshot from both sides. They played soccer as well, took shots on each other on the strength of both legs.

It made sense to Henry, as he attempted to develop Danny into a perfectly ambidextrous person, that he should also implement the same bimodal balance into his own life. He began brushing his teeth, using his fork and spoon, and opening doors with his left hand. He dialed phone numbers, tightened screws, and replaced light bulbs; he combed his hair, clipped his toenails, and held his coffee cup with his weaker hand. When he found himself using his right hand in some daily endeavor, he attempted to complete the task with his left, and one summer he built an entire deck as a left-handed carpenter. He'd even taught himself to use a circular saw backwards—like a lefty carpenter he'd seen years before. He consciously switched hands when he found himself about to pour a glass of milk with his right hand. He began to throw the ball left-handed when he had a catch with Danny. He became more conscious of those activities that naturally expected more of his right hand than his left. He'd put his key in the door with his right hand, catch himself, and take it out again. He'd return it to the keyhole with his left hand, and open the door. For years he'd worn his watch on his left wrist, so he moved it to his right. He realized also, that when he put his shirts and pants on, he always slipped his left limbs in first, so he reversed the entry limb. He began to thread his belt around his waist from right to left.

They made a game of it until it was second nature for Danny to do these things as easily from one side as the other.

And even Danny's affection for both Chicago baseball teams—though he favored the White Sox—suggested another kind of balance.

And Danny grew.

In the early spring of 1988, Danny was drafted by the Texas Rangers tee-ball team of the Forest Park Little League, and with some direction from Henry, Danny began to bat right handed when their team took the dugout on the third-base side, and lefty when they took the dugout at first base. Henry helped the coaches out, and when he could, he chose the dugout with Danny's bimodal progress in mind.

Except for bursts of energy, most of the tee-ball players would have been fine playing only one inning. Danny was an exception, though; he couldn't get enough of the game. When Danny played the field he seemed to know where the ball was going by the time the batter made contact. Henry laughed at the comments of the parents in the stands.

"That kid's a monster."

"Look at that kid at short! He could play this team by himself!"

Even Lori seemed proud to hear the other parents speak of Danny's ability on the field. On her better days, she would relate their comments to Henry.

"That guy with the crazy eye pointed at Danny," she said to Henry one night. "And said, 'That's the way the game was meant to be played.' "

"Another guy," she told Henry, "walked up to his son in the dugout and said, 'You see, Jack, *that's* how to get in a ready position! *That's* what I'm talking about!' "

Danny's team had two games a week during that first tee-ball season, and Henry took him to the batting cages at every chance. And they kept at pitching, too, though it would be three years, at least, before Danny could actually pitch in a little league game.

As August unfolded into September, Henry turned his thoughts toward remodeling the basement so that Danny would have a place to play when the weather turned. What he told Lori was that he was thinking about straightening up the basement a bit, so that Danny could have some space to run around through the winter.

And over the first few weeks of the new school year, Henry went to work.

To make room in the long rectangle of the basement, he created a miracle of a storage system in two side rooms, so that all of the Granvilles' more idle possessions gathered over the course of their separate and connected lives could be cleared from the arena and kept in two smaller rooms to the side. There were pulleys and hinges and hooks. Drawers rolled from under shelves. Bicycles hung from the ceiling. Garden tools rested in racks anchored to the walls. Boxes were labeled and stacked on shelves. From floor to ceiling and wall-to-wall, sense was made of every inch of space in these inner rooms.

But the method of storage was not the most remarkable quality of the remodeled basement. It was early November when Henry applied what he thought was the finishing touch on Danny's last day of summer break. He laid close-cropped artificial turf along the floor of the main room and constructed a portable pitcher's mound so that as Danny's strength and accuracy improved, the mound could be set further back from home plate to allow for pitching at greater distances. The mound was raised several inches off the floor. A lever on the side of the mound locked the wheels into the hollow underside of the mound to stabilize the device.

But it was Lori who brought the basement stadium to life.

Seventh

DANNY STARTED JUNIOR KINDERGARTEN IN SEPTEMBER, WHICH SENT Lori into a weeklong funk. She picked up a few hours more at the bookstore, which took some edge from the sadness, but then October came. And through its rains, its wind and cold, and the hard of its fall—the certainty of the endless gray winter ahead—the fatigue returned and she wanted only sleep. By November she wanted to cry as well. When Henry's alarm went off every morning so he could get Danny ready for school, Lori buried herself under the covers until she couldn't put rising off any longer.

Henry, it seemed, had all but given up on her. When he was home, he was either working on the basement, preparing for his classes, or playing baseball with Danny. Pushing Danny out into the world, is what it felt like. There were days, it seemed, she had energy only for tears and sleep.

It was difficult for Henry to see, but in what ways she could, Lori fought against the autumnal sadness. She wore sundresses late into September. In the park, at the bottom of the Circle Bridge she found the least shaded bench and tilted her head toward the sun. The sun seemed to help.

But for all her fatigue and depression, Lori couldn't get back to sleep the day that followed Henry's installation of the Astroturf carpet in the basement. After Henry and Danny said goodbye that morning she sat awake in bed and for more than an hour considered the great waste of an off day she could not sleep through. Why did Henry have to wake her up before taking Danny to school? Tomorrow she would ask him to not kiss her goodbye on Fridays when she wasn't working. She tried to will herself back to sleep. She tried reading in bed. She took a warm bath. And finally, after a cup of decaffeinated tea she gave into the day, and just before ten o'clock hauled Danny's hamper of tiny clothes into the basement to launder its contents.

She'd expected cold hard cement at the bottom of the stairs leading to the basement. When she felt, with the slippered toes of her right foot, the warm give of the turf carpet she shrieked. Her left foot was already moving toward purchase, so when she pulled back her right foot she stumbled onto the wicker hamper that fell from her arms. She stood and flipped the light switch.

Against the gray and lifeless memory of the floor, the carpet was a deep and tender and living green, so green it seemed as though Henry had laid sod across the unforgiving floor.

She uprighted the hamper and sat on its lid, rubbing at the wicker abrasion on her chin. The basement appeared enormous, emptied as it was, of all but the sink and washer and dryer. It had become a long, deep yard. It had become the backyard of a house where children dwelt, a field of summer grass, a children's park inside of a house, a valley in the country.

Henry had smiled at the poetry of Lori's telling.

She felt that Henry made summer of a basement, and Lori sat upon her wicker box seat in the new stadium, looking at the expanse of the field. It did not strike Lori as odd that she would weep in such a place. She felt as though it were possible—if she was did not take care, that she might fall asleep, and stay there through Danny's boyhood. She was afraid, she told Henry, that if she were careless, while her husband and son *lived*, really lived—playing and building and making and living— she just might sleep away a life. And she cried at that possibility. On her wicker seat, she wept and promised she would not sleep away her life.

She had allowed her sadness to take over everything, to blind her, to put distance between her and Henry, between her and Danny. She had given her sadness the power of anger.

Lori rose from the hamper and walked along the basement floor to see the rest of what Henry had done. Four crude bases made of cardboard were placed in the shape of a diamond on the infield. Foul lines made of strips of athletic tape undulated across the floor without regard for perspective. The on-deck circles were misshapen cutouts of white poster board, and the baselines and dugouts seemed they were scrawled in chalk by the hand of a child. She laughed at Henry's stick figure sketches of baseball fans on the walls.

As Lori moved from crying to laughing the tears flowed, and even through the tumbling emotions she wondered at the overlap of tears. It was as though there had been some miscommunication with the tear ducts, as though they had not been told their reason for being had become another thing—that their services were no longer necessary. And it was laughter that broke through. She was laughing.

And still the tears came as she laughed at Henry's foul pole past third base. He'd tacked a long strip of cardboard from ceiling to floor, and with a sharpie marker had written *foul pole* up and down the length of it. Across the room he'd tacked another just like it for the right field line.

And even as she put her finger on the laughter, the tears came. Lori felt, then, that she had been given the gift of vision, the pure vision of what was possible, and she held it for comparison against the vision of what she knew she would become if she gave in to the sadness, what she would become if she'd kept sleeping.

The joy that finally broke through was about the dugouts and the stick figure fans, the cardboard foul poles that needed words to be real, the scotch-taped silliness of the unfinished wonderland, but mostly the joy was that it was not too late. She could do this.

She splashed her face with water and dressed into an old pair of jeans and a tee shirt, and in twenty minutes was walking the aisles of the Home Depot on North Avenue. She bought two gallons of paint the color of a baseball player's sky, and with colorless regard she filled the bottom of her cart with a dozen quarts of paint from a shelf of mixed mistakes. She bought brushes in four sizes and turned up the radio volume in the car on the way home. She stopped in at Hildebrand Sports and bought a rubber home plate and three padded bases.

Henry and Danny were banned from the basement that weekend.

Lori came upstairs for short breaks to eat and feed and ask how days had been. When she finished her work on Sunday afternoon, she walked upstairs and took Danny's hand in one of hers and took Henry's hand in the other.

"Close your eyes," she said, and she led them into the basement.

"Don't peek," she said on the stairs, and when they touched the turf carpet on the basement floor, she said it again. Obediently, Danny covered his eyes with his hands. Henry hooked his arm into Lori's and she guided him to the center of the field, where she finally allowed them to open their eyes.

Danny opened his eyes and said nothing. He turned around in the space he stood until he had seen all sides of the stadium three times. And when he finally seemed to see that it was true—that the basement was not a dream—he laughed and ran the bases in slow motion.

Henry looked at the boundless expanse of the stadium. He laughed a wide-eyed and silent laugh, looking from Lori to the walls and from Lori to the ceiling, and from Lori to the limitless sky beyond the bleachers.

No more did his eyes settle on anything, though, than they did on his wife, as though even against the extraordinary transformation of the space, what had been discovered in his wife was greater still.

He walked to left field and looked to Lori as he slowly brought his fingers to the foul pole.

"You can touch it," she said. "It's dry." And Henry touched the foul pole and laughed.

A horizon line had been set on the walls with remnants of Astro-turf carpet. Above the horizon, on the walls and ceiling, there were white clouds sponged in a summer sky. It seemed to Henry as though the basement walls had fallen away and the ceiling disappeared. All that had given limit to the room was gone.

A thousand featureless fans stood in the background of the stadium stands, and in the foreground they had faces, real and alive. Here the face of a greasy-haired beer vendor, sweat-drenched and scream-ing, reached through the crowd and into the basement. And here a girl in a tank top wearing a long, blond ponytail threaded through the back of her baseball cap reached her glove into the field for a foul ball. Here was the face of Henry's father keeping official score, and next to him, Lori's father.

Along the outfield stands Lori had painted the ivy of Wrigley Field with shadows that lifted the leaves off the surface, and high on the back wall she painted the exploding scoreboard of old Comiskey Park, complete with pinwheels and clock. The door to Henry's office was the entrance to the bullpen when it was open and a concession stand when it was closed.

Henry laughed at what the space had become.

Danny was still laughing, still running the bases in slow motion.

It was ten that night before Danny's racing heart stilled enough to allow for sleep. When Henry finally left Danny's room and returned to the basement to see it again, he found Lori softened by candlelight, he found her showered and bathrobed and sitting on a picnic blanket in center field, a glass of wine in her hand. Reaching toward Henry.

Henry took the glass and sipped his wine as he walked along the field in wide-eyed wonder, and when he returned to her she had loosened the cloth belt of her robe. In the candlelight she sat with her breasts half revealed and she told Henry how alive she had felt that entire weekend. She pointed at features of the baseball stadium he might not have seen, and Henry smiled and listened. She lay back against him and sipped wine while Henry brushed his fingernails across her chest and marveled at what the weekend had become. And when the wine was gone, Lori sat up and unbuttoned Henry's shirt. She pulled away his pants and boxers and rolled them into a pillow. And under the influence of a bottle of wine, and to the witness of a sold-out crowd at the first night game of the winter season, on a red-and-white-checkered tablecloth in the middle of the basement stadium, Lori Granville lay back on the floor, with Henry's clothes for a pillow. She untied the loosened cloth belt at her waist, opened her robe to her husband, and reached to him with her fingers.

"Come here," she said. And Lori closed her eyes as Henry slowly and tenderly obliged.

He took great care with the gift she had given to him that night. It had been so long. If Henry could have just watched her all night he would gladly have done so. But Lori wanted all of him. She told him so. And Henry entered her slowly, reaching greater depths with the tenderest care, settling at each definite space to kiss her on the corner of her lips, or to wipe away a silent tear that stuck at the edge of her eye, or to stretch time.

And Lori seemed to feel each minute shift within. Puffs of sound seemed to come from within. The whispers of a body, perhaps, that was grateful for the gift of time. When Henry's hips were pressed against hers—his cheek in the hollow of her shoulder—Lori opened her eyes and set them on the historic sky she had painted, she put her hands to Henry's hips.

"Are you okay," Henry said.

"Yes," she said. And she fingertipped lines from his hips to his ribs.

"I want you to see this," she said, and slowly she pulled from beneath him and Henry took her space on her white robe on the picnic blanket on the field of grass beneath them. She knelt over him and as slowly as he had entered her just moments before, she lowered herself onto him, she eased him within. And when her hips had pressed against his again, she told him to open his eyes.

"I want you to see the sky," she said.

And Henry looked at Lori above him. She leaned over him and pressed her lips against his ear. "I want you to see the sky," she said again.

And Henry put his hand at the small of Lori's back and looked over her shoulder at the sky. He held her against him until she was still. When she began to sway against him again, Henry held her so that her movements were easy and slow, as if, on the chance that she left again, and never returned, he wanted to give her something to recall.

When the trembling came, Lori cried.

"Are you okay," Henry said.

"I think so," Lori said. "I think I am."

Before the smell of semi-gloss paint left the basement, Lori went to work turning Judy's old bedroom upstairs into an art studio. She painted the room and bought a canvas tarp and tacked it on the floor. She opened an account at Pearl Art Supplies and bought an easel and pencils and pens and paints, chalk and clay and brushes. She returned art to her life.

And she would bring art into Danny's life, as well. Among the pieces of Judy's furniture that Lori did not let go was an antique children's desk that had been used by all of Judy's children. Lori brought it into the studio and it became the centerpiece of Danny's space in the studio. On countless afternoons that followed, Danny would greet Henry after work with sketches he had made, dinosaurs and cars and superheroes and baseball players.

"We had a picnic in the studio upstairs," Danny would say. "Close your eyes, Dad." And Henry would close his eyes and swear to their closure several times until they reached the kitchen where Danny's latest artwork struggled against refrigerator magnets.

"Tada," Danny would say and Henry would open his eyes wide and tell Danny it was the most beautiful thing he had ever seen.

And Lori would stand at Henry's shoulder with her hands on her hips and her head tilted proudly.

It was impossible for Henry to think about the time Lori and Danny were spending in the studio upstairs without wondering how it fit into the symmetry campaign. Sometimes he looked at Danny's drawings for great lengths of time, wondering if he could tell, by attending to them closely, whether they were drawn with his left or right hand. But he never pressed the issue with Lori. She'd been spending more time with Danny. She seemed happier than she'd been in years, and against the question of whether Danny colored with his left hand or his right, the weights of her happiness and her return to them were heavier things.

And Henry interpreted Lori's creative participation in the basement stadium as a kind of permission to raise Danny's athletics to another level.

Along the rear and side walls of the basement, Henry hung double-netting on a pulley system to protect the walls, and set up a hitting tee at home plate. After dinner he would take Danny in the basement stadium and set whiffle balls and tennis balls on the tee while Danny took fifty swings from the left side and fifty from the right.

Using PVC pipes and netting Henry built a pitching screen, behind which he sat on an overturned bucket and tossed soft cloth balls to Danny. After Danny took another fifty swings from each side of the plate, Henry would back up and pitch another bucket of balls with a little more speed on them.

They worked on defense as well. After their work at the plate Danny would take the field while Henry peppered a bucket of grounders to him. Danny wore his glove on his left hand and threw the imaginary runners out with his right. Then he switched out his glove and fielded a bucket of balls from the other side, never questioning the balanced attention his father paid to everything, the insistence on this glove now, on taking swings from this side now, on writing with his pen in this hand, on combing his hair with this hand, kicking the ball with this foot, shooting a lay-up from this side.

And the young athlete spent the winters of his boyhood in the basement stadium where it was always summer and mostly sunny. Where the sky was always blue.

Eighth

As DANNY GREW, HENRY WORKED HIS PERSONAL RESEARCH ON handedness into his science classes at U-High. To his elective, the Social Life of Animals, he added a section on sexual dimorphism and beauty as they related to physical symmetry in kingdom animalia. To his biology course he added a section on the human brain and the functions of its hemispheres. And in his Primate Behavior and Ecology class Henry squeezed a two-day section on ambidexterity among the Western Lowland Gorillas. Only once, though, did Henry bring up the issue of his son's personal ambidexterity campaign. It happened in the spring of 1992, the year Danny Granville turned nine.

Primate Behavior was an elective for students on the soft-core science track, and the roster typically boasted its share of slackers and lazy schemers.

At first, it seemed to Henry that Michael Finnegan would fit right in with the rest of the clowns. Henry put up with his smartass comments the first day of class that semester, but shut him down the next time they met. Before five minutes of class had passed, Finnegan raised his hand and Henry called on him.

"Do you like Black Sabbath?" Finnegan said.

Henry looked at him for a moment as if to say *are you kidding me?* And feeling he'd made his point, Henry continued the lesson. But minutes later Finnegan raised his hand again.

"Is this about Black Sabbath?" Henry asked, and the class laughed.

"No, sir," Finnegan said.

"Go on, then," Henry said.

"Knock knock," Finnegan said, and in a very quiet classroom,

Henry walked slowly to Finnegan's desk and leaned to whisper in his ear.

"I want you to listen closely, Finnegan," he said. "I don't know who you think you are, but I'm guessing you fancy yourself the class clown. You say something funny, and the class laughs, and you think well of yourself for having made them laugh. But here's the thing, Finnegan. Though I've only known you for two days I think you're an ass. And you're not funny. And perhaps—because you don't know me, either—you think I'm an idiot and don't deserve your respect, but I can assure you that I'm not an idiot, Finnegan, and neither will I be publicly mocked by one. And finally, if you're taking this class in your senior year, I suspect that means you need to pass it in order to graduate, which means you need *me* far more than I need you, see?" Henry continued in the quietest of whispers, "So you just sit here, and keep your mouth shut, okay, Finnegan?"

It seemed as though Finnegan's lips moved slightly in the direction of a response, but no sound came forth.

"Nod your head if you understand what I'm saying, Finnegan."

Finnegan nodded his head.

"Excellent," Henry whispered.

After that the whispering Finnegan was well behaved. There were days, in fact, that he showed signs of life—scholarship, even.

Since Henry's discovery of his son's ambidexterity, he had been addressing the foraging sphere of the Western Lowland Gorilla as an introduction to a section on bimodality in the animal world, and the day he address this in class Henry thought he had noticed something in Finnegan's eyes. The boy seemed *locked in* from the moment Henry drew his crude ape in a tree on the white board. Finnegan seemed to be taking notes furiously, flipping the pages of his spiral notebook as space ran out on the previous sheet.

Five minutes before the end of class Finnegan raised his hand.

"Michael," Henry said.

"Question, Mr. Granville," Finnegan said. He looked off toward the window and addressed Henry as though he were suspended in the air outside. "This may seem random," Finnegan said, "but are there any switch-pitchers in baseball?"

Henry felt his heart race.

"You use the word *successful*," Finnegan continued, "to describe the Lowland Gorilla, and you address how the prospects of its foraging success are improved because of its bimodal ability, and I was just thinking about how that relates to man."

Henry nodded slowly, crossed his arms over his chest to still his racing heart.

". . . and it seems so obvious to me that it would be awesome for a baseball player to be able to pitch with both arms."

Henry nodded again.

"I can't believe that in all these years of baseball I've never heard of anyone actually being a switch-pitcher," Finnegan said.

Henry smiled.

And while Michael Finnegan began to offer the mathematics he had scribbled on his notebook for his hypothetical switch-pitcher, Henry considered how lovely it would have been to dismiss the class and spend the rest of the afternoon talking about the myriad implications of a high-caliber switch-pitching athlete.

Henry had never discussed the symmetry campaign with Lori. For one, she was terrifically opposed to competition; Henry was certain she would have interpreted his interest in Danny's bimodal development as an endorsement of a thing she hated. She would say that Henry was living vicariously through Danny. Henry couldn't argue with her.

In fact, Henry hadn't discussed the campaign with *anyone*. And now that Finnegan had brought the issue into the classroom, had said the words *switch-pitcher* aloud, it felt for a moment like consent to speak about the thing that had consumed Henry for nearly a decade. Was it possible that Finnegan was experiencing in this moment all that Henry had experienced in the days that followed his discovery of Danny's left-handed throw? Was it possible that the kid's mind was reeling with the same frenetic possibility that Henry's reeled with that day?

"Do you know what I mean?" Finnegan said.

"Say that again," Henry said.

"A switch-pitcher could probably start sixty-eight games in a regular season," Finnegan said.

"I'm thinking more like fifty-eight games," Henry said.

"Why fifty-eight?" Finnegan said.

"I figure he'd need more time to rest between starts, not just for his arm but for his back and lower body as well."

Finnegan nodded. "Makes sense," he said.

"The kid would have to be talented and disciplined," Henry continued. "And he'd have to be in amazing shape. But he's already headed in that direction. He throws as well lefty as he does righty, and he's already throwing in the high forties, I clock him once a week with a radar gun in the basement stadium, and if Danny wins only sixty-two percent of his major league starts, he'll end the season with thirty-six wins. How's that for a season?"

"Danny?" Finnegan said.

"What?" Henry said.

"You said *Danny,*" Finnegan said.

Henry said nothing.

"Your son's a switch-pitcher?" Finnegan said.

And just like that Henry's secret had become a thing revealed. Seldom at a loss for words, and well-schooled in the art of classroom management, Henry froze while his secret lay exposed to the world, hung in the air for anyone to see, steal, or exploit.

He looked at the clock. Any second now.

"You raised a great point, Michael," Henry said while turning back to address the class. "Write this question down in your notebooks," he said. And the sound of pencils and pens shifting on paper whispered through the room.

"What are the measures of success for a Western Lowland Gorilla?" Henry said. "And how, in our daily lives, might we be more successful if we look to members of Kingdom Animalia for lessons on adaptability?"

The bell announced the end of the period. From his desk Henry watched Michael Finnegan walk out of class looking at the still-opened notes at the top of his short stack of books and tilting his head toward further wondering.

After class Henry walked into his office with a mass of anxiety in his chest. It felt as though something hot and yellow had come to life just behind his sternum and was growing steadily from the moment Finnegan had asked about Danny. At his desk Henry muttered "fuck" into his hands. From behind him came the voice of Emily Seltzer, the new English teacher who had been assigned to the only open faculty desk at U-High, in the science office next to Henry.

"You okay, Henry?"

"Oh, sorry Emily."

She propelled herself on her wheeled chair—like a child, Henry felt—to his side.

"What's up?" she said.

Henry looked at Emily and smiled. "Nothing," he said. "Why?"

"My mentor teacher, whom I've never heard swear, comes into the office, buries his head in his hands and says *fuck*. I'm going to say something's wrong."

"Sorry about my language," Henry said.

"No need to apologize," Emily said. "I'm actually a fan of swearing."

"You want someone to chat with," she continued, and Henry smiled again.

"I'm good," he said, and with a quick push of her athletic legs, she was back at her desk across the room.

What was worrying him? Was it the fear of exposure? Shame? Is that what it was? Would he feel shameful if the world accused him of pushing his son toward something unnatural? If he couldn't even be totally honest with Lori about the symmetry campaign, what made him think the world would understand? Or was he worried that someone else would come along and beat him to the punch? Was he afraid that Finnegan would embark on his own campaign?

Finnegan was absolutely right about one thing: it was ludicrous that in this sports-obsessed world no one had ever really seriously considered the question enough to set off on a lifelong crusade to develop an athlete into a switch-pitcher. Why was that? Did it require a convergence of things—events, knowledge, temperament, history—things so specific and precise that they'd never before come together? And that only now, in the person of Danny Granville, the forces had come together to allow for the realization of the thing?

It seemed to Henry that this might have been so. And for the first time, with the mere public inquiry of the possibility of a switch-pitcher, Henry worried that the forces necessary for its realization might converge in someone other than Danny. Someone would figure it out one day, and Henry—the scientist and sportsman, the father, wanted to make his point before any other man.

But it was more than this. Henry's unwitting inclusion of Finnegan into his secret made him worry about how the rest of the world might respond to a young switch-pitching superstar. What if the media got hold of this hotshot nine-year-old who could throw a baseball from both sides, and what if they pumped him up like they'd done with young athletes before?

On that Tuesday afternoon in April, Henry Granville began to imagine the danger of Danny's discovery by the world. He would hold the secret. It would become his great hoarding.

Danny met Patrick Decker at the first day of kid-pitch baseball that year. Joe Sansone, the coach of the Padres' nine-year-old team, paired the boys up on the first day of preseason practice and told them to warm up with a catch.

The players began warming up by short-tossing balls to one another. Decker was a mess. Not a single ball traveled more than ten feet from his hand. The baseball slipped disobediently from his fingers every time he attempted to throw.

Danny watched him closely. "Keep going," he said. "A couple more."

Danny focused on the path of Patrick's throw from his wind-up to his release point. He saw the motion as though it were a collection of countless still photographs, each frame distinct in some tiny way from the one it followed, like flip art.

After retrieving Patrick's final throw, Danny walked up to his new teammate.

"Hang on," Danny said, reaching toward Patrick with the ball. "Hold this like you're getting ready to throw."

Patrick froze with his hand on the ball, two fingers at the top of it and his thumb at the bottom. Against the spanking white of the brand new baseball, Patrick's fingers were long, thin night crawlers.

Danny tucked his own glove under his arm and faced Decker.

"Is that how you hold the ball right before you throw it?"

Decker nodded.

"Just like this?"

Decker nodded again.

Danny put the ball in the pinch of his thumb and finger and pulled it without effort from Michael's hand.

"Get a better grip on it," Danny said. "And spread your fingers a little more." Danny stepped away from Patrick.

"Now let's give it another shot," he said. But as Danny stepped away from Patrick, a dozen frames of the flip art of his teammate's throw flashed before his eyes.

"Hold on," Danny said. "Let me see that grip again." And Patrick held the ball toward Danny.

"Let's give this a shot," Danny said. "Put three fingers on top of the ball, like this," he said, and he modeled the grip for Patrick.

"Like this," he said. "Rest your pinky on the side of it, and hold the ball tighter in your hand before you let it go."

It was not how a ball should be thrown, Danny thought as he put his glove back on, but something in Patrick's wormy fingers was keeping him from throwing the ball without distance or accuracy.

Decker's next throw sailed into Danny's glove with a slap against the leather basket, and Danny laughed. He threw the ball back to Patrick.

"How'd that feel?" Danny said, and Patrick smiled.

"Throw it over my head this time," Danny said, and Decker's next throw sailed over Danny's head, three times the distance of any ball he had thrown before.

On Opening Day Danny went three for three at the plate and pitched a complete game from the right side and the Padres won four to zero.

After the game he asked his father if he should pitch his next game lefty.

"I've been thinking about that, Danny," Henry said. "But I think you ought to stick with righty."

"And not pitch lefty at all?" Danny said.

"I just think we ought to work on your right side during games and see how that goes," Henry said. "If you start struggling as a righty then we'll play it by ear, know what I mean?"

After the game Danny balanced himself by throwing left-handed pitches to Henry in the alley behind Lathrop. After forty-six throws Henry stood from the overturned bucket and started walking toward Danny.

"That's only forty-six pitches," Danny said.

"That's how many pitches you made during the game," Henry said.

"I threw forty-seven, Dad," Danny said.

"Are you sure?"

"I'm positive," Danny said.

Henry set up the bucket and sat down, punched his hand in his catcher's mitt and held the target before Danny for one more pitch.

And so Danny's right arm became his game arm that first season of kid-pitch, and his right remained a secret, shared only with to his father in the alley behind Lathrop Street or with Patrick in the downstairs stadium, where there were night games, and where baseball could be played in the rain.

On their way to the park for a late April game against the Dodgers, the Granvilles drove past Kurt Lewis, a fourth-grade classmate of Danny's. Kurt played for the Dodgers, and even from a half block away Danny knew it was Kurt. He was tall and thin, his shoulders slouched mopily. Kurt was alone and coatless. Armless, too, it seemed. Against the gray chill of the April morning he had his arms pulled inside his jersey for the warmth of his skin. He held his mitt—a White Sox giveaway glove, more plastic than leather—at the hem of his jersey.

When kids at school imitated Kurt's loping stride they did it with springy exaggeration, laughing as they bounced in the air. Sometimes even Kurt smiled at their mockery. But as they drove past him that morning and Kurt Lewis looked into the car there was something too sad to smile about as far as Danny could see. He waved, and Kurt lifted his hand in a slow wave to his classmate, but as his arms were pilloried in his shirt he could only flick his baseball mitt at his hip and nod his head sadly.

At the park, Danny watched Kurt take batting practice swings. He was terrible. From start to finish his swing was a flailing, spastic, misinformed, and futile exertion of energy. Forty or fifty people would be at the game that day but none of them would be Kurt's parents. The word at school was that Lewis's father was in prison, and if he had a mother no one knew.

Kurt dropped his bat without hitting a single ball during batting practice. He took off his helmet and recovered his glove from the dugout and shuffled to right field to chase fly balls with his teammates. When Danny closed his eyes, the image of Kurt walking to the ballpark returned to him; the odd, moping gait, and sadness in his eyes as he watched Danny pass in the car. The flickering wave of his glove at his hip.

If Danny could have made everyone else go away for an hour, or freeze them right where they were—everyone but Kurt—if he could just stop time for twenty minutes, Danny would have shown him how to swing a bat with his whole body. He would have taught him how to *load up* and he would have made it so Kurt would come to the plate and hit the ball the ball so far and so hard that no one would ever make fun of him again.

But with the game just ready to start there wasn't even time for an apology, which is the other thing Danny wanted to do with frozen time. He wanted apologize to Kurt for everything Danny had. For his family car and for his coat, for his .800 batting average from the left side and his .800 average from the right. And for having a father and mother at the game today.

And while Danny wished for the momentary cessation of time he closed his eyes and felt a silence wash over Forest Park. From the stands behind him the chatter of parents disappeared with the choral disorder of two dozen boys before a baseball game. In the silence, the image of Kurt performing his terrible swing appeared before Danny, this time as a series of consecutive-motion still shots that captured the full path of Lewis's swing like a rapid-fire flipbook. Each frame lay before Danny's closed eyes—tinily distinct from the one before—as clear as Polaroid snapshots. Lewis's ten batting practice swings had etched themselves into Danny's game day memory.

If Danny could have wished for anything that day it would not have been to pitch a perfect game or to hit a grand slam to win it in his last at bat of the game. If he could he would have willed Kurt Lewis to get a hit. Each Dodger who came to the plate to face Danny on the mound after Kurt Lewis's first at bat was an irritation, a thing between Danny and his single goal for the game: to feed Lewis a ball the kid could hit.

Lewis flailed away at Danny's first pitch to him in the fourth inning. Danny watched his second swing closely. The same swing. He watched Lewis's fourth swing. As convulsive and terrible as it was, there was a sameness in the swings. Each swing took the same wild path as the one before. Each swing missed the ball completely and certainly. It seemed to Danny that what stood between Kurt and contact with the ball was a miracle, and with the Padres close to beating the Dodgers by slaughter rule, Danny might have only one more chance to pitch one for the kid.

While the Padres were at bat in the bottom of the fifth, Danny eyed Kurt as the Dodger stood in right field. The late morning sun poked through a cloud in a band of light just past the second baseman, and through that band of light a crow flapped into the sky and cawed above Kurt Lewis. When its shadow flitted over his head Kurt flinched. His glove twitched into the air above his shoulders as if he were trying to catch the darting thing. Danny smiled at this same bird that had fooled every boy who had ever played the game, the bird whose shadow looked so much like the shadow of a baseball, and Danny closed his eyes to read the flipbook of Kurt's swing again, and to focus on the lesson of the crow that had made Kurt Lewis flinch.

The only way to correct the timing of Lewis's swing was to fool him. He would make Kurt think that he was about to throw the ball, but Danny would hesitate for the same split of a second that Kurt held his foot in the air before swinging.

Danny struck out the eighth hitter to start the top of the sixth, and when Kurt Lewis came to the plate Danny held his glove in front of his face. In the shadow of his leather mitt the flipbook frames of Kurt's swing returned once again. Danny lowered his glove to his chest and reeled back for the first pitch. At the point of release he flicked his hand back as if to throw, but he held it there, and as Kurt lifted his leg to begin his flail Danny hesitated, only releasing the ball when Kurt had moved through several frames of his swing. The ball floated toward home as Lewis's bat chopped its way across the plate, high over the strike zone, and for a moment, the chatter of parents and siblings in the stands on either side of the field that had blanketed Forest Park for most of a morning ended, and the silence that Danny had imagined in a wash over the field, had for a moment become a reality, when his fifty-ninth pitch of the game smacked against the spastic swing of Kurt Lewis's bat and dinked over the head of the shortstop while Kurt Lewis ran, smiling, to first base.

Even the Padres fans cheered in the stands when Kurt Lewis

reached base. Fans on the Dodgers side were on their feet in the bleachers, and beneath his own feet, Danny Granville could almost feel the padded base that Kurt Lewis felt beneath his.

He struck out the next batter and when the final hitter popped out to the mound to end the game, Danny walked to Kurt Lewis and put the ball in his glove.

"Nice hit," he said. "Put this in your pocket."

For Danny, that first season of kid-pitch baseball was shorter than a summer had ever been. After games he balanced himself by throwing to Henry or Patrick in the alley behind Lathrop. With autumn came park district soccer and flag football and with winter came basketball and floor hockey, until volleyball finally welcomed back spring and the promise of baseball. Henry observed Danny as he always had, charting his attention to balance and symmetry as any good scientist would. Each sport held its own allure for Danny, who applied to them the same energy he did baseball. Soccer's attention to the legs seemed to thrill him. In basketball, his use of both sides of the court, his ability to shoot with either hand, make layups on either side of the basket, and dribble with both hands allowed him to foil his opponents every time he held the ball. Within these mini-seasons of park district athletics he studied every sport with a scholar's discipline. The complexity of football—its sheer numbers of players in great spatial concentration—captivated him. It was nearly impossible to defend him on the field; his peers felt it was unfair to go against him, and a gift from above to be with. He could throw, pass, kick, catch, run, leap, shoot, hit, field, and catch like a man among boys. There were trophies and uniforms and sports banquets, there were MVP awards and plaques and ribbons.

Henry charted each contest closely, and he soon began to learn that even Danny's attention to balance was an academic discipline. If he punted a ball a greater distance with his left foot, he tried again with his right foot until he reached an equal distance. Within the course of each game Danny made corrections at the imbalances of each sport, so that there was little disparity between his power movements from one side to the other. And what he couldn't correct within the parameters of the game, he corrected without.

One day that August, after Danny and the Forest Park All-Stars played a doubleheader against the River Forest All-Stars, Henry took a carload of Danny's friends to U-High where the boys played basketball and baseball in the field gym, and finished up the day swimming laps in the varsity pool.

At home Danny asked his father if he could help him before dinner. He'd pitched right handed as usual, in the opening game of the double-header, and the afternoon at U-High had thrown him off a bit. Would Henry help him even up in the alley? After a half hour Danny said he felt fine.

"I'm tuned up," he said, and Lori called them in to eat.

At dinner she was quiet.

"Is something wrong?" Henry asked.

"No," Lori said.

"You sure, Mom?" Danny said.

"I'm fine, sweetie," she said to Danny.

After dinner Danny sat on the floor at his mother's side and Lori combed his hair with her fingers; he was asleep in minutes. From the other end of the couch Henry watched television while Lori glared silently with her arms folded across her chest.

"Are you sure nothing's wrong," Henry said.

Lori said nothing.

When Henry joined Lori in bed she didn't look up.

"I wish you'd just tell me what's wrong so we could deal with this without the silent business for three weeks."

Lori did not raise her eyes from her magazine.

"You sounded fine on the phone this afternoon," Henry said.

"Well, I wasn't fine, Henry."

"What's wrong?"

"I just feel like you're pushing him, Henry."

Henry kept his finger in his book.

"Did Danny say something to you?" Henry said.

"He wouldn't say anything about it, Henry."

"Well, then how do you know I'm pushing him?"

"Jesus, Henry. He pitched today, he played in a doubleheader, he played for three hours or whatever at U-High, and then you take him out to have a catch with him behind the house for a half hour. Do you really need me to tell you that's a lot for one day?"

"They had a blast today, Lori. It was a perfect day for a kid."

"He was asleep within minutes after dinner."

"You were scratching his head, Lori. I can't remember exactly what that feels like, but I suspect I might have fallen asleep, too."

"What does that mean, Henry?"

"It doesn't mean anything."

"Don't turn this around, Henry."

"I'm not turning anything around, Lori. I haven't done anything wrong."

Henry shifted on the couch so that he looked away from Lori, and from behind him came Lori's voice.

"You're pushing him too hard, Henry. That's all I'm saying."

Henry rose from the sofa and faced Lori. "Tell me this," he said, and he stood there for seconds while Lori looked at him.

"From the day Danny was born," he began. "Until this day. Have I ever told you how to be a mother?"

It was Lori's chance to turn away from him, then.

"I'll answer the question for you," Henry said. "The answer is never, Lori. I have never told you how to be his mother. So how about you do me the same favor."

"He's just a boy, Henry. That's all I'm saying."

"Boys play," Henry said, walking from the room. "That's what boys do."

Ninth (1994)

There was a time, Henry remembered, when Lori had desired him. To this he returned time and again. He had even been the subject of her art. She had painted portraits of him; he had been the object of her thoughts. She had spent daytime moments thinking of making love to him. She used to tell him these things. She had worn sundresses for him, had flirted with him in those early years before Danny was born. He had come home from work on late summer afternoons and found her waiting for him, topless on the bed, pretending sleep, her hands tucked under her chin. How he had loved those times with her. Other men might have only made moments of them, but Henry turned them into hours. When she had pressed him to finish, when she had gripped her fingers into the small of his back, he had stilled her, had made long languid hours of moments. How many times had she cried out of love when he finally gave himself to her, when he finally pressed all of himself into her, when the tremblings and quiverings were finally unloosed. She had wanted him once.

Now, when she did kiss him, it was perfunctory. A bone thrown at the starving dog of a marriage, her lips tight and dry. And when he touched her in the morning or at night or in the middle of the day, he was made to feel as though he'd made a mistake, just to touch her.

And still, he wanted to tell her he loved her, that she was pretty, prettier than ever. He wanted to buy her flowers, to brush her shoulders at Danny's games. He wanted to be unlike the men who never touched their wives. But each time he tried he felt her pull away from him.

How many times had he stopped himself from caressing her?

And just when he'd become convinced she no longer desired him, or worse, she no longer loved him, she would have a moment of sweetness. She would reach for him when he expected it least. A phone call to him at work to ask if pork chops would be okay for dinner tonight. Or she might kiss him warmly when he returned after school. Or they'd have a glass of wine and she would put her fingers to his back and nod familiarly, like a girl on a date.

A real kiss—or some other ephemeral sweetness from her—was enough to remind him he loved her, and he would tell her so. And instead of considering love lost he drove to work thinking, perhaps we'll make it, she and I.

She had come alive, briefly, after painting the stadium. She'd taken him into the basement in only her robe, with the intention of giving herself to him like a new bride. And on the morning that followed she hugged him from behind as he washed the breakfast dishes, and stayed there holding him until he turned around and held her. She wanted to be held, it seemed, and he held her. He thought she had returned. But all of her returns were tricks.

There was a night in a bar. He'd nearly pleaded with her to go out for a drink. Twice she'd nudged him with her elbow, like a buddy. And another time he'd asked her to rub a kink from his shoulders, and her hands felt like a mannequin's hands. He thought then that she had forgotten how to touch him. Or worse, that she'd found another man to touch.

To this he had been reduced.

And Henry wondered about the week that followed the completion of the basement stadium. Where was the woman who'd taken him, eyes closed, into the basement? Where was she now?

That was the bitch of it, the constant speculation on their relationship. After every episode—every kiss, dry and tight or warm and sweet—he had to rethink their marriage, had to come up with a new theory, a new insight, a new something to allow him to make sense of the long weeks that passed between sweetnesses, until she surprised him again.

Henry could not reject the possibility that there was someone else. He'd found a card from an artist named Dels in her purse. Was that a woman's name? Dels? She'd begun going out with the girls from work, had been going to the Art Institute more often, had been going to openings at galleries in the city, had been missing Danny's sports events at the park district. How could there *not* be someone else?

He had tried to share in her love for art. He had offered to go to a River North gallery with her to see an exhibit on some artist late last August. She protested, but acquiesced in the end. When they arrived, Henry was immediately sorry he had come. He felt as though he'd invited himself, which he had, and so he allowed Lori her space at the gallery. He looked around on his own, stood in front of the images and paused, as others did. He didn't understand art, didn't understand its narrative. He understood something about music and literature and drama and cinema, the structure of these art forms, and how they moved people, but visual art was beyond him.

When he met up with Lori again that night at the Art Institute, she was sitting on a bench in front of a painting of a man scolding a boy—his son perhaps—and Lori was crying. In the car on their way home she was silent.

"Is something wrong?" he'd asked, but Lori only shook her head.

Henry wondered if he had married someone who didn't love him. Or couldn't. He wondered if she could love him if he were an artist.

That night, Henry dreamed about Emily, the new chemistry teacher at U-High. In his dream, Henry was reading on the couch and drinking a cup of coffee when Emily knocked quietly at his front door. She told him she was on her way back from the café where she waited tables part time and thought she would stop by since she was in the neighborhood. Even in his dream Henry knew the café was nowhere near Forest Park, but he said nothing about it. Neither did he say anything about the violin she had on her lap when joined Henry on the couch.

"Is this okay?" Emily said. "Is this okay that I came by?"

But even as Henry said that it was fine, he hoped that Lori would not hear Emily's voice on the couch. Even as Henry said that it was fine, he hoped that Lori would not get up to use the bathroom and look into the living room where Emily sat so close to him on the couch.

Twice that August, Henry drove to the Uncommon Ground Café for an omelet and a cup of iced coffee. The second time, Emily waited on him.

As the school year began, the snap of baseballs into leather gloves tumbled into the afternoon sounds on Lathrop Street, and soon after, the swish and brush of leaves being raked. The trebled hiss of water through the radiator. The tickings of the cuckoo clock in the dining room, always clearer in the fall. After work, Henry found Danny and Patrick Decker in the stadium having a catch, taking swings off the batting tee, or well into some world championship whiffle-ball game.

Danny's attention to balance remained steadfast. When Henry came into the basement stadium to work in the bullpen office he rarely passed the boys without checking in on Danny.

"You guys doing all right?" he would say.

"Fine, Dad," Danny would say. "Just balancing myself."

Balance, though, was not the only thing on Danny's mind.

Despite Henry's frequent cautions against throwing anything but fastballs and change-ups, in his absence the boys experimented wildly. Many days the basement stadium became a pitching laboratory. Danny experienced, that winter, the thrill of making another boy buckle at the knees and flail at pitches that deceived in a dozen ways. He was fascinated by the possibility of the great hook—both boys were—the unpredictable float of the knuckle ball, the cut of the cutter.

And as boys were wont to experiment in this way, it did not shock Henry to enter the stadium one afternoon just as Danny released a right-handed curveball in Patrick's direction. What did surprise him was the trajectory of the curve. As the ball seemed headed straight for Henry's face, he ducked back out of the doorway to the basement. Patrick, though, who knew something about Danny's curveball, stayed in position behind home plate while the pitch curved mightily into his glove. At seeing Danny staring at something over Patrick's shoulder, the receiver turned around.

"Hi, Mr. Granville," Patrick said.

Some part of the glare Henry had intended only for Danny, though, was present when he looked at Danny's friend.

"Patrick," Henry said.

The rest of the glare he saved for Danny.

"We've talked about that pitch haven't we?" Henry said.

Danny nodded. Henry had told Danny countless times of the damage throwing curveballs could do to a boy's arm.

"Who taught you how to throw that?"

Danny smiled and shrugged. "Nobody."

"Been practicing?"

"Not a lot."

"Not a lot?" Henry said.

"Kind of a lot," Danny said.

"Can you do that lefty?"

At Henry's shoulder, Patrick nodded as though the question were asked of him.

"Yeah," Danny said.

Henry looked at Patrick and then back at Danny.

"Let me see that again, Danny," he said, but when Danny shifted to prepare for the throw, Henry stopped him.

"Wait," he said. "Just to be clear, Danny. I'm giving you permission to throw a curveball this one time," he said. "Do you understand that?"

Danny nodded.

"One time," Henry said again. "Let's have a look at it."

Patrick leaned into the equipment bin in the corner of the narrow room, tossed Danny his lefty glove, and crouched in preparation for the pitch.

And with the qualified blessing of his father, Danny threw a curveball that would have stymied any hitter in Forest Park. It smacked into the brown leather target of Patrick Decker's mitt.

"How the hell?" Henry said. He pointed at Danny. "Don't let me see you throw that again, Danny," he said. "You hear me?"

"What about a cutter?" Danny said.

"You have a cutter?"

"Yeah," Danny said.

"Let me see it," Henry said.

The movement on Danny's cut fastball made Henry laugh.

"Holy shit," he said. "I mean *crap*. Holy crap."

Danny and Patrick laughed.

"Anything else up your sleeve?"

Danny showed his father a slider Danny threw from the left, and three change-ups from each side, one that broke nearly as much as his curveball.

By the time Henry had seen them all he was shaking his head and smiling. Patrick was laughing as though he'd been saving a punch line for a week.

"I think you'll be okay without that curveball huh, Danny?"

"Yeah, I should be all right, Dad," he said.

BOOK TWO

Tenth (1996)

TWICE A WEEK THROUGH THAT FALL AND WINTER, HENRY TOOK Danny to Stella's batting cages where he worked himself up to the fast machines that shot out sixteen pitches at ninety miles per hour for a one-dollar slug. Against the clang of balls off the aluminum bats in the other cages, the crack of the dimpled yellow balls against his ash Louisville Slugger pulled at the attentions of all the players waiting for their turn at bat. Near the back wall of the cage, a giant gong, eight feet around, painted in the red and white concentricity of a target, hung from the ceiling, and on Fridays, Danny spent his last two slugs aiming for the gong, and when he was on, he blasted line drives one after another against the gong, first from the right side of the plate and then from the left. Even boys at bat in the other cages stopped to watch as the echoes of Danny's line drives filled the warehouse with such a racket that mothers and fathers and players alike put their hands to their ears while they laughed in disbelief at what the eleven-year-old could do with a baseball bat. At Stella's, where young ball players were practiced at ignoring the achievements of others, Danny finished his cagework to the cheers of boys.

One of the regulars at Stella's was a boy from Berwyn named Mickey Wells, a thirteen-year-old catcher who played travel ball for the Bensonville Bulldogs. He used the machines as much to work on his hitting as his catching. The first time Danny saw him there Mickey had his gear on and was dropping slugs in the machine and crouching behind the plate to receive pitches in his glove. After catching them, he'd spring up and throw the ball over the pitching hut to nail the imaginary runner.

When they'd seen each other at the cages three Mondays running, Danny and Mickey began to greet the other with nods as they waited for their respective turns in the fastest cage, and by the time January blistered its way through Forest Park, they'd learned each other's names and become friends. In similar fashion, the fathers of the boys also became something like friends. Mickey's father introduced himself as "Beef. Beef Wells," and while the boys worked in the cages, their fathers leaned on the railings behind them, talking of baseball.

Several times, Wells encouraged Henry to consider playing for the Bulldogs. The team played sixty-two games from April to August, competed in tournaments with trophies on the line nearly every weekend, and had a shot at the travel ball world series at the end of the summer. While Beef pushed the team with Henry, Mickey pushed it with Danny, and against a sixteen-game Little League schedule and one practice a week, it didn't take much for either Granville to be convinced that a tryout was worth a shot.

The Bulldogs practiced once a week at an indoor baseball facility in Villa Park called Rookies, and in the car on their way there, Danny pressed his fist into his glove and looked at his father. It had been a warm February and the streets were wet with snow that disappeared on the highway. The streetlights flashed a blue glow and intermittent shadows of water droplets and windshield wipers across Henry's face.

"How do you feel?" Henry asked.

"Am I going to pitch today?"

"They'll probably have a look at you," Henry said. "I think so."

"Just with my right arm?" Danny said.

Danny's eyes were locked on the yellow threaded embroidery of his glove, but he felt his father glance his way.

"Yes, Danny. Righty."

Danny turned his fist in his glove and looked out the window.

"Look, Danny," Henry said. "I know where you're going with this." Danny traced his finger along the stitches of thread. "I know you want to pitch lefty for this guy, too, but you only need one arm to make the team, Danny."

Henry pulled up to the entrance and shifted the car into park.

Danny twisted his fist in his glove again and looked at his father.

"What's the point of all of this, Dad? What's the point of me throwing with both hands for all these years? What's the point of me brushing my teeth with both hands and combing my hair with both hands, and kicking footballs with both feet, and shooting free throws and fielding grounders and wiping my ass with both hands?"

Danny looked away from Henry when he swore.

"I'm sorry for swearing," Danny said. "But I'm afraid. I'm two years younger than these guys, and I thought the whole point of all this work was so that I'd be good from both sides. What's the good of it if I can't ever use it in the game?"

Henry looked at his watch.

"Look, Danny," Henry said. "All I can tell you now is that you've never needed anything more than your right arm to get you through any difficulty on the ball field."

"Well this isn't Forest Park in-house baseball anymore, Dad. These guys are good. They're serious; they play all year 'round. They're gamers."

"When you can't do it with your right arm, Danny," Henry said, "and we need to switch it up, we'll talk about it again okay?"

Danny looked back to his glove.

"Look at me, Danny."

Danny raised his head to Henry.

"Trust me," Henry said. "If there's two kids on that team that are half as good as you, I'll let you drive home tonight."

Danny smiled.

"I don't want you throwing lefty except to me or Patrick. I don't even want them to *know* that you throw lefty."

Danny looked out the window at the entrance to Rookies. "Does Mickey know you can throw with your left arm?"

"No."

"Let's keep it that way," Henry said.

"I better get going," Danny said.

Henry nodded. "I'll park the car and meet you inside."

Danny opened the door, and walked away from the car.

Inside, Beef Wells introduced Danny to the manager of the Bulldogs. Coach Sullivan was short and thick, and freshly shaven. He smelled of unsmoked cigars and mouthwash. His belly, tight and muscled, extended inches past his belt. Henry walked with the men and Danny to a batting cage in the back of the room. Wells turned on the manual-feed machine and adjusted the dials while Sullivan and Henry stood outside the cage and watched.

"Take a look at the first pitch," Beef said. "And then lay down three-four bunts."

Danny tapped two bunts down the third base side of the cage.

"What's with the wooden bat?" Sullivan asked Henry.

Henry shrugged. "That's all he uses," he said.

"Old school," Sullivan said. "Nice."

After two bunts down the first base side, Danny looked at Coach Sullivan.

"All right," Sullivan said. "Swing away."

Danny ripped a line drive up the middle of the cage, and Beef flinched. Before he fed the next ball into the spinning wheels of the pitching machine, he adjusted the protective screen, but when Danny's next line drive bulleted off the aluminum edge of the screen Beef flinched again.

"Shit!" he said. Outside the cage Sullivan laughed, and Henry smiled.

Danny took twenty total pitches from the right side of the plate and raised his hand to Wells.

"Lefty?" Danny said.

"Yeah," Wells said. "Take a few lefty."

Danny laid down four bunts from the left side and after knocking twenty pitches squarely off the sweet spot of his bat he stepped away from the plate.

"That's good," Sullivan said.

Wells flipped the switch on the machine. Its rubber wheels whirred to a slow spin and stopped.

Sullivan led the Granvilles to the infield cage where he warmed up Danny's arm with fifty throws back and forth, then started knocking grounders to Danny across the Astroturf carpet. Beef stood next to Sullivan to catch Danny's throws. Between Danny's plays Beef and Sullivan leaned toward one another and spoke.

Sullivan hit twenty-three grounders, set down the bat, and stuffed his thick hand into a catcher's mitt. In the pitching lane along the wall he took sixteen long strides away from Danny and crouched into a receiving position, and with Beef Wells and Henry looking on Danny right-armed fifteen fastballs into Sullivan's glove.

"How you feel?" Coach Sullivan asked Danny after the next pitch.

"I feel good," Danny said.

Sullivan turned to Henry. "Kid looks good," he said. "Does he wanna stick around for practice?"

"What do you say, Danny?"

"Yeah," Danny said.

"That'd be awesome," Sullivan laughed, and by the time the Granvilles walked out under the blue awning into the February night, Danny was a Bulldog.

Eleventh (1996)

THE LAST FRIDAY MORNING OF THAT APRIL WAS A FIST IN DANNY'S chest. Or a balloon the size of a fist. That's what it was: a balloon inflated somewhere above his stomach that made breathing something to think about. There was a note from his father on the kitchen counter.

He was with a colleague from U-High at a two-day retreat for science teachers in Indiana, and wished him luck at the weekend Rockford tournament. "If you win big on Friday and Saturday," he wrote, "I'll see you in Rockford on Sunday."

Danny checked his parents' bedroom anyway. Gone. Only his mother was there. He smelled his father's absence in the uncoffeed kitchen. Felt it in the unsteam of the bathroom. Listened to it on the ride to school in his mother's silent car.

The early April sun was a blanket over the playground at recess. Danny had a catch with Patrick Decker along the fence that separated the middle and lower schools. After ten warm-up tosses, Danny started pitching. He snapped balls into Patrick's glove with game-time pace. Twice Patrick winced in pain, but Danny fired twenty-two more pitches, wordless and right-handed before Patrick spoke.

"You should have told me to bring my catcher's mitt," he said.

But Danny said nothing. He fired eight more throws.

"My hand's starting to hurt," Patrick said.

"Sorry," Danny said.

They leaned against the fence that separated the middle school playground from the younger kids, and watched a group of fourth graders playing kickball. An outline of the United States was painted on the asphalt in front of them. The boys were silent.

"What's wrong?" Patrick said.

"Everything," Danny said.

Everything was wrong. His father was in Indiana for the weekend and the Bulldogs were playing in one of the biggest tournaments of the year, and the first team they were playing was the Wisconsin Rockhounds who the Bulldogs had never beaten. They were supposed to be huge guys, Danny told Patrick. They all shaved and had legs like trees, and had won the tournament for three years running, and the lineup was supposed to be stacked with lefties. And the worst part was that his father wouldn't let him throw left-handed against them, and he wasn't sure he could beat them if he pitched righty, and this was his first opportunity to pitch against the Rockhounds. And he also wasn't sure how he was supposed to stay balanced this weekend when he wasn't supposed to let anyone on the Bulldogs know he could even throw lefty.

But as many words as there were, there were none for the fist in Danny's chest, the inflated balloon at the top of his stomach.

In the car, on their way to the Rockford tournament, Danny's mother was like another person. Someone else's mother. She was chatty and excited about baseball and the spring and hadn't it just been a beautiful day and how was school and what did sixth graders do during recess and what was the name again of that math teacher who was supposed to be so mean and what was the schedule for the rest of the games this weekend and maybe Dad would be home in time to catch the game Sunday if the Bulldogs were still in the tournament, and by the way she'd packed a cooler of Gatorade that should get Danny through the weekend. She wasn't sure if she was going to be at the games on Saturday, but if she couldn't make it Mickey's family would drive him to the fields. When she woke up she would stop at Alpine Deli to get sandwiches for them to eat between the games, and she'd be there in time for lunch. And was something wrong? He was so quiet.

But there was nothing wrong. There was nothing wrong.

An hour before the first game of the tournament the balloon was still there, the warm glory of the earlier day was an April trick, feigning love just to crush a city, its fraudulent sun now a cold shadow, cheerless and wintry. A Bulldog grandfather, heavily coated, sipped something warm from a thermos. Lori Granville bought a cup of hot chocolate at the concession stand and sat in her canvas chair and braced herself against the cold. She curled her shoulders in toward each other, as if to close herself within them.

Danny loosened up on field one, did sprints in the outfield, took soft-toss swings against the batting net, and threw twenty warm-up pitches to Mickey in the bullpen.

In the batting cages off the practice field a right-handed pitcher threw batting practice to the Rockhounds. Danny watched four lefties take swings. Every one of them seemed to crush the ball in the cages.

He looked into the dugout bench of field one where Mickey was unbuckling his shin guards and singing "Take Me Out to the Ballgame."

Mickey grabbed his glove and jogged toward Danny, blowing steaming breath into his ungloved hand.

"Check 'em out," Danny said. "They're taking cuts from only twenty feet away from a right-handed pitcher."

"They're getting ready for your fastball," Mickey said.

Danny felt the balloon swell with another press of air.

When the umpire yelled, "Play ball," the Rockhounds huddled into a mass of light blue jerseys around their coach at third base and began chanting some memorized thing—a war cry. They sprang off the earth as one to some metronomed internal beat, a choreographed chanting machine. Behind them, a column of fifteen baby-blue helmets sat on their dugout bench against the chain-link fence. Behind that, Rockhound fans sat in a sea of blue hats and coats and welcomed the start of the game with cheers that seemed capable of triumphing over the wind.

The leadoff batter was the smallest of the four lefties Danny had watched take batting practice. He was limber and expressionless in the batter's box. From the Rockhound dugout a chant of "Ke-vin! Ke-vin!"

Danny blew into his right hand and eyed Mickey Wells. Crouched and smiling behind the plate, Wells pounded his fist in his glove and signaled nothing. He would let Danny start the game on his own terms.

Fastballs and change-ups, Danny thought. Let them put the ball in play. He would throw strikes and let them hit the ball if they could.

His first pitch came in high. Mickey stood and gestured to Danny to keep his pitches low.

Danny breathed warmth into his right hand again and threw another fastball. High again. Ball two. Cheers from the Rockhound fans. Wild.

The wind. Danny's right eye teared. He rubbed it with his shoulder and pitched again.

Outside. Ball three.

Mickey stood and ran to the mound.

"Nice and easy, Danny," he said. "He's gonna sit there all day until you make the umpire say *strike*. Let's go."

Danny fired another fastball down the middle of the plate and the leadoff hitter swung, knocking the ball down the right field line for a single.

Coach Sullivan's voice from the dugout. First game. Leadoff hitter. Coach Sullivan swearing.

Danny wiped another wind tear from the bottom of his eye. Another lefty. Big this one. Staring back at him like an enemy. Make him hit it. Fastball.

"Strike one!"

Staring back like he's angry. Change-up. Danny looked at his teammate at first base. Big leadoff there. Change-up, watch for the steal.

Danny threw a change-up. The big lefty swung and missed. Strike two.

Tears every pitch. As though the wind were on the Rockhound team. Mickey signaling something. Danny wiped his eyes again. Fastball inside. Mickey calling for an inside fastball.

Danny lost it high. Mickey had to stand to keep the runner

from stealing second. One ball, two strikes.

Water in his eyes. Another fastball out of the zone. The number two hitter swung and tipped the pitch into the stands. Foul ball. Water. Every pitch, more tears. Foul ball. No one else wiping his eyes. Foul ball. He's swinging at everything. Mickey signaling. Tears. Danny pulled off his glove and wiped his eye with his right hand and put the glove back on. Signal again, Mick. Outside fastball. Ball two, strike two. Runner at first. Big lead. Another fastball.

The big lefty swung and hit a hard grounder to third base, but it was too late to get the runner at second. The third baseman threw the ball to first but it came in off target and pulled the defender away from the base. Safe.

Sullivan threw his clipboard against the Bulldog fence and champion cheers exploded from the Rockhound dugout.

Third batter. Another lefty. Not so big as the number two batter.

Danny threw a high fastball and the batter swung and missed. Strike one. He wiped his eye and threw another fastball.

Foul ball. "Strike two." Another tear. Mickey signaling.

Can't see it. Change-up. "Strike three."

Danny looked at second base. Big lead. First base. Big lead. One out. At the plate another lefty. First four batters, lefties. No end to lefties. This one huge. Fastball. Outside. Ball one. Have to be careful with this guy. Two men on base. Another huge lefty at the plate. Clean-up hitter. Careful.

Ball two. A tear. Mickey signaling something again. Can't see.

Fastball inside. Ball three.

Careful here. Three and oh. Has to be a fastball, though. Can't walk anyone.

Ball four.

Danny wiped a tear from his cheek. Another.

Behind his eyes there were more. He could feel the cold wet of them. Sitting in a pool of water around his eyes. Inside his head he felt it there, cold and wet. Thick and syrupy, like blood. There was a Rockhound on every base. No end to any of it, to lefties, to wind, to the cold wetness flooding the back of his eyes and running down his cheeks.

By the end of the second inning, the Rockhounds were ahead 3-0, and by the middle of the fourth they'd stretched their lead to 5-0. The Bulldogs were sluggish at the plate until the fourth inning when the first baseman hit a two-run triple, and at the end of the inning it was 5-2.

Every inning was a struggle on the mound, every Rockhound a fight. Every player seemed somehow to know what pitch was coming every time. He wasn't pitching, he was *throwing* at them with his right hand. He was pushing the ball. It felt as though he were pitching in a bad dream, like the dream where he was riding a bicycle with no pedals, or the one when he was fighting a dream villain and could hardly move his arms. He was pitching underwater. He had nothing in his right arm to throw at them. Twice he took his glove off and considered throwing a ball lefty. He could do it with his left hand.

Mickey's fingers, signaling between his thighs, waved like rills of heat over asphalt—helpless and alien ripples without meaning. Rockhound cheers, pounding feet on the aluminum stands. Coach Sullivan swearing from the dugout. His smell. Smoke under chewing gum and the angry shape of his mouth and another guy on base.

Nothing left in his arm. He could do it with his left arm, though. He knew he could. His mother. Gone. Her chair. Gone. In the car keeping warm. His father. Gone. Danny's promise not to pitch left-handed. No end to any of it. The wind, the tears, the Rockhounds. The screams of the baby-blue crowd roared like a current, raged beneath the icy wind, and when Coach Sullivan held his hand before the umpire and walked onto the field and pointed to the third baseman to replace Danny, the fist beneath the cage of bones that was meant to contain Danny's heart had swelled into a hardened mass of muscle, and as he walked to first base he felt the fist inside his breast surge through the left side of his chest and through his shoulder and into his forearm, thrusting into the hand he held clenched at his hip, swinging like a certain and pendulous weight into the bone of his own left eye and landing with a crack that made four women in blue wince with the primal pain of broken-hearted mothers. Twice more then, Danny made them wince. It might have been four times, perhaps more, if Mickey Wells hadn't thrown down his mask and run to first base to hold Danny in a hug that held his arm in mandated concord against his chest.

Mickey turned Danny around and faced him, then.

"Danny!" he said. "Shake it off! It's over. We need you here, now!"

Over Mickey's shoulder, Danny's mother had her hand over her mouth. She had seen what the other mothers had seen.

Danny played the rest of the game in a fog. The Rockhounds scored two more runs and the game ended 7-2.

After the game Danny looked for his mother but she was gone.

During Coach Sullivan's postgame speech Danny stared at the diamonds of the chain-link fence until he fell from focus. He felt Mickey's eyes on him the whole time. Stay warm, Sullivan was saying. Find someplace to stay warm until the eight-thirty game under the lights. Now they were in a spot. Now they had to fight through the back draw. They had to win tonight and they had to win their two games tomorrow and they would probably face the Rockhounds again on Sunday.

After the Bulldogs cleared the dugout, Mrs. Wells told Danny his mother had gone home.

"We'll take you home after the game," she said.

Mickey Wells walked toward them, looking at Danny the whole time.

"You all right?" he said.

"Come with me a minute," Danny said. "Bring your bag."

They picked up their bags and walked from the field without speaking. It was almost dark and the wind was still, but it was cold. Danny led Mickey to the remotest of the baseball diamonds. He put on his glove and pointed at Mickey.

"Put on your glove, and don't say anything," he said, and Mickey put his hands up like he was under arrest and slipped on his glove.

"Just a little catch to warm up," Danny said, and with his right hand he threw a baseball, softly, to Mickey.

"Hey, not bad," Mickey said.

"Don't say nothing," Danny said again and he threw another ball to Mickey Wells and Mickey said nothing.

After ten warm-up throws Danny stepped off the mound and flicked his gloved hand at Mickey.

"Ten pitches," Danny said and Mickey crouched and punched his glove. "Don't say nothing," Danny said.

He threw a fastball that snapped in Mickey's glove.

"Holy shit," Mickey said. "That's faster than righty."

"I told you don't say nothing, Mick," Danny said, and he threw another fastball and Mickey said nothing and then Danny threw a curveball.

"Holy shit," Mickey said again.

"Shut up," Danny said, but he was smiling and Mickey started laughing and then they were both laughing.

"You could beat the Rockhounds lefty," Mickey said.

"I know I could," Danny said.

Mickey looked at the ball in his hands and then he looked at Danny. "How come you never told me you could throw lefty?" he said.

"My dad doesn't want me to pitch lefty in games. He doesn't even want anyone to know I could do it."

"Why?"

"Who knows?" Danny said.

"My dad would be creaming in his pants if I could throw lefty," Mickey said. He took off his glove and pretended a left-handed throw. "You gonna go lefty if we meet them again?"

"I don't know," Danny said.

"The Rockhounds won't know what hit 'em, Danny Boy," he said.

"Don't say anything," Danny said. He bagged his glove and

shouldered his bag. "Anyway, I don't have to think about it unless we're still alive on Sunday afternoon."

"We'll make it to Sunday," Mick said.

After the Bulldogs won the night game easily, Mrs. Wells drove Danny home in a cold and silent car. She waited until Danny was in the house before pulling away, and Danny waited in the hallway a moment before opening the door. When he entered, his mother was on the couch.

"Did Dad call?" Danny said.

"No."

Danny stood in the doorway and looked ahead. He set his equipment bag on the floor and stood there, keeping the left side of his face hidden from his mother.

"Look at me Danny," she said.

"I can't," Danny said.

"Look at me," she said, and Danny stood stiffly in the frame of the front doorway.

As Danny slowly turned his face toward his mother, she closed her eyes and put her fingers to her temples and rubbed. Danny felt the bruise press against his eye in the heat of the living room.

Lori shook her head and walked to Danny. She put her hand on his cheek and tilted her head to better see it.

"Damn it, Danny," she said, and she took her hand away.

"I'm sorry, Mom."

"Do you have any idea what it was like for me to see you punch yourself in the face?"

"I was frustrated."

"Why, Danny? Because you're not perfect?"

"No, Mom. Not because I'm not perfect," he said. "Because I could have beaten them if I threw lefty."

"Why didn't you just throw lefty then?"

Danny looked at her.

"It's not that easy, Ma."

Lori touched Danny's cheek again.

"Let me get some ice," she said. "Sit down."

From the couch, Danny listened to his mother's footsteps in the hallway, the freezer door opening, the crack of the ice as she twisted the tray, a cube falling into the aluminum sink and knocking around the basin and another falling to the floor and sliding across the kitchen. The rustle of the ice in a plastic bag and her steps again coming toward closer.

Lori folded a bandana around the baggie of ice and handed it to Danny. She sat at the other end of the couch. She patted her lap and Danny lay his head there and lifted the ice to the side of his eye.

Lori combed Danny's hair with her fingers.

"Are you pitching tomorrow?" she said.

"No," Danny said. "I'll pitch Sunday if we win our games tomorrow."

"Will you play the Rockhounds again?" she said.

"If we make it that far," Danny said.

"Can you pitch left-handed against them if you play them on Sunday?"

Danny was silent under the slow massage of his mother's fingers on his forehead.

"I was thinking about it," Danny said. "That's why I was hoping that Dad called. I wanted to talk to him about it."

"Do you want to pitch lefty against them, Danny?"

"I think so," he said.

"Well, then you should," she said. "You're not playing baseball for your father, Danny."

Lori lifted the ice and looked at Danny's eye. She shook her head at him. She spoke through her teeth.

"If I ever see you pull something like that again, Danny," she said. "You'll never play another game of baseball as long as you live."

Danny opened his eyes and nodded.

They were silent for a moment. A car drove past on Lathrop. An alley cat meowed, and then there was quiet.

"Will you be there tomorrow?" Danny said.

"Yes," she said. "I'll be at the second game with sandwiches."

"Good," Danny said.

It was gray on Sunday morning. Cold, and as wet as a day could be without rain. Mickey's father picked up Danny this time, and Mrs. Wells and the baby were in the car, too. Mickey's little brother was buckled in his safety seat between Mickey and Danny.

"What's his name?" Danny said.

"My dad calls him *Oops*," Mickey said, "but my mom calls him Sam," and from the front seat of the car Coach Wells laughed and Mrs. Wells hit his arm.

"How old is he?" Danny said.

Mickey shrugged. "How am I supposed to know?"

Danny held a baseball in his left hand and shaped and reshaped his fingers around it. When Mickey caught Danny's eye, though, he took the ball from Danny's right hand and put it into his left. Then he winked.

The weight of the ball in his left hand. Could he do it?

When Mickey looked his way Danny gave him the baseball.

"If it doesn't feel right during the first inning," he whispered. "I'm going to switch back to righty for the rest of the game."

Mickey winked and made a clicking sound with his tongue. He held the ball in his hand and rolled it along the base of the window.

A half-hour before game time, Mickey told Coach Sullivan he was taking Danny off the side to throw a few, and just before the game started, while Danny warmed up his left arm, the sun broke through a thick drape of clouds.

In the huddle with the officials, Coach Sullivan won the coin flip for home field advantage. Danny sat on the bench holding a ball in his left hand and flicking his wrist like he was about to throw a curve. Every time Sullivan passed Danny the coach looked at him thinking he was going to make eye contact, but Danny pretended he didn't notice.

"You okay, Danny?" Sullivan finally said.

"I'm good," Danny said. "How about you?"

"I'm fine, smartass," Sullivan said. "You owe me one," Sullivan said.

"I know," Danny said. "I owe you one."

The Bulldogs took the field first. Behind him, Danny's infielders took grounders from the first baseman, and Danny right-handed several warm-up pitches to Mickey Wells. Behind the plate Mickey received the throws without his facemask on. He stood up quick and hard after the first one popped in his mitt, and he whipped the ball back to Danny from a standing position in front of home plate.

"Nice, Danny Boy!" he said. "No one's touching you today."

In the Rockhounds dugout the leftfielder was playing air guitar with a baseball bat and the manager yelled from the coach's box at third.

"Eyes on every pitch, Rockhounds!" he said, and the leftfielder put his bat down and fifteen Rockhounds gripped their fingers around the links of the dugout fence as Danny shot another right-handed warm-up pitch into Mickey's mitt.

"Nice!" Wells shouted, and he shot the ball back to Danny and took two more throws from him.

After Danny's final warm-up pitch, Mickey jumped up and whipped the ball to second to catch the imaginary base stealer at second base.

When the umpire yelled "Play ball," Mickey turned to him.

"One second," he said. "Gotta get my mask."

When he returned from the dugout Mickey held his mask in his catcher's mitt. In his right hand he held Danny's left-handed glove. He sprinted to the mound. Wells put his mask on, and turning his back to the Rockhounds' dugout he covered Danny's head with his catcher's mitt and pulled him closer. The bill of Danny's cap touched Mickey's facemask.

"They ain't gonna know what hit 'em, Danny," he said. He switched gloves with Danny and ran to the dugout to throw the unwanted one over the fence.

Mickey took his position behind the plate. Danny stood with his heels on the rubber strip and the ball buried in his glove.

The first hitter to face Danny was the left-handed leadoff man who had reached base three out of four times in Danny's debut two days earlier. He'd had four solid at-bats against Danny and with the easy groove of his preparatory swing, he seemed confident about his prospects for today as well.

For a moment Danny wondered if it was too late to change his mind, but Mickey was behind the plate waiting for a left-handed pitch, calling for a fastball high in the zone, and now Danny had a glove on his right hand.

On the bench, the Rockhounds and their chant of *Ke-vin! Ke-vin!*

Danny let his hands fall to his hips. Then he lifted his gloved hand to his chest, as if to say, *Glove here, Kevin*. He lifted the ball in his right hand. *Ball here, Kevin*, and he set for the first pitch of the game, taking his time to give the batter every chance of seeing what was about to head his way.

Danny stepped into his wind-up and fired a left-handed bullet in the top half of the strike zone.

The umpire leaned to his right and pointed at first base. "Strike!" he shouted, and Wells pumped his fist so that Danny could see.

The batter looked at his manager in the coach's box at third base.

Mickey called for another fastball in the same spot and he got it, and then a third, and before anyone but Mickey Wells and the leadoff hitter knew it, Danny had struck out a Rockhound with three left-handed pitches.

When Danny threw the first pitch to the second batter, Coach Sullivan knew it, too. He stood next to Coach Wells at the dugout fence, both of them staring at Danny in disbelief. Mickey was smiling.

The number-two hitter struck out as well and the batter in the three spot hit a change-up that dribbled to first base for the third out of the inning. In the dugout Coach Sullivan started walking toward Danny, but Mickey put his glove in Sullivan's chest to keep him away from Danny.

"Don't say nothing, Coach," Mickey said. "Wait until after the game," and Sullivan nodded. Mickey sat with Danny at the end of the bench.

"What was that all about?" Danny said.

"I told him not to talk to you until after the game."

"Why?"

"So you don't have to listen to him," Mickey said, and Danny laughed.

By the time the Bulldogs were on the field in the top of the second inning, the Rockhounds all knew that Danny was throwing lefty. Still, each Rockhound batter who approached the plate seemed to flinch before the first pitch, as though uncertain where the next pitch would come from.

Danny worked through the first three innings facing the nine-batter minimum, and by the time he got around again to the top of the batting order he felt as though he'd discovered something, a connection between him and the batter he'd never known. It felt as though he had been pitching against the current for years, or that he'd been pitching without a current at all, that he'd been plodding along, pushing it out, and now someone had plugged him in. It wasn't just that he was facing batters live from the left side, finally. It was something else. He felt he knew what each batter had in mind, knew every miniscule shift in the nuanced fight between him and the batter.

And Mickey was right there with him, calling the same pitches Danny would have thrown. Only twice did Danny shake Mickey's sign.

In the stands there was no sound from either side. There was only the batter in the box, Mickey in his crouch, the umpire leaning over Wells. Danny wanted Friday back. He felt as though it wouldn't be possible for him to lose another game from either side for the rest of his life.

When he faced Traub the second time through, Danny had him on a one and two count when Mickey called for a fastball low and away. When Mickey set up to receive the ball outside, though, Danny noticed Traub's front hip shift slightly toward right field; he was looking for something low and away. Danny didn't shake off Mickey's call. He threw a change-up that headed low and away until Traub started his swing. The pitch dived and hit the ground before it reached the plate.

When Fisher appeared at the plate again Danny felt the number-three hitter hesitate in the reception of signals from the third base coach, and beyond doubt he felt that a curve ball to the outside of the box was what he needed to get the batter to strike out looking. Mickey called for it and Danny answered and that was that.

The Rockhounds couldn't keep a secret from Danny, it seemed. It felt as though he were able to read minds on the mound, to track, even, each change of the hitter's mind. Before the ball left his fingers he knew what the outcome would be.

When Mickey ran to the mound after the final batter of the game struck out, and handed the game ball to Danny, the teams shook hands and walked to their dugouts for their equipment.

In the Bulldog bleachers most of the fans stood packing coolers and folding jackets and blankets over their arms. But standing over Danny's mother in her canvas chair, in the full strength of the sun, was his father. Danny felt a rush of blood pulse inside the glove on his left hand, felt another surge of blood throb at the bruised ring around his left eye. There was nothing to hide and no way to hide it.

He had pitched a complete game with his left hand and he had never felt more balanced in his life. He had never felt better on the mound than during that game.

At the stands Danny hugged his father.

"Nice game," Henry said.

"I pitched left-handed, Dad."

"I know."

"I'm sorry," Danny said.

"It's okay."

"You weren't here, Dad," Danny said. "I would've talked to you about it."

"It's okay. It's fine," Henry said. "How did it feel?"

"It felt awesome, Dad," Danny said.

Lori uncrossed her legs in her seat.

"That's enough about baseball," Lori said.

"It felt like—"

"That's enough," Lori said again. "No more talk of baseball."

In the dugout Danny packed his equipment and headed back toward the stands.

His father's hands were on his mother's shoulders.

His father had returned. Was rubbing his mother's shoulders through her winter jacket. And though it was warm—though for a moment April seemed kinder and sweeter than ever—from the dugout where Danny observed his mother beneath his father's fingers it seemed as though she had not yet fully unclenched her shoulders to the sun. As though she were certain the sun was a trick of early spring, a ruse. As though she were bracing herself against the one certainty of April: it was there to crush you.

Twelfth (1996)

Since that past February, Henry had gone to the Uncommon Ground Café to see Emily Seltzer every Sunday morning. They'd been planning an interdisciplinary presentation they would be giving at an Indiana high school teachers' convention late that April. On the date of their last meeting he had fallen asleep, waiting for her, on a bench in the shade of a maple outside the cafe. Where he awaited her, generous crumbs of the morning sun had found their way through the leaves of the tree, and Henry had closed his eyes at their flickering warmth.

It was 11:05 AM when he awoke to find her standing above him. She had opened up two sheets of the Chicago Tribune and covered him with them. Henry closed his eyes again quickly, pretending sleep, and pulled the edge of the newsprint to his chin and grumbled sleepily. When Emily laughed, Henry stretched and yawned like the happiest homeless man in cartoon land.

"I didn't wake you, did I?" she said.

"No," Henry said. "I was just about to get up."

Henry looked down and folded the newspaper sheets neatly. He tucked the folded sheets under his thigh and Emily sat next to him on the bench.

"What are you doing here, Henry?" she asked.

"What do you mean?" he said. "The presentation is next weekend."

Emily breathed deeply, closed her eyes, and lifted her face to the flickering sun coming through the maple leaves. Her eyes were still closed as she spoke.

"We could have been meeting all along at U-High," she said.

Aware that her eyes were still closed, Henry looked at Emily. Her earrings, shapeless blue gems, dangled from hair-thin silver wires and sparkled in the sun.

"That's what I mean," she said. "What are you doing here, Henry?"

"I don't know," Henry said.

But he did know. Though he would not say this to Emily—he could not deny the excitement, the undercurrent of some sexier energy beneath the talk, beneath the interdisciplinary presentation for which they prepared.

She was more than an hour early for her shift that day, so they sat inside, at a table covered with butcher's paper. And there, Henry came as close as he cared to telling her what he had been doing there every Sunday for two months. He told her about his life on Lathrop, about Lori, about the marriage he thought he had signed on for, and the one he ended up with.

He did not tell her about the symmetry campaign. But while he sat there with Emily, it was never far from his thoughts. It was possible, in fact, that talking about the campaign was the reason he was with Emily all along. She was there when he nearly spilled the secret to that Finnegan clown three years before. What a joy it might have been to just have another human being with whom he could talk about Danny. And someone who might appreciate it for its narrative value.

Henry told Emily that it was nice just to have someone to talk to. There was definitely that.

"I suppose that's what I'm doing, Emily," he said. "Enjoying your company. Being in it."

Emily said she'd be lying if she told him he'd been alone in that enjoyment. She'd had fun planning this presentation with him, too. But it was dangerous what he was doing, and he should probably—they should probably—take better care. They should probably do this presentation and be done with it. She liked him. She could actually see herself with someone like him.

So by the time the weekend conference came up, they had already cleared the air. They had put words and parameters to this thing they had been doing.

Still, Henry said nothing to Lori about who he would be traveling to Indiana with on the weekend of the Rockford tournament. And it was this secret that weighed heaviest on Henry's mind at the Independent Schools Conference on Interdisciplinary Education. It was this secret, along with Emily's measured and sensible response to Henry's crush confession that troubled Henry through the conference weekend. As he walked around downtown Indianapolis with Emily between workshops he stopped in nearly every boutique to find something for Lori, some gift that might stand for his promise to return to her.

It was Emily, in the end, who selected that gift for Lori: a pair of earrings not so unlike the pair Emily had worn on their last meeting at the Uncommon Ground Café. When she pointed them out to Henry, he looked at her to see if she recognized the similarity, but Emily had not raised her eyes to him.

"Definitely," she said. "Definitely get those."

On Sunday morning Henry had called home from the gate at O'Hare Airport, and then again at curbside in the United terminal, but no one picked up the phone on the other end, so he boarded a taxi and headed for the Rockford Baseball Complex, crossing his fingers for more than just a baseball game.

When the taxi pulled into the Rockford Complex, men's softball teams were preparing for games on every field but one. On the championship diamond the Bensonville Bulldogs—with their black pants and hunter green vests over orange tee shirts—walked off the field after the third out. Henry paid the driver and walked as quickly toward the diamond as the swinging substance of his travel bags allowed.

Lori was sitting in her chair at the side of the aluminum bleachers. Henry set his bags down and kissed Lori's cheek from behind and she flinched in her seat. The quick intake of breath entered her throat like sound and swelled her diaphragm.

"Jesus, Henry," she said.

"Sorry about that," he said. "I wanted to surprise you."

"I don't like surprises, Henry."

"Sorry about that," he said.

Lori breathed and changed the cross of her legs.

"Hi," she said, but it was too late for the welcome home he had imagined, the kiss he had hoped for. Fighting against the urge toward silence, Henry settled his hands on her shoulders.

"Hi," he said.

He had planned to tell her everything. But then Danny walked onto the field with his glove on his right hand and the ball in his left and Henry's heart raced at the cage of his ribs. His throat lumped, and Lori, as though she'd felt through the twitch of Henry's fingers on her shoulders, the accelerated pound in the cadence of his pulse, turned her head slightly toward him but kept her eyes on Danny.

"I told him it was okay," she said.

On the mound Danny hardly paused between pitches. He took the signs from Mickey, nodded, got set on the mound, and threw. Henry watched closely as Danny struck out the first batter of the inning. Half thrilled, half filled with anxiety, Henry wished he could appreciate the event unfolding before him. He wished he could record the moment on video so that he could see it again, really see it. For now, though, his vision was trumped by thrill and anxiety, by the secret finally revealed to this small corner of the world.

Henry lifted his hands from her and stuffed them into his front pockets. He bunched the cotton innards of his pockets in the clench of his anxious fingers.

"Do you see his eye?" Lori said.

"What about it?" Henry said.

"You can't see his black eye?" she said.

"I see it now," he said.

Lori told Henry the story of the Rockhound game on Friday night. She told him about the lefties and their hits and she told him about Sullivan pulling Danny off the mound and she told him how Danny got a black eye.

"Do you know what that was like, Henry?" she said.

A two-seam fastball in at the batter's hands. Ball two.

"Do you know what it was like watching our son punch himself in the eye because he failed to win a game?"

A brilliant change-up and the lefty whiffed at the pitch before it reached him. Two outs.

Another lefty came to the plate.

"Are you listening to me, Henry?"

Is it my fault? is what Henry nearly said. Instead he imagined sitting in her chair and watching Danny's fist pump into his eye, and the possibility occurred to him that he was as responsible for Danny's self-inflicted black eye as Danny was. That it very well might have been Henry's fault.

Henry set his hands on Lori's shoulders again. Slowly, he felt the tension in her shoulders lift.

"Yes," he said. "I can imagine what that was like." He brushed his thumb against the skin of Lori's neck. "I'll talk to him," Henry said.

They would not talk about baseball that afternoon, though, for Lori insisted they spend the rest of the day free from all talk of baseball.

Danny and Lori spent much of the afternoon drawing in the studio upstairs while Henry prepared for his next week of classes at U-High. But while Lori was preparing dinner, Henry heard Danny's son's footsteps on the Astroturf outfield of the basement stadium. He pulled a plastic bag from his backpack and threw it to Danny the moment he appeared in the doorway.

"You looked good out there, this morning, Danny."

"Thanks," Danny said. "It was crazy, Dad."

"Open the bag, Danny."

In the bag was a red hat with the *Indians* insignia.

"That's the minor league team in Indianapolis," Henry said, and Danny took off his Bulldogs hat and replaced it with the Indians' cap.

He pulled a chair away from the corner of the bullpen office and set it closer to Henry's desk, but through the thirty minutes during which he related the account of the Rockford tournament, he never sat in the chair.

"Nothing seemed right on Friday," he said. "Nothing."

It was cold and windy, he told his father, but it wasn't that—he had pitched in that weather before—he just didn't feel right. He didn't know if it was because he was nervous about the tournament, or because he had to step it up in order to succeed at this level. Or maybe it was because the Rockhounds had so many lefties on their team, and they were giants, too; they were like full-grown men. Nothing was right. Every player who came to the plate was another problem he couldn't solve, and he felt as though he had made a great mistake leaving Forest Park's Little League. That's what he was thinking, at first, that he had no business playing with the Bulldogs. He couldn't connect with any of the batters he faced. He felt like he didn't have a game plan with the players, that he had no idea what they would be looking for, or what he should do.

"They were rocking me, Dad," Danny said. "And I got frustrated." Danny pointed to his eye. "That's when I did this."

Henry nodded so slightly he wasn't sure it registered.

"And that's why I pitched lefty today."

Danny was animated in the bullpen office. He stood like a pitcher and threw a montage of imaginary pitches at the wall behind Henry.

"Once I started pitching left-handed to them," Danny continued, "it felt so good and so easy out there, that I wanted to pitch righty, too. Even though I lost to them two nights before I felt like I could even beat those guys throwing righty on Sunday if I wanted to. That's how good it felt. I wanted to have Friday back. I wanted another chance to throw righty to them. It was like I wasn't even thinking about what I was going to throw. Mickey called the pitches and I threw them. I think I maybe shook him off one or two times and that was it.

"It was awesome, Dad."

Danny finally sat in the chair.

"It was awesome."

Henry rested his chin on his hand on his elbow on his desk, and smiled at Danny.

"Now what?" Danny said.

"I don't know," Henry said. "Now I guess we change the game plan."

In the alley behind Lathrop they started off ten yards from each other, Danny wearing his glove on his left hand and throwing with his right. They had a quiet catch for a while and when Danny backed up two steps to throw at a greater distance he pointed to the lilac bushes in the backyard.

"Did you see the lilacs?" Danny said. "They sprouted over the weekend."

The earliest signs of them, tiny buds at the tips of a thousand black and bony branches, had pressed through to the air over the weekend.

"I smelled them before they sprouted," he said.

The ball was ready for release in Danny's hand, but Henry held up his glove for him to hold off the throw.

"What did you say?"

"Before the game on Friday I smelled them," Danny said. "It was Friday afternoon and we were on our way to the game, and I asked mom if she smelled the lilacs and she said no, and I looked at them closely to see if they'd sprouted yet, and there was no sign of anything, just the dried-up knobs from the winter, and I said to Mom, you really don't smell them? And she said no, and by the time Coach Wells and Mickey picked me up on Saturday morning a few buds had poked through the branches."

Danny took two steps back and began to throw again. They stopped for a moment to let a woman on a Vespa ride past. She wore a winter coat and gloves and smiled at them.

"You know what pitching is?" Danny said. "It's about solving problems," he said. "That's all it is."

He stepped back again and threw the next ball with added pace.

"You know what I mean, Dad?" he said, and Henry nodded to let Danny know he was listening.

"It's about solving a different problem every time a batter comes to the plate," he said. "This one you have to stay away from pitches high in the box, this one likes them low, this one could take a pitch to the opposite field if you aren't careful, and this here guy is ahead in the count three and oh and now what are you gonna do? And here you got three men on and nobody out and speed on the bases and the score's tied and now what?"

On a sunny day, the sky would have been bright for another hour but it was the color of smoke, a great blanket of cool breath, a leftover of winter. It was the color of nothing and nearly too dark to have a catch, but Henry struggled to maintain eye contact with the ball.

"It's pretty much like math," Danny said. "Or science or language arts, or anything in school. You have a little bit of information and you have to figure the rest of it out," he said. "It's just like school."

From there, Danny veered into the subject of school. He went through his daily schedule, stopping at each class to talk about the teacher and the students. He talked about how great his lunches were, compared to other kids. Danny liked his turkey sliced thin, not shaved, and Patrick Decker brought the strangest lunches to school. He brought half-pints of milk and drank them after they'd been his locker all morning, and he always had a Ziploc baggie with vegetables in it. Green peppers and celery sticks and carrots.

Henry, straining to make out the ball against the graysmoke sky, half-listened to Danny.

Inside the apartment Lori was upset, stuck on the veniality of Henry's pushing Danny too hard, when all along, Henry was just beginning to learn, his greater sin had more to do with holding Danny back. Lori was fighting against anger and sadness. While frying pork chops and grilling onions to a crisp and glassy brown, She steamed broccoli and stirr chocolate pudding, pouring it into oversized blue wine glasses. In the bullpen office downstairs Henry had blue earrings for her, and in his heart he had another secret. He had planned to give them both to her.

When it was too dark for Henry to catch the ball, he and Danny walked into the house, which smelled like a welcome home to Henry. He kissed Lori in the kitchen and for the first time in he couldn't remember how long, he wondered at the chance of their making love. Later, though, Lori sat up hard in bed; her back straight and tight against the headboard and her knees raised to steady her book, *The Inner Buddhist*, at her thighs. She was silent until Henry settled in beside her.

"Did you talk to Danny?" she said.

"Yes," Henry said. "He was frustrated. That's all."

"He gave himself a black eye, Henry."

"I know, I know," he said. "He doesn't like to lose, Lori. He wants to win."

"It's not normal."

"He'll be fine, Lori."

Lori returned to her book. "I've decided that I won't miss any of his games this summer," she said.

"So that you can see him play?" Henry said. "Or to protect him from me pushing too hard?"

"I won't allow that behavior, Henry," she said. "I told him that if he ever does something like that again I'll pull him off the field and he won't play another baseball game for the rest of his life."

Henry allowed a few minutes to pass before he put his fingernails to work on the back of her legs while she read, and though a moan escaped from her lips, her knees never moved. She closed her book, and then her eyes. When Henry stopped scratching her legs Lori opened her eyes drowsily.

In the sleepy silence that followed, a weekend's fatigue came over Henry and as he succumbed to it. As the first waves of sleep washed over him, Henry startled himself with his own voice and he awoke.

"Did I just say something?" he said.

"You said that Danny could smell the future," she said, and Henry smiled.

"The lilacs," he said. "Danny told me about the lilacs."

"Hm," Lori said.

"I'm sorry about this afternoon," Henry said, but Lori had already fallen asleep.

That summer Lori maintained her promise to attend all of Danny's baseball games, and Henry kept score for the Bulldogs in his chair next to hers. At first, he charted Danny's pitches from either side, noting each time the batter made hard contact, what the count was, if he reached base safely, and where the ball was hit. But he stopped keeping Danny's statistics three tournaments into the season when he learned that Danny had been keeping his own record of the games.

Before each game Danny copied the opposing team's lineup card into his own journal. He drew rectangles that represented strike zones and between innings he kept record of every at-bat of the opposing team. He noted the sequence and result of each pitch. He shaped his own fitness regimen around the workout routines of major league players. He had cardio workouts that varied according to his pitching schedule. He had workouts for off days before his starts, and balancing workouts that followed every game. And the summer rolled toward the autumnal. The winter to the vernal.

On Danny's first day of high school Lori drove him and Henry to University High. Through the entire ride she stretched her neck to look at Danny in the rear view mirror. When she pulled into the faculty parking lot, Lori got out of the car. Danny threaded his arms through the straps of his backpack and half-hopped to settle its weight.

"Do you have everything you need?" she said.

"I'm good, Mom," he said. And Lori kissed him.

"Have a good day, baby," she said.

It seemed to Henry, as Danny walked toward the entrance, that Lori stutter-stepped toward following him. He put his hand on Lori's elbow.

"He'll be fine, Lori," Henry said.

"Tell me again," she said.

"I promise, Lori," he said, and in the faculty parking lot it felt like an airport farewell while Henry held Lori crying silently in his arms.

There wasn't much to the school day. It was Orientation Day for the freshmen. Danny sat through shortened periods to meet his teachers and then through a student government assembly. He met his classmates, toured the library and computer labs, and walked through the field gym and fitness facilities. He ate lunch with a boy named Jeff Letourneau, whom he had played baseball against that summer. Jeff's sister, Eve, was a senior and they sat with her and her friends and the girls told Jeff and Danny about the teachers who sucked and the teachers who were great. One of the girls said she had seen her history teacher driving on the highway once, and he was picking his nose and rolling the product between his thumb and finger and singing to a song on the radio, and all the girls laughed. One girl made fun of the girl who referred to the thing he rolled in his finger as *product*. Another girl said that *product* was a much better word than any other reference to the thing. Another girl said she had seen the history teacher do the same thing through the window on his classroom door.

At the end of the school day Danny took the train home with Henry, and after the train there was a bus from the station to their house on Lathrop, and on the bus just blocks from his house Danny saved a girl's life.

They had been riding the bus along Desplaines Avenue in seats facing the aisle for three blocks when a girl with a brown skirt and a long-sleeved white blouse boarded the bus and sat across from them.

Behind Danny a shaft of the sun angled through the window over his shoulder. Danny looked to his right, near the rear wheelhouse, where something rattled like a tiny screw in a coffee can. When Danny looked back at the girl she had button-sized headphones in the hollows of her ears and *The Great Gatsby* was opened on her lap to its earliest pages.

Something seemed to deaden all sound around him until the

silence was deafening. It seemed as though hands or cushions had been pressed against Danny's ears. But something raged under the silence. An inner scream, or its opposite: a balloon of silence that inflated in his head and stole all sound from the world.

East on Madison, something white, a dream-like blur, a spector not yet visible, and to his right: the screw in a coffee can. Across from him, the girl's hand reaching for the rubber-coated wire to let the bus driver know she wanted to get off at Madison.

The scream beneath the bus.

A white blur.

The girl closed her book and stood in the aisle and waited for the bus to slow toward Madison Street. Danny spoke but didn't hear himself. He spoke but wasn't sure if the girl could hear.

"I'm sorry?" the girl said, and she took the headphones out of her right ear and looked toward the front of the bus to see that she wouldn't miss her stop.

"You dropped something," Danny said, still not sure if he'd said anything. The scream. The squeak and hiss of the bus braking at Madison. The girl torn between the aisle and the front exit of the bus at Madison. She looked at the floor of the bus where there was nothing.

"Something fell from your book," he said.

The girl stepping toward the front of the bus. The scream. The blur. Danny's fear that she might leave the bus at the wrong time. The intolerable scream beneath and above and around.

"Something fell," he said, holding his hands against his ears, and louder this time. "I saw something fall from your book."

The girl looked at the floor again.

"Where?" she said, and she turned around, looked up and down the aisle. "There's nothing on the floor, you freak!"

Danny stood to put his hand on her arm to stop her from walking and he felt his father's hand on his own arm.

"What are you doing?" his father said.

"She dropped something!" Danny yelled, and every face on the bus turned toward him.

"Something fell!" he said, as if in response to everyone.

The girl held onto the pole and pivoted toward the front of the bus.

There was a squeal of tires then, and screams. Human screams. Screams not meant for Danny alone. Screams for the rest of the world to hear. The screams of passengers on the bus. There was the clash and grind of collision, then, the clang and scrape of metal. A white pick-up truck crashing into the streetlight on the corner, and below the crash, the tremble of the ground beneath the bus. The truck wrapping around the pole, its headlights curling into a perfect fit around it. The pole holding the front of the truck like a pivot, and the tail of the pick-up sweeping the corner of Madison Street and whipping in an arc across the corner, and another crash: the back of the truck banging into the front doors of the bus. A cataract of glass hailed across the entrance, along the steps of the bus and at the driver who shielded himself with his arm to keep the peppering glass from his face.

The front of the bus where the girl was not standing now. The girl. The girl was safe. She had fallen back into her seat. Bumped her head on the glass behind her. The white wires of her headphones at her neck. Her hand on her head. And her tears.

She was staring at Danny. The thing he had done.

Between them there was something on the ground. The girl's I.D. card from school. Danny leaned over and picked up the card. He walked across the aisle and handed the fallen thing to the wordless girl, who accepted the card slowly, as though she wished it had not belonged to her. Staring at Danny she shouldered her school bag and exited the bus from the side door. She was the first to leave the bus, and while she was on the sidewalk she stared at Danny through the window. He sat still next to his father while the girl walked backward through the chaos of metal and glass and people. There were tears on her cheeks but it didn't seem as though she was crying. She was look-ing at Danny through the window of the bus and her I.D. card was still in her hand. She held it between her thumb and her finger like a talisman.

They were both, Henry and Danny, still watching the girl from the empty bus when she finally turned around and started walking forward down Madison Street.

"Let's go, Danny," Henry said. He put his arm across Danny's shoulder and they walked off the bus. At Adams Street Danny looked over his shoulder. Police cars had arrived at the scene and hundreds of pedestrians gaped from the space at Lee's Mobil on the corner.

"Do you think we should go back?" Danny said. "As witnesses?"

"They'll want to talk to people who have a better idea of what happened," Henry said.

"I know exactly what happened," Danny said.

"Let's just go," Henry said. "They'll be fine."

As they walked home the wind picked up from the west, and Danny kept looking over his shoulder at the mess of Madison Street.

A Ryder rental truck was parked in front of the house with a yellow station wagon in tow, and a girl was walking across the Granvilles' lawn with a box under one arm and a bundle of hangered clothes over her shoulder. Her hair was short, she was nearly bald, but Danny could see that her hair was black, or would have been black if there was more than just a shadow of it. She had a nose ring. Her eyebrows were full and her lashes were long and thick and there was more hair on her eyelids then on all of her head. Danny had never seen a face like hers.

She lifted the many-hangered pile of clothes and steered them into a gust of wind to keep them from flying away and walked up the stairs and into the stairwell to Judy Copeland's second floor apartment.

"Who was that?" Danny said.

"Who was what?" Henry said.

"The girl who just walked up into Judy's apartment."

"It must have been the girl Mom was talking about," Henry said.

"The new tenant. "Her name is Bridget," Henry said. "I think she was teaching an art class Mom took."

Inside, Danny sat on the radiator at the window and answered his mother's questions about his first day of school. As they spoke, he held the curtain aside and looked for the girl. When it seemed his mother had finished questioning him, Danny asked if he could help the girl upstairs move in.

Lori looked at Henry and Henry shrugged.

"Why not?" Henry said.

Outside, Danny met her on the porch.

"Hey," she said.

"Hey."

"You must be Danny."

Danny nodded.

"Bridget Pentecoff," the girl said. "Are you doing anything?"

"I came to see if you needed help," Danny said.

"Yes, I do," Bridget said.

Her station wagon was yellow with fake wood paneling on the side, and the back of it was stuffed with her things. Danny moved some boxes to the side until he found a heavy one and this he slid to his thighs and lifted. Bridget was behind him with another armload of clothes she pulled from the front seat. He let her climb the stairs in front of him and when they came down for more things she seemed startled at the doorway, as though she were surprised to find the stairs had ended. Two trips later she did the same thing.

"What's wrong?" Danny said, and Bridget laughed through her nose.

"It's the wind," she said. "It sounds like cars."

On another trip Danny carried an easel into her apartment. He told Bridget about Judy Copeland, and that he and his mother used to use one of the rooms up there for their own little art studio, too.

"She called it our Friday Place," Danny said.

Bridget said it was okay if he still came up there to paint and to draw.

"That would be okay with me," she said. "Your mother, too. She could still come up, too."

For a while, they coordinated their trips so that they walked them together, and Bridget asked him questions about school and sports. He told her that it had been his first day at U-High and that he was play-ing travel ball now, but that it wasn't with school, and that would prob-ably go on through October, and then in the spring he would play baseball for U-High if he made the team. He was pretty sure he would make the team.

She was going to be a freshman, too. She was just starting at the School of the Art Institute. She'd been teaching art classes for adults that summer, which is how she met Danny's mother.

When the station wagon was emptied they moved to the truck for the rest of her things. Among the clutter were red toolboxes filled with art supplies. They each carried two boxes upstairs and set them on the canvas tarp Bridget had already duct-taped to the floor. She put her hands on her hips and sighed heavily. She was wearing boys' blue jeans, faded thin and baggy, and just to look at her and her smile it seemed to Danny as though he was staring at her, and he looked away hastily.

"This is crazy," she said.

"What?"

"Go get your art supplies, Danny," she said. "I'm not going to move another inch until you get all of it and put it in this room," and that's what Danny did.

Bridget told him, when he returned to the room with his easel and pencils and sketch pad and found her standing in the same spot with her hands still on her blue jeans, on her hips, that he should think of the room still as his studio, and that's what he should call it, she said, his *studio*, and Friday's were probably still going to be the best days to use it, actually, she said then, because she had classes every day but Friday, and after a week of jumping through hoops at school, she would need the day to unwind and to create. If he wanted to come there after school on Fridays to paint or to draw, she would even give him lessons. Danny told her that would probably be good because he got frustrated sometimes with drawing.

As they moved the last of her possessions—a tilted mound of hangered clothes, a CD boom box, a shoebox filled with scissors and tiny light bulbs, twist ties, a flashlight, a small hammer, scotch tape, and countless tiny things he could hear tumbling over each other at the bottom but couldn't see—Bridget asked him about the things he drew.

"Nothing really," he said. "Just whatever. Trees, baseball fields, stuff on a table."

"What frustrates you about it?" she said.

"Mostly people," he said. "They never look how I want them to."

"I know what you mean," she said. "I can maybe help you with that."

Bridget folded a stack of clothes over her arm.

"Hand me that junk box," she said, and Danny picked it up and tucked it under Bridget's arm. She smiled, and the cone of light from the streetlamp above threw shadows of her eyelashes across her cheeks.

At the top of the last pile of clothes that remained was a sleeveless white shirt. Danny hooked his fingers into the tunnel of hangers below it and lifted the hangers over his shoulder. The front of Bridget's blouse draped against his back. The weight of the rest of the clothes pressed against his back like the weight of a girl.

In bed that night, Danny closed his eyes and thought of Bridget. He could see the black shadow of her hair. Could almost feel it. He could see her smile and her eyes, which were brown, but how bright they were! He could see her flinch at the sound of wind as though she was from a place where it didn't blow.

Thirteenth

WHILE THE FOOTSTEPS OF DANNY AND BRIDGET TAPPED UP AND down the stairs above the Granville's apartment, Henry looked around for some grocery item that was needed from Jewel Foods. There was laundry detergent and bath tissue. There were dryer sheets. The dish soap was running low. He poured the remaining soap in the kitchen sink and told Lori he was going to take a walk to the store. The apartment was too small a thing to be in.

What had just happened? What had just happened on that bus? What made Danny say he had seen something fall before it had fallen? Had he seen the truck coming? Had he determined, somehow, its speed and location and anticipated the result? Was it about physics? How could he have seen such a thing from Adams Street? They were at Adams Street, two blocks away when Danny began to panic over the I.D. card. It had not even fallen yet! He could not have seen a truck coming down Madison Street from there. Had he seen the whole episode unfold before it happened? Otherwise, why the panic in his voice? Why didn't he just pick the damn card up himself and give it to her unless he knew he had to stall her so that she wouldn't walk to the front of the bus? Was he able to see things before they occurred? Was it like the lilacs he had smelled before they sprouted?

What had Henry set into motion when he had first considered the foraging sphere of the ambidextrous Western Lowland Gorilla? He was thinking only of function. The ease with which the ape ate from a tree. He thought only that he would provide Danny the possibility of ambidexterity. The he would give him every opportunity to pursue even-handedness.

All he had hoped for was that Danny would become a decent athlete. That was it. Is this what had come of Henry's unresearched, almost ignorant symmetry campaign? It was just a stupid and unfounded hypothesis, but had all of it come true? He had toyed like an idiot with things that were infinitely beyond the scope of his own comprehension.

Danny had been given a gift, and with it he had saved a girl's life.

What had gone through his head on that bus? Was it pain? Did he feel the burden of responsibility that came with a gift? Had it effected such pain that he had no choice but to repress it immediately? And Bridget had come along like an angel and allowed him to forget the afternoon.

How was he to manage the life of a boy, a boy-hero, who had been given a gift?

"Gift," Henry said to the night. "Some fucking gift."

There. He had put words to it. It was a fucking gift. But how was he to do this by himself?

It occurred to Henry Granville, then, that perhaps a *burdengift* had been handed to Danny. To both of them. There was a reason Henry was there, with him, on that bus. The accident required his witness. He needed to be shown the gift in that extraordinary way so that he could protect Danny, so that he could prepare him for the world, perhaps even to fend the world off, until Danny no longer needed his protection.

And in that moment Henry also awakened to the pain that belonged to his wife all along. It was not depression, nor was it some great postnatal sadness she had been fighting since Henry put surgical scissors to the purple cord that connected her to Danny.

All along she had wanted nothing for Danny but a boyhood. She did not want a boy who walked before he turned seven months old, or a boy who could have a catch at thirteen months old, or a boy who could throw with either arm. She did not want a boy who could see through things like time or smell the future. She did not want greatness for him, and she did not want to lose him to the world on account of his gift. If she could have kept him in her womb to protect him for the whole of his life, she would have. She'd been fighting against sadness for years and what had Henry done to give her any of this? He had pushed Danny.

In the bullpen office, Henry pulled several U-High yearbooks off the lowest shelf of a bookcase and reached behind them for a plastic bag. From it he pulled the blue earrings he had purchased for Lori in Indianapolis and walked toward the stairs. He would pour two glasses of wine, one for himself and one for Lori. He would give her the earrings. He would make it up to her and tell her everything, and she would be his angel. They would do this thing together.

Upstairs, Henry slipped the earrings into his pocket and walked into the kitchen to pour two glasses of wine. When he brought them into the living room, Lori was standing at the curtains in a flannel nightgown Henry had not seen since the end of winter.

"Do you think he's fine up there?" Lori said.

She turned around at the silence behind her, and Henry, two glasses of wine in his hands, responded.

"I think he's okay up there, Lori." He handed her a glass.

"What's the occasion?" she said.

"An apology," he said.

"For what?"

"Come here," he said, and Henry walked into the kitchen and Lori followed. He set his wine glass on the kitchen table.

"Could we sit here a bit?" he said.

Lori sat in the chair he had pulled for her while Henry settled his hand over the hill of the earring case in his pocket, and while Danny helped Bridget Pentecoff move her world into the apartment upstairs Henry asked Lori to please just listen while he spoke. He asked her to please not say a word or shake her head. Just to listen. He had much to say.

"First this," he said, and Henry removed the earring case from his pocket and reached it toward Lori.

"I bought them for you in Indianapolis," he said.

When Lori put the earrings on, the guilt of the secret of Emily all but vanished.

Lori smiled and put her fingers to her chin, batted her eyelashes. She walked to the bathroom mirror and returned with a kiss for Henry.

"Second?" she said, and Henry looked at Lori's earrings.

"They look beautiful," he said.

"Second?" Lori said again.

"Second," Henry said. "I wanted to have a catch with Danny," he said. "That's all I wanted. I couldn't wait to have a catch with him."

"What are you talking about, Henry?" Lori said. She elbowed her arms on the table and held her hands in a kind of prayer while Henry returned in time some thirteen years back.

"Remember the night we walked to the Brown Cow when Danny almost darted out into the street?" Henry said.

Lori nodded and sipped from her glass of wine.

And Henry recalled Danny's left-handed throw of the rubber ball he found at the curb, and he told Lori how he'd felt about seeing Danny throw lefty that first time. He told her about the ape and the foraging sphere. He told her about his idea of symmetry and the cross lateralization of the hemispheres of the brain. He told her how good Danny was at baseball. Sure, she had seen him play all along, but did she really know just how good he was?

"Do you understand how good he is, Lori?" he said.

Of all the thousands of kids he had played against—kids from every little league and travel ball game—Henry had never seen anyone better than him. Never. At the plate, on the mound, in the field. Never saw a better player. Anywhere. People gawked at the batting cages.

"The parents of opposing players cheer for him, Lori. Parents don't do that," he said, "but they do it for him. And maybe I'm wrong about this, too," he said, "but when Danny's on the field or at the plate or whatever, it seems that he has access to some knowledge that other pitchers don't have. And when he's pitching on that mound it's not even fair how good he is, Lori. It's like he knows everything. What the batter is thinking, what kind of pitch he's expecting, where he's going to hit it, and when he's going to swing. And he knows what the umpire is thinking, too, and what kind of pitch he could use to stretch the strike zone. And when he's in the field he can read the direction of the ball before it hits the bat. At the slightest twitch of the hitter's feet, the slightest shift in his stance, he knows where it's going, and he'll say, *heads up center field* or, *heads up second base*, and that's where the ball will go. And when he's at the plate he knows what's coming and that's why he's so good at the plate, too."

"Please don't roll your eyes, Lori," he said.

And then Henry told her about the accident on Madison Street.

"You're going to think I'm crazy," he said. "But just listen."

Henry told her about the girl on the bus, how Danny told her she had dropped something and how he'd pleaded with the girl to pick it up.

Lori stood up and pushed her chair in slowly, looking at Henry as she stepped back toward the kitchen counter, as though she had already begun to feel the weight of revelation and wanted to take it in standing.

Henry stood and faced her.

"There was nothing on the floor, Lori," Henry said. "Nothing. And Danny was almost crying. I put my fingers on the crook of his arm to hold him back, he was creeping out this girl, and I was starting to think the same thing as that girl, that Danny was a crazy person.

"She called him a *freak*, but if Danny hadn't said anything, she would have walked to the front of the bus and stepped out into the street and a truck would have pinned her against the bus."

Lori crossed her arms tightly across her chest, uncrossed them, crossed them again, and rubbed her arms as though she were trying to wipe away Henry and the thing he was trying to say. Finally she pressed her hands to her ears.

"Please, Lori." Henry touched her hands. "Please just listen to me. I'm telling you the girl would've been dead if Danny hadn't stopped her, and if she had lived she would have been paralyzed."

Lori was crying. "What are you saying, Henry?"

"I'm saying that Danny knew what was going to happen."

"No, he didn't," she said.

"He did, Lori."

Lori, sobbing, shook her head.

"Please don't cry," Henry said.

"He's just a boy," she said.

"No, Lori," he said. "He's not just a boy."

Lori looked up at Henry.

Lori's arms were crossed, and as she leaned against the counter she wept into her crossed arms. Henry watched her tears fall into her arms until her body finally stilled. Henry wiped Lori's arms then. He held her then and beneath the leaning weight of him she did not uncross her arms. She held them there, locked against this discovered news of her son.

"I'm doing the best I can over here," Henry said. "I need your help. I don't know what I'm doing, but there are special people in this world. I know you believe that, too. There are special people in this world, and if I'm right, if Danny is one of them, we need to be careful. And we need to make sure he's ready for whatever it is he's supposed to do."

"He's just a boy."

"I'm sorry," Henry said.

"He's just a boy."

"It would be fine if he were," Henry said, and Lori uncrossed her arms to Henry's embrace and he held her through the fits and bouts of a new trembling. He held her until her body quieted into his.

"It would be fine if he were just a boy," Henry said again. "He's more than that."

When Henry climbed under the covers next to Lori, she rolled, sleepily and naked, against him.

"Is Danny back?" she said.

"Yes," he said, and he held his wife as he hadn't held her in years. Which is to say he held her.

Lori lifted herself onto Henry's pajamed and tee-shirted body and asked him if he wouldn't mind holding her like this for a while, if he wouldn't mind touching her and running his nails along her body for a while. If he wouldn't mind kissing her a while before she removed his sleeping pants and slipped herself onto him and made love with him.

"I wouldn't mind," Henry said.

Against his pajamas and tee shirt, Lori was more naked a woman than he had ever known, and all that he could touch with his hands he touched.

"I'm reading about Buddhists," Lori said, as she began to pull at his pajamas. "And I wonder if we could love like Buddhists?"

"And how do Buddhists love?" Henry asked.

And Lori described to Henry, as she understood it, how Buddhists made love. The Buddhist husband, she explained, stayed inside the Buddhist wife for great stretches of time. It was silly, she said, to even put a measurement to the duration of their lovemaking. It was silly, she said, to use the language of time to get at the thing that Buddhists hoped to achieve in the arms of each other.

"Let us love like Buddhists, then," Henry said, and while they made love, Lori cried silently. She touched Henry's face with her wet cheeks while they made love, and while Henry was inside Lori he told her it seemed as though she were inside of him, too, that it seemed to him they each were inside one another.

And when they heard Danny footsteps on his way to the bathroom Henry stilled himself within Lori and Lori stilled herself within him, and at the sound of Danny's return to his room Lori sat up and began again to stir her hips against Henry's.

Danny did not see Bridget again until the Wednesday that followed orientation at U-High. But it was not for wont of looking. On errands for his mother—stamps from the post office, outfits from the dry cleaners, take-out from La Piazza, coffee from Caffe de Lucca, lemons and rosemary from Jewel—he would stop at the sidewalk and look for rectangles of light in Bridget's evening windows. He turned his head at every opening of a door that might have been hers. He listened for the screeches and creaks of the back stairs. He had begun to wonder if he'd dreamed her up. Maybe the late night footwork on the floor above him was the long dormant ghost of Judy Copeland, finally come to haunt the apartment upstairs. On the train to school, at the cafeteria table, in his bed at night, in line at the grocery store—he tried to call upon Bridget's image but could not. He retrieved her words—some of them—and remembered pieces of her: walking up the stairs ahead of him, boxes in her arms, the black shadow of hair, the street-frayed hem of her blue jeans. With his eyes closed he followed her all the way up the stairs where he thought he remembered her turning around to smile at him, but as soon as she began to turn her head back at him, the image would disappear.

After dinner on Wednesday Danny was on the porch taping the barrel of a new wooden bat when Bridget walked up the stairs.

"Hey," she said. "Friday?"

"Friday," Danny said.

Bridget said, "Seven," then, and smiled.

Danny filled the time between this smile and Friday with recollections of that image of her on the porch, and imaginings of when he would see her again. And like the minutes before a White Sox game—while he waited in line at the turnstile, or ran along the gray-brown cement of the concourse, or took in that first sighting of the field—he imagined the walk to her apartment in slow motion. The light would be on at the landing outside her door and with each step on the twenty-seven carpeted stairs it would draw nearer. He would knock at her door and listen for her steps and she would pull the door toward her and there would be a line of boxes still unpacked in the hallway and they would squeeze past them, and Bridget would lead the way into the living room, which was as far as he could imagine the night.

But when Friday came, only the walk up the stairs and the drawing nearer of the hallway light was as he'd imagined. Upstairs, the door was already open several inches and when Danny knocked he tapped it open several inches more. It swiveled away from him more than he'd expected so that he felt he was opening the door without permission to enter, and so he pulled it back toward him.

"Come on in, Danny." Bridget's voice from the living room. "Close the door behind you."

Classical music. The hundred-year-old smell of Judy Copeland gone. Rice and some kind of chicken now. Salad dressing. There were no boxes in the hallway. Ahead of him, there was a long table made of untreated lumber and topped with floor tiles in the middle of the room. Behind it, Bridget, sitting cross-legged on the floor between the two windows, half-hidden by a legless easel. Her back straight, like the body of a dancer or a pianist. She peeked from behind the easel.

"Hey," she said. A smile, and she returned to her work.

"Hey."

She seemed to balance herself with two fingers of her left hand, a peace symbol fingertipping the floor at her side.

"Come here a second," she said, and it was the perfect thing to hear her say. She wore jeans and the sleeveless white shirt he had carried from her station wagon on the day of the move. An airborne ballerina was coming alive on the easel before him. Bridget's hands moved quickly and lightly over the canvas, they seemed free and unstilted, as though she were drawing from interior place, as though some inner instructor was driving her. The dancer's legs were spread in a forward split that spread the dress beneath her like a lace doily. She stretched backward in a near perfect fold and looked skyward like an offering, like a flower.

"Wow," Danny said, and Bridget laughed through her nose.

Her hair seemed to have grown since she'd moved in just one week before. It swirled darkly, like nighttime ripples, from the center of her skull. She tilted her head and rubbed a finger along the thin shadow the dancer's arm made across her leg, and when Bridget tilted her head to look at the shadow she had rubbed, Danny tilted his head the same way.

"It seems as though it should be raining," he said.

"What do you mean?"

"I don't know. The expression on her face," he said. "No. Not her face. She doesn't even have a face. Her body, I guess. Her arms back like that, and the bend of her body. Like it's raining and she wants all of it.

"All of the rain?"

"Yes."

Bridget angled her head. "Let me finish up here and then we'll do a drill I learned this week at school."

Danny nodded and said nothing. While Bridget touched at the shadows in the folds of the ballerina's lacy dress, Danny noted the shadows along Bridget's neck, the strain of Bridget's skin stretched over cartilage and ligaments within as she titled her head for a shift in perspective. Tiny holes were pierced in her earlobes but she wore no jewelry.

"How do you do that?" he said.

"What do you mean," she said again.

"Her face is unfinished but I can see that she's happy."

"Hmm," she said again. "I wasn't thinking of her as happy."

"No?"

Bridget titled her head again. "I guess I wasn't thinking of her as anything." She set her pencil on the easel's ledge and rose from the floor.

"Let's sit at the table," Bridget said. She sat on a stool and tapped her fingers on the seat of another and Danny sat down. "I was thinking we'd start off with a drill or something like that every Friday, and then in your studio you can just work on whatever, if that's okay."

"Sure," Danny said, and Bridget flipped over the cover of a new sketchpad.

She slid a book toward Danny and opened it to a photograph of Dr. Martin Luther King, Jr., with his fingers locked under his chin. Bridget turned the book upside down and set it to the left of the sketchpad.

"I want you to draw this," she said. "There was a painting of this photograph at a soup kitchen I worked at on Monday, and I thought of doing this exercise with you. I want you to draw it upside down."

"Why upside down?" he said.

"Because sometimes when you draw things from the correct orientation you think too much about what you're drawing. It's supposed to allow more creative capabilities to take over, because you're not thinking so much about how something is supposed to look. You just draw exactly what it is that you see. All you need to know is what's right there in front of you."

Danny held his pencil in his right hand and stared at the photograph.

"Go ahead, start from the top."

Danny pointed to King's head at the bottom of the photograph.

"Here?" he said.

"Well, you know," she said. "The bottom," and Danny laughed.

When he brushed his hand over the blank sheet of paper, Bridget returned to her easel on the floor behind him.

"You'll be tempted to turn it right side up," she said. "But don't. It'll mess up the point of the exercise."

Danny was certain he would be unable to draw anything with Bridget sitting behind him. Cross-legged with her white shirt and jeans, her neck and hair, her pierced and earringless ears. He wanted to look at her, return to where he had stood behind her, learn by watching her draw.

Before he set his pencil to the sketchpad, Danny stared at the disoriented photograph for a moment. Upside down as it was, the shock of light on Dr. King's face was only broken by the shadows of his eyes, his hair a crescent moon at the bottom of the page, a black smile. He considered the oval of King's face and the wide and angled spread of his fingers, the papery folds of skin on the hammer of his hand. He set his pencil to the paper and began to draw. Lightly, the heel of his right hand whispered across the page like a slipper. Softly his pencil touched paper and he began to draw, to follow the lines at the top of the image and the curves at the bottom. King's features were lost as Danny began to draw. It wasn't a nose he was drawing, or eyes, there weren't fingers, ears, or hair, there were only curves and lines and shapes and angles. Where one line ended, another began. There were spaces and edges of spaces, relationships between lines and arcs and the edge of the paper.

Behind him—once—there was Bridget. Standing over his shoulder. A flash of Bridget at his side and then Bridget walking through the hallway to the kitchen, Danny watching her until she turned around a kitchen corner. And he returned to his drawing to thumb-rub shade at the side of his inverted King, to pencil darkness into space.

When he was finished, he sighed, more heavily than he had intended.

"Finished?" Bridget said.

"I don't know."

Once more, Danny set his pencil to darken a space in the upper left corner of his sketch.

"I think I'm done," he said.

"Did you draw this with your left hand?" Bridget asked.

Danny looked at the pencil in his hand.

"I guess so," he said.

"You started with the pencil in your right hand," she said.

"Did I?"

"Yeah."

"I guess I drew it with both," he said. "I'm pretty good with both hands."

Bridget reached to the table to upright the sketch.

"Yeah, I'd say so," she said.

She walked around the table and tilted her head at the drawing. Danny tilted his head, too. A mirror across from Bridget.

She looked in his eyes and smiled.

"What?" he said again.

"It's good, Danny," she said. "It's really good."

"Should I work on something in the studio, now?" he said.

"It's eleven o'clock," she said.

Danny looked through the windows behind him, the dark curtain of night sky.

"Next week," she said.

Downstairs, Danny opened the mirrored bathroom cabinet and squeezed toothpaste onto his brush. He ran cold water over it and closed the cabinet door until the mirror was revealed and the metal catch clicked into place. On the side of his nose there was a thumb smudge of pencil lead. Like a shadow. Why Bridget had smiled.

When Danny climbed the stairs to Bridget's apartment the next Friday, he found the door ajar as it had been the week before, he knocked again, holding the doorknob this time so it wouldn't swing open further. Bridget's voice called him closer again.

"Hey," she said. The word came from her mouth like a tiny split chord and Bridget lifted the back of her hand to her throat as though she'd made a mistake.

She wore a paint-stained tee shirt the color of butter. It was loose fitting and revealed the white strap of a bra on her left shoulder. She'd begun painting her ballerina. Danny stood behind her and watched, fascinated by what came of the simple application of paint, the touch of her brush to palette and then to canvas. How the ballerina came alive with color. Through the window behind Bridget, the sun was a cloud-scattered flower in the sky, and somehow she seemed responsible for that as well. Some part of him wanted to say something. That ballerinas dressed like brides, it seemed, and why did she think that was? And had she ever been a dancer? And was that "hey." that came from her, that tiny song she had sung to greet him tonight, was it the first thing she had said all day? It sounded as though it might have been. But Danny said nothing. He waited for Bridget to set her palette on the floor at her side and her brush on the easel's ledge.

"Hey," she said, rising from the floor. "How's it going?"

She had taped a single sheet of sketching paper to the table in the center of the room.

"Let me get a drink real quick. You want something?"

"No. Thanks," he said.

She returned with a glass of water, a folded square of paper towel shaped to its bottom, and set it on the table.

Danny opened his hand to the sketch paper taped to the table.

"What's this for?" he said.

"A contour drawing," Bridget said. She sipped the water and set the glass down. "You're going to draw a picture of your own hand today, but you can't look at what you're drawing."

"Why not?"

"It's an exercise in seeing. The point is for you to focus entirely on the thing you're drawing. It doesn't matter what ends up on paper."

The diamond in her nose was the tiniest jewel in the world, the crumb of a jewel, and as Bridget directed Danny, it flickered in the light.

"You have to do this exercise slowly, Danny. It requires the slow-est movement of your eyes along every edge and line and wrinkle of your hand, and your drawing hand records every slight change your eye observes. The point is to see things exactly as they are."

"Which hand should I draw?" he said.

Bridget laughed softly and briefly and shook her head. "Why don't we draw your right hand today," she said, "and we'll draw your left hand next week."

Danny pulled the stool from beneath the table and set his left hand well within the edges of the sketch paper. He turned completely away from the paper at his hip facing skyward. Bridget adjusted the height of the other stool and placed it under Danny's hand, and returned to her easel on the floor.

The contour exercise began as did the upside down drill, with Danny thinking he would be unable to concentrate with Bridget so near. With his hand reaching out over the stool and Bridget hidden behind her easel over his right shoulder, it seemed as though he were waiting for her to set her hand in his. But, as with the other drill, he was soon lost in the curve and bend, the depth, angle, and shadow of his fingers. The bone and skin of them.

As he blindly sketched his hand he found himself attending to the line and color on the surface—the minute atlas of palm- and finger-prints—but to the workings of line and color beneath his skin as well.

And unaware of the passage of time—unaware, even, of his own drawing hand—when Danny felt he had rendered all he had seen onto the sketch paper, he sighed and stretched, cracked the knuckles of his fingers and rubbed his hands together. He looked over his shoulder toward Bridget, but she was gone. She'd left a note for him on the table. She'd had enough of her ballerina for the evening, had watched Danny sketch his hand for an hour, had gone to sleep at eleven-fifteen. He should work as long he wanted. The door would lock, he knew, when he pulled it closed behind him.

Eleven fifteen? What time was it now? The clock radio. Twelve-twelve. On the table, the sketch he had made looked something like the mess of a mangled hand behind a broken window screen. Twelve-thirteen now.

Past the hallway Bridget lay asleep, a long rectangle of darkness marking her open bedroom door. He had waited a week for this day, and in a room filled with her he had watched his hand for five hours. Now she slept beyond that bar of darkness. How long might he have been able to watch a sleeping Bridget?

Downstairs, his mother was barely awake on the couch. She sat on her legs, book on her lap.

"It's past midnight, Danny," she said.

"I know, Mom. I was drawing my hand," he said. "Go to bed, Mom."

"You, too, sweetie," she said. "Goodnight, Danny."

Fourteenth

FROM THE FIRST DAY OF FRESHMAN YEAR THE WORLD SEEMED TO open its arms to Danny Granville. Jeff Letourneau, the captain of the varsity boys' baseball team said hello to him in the hall and called him by name, and introduced Danny to what seemed like everyone. In the cafeteria, Jeff's sister Eve and her girlfriends, all juniors, waved him over to their table on the first day and never let him sit alone.

By the second week of September, Danny knew everyone at U-High who would be playing baseball in the spring. Though the first day of the official start of the season was five months away, there was a buzz that filled the air like static when Danny saw another player in the halls of the school. The juniors and seniors on the varsity team nodded to him when they saw him between classes. They tapped his shoulder and said, "What's up," when they saw him at his locker.

The school days were filled with biology and humanities and Spanish and algebra, reports, presentations, essays, tests, and quizzes. For health class he designed a workout routine for the pitchers that incorporated strength, speed, agility, and quickness training, along with cardiovascular exercise, stretching, and plyometrics. He studied ballistics and explosive training, and with his father's help, designed a resistance station for the fitness center using cables, pulleys, dumb-bells, and medicine balls.

And to the world that seemed to have been giddily awaiting Danny Granville's arrival at his final boyhood, was added Bridget Pentecoff. Every Friday night began with that trek up the stairs, the push of the slightly opened door, the walk through the hallway into her living room, and then Bridget painting at her easel on the floor. He would pull up a stool and sit behind her and watch silently for a while. From the CD player in the corner of the room classical music streamed, floated around and above her, and filled the room like light. Like dry rain.

Bridget speaking of art while she painted, and Danny listening.

Bridget answering Danny's uncountable questions about paint.

Bridget startling him by jumping up at the mention of an artist's name, and searching for a book of his work.

Bridget patting the stool next to her for Danny to sit in while she flipped through the pages of an art book.

Bridget with dried paint in her fingernails.

Bridget with a smudge of charcoal on her neck.

And Danny would warm-up with some version of the contour exercise, which often consumed much of the night. He brought old baseball gloves, bats, and balls upstairs to draw as still lifes. He spoke to Bridget of baseball at U-High and how the team had already begun to prepare for the spring season.

Bridget told him one night that she had never been to a professional baseball game and Danny told her he would take her to a White Sox game in the summer, or maybe even the spring.

"Wait'll you find out what you've been missing," he said, and several times that night he shook his head in disbelief at the discovery of her limited baseball history.

Late that fall, Danny spent all of two Fridays and three hours of another on a single drawing of a forgotten baseball glove sitting under bleacher stands. When he finally completed the drawing in November, Danny asked if she'd like to celebrate its completion by going to the batting cages.

Bridget eyed the scattered and tiny bits of her own project on the studio table, a drawing collage assignment. She looked back at Danny.

"Right now?"

"Yeah," Danny said.

"It's like ten o'clock," she said.

"We got another hour," he said. "Let's go."

A long table of colored helmets and three racks of baseball bats lined the walls of the walkway. She ran her fingers along the tops of the helmets and asked Danny how he knew what size bat to use, and what were the differences in the speeds of the pitching machines, how many pitches did you get with one slug, and how often did Danny come here, and who was that man that said hello to him, and those high school kids, and did he know everyone who came to Stella's. They watched a girl and her father hit softballs in the last cage to their left. She asked why some of the helmets had protective bars like football helmets and why some didn't. She asked if this was how fast they pitched in high school, and did the machines throw more than one kind of pitch; why was Danny using a wooden bat when all the other bats were metal, and why didn't he use one of Stella's helmets, they seemed much nicer than the one he was wearing, and if she put a slug in the slow cages did he think she would be able to hit one of the pitches.

Danny smiled at the quantity of questions and answered them all. He bought six slugs with a five-dollar bill and took a wooden bat from his bag and opened the gate to a medium cage. He bunted six pitches lefty and turned around at Bridget's voice. She wore a yellow helmet with a full cage across the mask and leaned on a metal baseball bat.

"You know you're not very good," she teased. "You make it seem like baseball is your life and then you hit these little dinky things that go nowhere. You hardly even swing the bat."

Danny turned around and smiled and the next pitch thudded into the rubber backstop against the fence.

"See what I mean?" Bridget said. "You missed that one completely."

Danny smiled and prepared for the next throw.

"I think I'm going to go back by that girl to see some decent hitting," Bridget said, and Danny started to swing.

There were two boys hitting in a medium cage to their right, and farther down, in a slow-pitch cage, a girl watched her boyfriend hit balls lefty. Danny took a few easy swings from the left side and a few from the right before the red light on the machine noted the end of his pitches.

Danny opened the cage and touched Bridget's wrist.

"Let's move down one," he said, and they walked to a fast-pitch cage. Danny dropped a slug in the machine and stood at the yellow plate painted on the cement floor. Danny blasted six line drives from the right side and six from the left. With another slug he hit a dozen balls against the left field wall hitting right handed, and then a dozen to right field from the other side. With his fifth slug Danny aimed for the target gong at the back wall in center field, hitting it first from the right side and then from the left. When his slug ran out he looked back toward Bridget and realized the people in the other cages had stopped hitting baseballs and were watching him, too.

Danny opened the cage and steered Bridget to the bat racks to pick one out for her.

"You started picking it up at the end there," she said.

"Yeah," Danny said. "It takes me a little while to warm up."

"You'll be fine," she said, and Danny smiled.

In the slow cage against the wall to their left, Danny showed Bridget how to stand at the plate, and when she was ready, he put his last slug in the machine and watched her laugh through the missing of a dozen pitches.

"Maybe you're a lefty," Danny said.

"Yeah, maybe you're right," Bridget said.

Lori's response to the night of the accident surprised Henry. He feared it might reignite the sadness of her years as a young mother. For starters, it had been Danny's first day of high school. That alone was event enough to make a mother cry. Then the accident. And then Bridget. Pretty enough to steal away the heart of a son. Even Henry worried about the day Danny's heart might break.

Before Henry opened up to her that night, revealing his own fears, Lori had already begun to worry about Bridget. Danny had not even helped her carry the first load of her possessions upstairs before Lori's heart felt the pinch of Bridget pulling Danny further away.

Now Danny rarely came down before midnight on Fridays, even when he had an early morning game or practice on Saturday. Who would ever have thought that Lori would think this, but maybe Bridget had come along at a good time for all of them.

On Saturday mornings his artwork—sketches, drawings, and paintings—would be spread on the dining room table waiting for Lori to rise from bed for her first cup of coffee, waiting for Lori to walk around the dining room table tilting her head at the images to see them in some newer way, waiting for her to look at them like a proud mother, and an artist herself. And it wasn't just on Saturdays that Lori would awaken to these surprises of Danny's artwork. She would find them on school days as well, for after the homework and catches with Henry, after the batting cages, practices, and workouts, Danny would draw in his room before going to bed.

"He's already a better artist than I ever was," she had told Henry.

"Look at this," she said one morning. She held a pencil drawing of Bridget sitting at her easel with her legs crossed on the floor.

"He understands line and light and color and shadow and perspective."

There was a passion, an emotional charge in his work already. He was discovering and understanding what so many artists never seemed to learn: the *gestalt* of art.

"And Bridget," Lori said. "The girl was born to teach."

Together, they paid attention from a new distance. They watched Danny from a close place, like new parents.

Henry's hand at the small of Lori's back, her fingers at the nape of his neck, his arm at her waist, her head leaning on his shoulders, his arm locked in the crook of hers, they touched. As though to remind themselves constantly in the sight of their son that they were not capable of doing this thing without one another. As though to remind themselves that it was not Danny alone who had been given a gift.

For Henry, the accident at Madison Street marked a change in the direction of his life as Danny's father. If, out of some idiotic and grand illusion of his young parenthood, he was responsible for putting the strange gift upon the shoulders of his son, he could no longer push Danny toward perfect balance after witnessing its frightening possibility on the afternoon of the accident at Madison Street.

And so Henry backed away from the symmetry campaign. He no longer tracked throws Danny made from one side or the other. He paid no attention to what hand Danny held his fork or brushed his teeth, or opened doors with. Instead of staying with Danny at Stella's and charting every swing of the bat, Henry dropped him off at the batting cages three times a week to hit balls with Mickey. While Danny worked through pitching sessions on Sunday mornings, Henry read the paper at Sophie's diner across the street.

On warmer days, when the café windows were open, Henry could hear from this booth the clinks of the dimpled hard-rubber balls off the aluminum bats across the street, and from this changed distance Henry observed Danny with new eyes. It seemed, at first, as though Danny paid very little attention to balance. At one morning practice with the pitchers on the team, Danny threw fifty-some pitches from one side, and then a few more while instructing. He didn't seem to keep track at all of the quantity or type of pitches he threw, much less attempt to do the same from the other side. He stretched after practice, and kept to his various workouts after school, but seemed to end the day without much attention to the other side of his body.

Through the week, though, Henry began to observe Danny's attention to symmetry in less conspicuous and comprehensible ways. For every day that was heavily sided right or left, there was another day in the week to work the opposite side. Whenever the school swimming pool was available Danny finished off the day with a swim. When it wasn't, he spent thirty minutes on the treadmill or stationary bike.

Late one night Henry woke up with his biology class weighing heavy on his mind. On the way into his office in the stadium he found the basement lights on, and Danny doing yoga in centerfield. Another night he found him in the same spot in centerfield, but not doing yoga; it was more like tai chi. His arms rolled slowly in gentle waves, hands twirling over one another in peaceful swirls, light and plotless, each slow movement unfolding gracefully into the next, and it occurred to him, Henry, that Danny's balancing act, all along, had very little to do with his father's prior and imbecilic attempt at a symmetry campaign.

How naïve, how pedestrian, for him to have thought all those years that he had seen to balance in Danny's life in a way that approached true symmetry. All along he had only switched silverware and sippy cups, counted throws and swings and steps and kicks. How to account, though, for curve balls and change-ups and sliders and knuckle balls thrown from one side? What part, really, did he think he had played in the balanced life of his son?

There seemed an untraceable logic to Danny's own attempts at balance, which Henry—for all of his note-taking and counter-clicking and positioning of silverware, for all of his former insistence on pre-cision, for all of his scholarly and fatherly interest—could not begin to follow. Whatever gaps Henry left open in his fumbling approach to symmetry, Danny seemed to pick up at Henry's retreat.

During winter break Henry drove Danny to Washington, Missouri.

"It's a surprise," he said, when Danny asked him why he was wasting two perfectly good days of his Christmas break on a trip to Missouri.

When they pulled into the parking lot of the Rawlings Glove Factory, Danny's eyes widened in the passenger seat. Inside they met Zip Evans, the master glove designer, at his workstation. He had the handle of a sawed-off wooden bat in his hand. There was a knob the size and shape of a baseball carved out at the top end of the sawed-off bat, and when the Granvilles came in Zip was wearing a baseball glove in his left hand and pounding the tool into the glove.

"A-Rod's glove," Evans said. "Breaking it in for him."

Above Evans' station, a dozen gloves tracking the evolution of baseball mitts were pegged to the wall. Evans took the Granvilles on a tour through the factory, a dark and high-windowed place that smelled of cattle and smoke and history and when the tour was over he reached below his desk and handed Danny a box with a thin strip of rawhide wrapped around it like ribbon. Inside the box was a custom-made six-finger glove.

"Made it myself," Zip said, and he took the glove from Danny the second he had it unwrapped. Zip held the glove at its first and last fingers.

"Here's where it differs from others," he said. He put the glove on his left hand. "When you wear it on your left hand, your thumb goes here, and when you wear it on your right hand," he switched the glove, "your thumb goes in this hole." He handed the glove back to Danny who smiled at the edge of laughter through his closer inspection of the glove.

There was a thumb on each side, a web in the middle of the glove, and pockets off each side of center.

"Your old man tells me you can throw pretty good from both sides," Zip said.

Danny shrugged his shoulders and pretended a throw from one side, switched the glove and pretended a throw from the other.

Zip laughed. "I'll be looking for you in the papers," he said.

Before spending the night at a Holiday Inn just outside town, they ate dinner at a Steak 'n Shake, where Henry suggested that Danny keep careful watch over his pitch counts as he prepared for the upcoming season.

"I know," Danny said.

Henry told him stories of kids who were finished pitching by the time they were fifteen because they overdid it.

"I know," Danny said.

It's not just about pitching until you feel pain, he said. By the time you feel pain it could be too late.

"I know," Danny said again.

"Danny," Henry said. "Let me talk to you about this for a while without you telling me how you know everything already."

Danny looked up at Henry from across the table.

"Sorry," he said.

"As far as I know, Danny, no one's ever done this before."

Danny set his burger down and nodded his head.

"Anything you or I know about pitch counts has to do with players who throw with one arm, Danny. Not two."

Danny nodded again.

"We don't know anything about this, Danny," he said. "And we have to be careful."

And so it was at a Steak 'n Shake in Washington, Missouri, that Danny agreed to be careful. He would hold himself to a pitch count of sixty if he had four days to rest before his next game, and fifty if he had three; and if he found himself in a position to pitch another game in only two days, he would hold himself to forty.

They watched a Bulls game in their room at the Holiday Inn while Danny worked in the leather of his new six-fingered glove. During commercials he stood between their queen-sized beds and practiced switching the glove from one hand to the other.

Six times, Danny looked at the glove in his hands and thanked Henry. Six times, Henry felt guilty for the half-truths that fathers took with them to sleep.

On a Friday night in January, Danny knocked at Bridget's door and walked in to find her sitting as she almost always was, on the floor at her easel. All but her left shoulder was hidden. She wore her faded yellow painting shirt, which looped lazily over her shoulder. Enough of her shoulder was exposed for Danny to know that she was not wearing a bra beneath her painting shirt. Or if she wore one, it was the color of skin.

Danny began the evening over Bridget's shoulder as he almost always did. She was not wearing a bra the color of skin, nor of any color. She was painting a threatening sky above a Mexican farmer and through the neckline of her tee shirt her breasts were visible. The farmer held an untied load of sugar cane in his arms. They were smallish and freckled along the lines where the sun of many summers had reached. She had dreamed the scene of the Mexican farmer. She spoke to Danny of the narrative of the image and what she took the dream to mean, and Danny watched as white and blue and black and red and green and yellow became sky, watched as Bridget worked unthinkable colors into the sky, watched as the clouds rolled in from the western heavens. He watched a roiling sky come to life at the tip of Bridget's brush.

Minutes passed as Danny watched Bridget dab her brush at the splotches of paint on her palette.

"Danny."

How she could make a bundle of sugar cane, a Mexican farmer, rolling fields of farmland, a moody sky from puddles of paint. As Bridget moved from palette to canvas, Danny lost himself in the paint-stained circle of wood at her lap, the source of the farmer's sky.

The second time she called him, Bridget looked over her shoulder to see Danny staring downward. It was then that Bridget looked down at the loose loop of her tee shirt.

She set the palette on the floor at her feet. "Be right back."

While she was gone Danny taped a piece of sketchpad paper to the studio table in preparation for a contour drawing of his left hand. He was looking at his hand while Bridget walked toward him through the hallway.

She set an eraser on the paper in front of him. It had the whiteness and shape of an egg and was tattooed with a Chinese symbol.

"That's the Chinese symbol for strength," she said. "At least that's what the chick at the art store said."

Danny smiled. "Thanks," he said, but he did not raise his eyes to look into hers, for as he saw Bridget walking toward him down the narrow hallway from her bedroom, his left hand held before him, he knew, from the stark white rectangle of bra strap at her shoulder, that she had not risen from the floor of the studio, in the middle of making a sky, for an eraser.

Fifteenth

AT DANNY'S FIRST HIGH SCHOOL GAME, HENRY STOOD BEHIND Lori. She sat on her folding chair with a blue comforter hooded over her head and draped over her body, the oval of her face reddening in the late March air. It was just as cold at the second game; an icy wind cut across Lake Michigan and through the fields from over Lake Michigan so Lori stayed home. Henry watched that game from the stands, Lori's voice hovering like a word balloon above his head.

Now you're just going to watch the games, right, Henry?

You're not going to stand behind the backstop and tell him how to hit, right?

And you're not going to count his footsteps or anything, right?

You're just going to sit and watch the games and not pace back and forth like a crazy man, right?

All of these promises were easy to keep with Danny playing shortstop again in the second game, but from the minute he woke up on Friday morning before the third game, Henry worried about Danny's first varsity start on the mound.

It was an away game against Francis Parker High that day, and though it seemed windless and sunny at the start of the day, it was still March, and the cold memory of that first game was still vivid enough to keep Lori away.

"Be good, Henry," she told him on his way to work that morning. He had given her a two-fingered salute in response. "Scout's honor," he had said.

Henry sat alone at the top of the stands. Two long-coated and business suited U-High fathers stood shoulder to shoulder to his left. Cigar smoke, sharp and leafy, swirled high and windlessly in the air above them.

Danny struck out six of the first nine batters he faced—five of them on three straight pitches. He retired the others on routine grounders that never made it past the frosted infield grass.

U-High scored twice in their half of the third inning and once more the next inning. When Danny faced the clean-up hitter in the bottom of the fifth, not a single player had reached base for Francis Parker. Danny had earned nine strikeouts of the twelve batters he'd faced.

By then, Henry was pacing the right-field foul line chewing sunflower seeds like a zealot, massaging his neck with the balls of his fingers and cracking his knuckles. When the inning was over, Danny was six outs away from a perfect game.

That's all we need, Henry thought. A perfect game from a freshman on a varsity team and it didn't matter how tiny the school was on the high school map; some coach or some high-powered, business-suited parent would phone an editor at the Tribune, and three pages in from the back of the newspaper there would be a six hundred-word spread for all the city to see.

Two more U-High players crossed the plate in the fifth, and by then the danger of Danny's perfect game hit Henry like a thing to own. The world would descend upon Danny. Six more strikeouts and the world would descend. There would be reporters and microphones and scouts, phone calls and cameras and note-taking and legal pads and college letters and then what? Were they ready for the *then what*?

Henry closed his eyes. What then, of the gift? Would the world roll out a carpet for Danny and blind him to anything more than baseball? As long as he could throw a ball eighty-five miles per hour with either arm and perfect games at fifteen—it would let him do whatever the hell he wanted. It had done the same for presidents and millionaires and movie stars. The world had done this before.

When Danny took the mound to start the bottom of the sixth Henry clenched his fists and spilled more sunflower seeds into his mouth. He scraped his tender and salt-swollen tongue against his teeth until it felt as though he had scalded it. He closed his eyes at the first pitch and listened to the cheers of U-High fans. When he opened his eyes the umpire was punching out another called strike. Sixteen straight outs.

Henry walked from the right field foul line past the fence that curved around the outfield. "Walk him, Danny," he said, "Just walk the kid."

He stopped at the fence along the left field foul line and clawed his fingers through the metal links. He had long lost track of Danny's pitch count.

"Come on," he said. "You're up five runs in a nothing game. Walk the kid. Or give him something to hit."

But seconds later, Danny struck out his seventeenth victim, and Henry mumbled, "Damn," into the icy air.

U-High's fans on the first base side were on their feet, and the Parker fans on the third base side, despite their differing allegiances, did not appear to be in opposition. After Danny retired the seventeenth straight batter the Parker fans were on their feet in the bleachers as well. Every spectator at the game seemed to cling to hope for just four more outs at the hands of the freshman on the mound. Every spectator but one.

Two hundred and sixty-five feet away from his son, Henry closed his eyes and held his hands, palms toward Danny, as though he were compacting air to the space between them and mumbled a message to his son.

"We need more time, Danny," he said. "Don't do this yet."

The eighteenth batter ripped a liner to U-High's third baseman on the first pitch, a fastball up and in. Eighteen.

What other father wished like this for the failure of his son? But what other father had been a witness to something greater than a perfect game? What other father had ever seen his son in the midst of a miracle? The girl on the bus. There were months of history between that bus ride on Madison Street and the game against Parker but its implications had not been forgotten, and though he wasn't certain what any of it meant, there was no doubt in his half-scientific mind that the same gift that was responsible for saving a girl's life was closing in on a perfect game of baseball.

U-High scored twice in the top of the seventh bringing the score to 7-0 before Danny took the mound for the final inning, and Henry pressed his hands once more toward his son, as if to hold off time.

"Please, Danny," he said again. "We need more time." Henry spilled the rest of his sunflowers seeds in his mouth and chewed them all without separating seed from shell, and the umpire crouched for the first pitch.

The batter showed bunt at a high fastball, but couldn't pull his bat away quick enough low to keep from popping out to third base.

Danny was two outs away from a perfect game.

"Don't do this yet, Danny," Henry said when the twentieth batter came to the plate, and like some gift of his own making Henry listened to the dink of the ball off the bat of Francis Parker's second baseman, listened to the dink of sound that silenced some one hundred people in the park as they followed the high arc of the baseball to short right field where it plopped in the cold grass without further movement. There was clapping on the Parker side—reluctant and obligatory. And when the only Parker batter to reach base stood still on first, the tepid applause for the batter was quickly replaced by cheers for the freshman on the mound who had strung a hundred fans along for much of a perfect afternoon.

Across the field Henry pressed his forehead against the cold fence. The broken perfect game came as such immediate relief to him that he felt groggy. He was a sleepy and atrophied version of his earlier self as he watched Danny's teammates spill onto the field around Danny in a huddled mass of raised arms and sound. Wasn't that what a father should want for his son?

After dinner, while Danny was with Bridget in her second-floor studio, Henry was downstairs telling Lori how he had paced back and forth during Danny's game like the crazy man she had warned him about.

"The press would have had field day with that story," Henry said. "A switch-pitching freshman throws a perfect game in his first varsity start."

Lori crossed her legs on the couch.

"I was thinking I should tell him about the accident on Madison," Henry said.

"And what will you tell him, Henry? That he can see the future?"

"If that's what it takes for him to get it, then why not?"

"I'll tell you why not, Henry. If he remembers the accident, there's a reason he's never brought it up, and if he's forgotten about it, there's a reason for that, too."

Lori turned her head to look at Henry.

"He'll put the pieces together when he's ready for it," she said. "Let him do it on his own."

Henry crossed his arms in the silence that followed. He nodded his head slowly.

"Promise?" Lori said.

"I promise," Henry said. "I might tell him to try to stay under the radar, though."

"That's fine," she said. "You tell him about the radar." And Henry laughed.

In the summer that followed Danny's sophomore year at U-High, he took Bridget to a White Sox game. He knocked at her door on a Sunday morning with a baseball glove in each hand and a White Sox jersey folded over his arm. Bridget held it at its shoulders.

"What does *Grebeck* mean?" she said.

"You're kidding me, right?" Danny said. "It doesn't mean anything. It's a player's name. Craig Grebeck. He used to play for the Sox."

"I was just kidding," she said, and she twisted her lips and furrowed her brow to let him know she wasn't kidding at all. "I'll be right back," she said, and she walked to her bedroom to change into the shirt.

When she returned wearing the jersey Danny almost hugged her but stopped himself.

"It's perfect," he said, and Bridget twirled around and curtsied.

"I cried the day I realized that jersey wouldn't fit me forever," he said. "It was big on me at first and then one day I put it on and it fit me just right, and I remember crying at how perfect it fit."

On the train into the city Bridget sat with her heels on the edge of the seat and her knees stuffed like baseballs in the web of the glove Danny had given her. Danny breathed into his own glove to smell what she smelled, and the train groaned toward the ballpark. When it looped around the downtown tracks it screamed.

As they drew closer to Comiskey Park, the arc of the stadium seats was a blue rainbow, the only splash of color in the great gray of the city.

Past the turnstile entrance they stepped onto the escalator toward the 100 level seats, and Bridget moved as if to climb the steps as they ascended but Danny pinched the tail of her jersey.

"Nonono," he said. "No fast walking here," and Bridget smiled.

On the gray-brown cement of the concourse, when the first green of baseball grass teased at them through the steam of polish sausage and hot dogs, Danny stopped Bridget again. He held two fingers to the crook of her arm.

"Did you feel that?" he said.

"Feel what?" she said.

"That," he said, and he smiled. "What it feels like before a baseball game," he said. "Did you feel it?"

"I think I did," she smiled. "Yes, I'm pretty sure I did."

The day felt like a date to Danny. He did not want it to end. On the train ride home he told Bridget he felt like painting and she smiled and said, "Me, too," and that's what they did.

He did not mean to spend the night. The last he'd remembered was Bridget leaning against the doorway and poking her head in the corner studio to tell him she was going to bed. His easel faced the doorway and he had peeked around it to see her. He was just finishing something, he had said, and would be done soon. He would lock the door on his way out.

"Night, Danny," she had said.

When Bridget got up to pee in the early morning Danny heard the bathroom door click shut. He was lying against the wall with his arms tucked into his chest for warmth, his face turned to the wall. The red numbers on the clock radio read 5:12. The light was still on. When he heard Bridget's steps coming toward him in the hallway he remembered his painting. He must have moved it into the center of the room to make space to sleep against the wall. Would she see it when she came into the room? And what would she think if she did? Danny's heart raced toward the waking day.

Bridget's footsteps stopped at the doorway to the corner room. He wondered if she would wake him, squeeze his shoulder and say his name. He wondered if she would whisper to him like a mother, *Wake up, Danny*. Instead, she waited in the doorway. He felt her there. Minutes it was before she turned and walked away. He listened to her footsteps. When she returned she had spread a blanket over him. The breeze of it was cool, and as she covered him with it he wondered if she had meant to touch his shoulder. She set a pillow next to his head. Danny felt her stop there. Her feet close enough to touch. He was certain she was looking at his painting there. Her arms crossed over her night-shirted body. His heart pounded.

He had drawn it from the memory of looking over her shoulder the night she was painting bralessly on the studio floor. She thought he had been looking at her breasts, for when she returned with the false gift of a Chinese eraser in her hand she had also returned wearing a bra. In the painting of her, he had covered her breasts with a bra, and had painted the Chinese symbol for strength on the cloth of the bra. Feigning sleep at 5:15 that morning, his heart was a hammer against his chest at the thought of Bridget seeing the painting.

When Danny was sure she had climbed back into her bed, he turned around to see that his painting faced the doorway.

Could she know, he wondered—from looking at the painting—that it wasn't her breasts he had been looking at? From the lift and changing arc of her protected breasts—the nuanced tilt of her shoulder—could she know that it was not her breasts he had been looking at, but her heart?

He pulled Bridget's pillow to his face, and his heart stilled. It smelled of her.

Sixteenth

SCOUTS FROM COLLEGES AND PROFESSIONAL BALL CLUBS STARTED appearing at U-High games during Danny's sophomore year. Mickey had told him it was bound to happen. That June, after Mickey had been drafted midway through the third round by the Chicago Cubs, he began his own campaign to see to it that Danny would enter the draft instead of go to college when he graduated from U-High.

While Danny played through his junior year, Mickey fought his way through Single-A and Double-A, and even dipped into Triple-A long enough for a cup of coffee.

In August that year there were pitching camps and hitting camps. There were letters from colleges and universities, there were ACTs and SATs and college essays. During winter break of his senior year, Henry took Danny on a tour of thirteen colleges in eight days, and they returned on a Thursday afternoon to a stack of letters from twenty more. One was an offer of a four-year scholarship to Kettle University, a school that had been a step on the just-completed Granville college tour. Danny flipped through the rest of the letters and found a sealed, unstamped letter with his name on it in Bridget's handwriting. He slid a knife along the fold and opened it.

> *Hey. I'm making dinner on Friday night to celebrate*
> *something. I hate to eat it alone.*
> *Six o'clock?*
> *_____yes _____no*
> *Bridget*

On Friday Bridget's stairwell smelled of rosemary and garlic. At her door she surprised him with a hug that was over as soon as it had begun—immediate and ephemeral—as though it had surprised her as well. A celebration hug, Danny thought.

Over a meal of Mediterranean chicken Bridget told Danny she had been accepted as a teacher's assistant in the Art Institute's graduate program. Danny clinked his glass of water to Bridget's glass of wine.

They talked through a Bulls game on television. Danny told her about the offer from Kettle and how it stacked up against his other college visits that week. Bridget sat on her leg in the corner of the couch and took tiny sips from her wine glass.

"Mickey Wells thinks I'm nuts for considering Kettle," Danny said. "He says that major league baseball scouts will be at my games this spring and that I probably have a shot at being drafted. He thinks I could be playing in the minor leagues by the middle of June."

Bridget asked what he thought about that and Danny told her the same thing he'd told Mickey: that he had just returned from a two-thousand mile drive with his father who had talked about the importance of a college education through more than half of those miles.

"He made me promise I'd go to college," Danny said, and Bridget smiled as though he had made the promise to her as well.

Despite Danny's letter of intent to Kettle, Henry worried his way through Danny's final season at U-High. As he leaned on the fence watching the team take infield practice before games, he was "Mister Granvilled" by what seemed like every scout in the country. He found their business cards in his wallet, on the refrigerator, in the pockets of his pants and shirts, and on two occasions Lori handed him cards when he joined her in her chair on the side of the stands.

With their clipboards and pencils and laptops and BlackBerrys and speed guns, the scouts were everywhere.

Reluctant to address the topic with his father, who had made his hopes quite clear, Danny learned all he could from Mickey.

"First of all," Mickey said. "You're gonna get drafted. Period.

And all I'm saying is you gotta keep your options open," Mickey said. "You sign a letter of intent for Kettle and the second you step into your first class you're stuck there for four years or until you're twenty-one. You sign at a Junior College and they can do a draft-and-follow, which is they don't sign you, but they let you go to the JuCo and they can monitor your progress through school and they still have a shot at signing you before you re-enter the draft."

Mickey shrugged. "I know your old man can't be too crazy about you going to Triton College, but it was all right for Kirby Puckett, you know what I'm saying?"

On a Friday night that April Danny was painting at the table in Bridget's living room studio while she was sketching with pastels, half-hidden by her easel on the floor to his left.

"Do you know what tonight is?" Danny said.

Bridget said, "Is it prom night?" and Danny leaned and looked in her eyes.

"Prom is next week, actually," he said. "It's my parents' anniversary."

After a moment of silence Danny leaned to see her face around her easel again.

"Would you have gone to prom with me?"

"Would you have wanted me to go?"

"I was thinking of asking you until I found out it fell on a Friday."

"You should go," she said.

"It's on a Friday," he said again.

Bridget returned to her easel.

In the silence, Danny called her name and he leaned over to see her face.

"Bridget," he said again, and Bridget said, "Hmm?"

"I'd rather be here on a Friday than there," and Bridget smiled.

He could have kissed her. Sitting there at her easel and smiling, he could have kissed her. It nearly made him cry to sit there with a brush in his hand and not kiss her.

Later that night he came close to kissing her again. They had drawn and painted until eleven o'clock and then sat on the couch in the dining room listening to music and talking until they fell asleep. Bridget awoke when Danny stood from the couch to go downstairs. He held his hand out for her.

"Walk me to the door," he said.

Bridget took Danny's hand and rose and he walked with her, tired and happy, to the stairwell.

At the door, Danny said, "I think I'll dress up next week," and Bridget smiled sleepily.

"Nothing too much," he said. "Just maybe a decent shirt and a jacket." He wrinkled his nose and nodded. "And maybe we'll go somewhere for dinner."

Danny held Bridget's fingers in his hand as she nodded and smiled again. The tips of two of her fingers in the tips of two of his. How easy it would have been for him to take her hand deeper into his, to slide her fingers into a lock with his. How much easier than a first kiss, this. How many Fridays remained? She would graduate soon and then he, and there would be the summer and then graduate school for her and undergraduate for him and maybe everything would change.

And because of this, because he thought it was possible that everything might change with the passing of three short months, he did not take Bridget's hand more deeply into his own. To lock his fingers with hers would have been a kiss, he thought, or would have become one. And if everything was going to change, Danny would not be made responsible for marking the moment of the change with a kiss.

If she kissed *him*, though. That was something else.

Bridget smiled. "Okay," she said. "Maybe I'll wear something nice, too." Their fingers slipped away from one another. "Nothing too much," she said, and as he turned and began to walk down the stairs she closed the door so slowly that there was no sound to mark its closing.

❖

The next Friday night, Bridget appeared at her door wearing a shirt that someone might have painted on her skin. It was sleeveless and yellow and printed with a splash of flowers in blues and greens and yellows that dropped petals everywhere. They looked to be falling from her shirt. Her skirt was the same color of ivy as one of the falling petals and Danny wished she would twirl in the hallway. It seemed that all of the petals of the flowers of her shirt would fall to the hardwood floor if she did and it would only be yellow.

"Wow," he said, and Bridget curtsied.

"Why, thank you," she said, and they walked to Cucina Paradiso in Oak Park because Danny wanted the night to have a long walk at either end.

At the restaurant Bridget ordered a glass of white wine.

"And you, sir?" the waiter asked.

"Water's fine, thanks," Danny said.

He unrolled his napkin onto his lap and slid his plate, his glass, his silver to the middle edge of the table, and smoothed his hands over the sheet of table paper that protected the white cloth beneath.

Bridget took a mechanical pencil from her purse and set it before him. In the middle of the table, as high as he could reach without pushing the clutter too close to Bridget, Danny began drawing the lines of the ceiling at the windowed wall behind her with the pencil in his left hand. As he spoke to her, he checked over her shoulders, squinted for reference, but drew the frame of the restaurant while he looked in Bridget's eyes.

"Next year," he said. Bridget swallowed a sip of wine, rested her elbows on the table, held her glass like a chalice, just a kiss away from her lips.

"What about next year?" she said.

"Next year," he said again, "I'll be home for Thanksgiving. And I'll be home for three weeks through winter break, too."

Danny penciled in the ceiling lights against the window over Bridget's head, over Bridget's silent lips.

"So there's that," he said, and Bridget sipped her wine.

"The spring'll be crazy because of baseball, but I'll probably be home for a couple of days around Easter, too," he said.

"There will be girls at college," Bridget said.

Danny had not yet begun to draw Bridget. He was sketching the folds of a heavy curtain, which hung purposelessly against the wall to his left. "Do you have colored pencils in there?" he said, and Bridget unclipped her purse and handed him three pencils.

"Yes," he said, "I've heard there might be girls there." Danny touched her fingers as he accepted the pencils from her. He set on the table in front of him. "But how many of them will carry colored pencils in their bags?"

Bridget said nothing.

"They will be just girls," Danny said.

Bridget rose from her chair as someone else's waiter walked past with a plate of black olives in his hand. She allowed passage to the waiter and then moved her chair to Danny's side.

"Scoot over," she said. And Danny made room for her chair on his side. He pushed the collection of tabled things—salt and pepper, a shaker of cheese, and a plate of warm bread—to the edge of the table Bridget had deserted, and he handed her his pencil.

"I have another," she said, and with a second pencil from her purse she sketched shade into the folds of the curtain he had begun.

Danny switched the pencil to his right hand and on that edge of the butcher paper he began to sketch the wine rack that made up the entire wall.

"They will be like the girls at other schools," Danny said. "They will be like the boys at your school."

The Italian waiter returned. Over their shoulders he watched them draw for a moment before taking their orders.

"They'll be like that guy," Danny said when the waiter left, and Bridget laughed.

"If you're not home on those Fridays, I'm not sure what I'll do," Danny said.

"They don't have to be Fridays," Bridget said.

Danny stopped drawing and looked at Bridget.

"No, I guess they don't," he said.

"I won't be far from home," Bridget said. She looked at the tables against the window and quick-sketched faces onto roughly sketched bodies.

"It will be tough on Fridays, though," Danny said. "That will be the day I'll miss you most, I'm afraid."

They looked at their penciling fingers swishing over the paper tablecloth as Danny spoke.

"I'll probably call you on Fridays," Danny said. "It's okay if you're not there, or if you don't pick up or anything, but I'm just going to call to say hi to you."

"But if you can't call, that's okay," Bridget said, looking at Danny's side of the drawing.

Danny nodded. He drew a waiter walking past with a plate of olives balanced formally on his fingers. When he leaned toward Bridget to draw the olives, Bridget suggested they switch seats, and so they did.

She filled in the squares of his wall rack of wine with bottles as he began to draw her in the seatless place across the table. Without looking at her, he began to draw Bridget Pentecoff exactly as she was. Her shirt, so painted on her skin with its falling petals, her black hair which she had begun to wear short and messily, as though she did not care how it looked. Without looking in her eyes he drew them. He drew her shirt as it curved over her breasts, and the wine glass as she had held it to her lips like a kiss, and the waiter brought their food and they pushed their plates above the ceiling they had drawn and they forked at their food from that distance— he at his pasta salmone, she at her grilled ravioli. Carefully, they ate. And slowly.

As they ate and drew, the waiter brought others to their table to see what the young couple was drawing. The waiter brought the bartender to see. The waiter brought his other customers to see.

When they returned to their stations and customers Danny smiled and told Bridget he was pretty certain the waiter was falling in love with her.

Bridget watched as he dotted a tiny nose ring into the Bridget he drew from memory.

"He's falling in love with both of us," she said.

When they finished their meals they waited for the busboy to clear the table and with their napkins they carefully erased any bread-crumbs the image had captured. Bridget rolled the sketch like a poster.

Back at her studio, they sat on the couch in the dining room. Bridget lit a candle and they watched television. When she fell asleep Danny took a pillow from her bedroom and set it at the end of the couch. He eased Bridget's feet from under her body and stretched her legs across the couch. He brought his easel into the room then and through the night he drew her sleeping. He made her shirt yellow and he turned the flowers that had once been on her shirt into butterflies and flew them above her sleeping body. Along the side of the sketch he wrote these words: *While Bridget sleeps, the flowers rise from her yellow shirt like butterflies* and he turned the easel toward her so that it would be first among the things she saw in the morning.

Before he left, he considered kissing her in her sleep but he was afraid that he would awaken her and she would see the thing he had drawn before the morning. He knelt at the side of the couch inches from her sleeping lips but did not kiss her. He turned out the dining room lights and blew out the candle and walked softly toward the door. He stepped into the hallway and nearly closed the door before he decided to return and to kiss her after all. He lit the candle again, brought the easel and the drawing of Bridget and the butterflies into her bedroom and he returned to the couch to kiss her.

Bridget awoke, it seemed, before their lips had even touched. She awoke, it seemed, at the sweet release of air in the diminishing space between their lips. Danny wondered if the kiss had come as a surprise, for though it seemed her lips had attached to his for the splittest of seconds, she opened her eyes quickly and wide, as though it were a thing she had thought might never happen.

When Danny pulled away from her, though, Bridget said nothing. She looked at him and then touched the tip of her finger to his lips.

"Why did you wait so long to kiss me?" she said.

Danny said nothing. He thought if he spoke that she might not touch his lips again with her finger. When she touched him again, though, Danny answered.

"I was afraid," he said.

"Of what?" she said.

"That it might end," he said.

"All kisses end," she said.

"Not the kiss," Danny said. "I wasn't afraid the kiss would end. I was afraid the *this* would end," he said, and with a roll of his fingers in the space between them, he gestured to the *us* of them.

"Oh," she said, as though she had considered the thought herself.

"Anyway," she said. "You needn't worry."

"Why not?" he said.

"Because that wasn't a kiss, really."

"What do you mean?" he said.

"You kissed me in my sleep," she said. "That doesn't count as a kiss."

And Danny leaned to kiss her again. An inch from her lips, Bridget flinched away from him.

"Wait," she said, and she pointed her finger to some indefinite place above and around them.

"Did you feel that?" she said.

"What?"

"That," she said. And she smiled. "That's what it feels like just before a kiss."

"I think I did feel it," Danny said. And he kissed her.

On the morning of his graduation, Danny got a phone call from Mickey Wells who had been following the major league draft on the Internet. When Mickey finally stopped screamed, laughing, and swearing in the phone, Danny learned they both had been drafted by the Chicago Cubs midway through the third round.

After graduation, the Granvilles returned home to a voice mail message from the Chicago scout who wanted to know if he could come by the next day with a contract in his hand. Henry stood at the kitchen counter with his hand on Danny's shoulder as they listened to the message a second time. And then a third.

Countless times they had covered the possibility that this day might come, and Danny agreed with Henry, each time, that it would be best to go to college. But standing in the kitchen and listening to the recording of the scout's voice on the answering machine, Danny wondered at the logic of passing up a shot at professional baseball.

After listening to the message a fourth time, Danny brushed his hands over his diploma from University High.

"Danny," Henry said.

"It's the Cubs, Dad," Danny said. "The Chicago Cubs."

"I know what—I can imagine what you're feeling," Henry said. "But this is about something bigger than baseball."

"I've been preparing for this as long as can remember," Danny said.

"I know," Henry said. "Baseball is still going to be here in four years, Danny."

"Four years is a long time," Danny said.

"Baseball will still be here, Danny."

"College will be there, too."

Danny opened and closed his diploma absently, its curved binding ticked with newness.

"I know how hard this is for you Danny. I'm arguing for four years of studying and playing college ball over professional baseball and an early shot at the major leagues," Henry said. Danny looked up.

"I want you to go to Kettle," Henry said, and Danny closed his diploma and the ticking stopped.

Seventeenth

THROUGH THE SUMMER, LORI PREPARED FOR DANNY'S DEPARTURE for college in small and daily ways. She sat with Bridget through a double header of Danny's so they could compile a list of things he would need for his first year at college, and they hardly paid attention to the game.

Lori held a pad of paper over her crossed leg, and as the game began she told Bridget about the time Danny went on a camping trip with some friends from school.

"I didn't help him pack his bags," Lori said. "I don't know if it was just a crazy week, or maybe I was sick, but we were just about to leave the house to take him to the airport when I realized he had packed his bags without me."

Bridget nodded like a mother, her eyes softening while Lori spoke.

"The whole week he was gone I could hardly breathe for thinking he was being eaten alive by insects or burned by the sun because I didn't help him pack.

"Well. Anyway," she said, taking a pen from her bag. "It's not going to happen this time."

And through the double header Bridget and Lori made a list of things he would need, and the moment they thought they had exhausted the list, one of them started at the discovery of some item Danny could scarcely do without, and the other would shake her head at how remiss they would have been to neglect that thing.

At the baseball silences between innings Lori reached to her left where Henry sat to remind him that he was there as well. She and Bridget clapped emptily at the sound of cheering. Henry interrupted

them once to tell they had just clapped for a homerun by the opposing team, and they laughed like girls at what might have seemed like
inattention.

After the second game, Danny joined them near the stands. He
stood behind their portable chairs and kissed Lori on her right cheek
and Bridget on her left. He put one hand to his mother's shoulder and
the other to Bridget's, and the symmetry of the gestures was not lost
on Lori.

She took dozens of trips to stores through June and July, never
buying more than two or three items each visit, as though to remind
herself that there was time still time. She bought bed sheets and toothpaste. Pens and a dust buster. Envelopes. She bought corduroy pants
and tee shirts. She bought stamps on another day. Towels and wash-
cloths. Soap.

If Danny was home on summer afternoons, Lori made him lunches.
Sat him down at the dining room table with sandwiches quartered and
toothpicked and spaced with potato chips and pickles. In the mornings
she might lean for a moment against the frame of his bedroom door
and watch him sleep. After her evening walks with Henry she would
look up at the second floor windows and smile to see Bridget standing at her easel.

From the day that followed their prom night kiss into the dark of
the mid-August morning he would leave for Kettle, Danny and Bridget
painted. In the shared hours between his baseball games and her night
classes, they stood in her living room studio with barely an easel's distance between them, and painted through June and July—she in her
yellow painting shirt, he in his brown tee shirt from the Louisville
Slugger baseball museum—while Danny waited for another kiss.

There were evenings Danny stood at his easel thinking only of
kissing her again. Or of the consequences of a kiss. Some nights he
dabbed at the canvas emptily and all of the art was in watching her, all
of the art was in thinking that the responsibility for summer belonged
to a single kiss. Some nights he wondered if they had kissed at all, or

if he had conjured the kiss from some wish.

It was on one such night of painting, and watching and wondering and waiting for a kiss, that Bridget seemed a chattier person than he had known. Two days remained to July and two weeks remained before Danny would leave for college

She couldn't believe her first graduate course had already ended; in two weeks she would be standing in front of students as their teacher—actually teaching, finally. And Bridget wondered if it was even possible to *teach* art, to really *teach* it. In that freshman class she observed last spring so many of the students didn't seem to get it. It was like they couldn't *see*.

"Do you know what I mean?" she said. "They turned in this pedestrian crap and the teacher couldn't seem to get through to them."

"Well," Danny said, "you've done a decent job with me."

"Different," Bridget said. "You were already an artist."

She dwelt there, at the edge of her sentence for a moment, as if there were more thoughts coming.

"Maybe that's it," she said. "Maybe you can only teach art to an artist."

Bridget tilted her head and fixed on something near the center of her portrait, but spoke to Danny without pause, as though she were feigning occupation with that specific moment of paint.

Anyway, this was going to sound weird and he could say no, of course, he could definitely say no, but she had something to ask him that he was probably going to think sounded a little weird, but she was just going to ask him anyway.

"What is it?"

Well, one of the first projects in the figure drawing class was going to be sketching a live model.

Danny felt Bridget's eyes on him.

"And you want me to be the model?"

Bridget laughed. "No."

"Why is that funny?" he said. "You're laughing at the idea of my modeling?"

"It's not that," she said, still smiling. "I'm not laughing at that at all. It's just that there are people who get paid for modeling. They're graduate art students and usually not that attractive, actually, and some of them are kind of—well, creepy, and pretty much just people who like being naked."

"Nice," Danny said.

"What I was wondering, though, is if you would sort of *pre* pose for me."

"For you?" Danny said.

"For me," she said. "Just me. Ahead of time, you know? Before the in-class model. Like, one of these days."

Danny was silent.

"I knew you were going to think it was weird," she said. "I just want to be ready for it."

Dozens of models had sat in on the classes she'd taken, but she had never led a class with one, and she wanted to be ready. She remembered the first time a nude model came in. She wasn't prepared, really. The teacher hadn't prepared any of the students for it.

"All I kept thinking is that I was in school and there was a naked man in the classroom. There was no real discussion beforehand. We were eighteen years old and away from home for the first time and were all jumping out of our skin, and all of a sudden they were marching naked people in our classrooms, and no one was ready for it. We just all sat around trying to play it cool, trying to pretend it was nothing, but I could tell we were all thinking the same thing.

"I want to be ready for it," Bridget said. "I'm not even sure it makes sense to me, so it's fine if you don't want to do it."

"Nude?"

"No, no, no. Not nude. Sorry. I meant for that to be the first thing I said. You don't need to be nude. Shorts maybe. Or like your baseball shorts," she said.

"It's more than just the nudity that I want to address with my students," she said. "What I really want to do is deal with this thing about *seeing*, like I was telling you."

She wanted it to be clear to them. She wanted her students to understand, fully, what she meant by *seeing*. And some of them would probably not understand it right away, and some of them would understand it in a year or two, and some of them might never get it. But it was her responsibility, you know? To do what she could to get them to see.

Did he know what she meant?

And maybe this would help and maybe it wouldn't, but if she had a live model to help her prepare for it, while she was gripped by this thing about *seeing*, maybe it would help her figure out exactly how to prepare her students for the project.

"I feel like I sound like a crazy woman," she said. "And I'd rather sound crazy here with you then in the classroom with a bunch of smart-ass artists."

Danny laughed.

"Maybe it's a bad idea," she said. "Maybe I'll never get past the physical, but at least there will be that.

"Then at least I'll be able to say things like, *see how the shadows this . . .* and *see how the angle of that . . .* and *see how the curve of the other thing . . .*

"I know I'm babbling on," she said, "but here's the thing. I've only ever looked at live models as a *student*. I need to see this one as a teacher. If my point is to teach my students how to see differently, how to see more accurately, I should do it myself."

"It's fine if you don't feel comfortable with it. You could say no if it you think it's crazy."

It wasn't that crazy, he said. Of course he would do it.

On the last day of July—a Friday as it turned out—the afternoon sun sharpened everything on Lathrop, but in Bridget's hallway it was dark and cool. Her door upstairs was closed. Danny knocked lightly and Bridget opened the door wearing jeans and a Kettle tee shirt Danny had given her.

"Hey," she said.

"Nice shirt," he said.

"Oh do you like it?" she said. "I know a guy who goes there."

"Nice guy?"

"Ehh."

Bridget's flip-flops slapped against her heels as she walked toward the living room ahead of him.

In the studio the sunlight was made soft by the trees lining Lathrop.

"You want some water or something?" Bridget said.

"Water's good," Danny said.

"I hope you wore clean underwear," Bridget said on her way to the kitchen.

"Oh," he said. "Was I supposed to wear underwear?"

Bridget had cleared the raw wood table in the studio, and had laid a canvas tarp over it like a tablecloth. One of the stools sat in the middle of the table.

Danny was glad she had teased about the underwear. At breakfast that morning, he had considered the awkwardness of undressing in the studio, which is why he'd worn shorts and a tee shirt—so he wouldn't have to change into anything else. To ease the tension more, Danny removed his shorts and shirt, so that by the time Bridget returned with two cups of coffee in hand, he was standing on the platform wearing only his sliding shorts tight against his thighs.

Bridget laughed. "We gotta do something about this shyness," she said.

Danny sipped his water and pointed to his glass.

"Good coffee, hon," he said, and Bridget smiled, walking around the room like a teacher getting ready for class to begin.

"I don't get it," she said.

"It's a coffee commercial," he said. "The guy is standing with a cup of Folgers in his hand and he's wearing boxers and he says that to his wife."

"Oh," she said. "And the woman gives him that look."

"I love that look," Danny said. "Like she's got a secret about making coffee, and the guy should know how lucky he is to be with her."

Danny set down the cup then, and stood as David might have stood for Michelangelo. Then as Arnold Schwarzenegger might have stood for a muscle magazine. Then he sat on the tabled stool as *The Thinker* might have sat for Rodin.

Finally, he stood as he felt a model in an art class should stand. Arms at his side, palms forward, his feet planted in an easy vee facing the windows.

"Good," Bridget said.

On her first slow walk around the table Bridget mumbled as she might have mumbled if alone. Between words she scribbled on the grid-lined pages of her artist's journal. She penciled notes in her book without raising her eyes to his. For a moment, she stopped to pull one of the window shades closed. Looked at Danny to see the effect of the changed lighting, and opened the shade again. She walked slowly around the table again sketching quickly for perspective and writing words in a growing tower on the right side of her sketchbook: line, angle, shadow, perspective.

"This is good," she said.

"What?"

"Nothing," she said. "You doing okay up there?"

"I'm good," he said.

She walked around the table still more slowly, still taking notes and making quick sketches.

On the studio table, shirtless, and in the center of Bridget's circling, Danny thought of Bridget's heart beneath her tee shirt—beneath the tee shirt she wore. His tee shirt. He looked for her eyes as she entered and walked across his line of vision but she did not look up. He wondered if, while she walked behind him again, if her heart pounded for release as his did.

And with Bridget's next emergence into his vision the wondering was gone. He knew for certain that Bridget's heart was pounding with life and something else and it had to do with Danny. He could not put words to the reason for the shift from speculation to certainty but in that moment he knew what Bridget felt.

He wished he could put her hand to his heart so that she might know his own.

I kissed you.

Her heart.

Lines, she reminded herself.

She was thinking of her own heart.

She had seen his painting of her heart.

How could a kiss not count?

Shadow, she reminded herself.

She was thinking she was too close.

Light.

He could see her heart from there. She knew he could.

Angle, she was thinking.

No eyes. If he looked in her eyes he would see her heart.

Reminders.

Lighting. See. Balance.

Balance. That was it. Get them to understand this idea of balance. See closely enough to notice the peculiarities of the human form. Become observers. Notice the difference from one side to the other. It required attention.

She was in front of him now. She was facing him. It seemed to Danny as though Bridget was half-speaking words—clipped phrases —if she was speaking at all.

Differences in musculature. Use grid-lines to show difference in musculature. One side to other. Tough to tell here. Not much difference.

Thighs. Muscles of the quadriceps. Left. Same relationship to grids as right. Calves. Same. Muscles of his chest. Left. Right. Same relationship to grids. Abdominal musculature.

"Hmm."

"What?" Danny said.

Had she said that aloud?

"What is it?" Danny said.

"Nothing."

Bridget walked halfway around him again and sat on her stool against the wall. She flipped the page of her journal and quick-sketched his back.

She slid the stool to twelve points around the path of the table, and at each of them quick-sketched Danny from a new angle, shaking her head as she began each new sketch, and for much of the hour that he stood there Bridget said nothing. After the twelfth sketch she spoke.

"You okay?" she said.

"Do you need a break?" she said, after minutes more.

"Let me know if you need to sit," she said later.

"You still good?" she said again.

Danny said nothing. He listened to the scribblings behind him. Listened to the turning pages, the slight slidings of the stool. Listened to the *hmphs* of sound caught in her throat like wordless questions.

Bridget was in front of him again, taking notes and sketching and walking around him as though she had never kissed him.

When Bridget had sketched from twelve points in the circle around him, she finally raised her eyes to his.

"What?"

"I'm glad I didn't ask you to pose for my class," she said.

"Thanks," he said.

"No," Bridget said. "I'll tell you what I mean in a minute. I want to be sure about something."

She set the pencil down and from the corner of the room picked up a Polaroid camera from its strap and took snapshots of Danny as she spoke.

"First of all," she began. "The girls wouldn't be able to concentrate. The models never look quite like you." She smiled. "And now that I think about it," she continued, "a number of the boys would have trouble with that, too." And Danny smiled.

Bridget took three more photos from angles outside of Danny's line of vision.

"Second," she said. "My whole point will be to get them to see *closely*. To see the thing exactly as it is, and then to draw the thing. And so I thought I might spend a great deal of time getting them to pay close enough attention so that they might see and understand the *asymmetry* of the human form."

Bridget held a Polaroid photo in her right hand and watched as it developed under her gentle breath. Walking around the table and gathering the other photos two at a time, and holding each of them at their white-framed edges in the pinch of her fingers, she placed them gently on the platform in front of him, shaking her head as she squared the eight photographs against the edge of the table at Danny's feet.

"And?" he said again.

Bridget held her finger up.

"One second," she said, and she walked away. When she returned from the kitchen with a tailor's tape over her shoulder. She started at his feet.

"Heel to toe, right foot," she said, and flipped the pages of her journal and wrote a measurement on one of the sketches she had drawn earlier.

"Heel to toe, left." Bridget shook her head and recorded the number again.

She pressed the zero mark of the tape measure at Danny's left ankle and traced the tape along the inside of his leg to his knee and did the same on his other leg. She measured the outside of his legs in the same way. She pressed the tape along the back of his legs from his heel to his backside.

And on she measured—ankles, calves, thighs in three places— lacing her measurements and pencilings with mumblings and smiles. Fingers, hands, wrists, forearms. When she came to his biceps she measured them flexed and unflexed. She measured the length from each of his fingertips to his elbows, each of his elbows to his shoulder blades.

She wrote measurements in her journal. She shook her head as she wrote. She said nothing. She stepped back and looked at him from behind. Danny looked over his shoulder at her.

Finally she pulled her stool in front of him and looked up.

"These measurements," she said, finally. "These. They're. These measurements from one side to the other are identical, Danny." She looked up at him. "I've never."

"One second," she said, and left the room again. When she returned she was shoeless and wearing a black summer dress. She curtsied once in front of Danny and then danced a pirouette around him. It was a wraparound dress tied at the small of her back with a black ribbon.

"Your turn to pose?" Danny said.

"Sort of."

Bridget sat on the edge of the table and rested her left foot on the stool she had been sitting on. She lifted the hem of her sundress to expose her leg to the thigh.

"Sit down," Bridget said, and she nodded at the stool on the table and circled her left calf with the tape measure.

"Eleven and three-sixteenths," she said, and Bridget wrapped the tape around her right calf.

"Eleven even." She looked up at Danny.

Bridget stood on the table and spread her dress to the side so that her right leg was revealed to the edge of her underwear.

She put the tape around her right thigh and measured it at its point of fullness.

"Twenty-one and just short of three-quarters," she said.

Twice then, Bridget swept her dress back from her left leg so that she might measure her thigh, and twice the skirt rebounded again to cover her leg. She growled at her disobedient dress to make Danny smile, and without warning or apology she straightened from her slight bend at the waist, and swept both sides of the skirt of her dress behind her, and using the satin string at the small of her back she tied the skirt of her dress so that her legs and underwear were completely revealed.

Bridget Pentecoff stood before him wearing what amounted to half of a dress, and measured her left leg at the corresponding thickness.

"Just over twenty-two inches," she said, and looked at him as though this last measurement was all the proof Danny needed.

"Do you see what I mean?" she said. "There are variations from side to side in every body part. And that's not just me, Danny. It's everyone."

She looked up at Danny again.

"Almost everyone," she said.

He was looking in her eyes. Bridget pointed to her sketch journal on the table.

"Look at the measurements for your calves," she said, and Bridget bent to pick up her journal. She flipped through the book until she found the page.

"Here," she said, and pointed to the measurements in question, and Danny stood on the table at her side.

"And now look at mine," Bridget said. "And we can go on and on with every part of my body."

Bridget caught his eyes again.

"Get the tape," she said, looking away from him. The tailor's tape spread like a flattened snake on the table. "Measure my arms."

She felt Danny's eyes working into hers, but she didn't look away from the tape. "Write the numbers in my journal."

"I'll remember them," he said. Still, he was looking in her eyes.

Danny pinched the tape in his fingers and brought it to Bridget's arms, wondering if the point of her undressing was an exercise in symmetry. There was nothing special about the discovery Bridget had made. Since he was thirteen months old his father had directed him steadily and scientifically toward balance. That a lifelong attention to even sidedness would result in anatomical symmetry was not a surprise. And even so, there were probably differences of a less measurable sort—differences a tailor's tape might not pick up.

Danny forgave Bridget her attention to this unremarkable discovery, though. She was an artist. But as he measured, gently, each of Bridget's fingers, at, and between, each knuckle, as he looped the tape around Bridget's wrist and penciled measurements in his head, as he slid the loop of tailor's tape up her arm and noted a dozen measurements from her wrist to her elbow, as he loosened the loop and set it above the crook of her arm, and slid the loop up her biceps and memorized a dozen numbers more as he approached the soft underside of the hollow of her arm, he wondered if there was any other point to Bridget's undressing than this lesson in symmetry.

He wondered, too, as he measured Bridget's arms, wrist to shoulder, if Bridget felt every shift in the loosening satin ribbon at the small of her back. If she felt its loosening at her hips, its skirt at the back of her legs as the ribbon's loosening allowed the dress's greater length. As Danny moved to her left arm did she feel the diminishing tightness of the dress away from her breasts, the whispering brush of the dress along the outside arc of her breasts? Danny would be at her left forearm soon. And then her elbow and then her shoulder, and he wondered if the unribboning would be complete by then.

Bridget's left arm was extended in a line along the horizon, and Danny's fingers were pressed against the tailor's tape around her left bicep when the ribbon untied, when the skirt fell, when the dress opened, and only in the loosest of all ways—in the flimsiest of all ways—were her breasts still covered.

Bridget extended her right arm—she was the letter tee against the wall—and her dress opened to reveal her breasts. She lowered her arms to her side then, stood as Danny had stood for her. Her palms open to him, her feet an easy vee on the table of wood.

Danny looked only into her eyes, while Bridget stood before him, breasts dis-covered for him.

Did she mean to speak? Did she mean to say, *Danny. Look at my breasts?* Did she mean to attend to the asymmetry of breasts, the normal and natural differences from one side to the other? Or did she know now that her point had already been made? Or that it was no longer important enough a point to be made.

Her dress was held only by her shoulders. Danny looked only into Bridget's eyes. She was light and relief against the dark of her dress— a long, light, loose, and open whisper of a dress. She was as beautiful and certain as anything he had ever known, and he looked only into her eyes.

"Look at me, Danny," Bridget said.

"I am looking at you," he said. His eyes locked into hers.

"You know what I mean," Bridget said. "Look at me."

Danny's eyes stayed in hers as he stepped slowly toward her open arms. Her chest against his, more of a woman's skin than he'd ever known. Behind her, the valances over the two windows facing Jackson were brows over the closed eyes of the windows.

Bridget took Danny's fingers in hers and stepped down from the table. Danny held the tips of her fingers in his and followed her onto the studio floor and into her room.

On her bed, he slid her dress away from her body and whispered to her.

"I kissed you," he said. "That was a kiss." And Bridget closed her eyes.

He whispered into her ear at first, as though he meant for her to *hear* his whispered words about the kiss he had given her in her sleep.

"I kissed you," he said again.

He whispered into her neck and shoulders then about the long time between kisses, and into the hollow of her arms about how the summer was soon to end and into her lips about how it was possible that he would never kiss another girl, and he whispered into her belly that his whispering was like a kiss, too, and he whispered into softer places, too: "And this is a kiss," he whispered to her breast, and this is a kiss," he whispered to her breast, and he whispered into each of her softness- es as though the things he whispered were intended not so much for ears as they were for those other places, or as though they were meant for him—for Danny; that he might hear his words as they returned to him from these places, so that he might locate himself aside her.

And Bridget tilted her head back on her pillows and stretched her arms to the side and then above her and then everywhere but around him, as though she felt that touching him would hold him to only one softness, as though she wanted him to have all of her places at once, and the small of her back arched into a bridge and under the bridge of her and over and between the curves of her and into the soft of her rushed Danny's whispers like late summer zephyrs, like music and light rain and Bridget shuddered.

Danny left for Kettle University on a Saturday morning two weeks later. While Henry packed the car Danny hugged his mother on the front lawn. Above Lori's shoulder Bridget was not at her window. One shade was drawn.

Between his feet on the passenger side of Henry's car Danny's backpack slumped toward its shoulder straps. He unzipped it and slid his artist's pad from the center pocket and quick-sketched the front of the house—lawn, tree, stairs, doors—to get at his subject: her empty windows. One shade open, one closed. Behind them somewhere—lying awake or sitting on the edge of her bed or drinking coffee at her kitchen table or painting at her easel—was Bridget.

At school, once his things were unpacked—sooner, even—he would render the scene in oil on canvas.

Danny put down his pad, slid the passenger seat back, and locked it into place, he stretched his legs and yawned. By the time Henry pulled onto the Eisenhower Expressway, Danny's eyes were closed. Awake, he kept his eyes shut through three towns before he spoke.

"Last night," he finally said, "Bridget and I stayed up the night painting."

He closed his eyes again and they passed another town before he spoke again.

"We hardly talked."

Still closed, Danny's eyes. But his words carried none of the haunted distance Henry expected of a sleeptalker. Minutes and miles stretched between his words.

"I hugged her when I left."

Danny adjusted his pillow against the window. Henry felt as though he were reading his son's journal.

"Like I'd hug you."

Henry shifted his weight in the driver's seat.

"I came downstairs at six o'clock this morning, and I heard her crying." Danny said.

The highway light posts flashed past.

"Not actually," he said. "I didn't hear her."

In the miles of silence that followed, Danny's breaths lengthened.

"I knew she was crying, though," he said. "I should have kissed her."

Danny's breaths deepened. Miles.

"I should have stayed upstairs and kissed her until it was time to leave."

Thickened into sleep.

They rode, father and son, toward the western horizon, which, despite the rush of white lines beneath the wheels, never drew nearer. Henry considered long drives with sons. There should always be long drives, he thought, to help fathers mark the passage of time; a 465-mile drive at least. For a mother it was different, perhaps. For Lori it would only have been a long goodbye—eight hours in the sight of a son with the driving sun calling its light on her oft-broken mother-heart, but with Danny's sleepy confessions of regret, the drive became for Henry a thing to remember, a birth or a birthday, a sacrament, a church emptied of every worshipper but two, a son asleep on his father's chest, the child's sweet breath on the other's neck—a song, a long beautiful song. And while Danny slept a certain sleep, Henry felt his son's infant weight against his chest, his actual chest, and he found himself holding his breath on westbound I-88 to keep from disturbing the sense of that weight.

For a moment, Henry considered turning the car around while Danny slept. He imagined Danny waking up in front of the house and looking back at Henry and smiling, running up the stairs to Bridget's apartment and kissing her, but he passed an exit without slowing down. It occurred to him then, that less than four hundred miles remained of Danny's boyhood, and Henry resolved to be wise with each of them.

When he spoke, he felt the dried and cracking path of the unwiped tears on his cheeks.

"The night before you were born," he said to his deeply sleeping son, "your mother and I made love." He wanted Danny to know that. That he was born of love. And Henry remembered those hours to his sleeping son: the drive to Good Samaritan in the rain, the tulips in the driveway of the hospital, the night in the birthing center and the day that followed. He told Danny the story of his first baseball glove and his first steps across the living room floor. He told him stories of Halloweens and Christmases and the first day of kindergarten.

"And do you remember the day you lost your boot in a snow-drift?" he asked him. "Here was your face," he said. "The face you made," and he returned to Danny the look of a boy who had lost a boot in deep snow. And did he remember the time he cried when a tee-ball game was canceled on the chance of rain?

"It's not raining now, you said. *It's not even going to rain*, you said. And it never did.

"Do you remember that, Danny?"

And did he remember the thousands of catches they had in the alley? And did he remember how he liked to ride with his father to the games but with mother back home? And did he remember how frustrated he was when his tee-ball coach said the game had ended in a tie again?

"It wasn't a tie, you told him. *It was 12-6. I kept the score*, you told him."

Did he remember saying he would rather continue playing and lose than end a game in a tie?

Henry recalled stories Danny had never heard, and stories Henry thought he had forgotten himself, until the words for them slipped past his lips—discoveries that swirled into the cubic space of the family car, which seemed to stand, then, for the moving space between a boy and whatever it was that Danny was soon to be.

If pressed, Henry might have said there was an untraceable chronology to the first two hundred miles of stories he told to his sleeping son. Danny was ten years old hitting a homerun in the rain and slipping in the yellow mud between first and second base, and then he was throwing a tennis ball across Madison Street in front of the Brown Cow Ice Cream Shoppe; he was reading a poem at the seventh grade literary festival and then it was his fourth birthday and he was riding a bicycle without training wheels on Lathrop. Then he was a toddler in the yard taking tennis balls from a bucket and throwing them across the street, first with his left hand then with his right.

And then Henry told him about the Lowland Gorilla and the symmetry campaign. He told him of the hopes of a young father for his infant son.

But as the sun overtook the Granvilles in the westward and effortless race to the other side of the world, everything—the sun, Henry, and all of the history of Danny's young life—seemed to be heading toward the one story that Henry had once hoped he would never have to tell. Each other story he told was another chance to delay the story of the girl on the bus at Madison Street, a chance for Danny to linger longer in burdenless boyhood, it was the story at the end of all of his stories, even the ones that followed it. It was the *more* to the story, and while Henry avoided the more of it, he knew he was only a father telling a liar's story to his son—a boy who could smell lilacs before they bloomed, and who knew crying without hearing it—and he was wasting the last long drive of his son's boyhood on a lie.

And wasn't it already a kind of lying, anyway, to remember stories to a sleeping boy? Wasn't it like a first kiss on the lips of a sleeping girl? It was no wonder that Danny slept now with the regret of not kissing Bridget when he had Henry as his model for honesty and truth.

Danny flinched awake for a moment, as though something had been thrown at his dreaming self. He stirred in the passenger seat, straightened his legs, stretched like a cat toward the back seat, and turned toward Henry.

"Did you just say something, Dad?"

"No," Henry said.

"You okay driving?"

"Yeah, I'm good," Henry said.

"You want me to take over?"

"No, I'm good."

When Danny closed his eyes again Henry knew it marked a return to sleep. A father who had watched his son through a thousand nights and a thousand naps knew the breathings of a boy in three-quarter sleep, knew the sound of false awakenings. Henry would drive while Danny slept the last sleep of boyhood. The story of the girl on the bus was not a story for a sleeping boy.

When Danny woke up at a gas station in Iowa, he had a box of Topps baseball cards balanced on his knee, and his father was scrubbing insects off the windshield with the station wiper. Danny rolled the window down and pointed at the box of cards so that Henry could see it.

"What's this?" he said.

"What does it look like?" Henry pulled two sandwiches from the cooler in the back seat and returned to the car.

"These are from 1990," Danny said. "Did you know that?"

Henry shrugged. "They were sitting on the counter and the guy was selling them for fifty cents a pack."

"Did they have any Bowman cards from 1951?" Danny said.

Henry laughed. "Nope. I checked," he said.

"Where are we?"

"Williamsburg, Iowa," Henry said. "Halfway to Omaha."

"Baseball cards for fifty cents a pack," Danny said. "We should move here." He pulled the lever on the side of his seat, and the backrest locked into a straightened position.

Henry smiled and pulled the car into a parking space that faced the store of the station and they ate lunch.

By two-fifteen they were back on I-80, driving silently toward the diminishing space between the sun and the west end of the earth.

Henry shifted his head slightly toward Danny, but kept his eyes to the road.

"Do you remember the day Bridget moved in?" Henry said.

"It was yesterday, wasn't it?" Danny said.

Henry smiled. "It sure feels that way," Henry said. He adjusted the rear view mirror, and then told Danny the story about the other girl they met that same day. Henry told Danny about the accident and how Danny had seen the girl's I.D. card on the bus floor before it had even fallen.

"There was nothing there, Danny," Henry said.

"Maybe there was."

"There was nothing there, Danny. Not until the truck smashed into the bus. Only then was there something on the floor."

Danny massaged his forehead with the fingers of his left hand.

"You don't remember any of this, do you?" Henry said.

"I remember crying on Desplaines," Danny said. He stared at the road ahead.

"Yes. On the walk home you started crying."

Henry's hands were at ten and two o'clock on the steering wheel. He was nodding his head slowly.

"I kept thinking maybe I was crazy," Henry said. "That it never happened. That I conjured it up out of nothing."

"I remember crying on Desplaines," Danny said again.

Danny opened the glove compartment and took a bag of sunflower seeds from under folded maps of Nebraska and Iowa. He sprinkled some in his palm, tilted his head back and poured them into his mouth.

"Why did you wait so long to tell me?" Danny said. He chewed one seed at a time, picked its two half-shells from his lips and transferred them to his empty soda can from lunch.

"I didn't know what to do," Henry said. He reached toward Danny for sunflower seeds and Danny shared them.

"I thought you had a gift," Henry said, but quickly corrected himself. "You *have* a gift. And all of a sudden it was so much bigger than baseball, and I was afraid for you. And your mother cried. She didn't want to believe me, and I didn't know what else to do but hold you back. I was afraid. You were beating everyone at every sport you played. And I thought maybe the two things were connected somehow, and I was afraid that if you really had some kind of gift and you never lost at anything, that the point of the gift—whatever the point of the gift was—might get lost and that you would be treated like royalty and, I started thinking you were meant for something great but I didn't know anything else, Danny."

"Why now?" Danny said. "Why are you telling me this now, Dad?"

Henry let Danny's question sit between them while the sun lowered imperceptibly in the sky. They were seventy miles past Williamsburg by then and Danny hadn't touched the box of baseball cards. On the seat between his thighs the cards were the unopened ephemera of the past, each one a still-packaged thing unknown to the men, each piece of paper a chronicle of a single man's history. Every pack had its heroes, its forgotten players, its sons of mothers and its fathers of sons, its stories. Henry wanted him to rip the box open like he would have done a few short years ago. He wanted Danny to arrange them according to the numbers on the backs of the cards, or by the teams of players as he had arranged them one year, to read the statistics on every card and test Henry on his memory of batting averages from the year before. He wanted to watch Danny's face light up at each wrapper he crumbled and threw to the floor.

"I don't know," Henry said. He pressed a button and wiper fluid fanned the windshield. The wiper blades stumbled and re-stumbled over miles of insects.

"I guess it just didn't seem right to keep the truth from you any longer, Danny."

Danny looked ahead as the day diminished before him. His fingers traced the box of baseball cards on the seat between his legs.

"I suppose I thought you'd be ready for it, Danny."

"Ready for what, Dad?"

"Just ready," Henry said. "Ready for the world, maybe. You're not like everybody else, Danny. You're not like anybody. This is what I meant when the Cubs called with an offer and I told you that life is bigger than baseball."

Danny smoothed his hands across the box of cards.

"This is what I was talking about, Danny. You're about something much bigger than baseball," Henry said.

And while Henry sat in the driver's listening emptily to the whisperings of the highway beneath the car, Danny listened to them from the passenger seat, but differently—wondering if highways had things to say.

Eighteenth

In Omaha, Henry and Danny checked in for the night at a Holiday Inn downtown. They had dinner in the hotel restaurant and when they returned to their room they watched the Cubs play the Houston Astros. They stood for the national anthem and chewed sunflower seeds, tonguing the shells into their palms and dumping them in the ice bucket on the table between them. They guessed at what pitches were coming.

At the commercial break during the final inning, Henry leaned against the wall outside the bathroom and brushed his teeth while he watched Danny view the game. There was more he could say to Danny—there was always more he could say—but he was happy to have not wasted this time with Danny.

Henry watched the last half inning from under the sheets of the hotel bed. After the final out he continued watching the television warily, as though the game had disappointed him by ending too soon. He said goodnight to his son from beyond the first layer of sleep.

Danny turned the volume down and flipped through a hundred channels, pausing—sluggish and deliberate—for seconds between each offering, and in this way he fought against the thoughts that fumbled and slipped and struggled for purchase behind the lambent reflections of the television in his eyes.

Tomorrow. Tomorrow. He would allow them access then.

After breakfast in the hotel restaurant, under a blanket of gray morning clouds that covered the sky, Henry drove Danny to his dorm at Kettle. In the western sky, shafts of light splayed like fingers through the clouds and hinted at something more than a blue-less day.

After checking in at the student center, they drove to Baker Hall. They were quiet as they transferred Danny's possessions from the car to the freight elevator, from the elevator to his room on the second floor.

When the last of his things were in his room, Henry twisted a rod at the edge of the window to let in the still-fogged world outside. In the middle of the empty courtyard the American flag draped like a towel from at the top of a flagpole.

His back was turned toward Danny as he spoke.

"Maybe I shouldn't have told you all that, Danny," Henry said to the window.

Danny walked to his father and put his hand on his shoulder. The weight of their greatest parting looming gray and heavy between them.

"About that first day of high school, I mean," Henry said.

"I know what you meant," Danny said.

"Maybe all I should have told you is to play ball and hit the books," Henry said. "And I love you," he added. "That's all you need to know."

While Henry spoke to Danny at the window—while he tenderly passed Danny's life into his own hands, across the courtyard a woman held the door to Farwell Hall for a man with hamper in one hand and a shopping bag in the other. Goodbyes were taking place on thousands of campuses around the world, Henry thought.

Tens of thousands, Danny thought.

At the campus entrance a blue taxicab pulled in and the Granvilles watched it approach the entrance of Baker Hall below Danny's window.

"That's my cab," Henry said.

"What?" Danny said.

Henry unpocketed a key and set it in the palm of Danny's hand.

"It'll be nice to have a car out here," Henry said.

"You're going to take a cab back to Forest Park?"

Henry shook his head. "To the airport," he said. "Mom's idea."

Minutes later his father was gone.

In his room, Danny left everything unpacked but his easel. This he set against the wall in the space between the window and his bed on the promise of what natural light might come to his room if the Nebraska clouds ever lifted. He took the sketch of his house and Bridget's empty window from his artist's pad and leaned it on the easel's ledge, and trading the Kettle pillow for the one he brought from home, lay on the sheetless bed in his dorm, the protective plastic sibilating beneath his shifting body. He tried to still himself to silence the plastic, but even as he concentrated on stillness the plastic whispered in response to every breath he pulled and delivered. Finally he removed the fitted plastic from his bed and lay back on the mattress, stilling himself so completely that the only sound in the room was the languid tick and ring of the weathered rope against the flagpole on the far side of the courtyard.

It was only then, alone in that alien and unparented place, that Danny Granville allowed the rush of yesterday's thoughts to crash unfettered into his consciousness.

The girl on the bus had been real. The silent and ineffable gray mass of image and sound that ran random and uninvited through the dark of so many of his mornings was not just some unintelligible dream he had shrugged off in his sleep four years running. The screaming silence, a flash of something white, the girl standing before him, the crash, the screech of metal, the girl falling back—the scrambled mess of images that came to him in shards of a vision was conjured neither by ancient archetypes or pre-game butterflies. It was real.

He closed his eyes hoping to invite the collection of dream pieces that he had become accustomed to disinviting for so long. As he strained to recall the images, the easy close of his eyes shifted into a clenching of his eyelids against one another. He was forcing it, desperately grasping at an uncapturable thing.

Lying on his bed in Baker Hall, Danny wondered what it was that kept him from remembering the girl on the bus. What could have happened that day to prompt Danny to tell the girl she had dropped something, when his own father, and the girl as well, knew that she had dropped nothing? If it was true that Danny had some gift, some ability to see into the future, shouldn't he have been able to recall what had given rise to the prescience? Didn't it make sense that he should also have access to the memory of such an important event? Or had the gift been given to the wrong person? Should the gift have been given to someone who was a little more aware of the signs that preceded it?

As he eased the press of his eyelids then, Danny felt the warmth of the sun slanting in through the window blinds. For an instant he wondered if it was a sign, but knew he would drive himself crazy if he expected a vision every time the sun appeared.

He opened his eyes. On his easel, bars of sunlight sliced across his sketch of Bridget at her window. He swung his legs over the edge of the bed and stepped toward the easel. Was there some message in how the shafts of sunlight affected the sketch?

Outside, the parking lot was filling with cars of freshmen and their families. From the hallway outside his room, steps, voices—muffled at first and then clearer as they passed his door.

I'm fine, Mom. I told you, I've got it. Jesus.

Danny pulled the cord to raise the blinds on the window, and the soft afternoon sun washed the room. Below, two men huddled over a small refrigerator, shuffling in quarter steps over the path to Baker Hall. Behind them, a ten-year-old girl and her mother carried lighter loads of a brother's belongings, a son's belongings.

What if he had been missing signs all along? What if he had slept through a dozen of them on the way to Omaha? What if that June call from the Chicago Cubs, two days into the baseball draft, was a sign? What if whoever was responsible up there for dishing out visionary gifts had been trying to get Danny's attention in a thousand ways since the day he got that phone call? Couldn't that have been a sign?

What was the point of a gift if he was incapable of understanding it? What if his father's insistence on college blinded him to a thousand signs meant to steer Danny straight to baseball?

What if Kettle was a mistake?

At eleven o'clock at night, an hour after the first day of orientation week ended, Danny called his mother. He wanted to tell her that nothing felt right, that he had spent the evening meeting strangers in awkward and unnatural ways, that he had just lost a game of musical chairs to a bearded cheater from South Dakota, he had been on an ice-breaking treasure hunt, a tour of the school, and had sat through twelve role-plays meant to relate the history of Kettle University. He wanted to tell her he didn't fit here, that he wanted to come home.

Instead, he told her he was fine. He told her he missed her already, but that so far things were otherwise fine. After he spoke with his mother, Danny spent the last hours of the night, and the first hours of the morning, painting. He did not call Bridget; he wanted his first week at Kettle to be about Kettle. If he ended up loving the place and thinking it was the perfect fit, then fine, but if he ended up hating it he would hate it on its own merits, not because he missed Bridget. He would call her on Friday. Like every other Friday of his high school years, that day would belong to Bridget.

Over the next three days, Danny considered the psychic weight of these potential signs: he was the only student working out at the baseball facility; on Monday, Tuesday, and Wednesday there were parties on the floor above him that lasted well past midnight; at lunch on Monday the milk dispenser in the cafeteria emptied just as Danny started filling his glass with milk. On Tuesday, in his composition class, three guys named Bob sat next to each other. At dinner on Tuesday the milk dispenser emptied again into his own glass. On Tuesday night he dreamed of butterflies and a rainstorm swept through the night. The rain continued through the next day. On Wednesday there was a girl in his sociology class named Bridget, and on his way to lunch, under the wooden slats of a bench, he found a dollar bill, wet and folded. When he returned to his room after lunch on Wednesday someone had sprayed the second floor corridor with buck scent.

After dinner on Thursday, the rain finally stopped. Danny drove into town to hit baseballs at the batting cages. In a medium-speed cage Danny lid down a slug of bunts from the left side and then a slug from the right. Next, he took full swings, hitting a slug of balls to left field and then a slug to right. He did the same from the other side of the plate. Six slugs into his workout, Danny moved to a fast cage and hit two slugs before moving again to the fastest cage. He found his rhythm against the 95 mph pitches after two swings. The pitches at that highest speed were a better fit for his swing and for his breathing and for the beat of his heart. He hit a slug's worth of pitches from the right side and a slug from the left, and it felt so good he was smiling. For the first time in days he was smiling.

After his swing he eased into his stance and shifted his feet and swung again. It was as effortless as breathing. It felt like nothing else had felt since arriving at Kettle. He was certain that he could hit the ball even if his eyes were closed, and so after the first pitch of his third slug in the high-speed cage, Danny closed his eyes.

He stood still in the batter's box and leaned slightly toward the path of the dimpled balls as they whipped through the air past him. He did not swing at the four pitches that remained on that slug. He slotted another coin and with his eyes shut he listened closely. At first he heard only the thud of the balls against the rubber rectangle suspended at the fence behind him, but as that next slug spent itself he began to hear the mechanic release of each pitch and then the whisper of the ball growing in volume as it approached him. He coined another slug. He listened to the first pitch and swung at the second, fouling it off behind him. The third pitch he roped against the far wall. And with the final twelve pitches of that slug, his eyes shut tight to the machine, Danny Granville laced twelve line drives across the fan-shaped outfield.

He slugged another coin and did the same from the left side. And standing in that batter's box an urgency occurred to Danny: he had to leave Kettle. He was hitting fastballs at 95 mph with his eyes closed. Did he need a clearer sign than that?

If his father was right, if Danny had a gift, then it made sense that he could overcome the odds that were stacked against high school players who had entered the draft before college. If anyone could do it, he could. He wasn't going to waste four years of life going to sleep with the smell of buck scent in his pillow and drinking with frat boys when there was a massive sandlot of a world out there waiting for him to play ball in.

Danny did not realize that he was laughing until he opened his eyes to put another slug in the box. To his right, the birthday boys, open mouthed, were staring at him, the girls were still going at it in the softball cages. Danny slotted another coin and stood in the box for righties.

He did not swing at any of the twelve pitches thrown on the strength of that slug. He stood still in the batter's box and leaned slightly toward the path of the dimpled balls as they whipped through the air past him. He listened to each of them *thwap* against the black rubber mat behind him. It seemed as though each thud against the rubber was more word than sound. He slotted another coin and with his eyes shut he listened closely to the twelve pitches meet their destinies against the rubber rectangle.

I don't belong here.

The message was his own. He knew that. It wasn't a message coming from the baseball gods; he knew he was putting his own words to the thwap of sound, but it was truer than anything he had ever known. And standing in that batter's box listening to fastballs pass him like words, Danny knew he would leave Kettle University in the morning. He didn't belong in Omaha. He needed to be playing baseball.

He would pack the car tonight and leave in the morning. Maybe he would work it out so that he arrived home at dinnertime and he would tell his parents then. And maybe he would surprise Bridget in her studio on Friday night, and maybe on Monday he would call the Cubs. He had 500 miles to figure it out.

He passed the night sleeplessly, certain at every conscious wakening that he would leave in the morning, but not certain at all that it was the right thing to do. By 3 A.M. he stopped fighting against the forces that kept him from sleeping, and in the dark of the morning he carried the last of his things in the backpack strapped to his shoulders and in a box he held in his arms. He opened the door with his hip and began to walk along the edge of the courtyard to the parking lot, and when he reached the end of Baker Hall he stopped. He closed his eyes and breathed in the night. In the easy eastward breeze that rolled steadily at him was no longer the smell of deer piss. In the air was the morning side of the smell of night. It smelled like the wet dark morning of late summer in a place that was not home, and he wondered if he took twenty steps backward would he breathe in that other smell, would it come back to him?

But he did not step back. He walked knowingly, deliberately, and steadily two hundred more steps to his car in the student parking lot, and when he had placed the box in the car he stood behind it with his palms on the trunk and breathed in his final pissless whiff of Omaha, Nebraska, and was made aware of a great silence. But for a whisper coming from the trees to his left, the campus was a perfect silence. He closed his eyes to the breeze and listened intently to the whisper. It was coming from the Ginkgo trees. He listened again and, opening his eyes, he stepped toward the island of trees at the southwest edge of the parking lot. When he reached it he stood beneath the Ginkgo tree and again he closed his eyes. He closed his eyes and listened. He closed his eyes and listened and turned his face toward the black and still-night sky and smiled and laughed at the sound of the Ginkgo trees' tiny and gentle clapping hands.

After leaving campus, as Danny pulled onto Interstate 80, he continued looking to the sky on the chance that some trace of the gift, some greater proof of his visionary potential, was evident in the heavens. Maybe the clouds would take the shape of an angel opening its arms toward him, its fingers curling him forward, pulling him eastward. But if anything, the Nebraska sky was a bruise, a punch in the eye of the world.

He turned the radio on. If the universe had the power to give a man the gift of vision, it had the power to send him some signal by way of a song on the radio. Danny scanned the dial at first for anything familiar, but there was only country music, talk radio, and evangelical sermons. He went back, though, thinking a message could come from any of them, and on his second time along the dial he settled on a station that was mostly static, wondering if he was gifted enough to hear some message in the static. But there was nothing.

He turned off the radio. Ahead, light from the unseen sun pulled at the blackened sky, appearing less to add color than to subtract from its darkness.

"What now?" Danny said to the changing day. Should he call his father? What would he say to him? That it didn't feel right? Would he tell his father, *Trust me, Dad. I had a feeling. It just didn't feel right.* Would he tell him that it rained for forty straight hours and the sun never shined and the milk ran out on him twice and then just today the sky was dark and then the sun came out and it was light again?

And what would his father say if he called him? Would he tell him to turn around and go back to Kettle? One year, Danny. Give me one year. Would he say that? And would Danny do it?

If he obeyed his father would that make it right? Who was to say that Kettle was the right place to begin with? How many colleges were there in the world? Even in the United States? Thousands? Tens of thousands? And would Danny return to Kettle then? Did his father know what was best for him? What about his mother?

Or Bridget?

What would Bridget say? She had left some dinky town outside of St. Louis, Missouri, to come to Chicago straight out of high school. Went directly to college and then directly to grad school without skipping a weekend. What would she say?

Did anyone know what was best for him? Or were they all muddling through life trying to find their own way? Fumbling through life with their fingers crossed. Stumbling, getting up, turning around, going back, making new mistakes every day and turning back to fix them when they could, and shrugging their shoulders, or screaming and swearing at the mistakes that could not be turned around?

The sky was a morning glory then. Or a violet. Petals of lilac clouds around an orange ball of a sun. A black station wagon with Illinois license plates pulled onto the highway in front of him.

"There's my sign," Danny said.

There was a Volvo in front of me with Illinois license plates, Dad. That's when I knew for a fact that I made the right call.

Ridiculous.

But on the chance that there was some significance, some miracle in the merge of his fellow statesmen, Danny adjusted his speed slightly in order to maintain a comfortable distance behind the Volvo.

He imagined sitting all of them down—his father, mother, and Bridget—around the dining room table and laying it out before them. Maybe he *would* just tell them it hadn't felt right. That was the truth of it, and there wasn't much more. Probably his mother would understand. He would ask her, *Would you have stayed there, Mom? If it didn't feel right, would you have stayed there?*

And what about his father? How serious he had seemed on the ride up to Kettle. And the night at the hotel. And the morning he left. Danny had never seen him like that before. What would he say when Danny showed up in Forest Park in the living room and told him he decided against college after all? After years of counting pitches and kicks and steps and swings would he feel compelled to drive him back to Kettle and tell Danny to hand over the keys to the car? Or did he really believe that Danny was ready to make decisions for himself? To do as he felt should be done with the gift? And might his father even be relieved that finally Danny was doing something for himself?

In Altoona, Iowa, the Volvo pulled off the highway and Danny filled his tank at the next exit. A road construction zone slowed him down until he reach Colfax, Iowa, and when the highway opened up to two lanes he found himself behind a blue minivan with Connecticut license plates. A girl and a boy were playing a game in the back seat and when they discovered they had an audience in Danny they played show and tell for him. The girl introduced three animals to Danny: a white bear, a brown bear, and a tiger-striped house cat, and then drifted below the window and allowed her brother to display his uncountable wrestling hero action figures. The children disappeared for miles at a time and then reappeared according to what seemed like caprice. After thirty miles had passed, neither the boy nor the girl appeared again, but now and then on the girl's side, one or another of the stuffed animals appeared in the square window of the van.

It seemed to Danny as though the animals were checking on him.

When the polar bear danced in the window, Danny said, "Still here, Missus Bear."

The sun, by then, was a ball in the sky, more white than yellow, and though Danny was hungry he didn't want the girl in the van—or any of her animals for that matter—to raise their heads and find him gone without a proper goodbye.

When the brown bear appeared again Danny was glad he had not exited when he had had the chance.

"I'm right behind you, Mister Bear," he said. And twenty miles later, when the cat checked on him, he said, "Still here, Tiger."

When the cat checked on him three times in a row and Danny realized the animals were appearing in no set order, and he tried to guess which would be the next to show in the window. Through a hundred and twenty miles, though—as the girl's hand raised one or another of the animals to the window, Danny's guesses were only rarely correct.

Just before the van signaled a right turn as it approached the Illinois Welcoming Center, the back of the girl's head appeared. Danny thought that if any of the animals was to show itself one last time it was certain to be the tiger-striped house cat, which seemed to have checked on him more times than the either of the bears.

Danny stayed on Interstate 80, keeping an eye on the back of the van as it pulled onto the welcoming center entrance.

"Come on, Tiger," he said to the blue vehicle. But when the girl sat up straight in the back seat of the mini van and turned to face Danny, she wiggled the paw of the white polar bear into a farewell wave and smiled.

"Damn," Danny said. "Some gift."

The boy raised his head in the window of the mini van then and Danny beeped his horn at all of them, the polar bear, the boy, the girl, and a milk crate full of wrestlers.

Which is when Danny's cell phone rang. He flinched to hear it that first time and it rang three times more before he reached into the seat behind him for his backpack, transferred it to the front seat, fumbled through the mesh side pockets and finally hit the send button to stop the ringing.

"Hello?" he said.

"Good morning, stranger," the girl's voice said. "It's me."

"Oh, Bridget," Danny said, and he felt the flood of a Bridgetless week of life, perhaps even a wasted week of life. He felt as though he had spent a week wandering in some empty and lonely and wild region, some uncultivated place. He had read Dante's *Inferno* in his sophomore year at U-High, and though he had not read *Purgatorio* or *Paradiso* he had borrowed a book of illustrations inspired by the *Divine Comedy*, and at the instant of Bridget's voice he felt as though he had lived through a week of the same black and white traverselessness, and here, in the sound of Bridget's voice and all that it stood for, was the light and the hope and the certainty he had been looking for all along.

"What's wrong, Danny?" she said.

"I love you," Danny said.

Nothing in the way of sound came from the receiving end of the phone for a moment and still Danny was certain he would not return to Omaha.

"Do you know what you just said?" Bridget asked.

"Yes," Danny said.

"Where are you?" she said.

"I'm not in Nebraska," Danny said.

"Are you in Forest Park?" she said.

"Almost," he said. "I left Kettle."

Another silence followed his words.

"Are you still there?" Danny said.

"I'm here," Bridget said. "Are you sure about this?"

"Yeah," Danny said.

"Did something happen?" Bridget said.

"Hard to say," he said. "I think something did."

Bridget met Danny at Louie's so they could talk before his parents learned about his decision. She was mostly quiet while Danny told her about his short stay at Kettle. Three times, though, she asked him if he was certain. Outside of her silence, the slight noddings of her head, the sips of her decaffeinated coffee, it was all she said.

"What is it?" Danny finally asked.

She was worried about his art, is what Bridget finally told him. It was the other stuff, too. She was worried that he wouldn't go to college at all once he started playing baseball for money; she was worried it would be too much to expect after he started making a living. But there would be no time for art anymore. It was this that worried her most.

Danny smiled while Bridget put words to the sadness of a wasted gift. In the basement of the house on Lathrop a blue tarpaulin concealed more than twenty-five paintings and sketches of her he had stacked against a wall in the storage room.

"What's so funny?" Bridget said.

"Nothing," Danny said. "All I can tell you is that I promise that won't happen."

"How do you know?" Bridget said.

"I just do," Danny said. "You'll have to believe me."

Henry needed more than that. Bridget called him at work and asked him to meet her at Starbucks after work on that Friday afternoon, but when Henry walked in the door of the café, it was Danny who greeted him from the table in the corner. He stood up and put his hands into a stop sign before his father.

"Don't say anything, Dad," he said. "Just listen."

He hugged his father then, and told him what happened at Kettle. He told him about the slug of baseballs he hit without opening his eyes. He told him about the buck scent and the Ginkgo trees and the parties that didn't end, and it seemed to Danny as though Henry sat nodding his head, almost imperceptibly, in the same silence that Bridget occupied at Louie's earlier in the day.

"What is it, Dad?" Danny said.

"It's a lot of things," Henry said.

"I'm going to go to college," Danny said. "It's going to happen, Dad."

And Henry nodded, it seemed.

"Promise me that," Henry said.

"I promise," Danny said, and Henry nodded his way toward a second silence.

Danny opened his hands and shrugged his shoulders into a question at his father. *What now, Dad?*

"Is this about the girl?" Henry said.

"Bridget?" Danny asked.

"No," Henry said. "The girl."

"The girl on the bus?" Danny said. And Henry nodded.

"It's a lot of things," Danny said.

"The girl?" Henry said.

"I think she's one of them," Danny said. And Henry nodded.

BOOK THREE

Nineteenth

ON SUNDAY AFTERNOON THE HOUSE TREMBLED WITH LIFE. LORI made sandwiches and put a leaf in the dining room table to extend it for their lunchtime guests, Lenny Porter, the Midwest scouting rep for the Chicago Cubs, and Adam Soloway, Mickey Wells' agent.

Henry was restless; while Bridget and Danny sat on the couch in the living room, he fidgeted on the edge of a chair in the living room. He asked Bridget if she would like anything to drink. He re-swept the dining floor. He asked Lori several times if there was something he could do. He checked to see if the doorbell was working though it had never failed in all the years they lived there. He looked out the window. He made a pot of coffee. He asked Bridget if she would like anything to drink. He called Adam Soloway to see if he was on his way.

For her part, Lori seemed more content than she had been in years. She seemed happy to be mothering again, happy to be laying out slices of lunchmeat and pickles and olives, preparing for something.

Len Porter arrived before Soloway. He shook Henry's hand at the door and then Lori's. "Pleased to meet you," he said, and then he shook Danny's hand.

"Len Porter," the scout said.

"Danny Granville," Danny said, and he turned toward Bridget with Mr. Porter's hand still in his.

"This is Bridget," Danny said. "My girlfriend." Bridget stood and walked toward Porter, but looked at Danny as she held her hand out for the scout.

"Are you ready to play some ball?" Porter said.

There was talk of the hierarchy of leagues in the Cubs organization, of rookie ball and Low-A, of Advanced-A, Double-A, and Triple-A, all of which, Mickey had filled Danny in on since his own minor league career had begun. There would be conditioning sessions and an evaluation, and "Who knows?" Porter said. "Maybe you'll get to throw a game or two in the fall."

At the small of Danny's back was Bridget's hand.

The clump of ice cubes in at the bottom of Porter's glass loosened as he tilted it toward his mouth. Water splashed onto his cheek.

"My hope," Porter said, wiping his mouth, "depending on how it goes in Peoria, is that they'll ask you to play winter ball in Florida. You do good there, and the suits go into the winter meetings with you at the top of their lists. Maybe you start off next season on the Tennessee roster. Maybe you start with the Iowa Cubs. There's your best case scenario."

Danny smiled and looked at his father as Henry put his arm around Lori, standing at his side. She curled her finger to her lips to keep from crying. Henry smiled.

"You ready to start throwing?" Porter said.

"No one's throwing anything now," Lori said. She squeezed Henry's shoulder. "It's time to eat."

"Good call, skipper," Porter said and everyone laughed.

Soloway arrived just after lunch and immediately began discussing the contract. Porter opened his briefcase and took notes on a white legal pad, nodding his head and looking at Danny now and then, and smiling at Bridget and Lori.

Soloway addressed his own notes, which he had gathered on Saturday night over dinner with Henry and Danny. He spoke as though he were the player, and Danny and Henry looked at each other smiling as Porter and Soloway discussed the potential terms of the contract.

"I want four years of college paid for," Soloway said, scratching his pencil across a page in a spiral notebook. "Room, board, books, everything, no matter where I want to go, no matter when I want to go there."

Porter took his own notes.

"I want a three-year commitment, with another contract if I shoot up to Triple-A before the contract's up."

Soloway wanted several things Henry and Danny weren't certain they had even covered with the agent the night before, and when they all seemed happy with the deal, Soloway made the call to the Cubs' general manager from Danny's room.

"Done," he said, when he returned, and there was the shaking of hands, there were hugs, there were kisses.

After a week of conditioning with the Bristol Sox, Danny flew straight to Peoria, Illinois, to join the Chiefs. In the locker room, two players looked up at him from the bench facing the wall of lockers. They wore sliding pants and baseball socks. One of them had a black goatee and wore a blue tee shirt; the other was shirtless and had a shaved head. A third player, also goateed, sat in a chair against the opposite wall in his boxers. He was in mid-sentence.

"I told him, *Fuck you*—"

The players looked up at Danny in the doorway and at the silence in the room.

"I'm Danny Granville," he said.

The man in his boxers looked at the other bearded player and said, "Anyway, I told him, *Fuck you, get your own fucking beer.*"

The speaker stood up then and pulled his boxer shorts down and reached into his locker for his sliding shorts.

The player in the blue tee shirt picked up a car magazine.

The hairless and shirtless man looked at Danny and nodded his head in the direction of a locker in the corner of the room. Granville was spelled out in black marker on a strip of athletic tape between the top shelf and the space beneath it.

From another doorway in the left corner of the locker room came the sound of ping-pong balls and laughing, distant sounds that seemed further away than a single room.

Danny walked to the locker and set his bags on the floor. He considered asking his new teammates where the coach's office was, but he said nothing. He walked into the next room, aware of the mumblings of the players behind him. In the attached room there were three washing machines against one wall and three dryers against another. There was another doorway and crude wooden shelves from floor to ceiling against a third wall. But for a black-framed clock circled with oversized numbers, and a single desk, the fourth wall of the room was bare.

Gabe Morris, the manager of the Chiefs, sat at the desk facing the wall.

"Mr. Morris?" Danny said.

"That you, Granville?" he said, still turned away.

"Yes, sir," Danny said.

Morris turned toward Danny and looked at him from head to shoes. He shrugged his shoulders as though responding to some question that had been playing in his head. He lifted the bill of his cap so that at the back of his head the arc of the cap hardly moved. Morris scratched at the hairline above his forehead.

"Don't call me *sir*," he said. "And I ain't no Mister, either."

The trebled and definite taps of a ping-pong game continued from beyond the laundry room.

"Come here," Morris said.

Danny walked to the desk. Morris appeared to have shaved recently but without the aid of a mirror. Tufts of hair, the color of gray squirrels, sprouted from the threshold of his nostrils in neglected patches.

"How tall are you?" Morris said.

"Six-two," Danny said, and Morris scratched his pencil on the card before him.

He scraped his chair back from his desk and turned it to square himself with Danny. He crossed his arms over his belly.

"You ready to go today?"

"Yes," Danny said.

"Either side?"

"Either side," Danny said.

Morris shook his head slowly.

"Unbelievable," he said, and picked up the yellow card on his desk. "Mid-high nineties from both sides?"

Danny nodded.

"Tell you what," Morris said. "We're up against a mix of right- and left-handed players this afternoon. You throw whatever the hell you want to throw. How's that?"

"I'll go righty," Danny said.

"Fine," Morris said. He rose from his chair and walked to the wall of shelves, and picked out a hat and pants and a jersey.

From the next room came a long, steady rally of ping-pong taps.

When Danny returned to the locker room only one of the three players remained. The bald man stood naked in front of a mirror on the wall staring at himself. He was completely shaved. Not a hair on his body. He held a bat on his shoulders and he rocked in his batting stance, drumming his fingers on the bat handle as though the mirror were an opponent about to face him at the plate.

Danny walked to his locker and pretended to be unphased by the shaven man.

"Who's the Goat?" the player said to his own image. He took a half swing and froze with his arms fully extended and the bat pointing at the mirror. "You're the Goat," he answered. He returned to his batting stance and said it again.

"Who's the Goat?"

Half swing.

"You're the Goat," he said, pointing the bat at the mirror again.

Danny emptied his baseball equipment into his locker and looked up when the hairless man approached him holding his hand out for the stranger in the locker room.

"Gray Whalen," the player said. "But everyone calls me *the Goat*."

Danny shook his hand. "Why do they call you the Goat?" he said.

"Why do you think?" Whalen said.

"Because you're totally bald?"

"Goats aren't bald," Whalen said, and Danny laughed.

"I guess not," he said.

"It stands for the Greatest Of All Time," Whalen said.

"Okay," Danny said.

Whalen nodded. "I'm catching for you today," he said.

Whalen made the sign of the cross, kissed his fingers, and began to dress for the game.

"There were two other guys in here when I came in," Danny said.

Whalen pulled up his sliding shorts and nodded.

"With the baby beards?" Whalen said.

Danny shrugged.

"Wishnick and Coles," Whalen said. "Pansies. The both of 'em. Rich kids from Kansas or some fucking place. They been looking over their shoulders since the middle of June, no shit. Every time they see a new face in the locker room. They ain't going anywhere and they know it."

Danny warmed up with Gray Whalen in the dirt track along right field and then stretched in the brown grass of the outfield before heading to the bullpen. Wishnick and Coles sat in metal folding chairs along the bullpen wall speaking silently and laughing. Players trickled out from the locker room in ones and twos and as Gray Whalen settled into his crouch behind the bullpen plate and Danny began to throw, Wishnick and Coles grew silent.

Danny started with fastballs, half-speed at first, building gradually to three-quarter speed, and holding steady there. From the clean snap of the ball into Whalen's glove, the sharp and distinct crack of it,

Danny knew what Gray was doing. He could have silenced the sound by letting Danny's throws hit the sides of his glove basket, but Gray opened his glove wide to let the pitches slap sharp and hard against the leather. Whalen wanted to feed whatever worries kept Wishnick and Coles looking over their shoulders at every new face in the locker room. Whalen was smiling.

After warming up, Danny and Whalen walked toward the dugout where a trail of the rest of the team clacked their spikes down the stairs and along the dugout cement. Gray elbowed Danny in the side.

"Don't look at anybody," Whalen said. "Let them do the looking, you know what I'm saying? Act like you been here before."

Danny nodded, looked at his shoes.

"Nobody ever wants to see a new guy in the dugout because it means that one more person might make it up before they do. It don't matter if you pitch and they play first base. Nobody here likes you," Whalen said. "I'm the only one who wants you to win tonight. Me and Morris. You look good tonight and me and Morris look good, too, you know what I'm saying?"

Danny looked into the glove on his right hand for fear he might look in some other place.

On the mound Danny spun the baseball in his right hand. The stadium was the biggest he'd ever played. Five hundred people in the stands.

By the time Danny threw his eighth warm-up pitch to Whalen, the buzz from five hundred fans was louder than anything he had ever heard from a pitcher's mound, but somewhere between the instant of his half-step to the hollow dip in front of the pitching rubber and his push off the mound, a hush fell over the stadium, and by the time his fastball had been released from his hand, the buzz of the stadium, if not the stadium itself, had faded. There were no longer five hundred people in the arena; there were only four. There was Gray Whalen behind the plate and the umpire behind him, there was a man with a bat at the plate, and there was Danny Granville. More alone now than he'd ever been.

He struck out the first batter with four straight fastballs that he spread around the strike zone. Whalen extended only one finger for the rest of the inning, and Danny complied. No batter reached base in the first.

In the dugout the only player to acknowledge Danny was Whalen. It seemed to Danny as if there were no boys left in baseball. As if there were only men, now. As if sometime between his last tournament that summer and his first game in Peoria all the other boys had left baseball.

By the end of the sixth inning Danny had thrown eighty-two pitches, struck out nine batters and given up only two hits. The Chiefs led 6-0 and Morris pulled Danny for a pitcher Danny hadn't met.

"Who's that?" Danny asked Whalen.

"Who's what?" Whalen said.

"The reliever," Danny said.

"Don't worry about it," Whalen said. "He's an asshole and he don't like you."

"Nice," Danny said, and Whalen laughed.

Danny called Mickey Wells after the game from Whalen's apartment, a dusty, unfurnished one-bedroom with rust stains everywhere; arches of it on the porcelain sinks, and mountainous stains on the sheetrock of the living room walls.

Danny sat on a milk crate on the cement slab outside the sliding doors of Whalen's apartment after his host made dinner: macaroni and cheese with canned tuna. After two rings, Mickey answered his cell phone as he had always answered.

"What's up?"

"Nothing's up," Danny said. "I'm looking for Mickey Wells."

"Holy fuck!" Mickey said. "Danny Boy! Where are you?"

"You first," Danny said.

In the two years since being drafted Mickey had stepped steadily up the minor league system to the Cubs Double-A affiliate in Alabama.

"Any day now, Danny Boy," he said. "I could be up at Iowa any day."

While Whalen banged dishes and glasses and silverware in the kitchen sink, Danny filled Wells in on what had happened at Kettle.

"Don't let anybody get on base," Mickey said.

"I'll do my best," Danny said.

"You know what I mean," Mickey said. "Somebody's gonna get on base, but you gotta always be thinking I'm gonna beat these ass-holes. Nobody's ever gonna go yard on me, you know what I mean?"

"Yeah," Danny said.

"You gotta get up here as soon as you can," he said.

"I know," Danny said.

That night, as Danny lay in his sleeping bag on Gray Whalen's living room floor, it seemed the trip from Omaha had taken place months before. In the bluish light of the living room cast from the near-full moon, the rust stains on the living room wall looked like Rorschach ink. Danny sat up on the floor for a moment, thinking about signs. Then he smiled and lay back down.

The next day was a rare day off for the Chiefs. In the morning, Danny ran three miles before breakfast and partnered with Gray Whalen through a leg workout in the weight room while the rest of the team worked out on their own. After lunch the position players took the field for fielding drills and sprints, and the pitchers and catchers worked in the outfield. If the rest of the Peoria pitching staff tried to pretend Danny wasn't there on Tuesday, it seemed harder to pretend on Wednesday afternoon while Danny ran through his routine with Whalen. He started with an easy right-handed short toss to loosen up his arm after yesterday's game. He walked up close to Whalen then and said he was going to loosen up his left arm if it was all right with him.

"Let's go," Whalen said, He shrugged his shoulders and Danny switched his glove. Whalen looked to his right to see if anyone was watching.

They started with a game of short toss and after five easy throws Danny stepped back a long stretch of a leg and did the same each return of the ball from Whalen. As the distance between them grew, the other pitchers, wrapped up until then in their own between-game routines, started to pay greater attention to Whalen and Danny. They were wondering at first, Danny knew, why he was throwing long toss the day after he pitched, and now they were putting it all together. He was throwing long toss lefty, but he had pitched against the Lake County Captains with the other arm.

By the time Whalen was at the warning track near center field, all of the pitchers were standing at short right field watching Danny with their arms crossed or akimbo.

On the cool down, Danny stretched toward Whalen after each throw until they met up in right center. Whalen put his arm across Danny's shoulder and walked toward the left field bullpen away from the rest of the players.

Danny smiled.

Whalen backhanded Danny in the chest with his gloved hand. "That's what I'm talking about," he said. "Let them do the looking."

Whalen looked at Danny's glove still fixed to his right hand.

"Let me see that thing."

Danny took his glove off and Whalen held his catcher's mitt out for a temporary trade. He tried Danny's glove on his right hand and then his left.

"This is fucking awesome, Danny," he said. "Just fucking awesome." He returned the glove to Danny and put his own back on his hand. "Morris told me you could throw from both sides, but I had to see it to believe it."

In the bullpen, while the pitchers, Wishnick and Coles, prepared for their start on Thursday by throwing to two position players, Danny stretched outside the bullpen. Between Coles' pitches to his receiver, he glanced back at Danny on the other side of the fence.

"How about a game of Williamsport," Danny said to Whalen.

"Let's do it," Whalen said. They positioned themselves at the third mound and plate and Danny began to throw lefty to Whalen from the shorter Little League distance. By the time Danny had thrown twenty fastballs the rest of the pitching staff had gathered at the bullpen fence.

While Wishnick's throws landed into his receiver's glove and while Coles' pitches slapped into his, Danny's fastballs cracked into Whalen's glove with a sound that seemed to belong to something other than baseball.

Denny LeCoure, a middle reliever, laughed and raised his eyebrows after every pitch. He looked around at the others as though he still wasn't sure if he had actually seen what he'd seen. In a moment, even Wishnick and Coles leaned against the fence and watched as well. They were smiling. When one of Danny's fastballs rocketed past with the sound of a soft whistle, Coles looked back through the fence at the others and said, "Holy fuck. Did you hear that?"

Whalen fought a full-blown smile. He was churchsmiling. And suddenly it seemed to Danny that the men were boys again, behaving as boys behaved in the presence of some good thing that could not be fought against. He felt it. He felt what Gray Whalen would later call the *buzz*. There was a buzz there on the field.

"You *know* what I'm talking about," Whalen would say. "A friend of my old man's played Triple-A in the seventies and Hank Aaron came down to do a hitting clinic with the guys and he was out of baseball for five years and he was taking batting practice and smacking shit out of these balls. Bam! Bam! Bam! Every pitch. Knocking balls out of the yard. Everybody in Triple A walking around like they were the man and all of a sudden a fucking *man* showed up, you see what I'm saying?"

On Thursday morning the West Michigan Whitecaps came in for a three-day against the Chiefs, and while the Whitecaps took batting practice, Danny had the Peoria pitching staff lined up against the dugout wall, watching while he charted their opponents' hits and pitches that fed them. The second time the Whitecaps came through the batting practice line, Danny passed his clipboard to Coles and told him to continue charting. Danny leaned toward Wishnick, who would start the first game of the home stand.

"Look at this guy in the box. Number fourteen," Danny said. "He's jumpy, huh? Twitching in there as far away from the plate as he can get. Nothing but fastballs middle-out."

Three more pitches to number fourteen and another player came to the plate.

"My guess is this guy here, twenty-two, is the leadoff hitter," Danny said. "He let the first pitch go each time he came up, and this is only batting practice. Set the table with a fastball and then come at him off-speed."

Wishnick nodded his head and jotted notes on a legal pad. LeCoure ran inside the clubhouse for pencils and pens and when he returned he distributed them to the rest of the pitching staff. They took sheets of paper from Danny's clipboard and folded them to take notes.

While the Chiefs were at bat that first game against West Michigan, Danny stood at the dugout wall with Wishnick at his side and shared his notes from the batters he faced during the previous inning.

Wishnick went six innings and got the win in the first game 4-2.

Danny faced the Whitecaps in the second game, pulling himself out after throwing eighty-five pitches over six hitless innings, and middle reliever, Miguel Villanueva combined with the closer, Tony Lorraine, to shut out West Michigan 4-0.

Pleased with the two wins against the Chiefs' division rivals, Morris allowed Danny to take batting practice with the position players. Danny sprayed line drives from both sides of the plate and earned himself a pinch-hitting role in the seventh inning of the game. Hitting lefty, Danny laced the first pitch into the left field corner and reached third base standing.

In the dugout, Gabe Morris lifted his hat and scratched at his nest of hair. Shaking his head, he seemed to fight back a smile.

By the time Danny called Bridget that Friday night, he had a 2-0 record and his first professional newspaper clipping, an article in the *Peoria Times* about the buzz in the Chiefs' clubhouse, and by the time he called his mother on Sunday night at 11 P.M. sharp, he was 3-0.

When he spoke to his father, Danny told him that a roving instructor from the Cubs had watched his off-day workout taking notes and making phone calls through his entire routine. He had heard that the Cubs' brass was asking about him.

Three days later, Danny had a 4-0 record and an ERA under two, and when he phoned Mickey Wells again, and said, "Guess where I am, now, Mick?" Mickey guessed right.

"You're a Warthog in Winston-Salem, you son of a bitch," he said. "Fucking A, Danny."

Twentieth

ON THE FLIGHT HOME FROM ARIZONA EARLY THANKSGIVING MORNING, Danny imagined a dozen ways Bridget might react upon seeing him that afternoon. She would look at him across the dinner table all night, and afterward, while he and his father cleared the table and washed the dishes in the kitchen, she would touch his arm as she passed him on her way to the couch where she would sit with his mother. And as the night settled on Lathrop they would be together again.

It was still dark when Danny exited the taxi from the airport and arrived at the house on Lathrop. Henry was at the window, fingering the curtain aside to check for Danny.

It had been nearly three months since Danny had seen his father, and in the bright light he seemed older. Had Danny been so wrapped up in himself that he had never noticed the creases around his father's eyes, the shadows below them, the neck that seemed now to belong to an older man. When Henry smiled, though, his eyes were a boy's eyes.

"Hey, kid," Henry said, closer to laughing than smiling.

Henry took Danny's bag and set them inside the doorway. He followed Danny into the kitchen where Lori was rubbing olive oil on the turkey. She hugged him armlessly, her oiled hands held daintily away from him like the freshly painted fingernails of a girl.

While Danny rested on the couch, Henry asked questions about the flight and the cab ride from the airport. He asked him about the Arizona fall league. From the kitchen came tiny clicks of knives against the cutting board, came the hesitant closings and openings of the oven door, came the suck and spit of bastings, came the random hum of the refrigerator, fauceted rushes of water, rills of aroma from onions sizzling in butter, and the nascent waftings of heat against a still-pink bird.

Henry and Danny talked baseball while Danny softened in the thick shaft of windowed sunlight from the sky over Lathrop, Henry smiling at every hint of hope in Danny's voice, at every success his son recalled. Danny fought against sleep there, struggled twice to open his eyes against the downward press of it, but each time, Henry smiled and said, "Sleep, sleep, Danny," and so Danny slept.

When he woke Danny peeled potatoes, cubed bread for the stuffing, watched pre-game football shows with Henry in the living room, and took three trips to Whole Foods: one for nutmeg, one for evaporated milk, and one for aluminum foil. He listened for the sound of Bridget's stockinged feet on the floor upstairs.

It was four o'clock when Bridget finally knocked on the door. All day Danny had planned to be the one to open the door so that he could greet her alone.

When she finally tapped at the door it was not with her knuckles. Two taps with the corked lip of a bottle of wine. Danny opened the door and there was Bridget, tee shirted tightly and skirted longly. She held bottle of wine in her right hand and an autumnal bouquet of flowers in her left. She twirled around with her hands full of things, and as she twirled she kept her eyes on Danny's as long as she could and as she twirled her skirt billowed out at the bottom. He hadn't imagined a scene like this, Bridget spinning there with flowers in one hand, wine in the other.

"Hey," Bridget said.

"Hey."

Danny reached for the bottle of wine and the flowers but Bridget set them on the hallway floor instead. When her hands were made free she reached for Danny's face. She peeked over his shoulders to check for Henry and Lori, pulled him toward her and shut the door behind him, then pressed her lips against his in a kiss that went farther than any of his imaginings had stretched. And she kissed away what worries came of absence.

"I missed you," she said.

Danny smiled.

"Remember that Gray Whalen guy I was telling you about who I played with in Peoria?" Danny said.

"Yes," Bridget said. "What about him?"

"In my second or third game he hit two triples and a homerun and there were reporters in the clubhouse getting quotes from him and snapping pictures and everything, and there were hardly reporters in the clubhouse, and when they left, Gray looked up in the locker room, smiling like he was on his way to the Cubs, and here's what he said: 'Don't nobody say nothing to bring me down, today. I'm having me a dig-me day.'"

"Is that what you're having today, Danny?" Bridget said.

"That's what *you're* have today," he said.

"Yeah, I guess I am," she said.

Danny reached behind and turned the doorknob.

"And you locked us out," he said.

"Who cares? We can eat upstairs," Bridget said. "I have leftovers from La Piazza."

Behind him the door opened to Henry.

"Damn," Danny said. "They're home."

Bridget smiled. She hugged Henry. She nodded her head and pointed her thumb at Danny. "Our guy is back," she said, and picking up the flowers and wine, her feet unseen beneath her skirt, she seemed to float into the kitchen, leaving father and son at the living room entrance smiling.

Through December and January Danny worked out with his old friend, Patrick Decker, now a commuter student at DePaul University. They trained at U-High when Henry could get them in the weight room or pool, or else at the Melrose Park Health Club, and on Danny's throwing days the old friends ran or drove to Stella's Baseball Warehouse where Patrick suited up with his old catcher's equipment and received for Danny.

It was on their way to Stella's that January when they turned on the sports radio station to hear the baseball analyst discussing Danny with callers.

One of the announcers had found Danny's high school fielding and batting stats, and in a conversation with the general manager of the Cubs offered the possibility of Danny playing shortstop or first base on his off days. The radio personalities argued the value of great hitting against great pitching. They challenged the Cubs brass to come up with a reason why Danny, if he was able to sustain a .300 batting average and hit for power, shouldn't be a pinch hitter when they needed one.

There was a buzz over Chicago, a Cubs-blue sky of it. After more than a hundred years without a World Series championship on the north side there was a buzz. With these new kids coming up in the system, with this homegrown kid with two arms, there was talk of the Cubs having something special.

In January, Danny helped Bridget move into a condominium she'd purchased on Division Street that she called her lakeside condo, even though Danny had to stand on a chair at the kitchen window to find the single square inch of Lake Michigan which could be seen from the place. But there was an abundance of light in the apartment's living room, and in those last few weeks before his return to spring training, Danny and Bridget spent as much time as they could painting and drawing and loving in its fullness.

In February, when the Cubs pitchers and catchers reported to Hohokam Park in Arizona, Danny Granville was among them.

Twenty-first

MICHAEL FINNEGAN WALKED UP THE STAIRS TO THE ELEVATED CTA
platform at Oak Park Avenue. He wore his old blue Cubs jacket. It was
meant for warmer weather, but tradition was tradition; every March
when the *Sports Illustrated* baseball preview came out, Finnegan
dropped his winter coat off at the cleaners and pulled his retro Cubs
jacket out of the closet.

On the platform Finnegan adjusted his flat Irish cap and rolled the
magazine into a tube. He tucked it under his arms and blew warm
breath into his cupped hands.

Thursday.

Two more fucking days until the weekend. Two more trips into
the city on the Blue Line to a nothing job as a clerk at the
Commodities Exchange where money was the bottom line and former
high school bullies ran in packs and ruled the day.

When he boarded the second car, Finnegan pulled his moleskin
notebook from his shirt pocket to record the events from the past three
days so he would not forget them. He would write a book about this
fucking place one day.

On Monday he had seen a whore in the company bathroom
blowing one of the guys from his office. On Tuesday one of the brokers screamed at Finnegan to shut the fuck up and later in the day
another broker stole a big money trade from a pretentious and
whiny trader named Bernstein. Not that Bernstein didn't deserve
mistreatment—he talked from his nose and corrected everyone's
grammar in his screechy and maddening voice—but no one
deserved a thirty-five thousand dollar fuck in the ass.

And then on Wednesday a giant pock-marked yahoo named

Valenti grabbed another broker by the necktie and tied him to the rail of the pit where three other guys mock-sodomized him.

This is where I work, Finnegan thought, closing his moleskin journal and slipping it into his jacket pocket.

A journalism degree from Northwestern and this is what I get. Eight years of this shit. How did that happen? What happened to all those plans to take his dinky sports column in the *Oak Leaves* journal and springboard it to a real career?

Finnegan unrolled the *Sports Illustrated* he saved for the Thursday morning commute.

At least winter was over. The baseball issue—an annual seed of hope—was in his hands.

He read the two-spread on the Chicago Cubs pitching staff which had been beefed up by the acquisition of three veteran aces, and a power-hitting catcher named Mickey Wells had finished the last season up in the Arizona Fall League and was on his way to the bigs as well.

Finnegan flipped the page and began reading about the biggest story out of the Cubs farm system: a switch-pitching prospect who had spent all of two months in the Arizona Fall League, and skyrocketed through the minors. Finnegan read it under the cloud of a notion that he was reading about someone he knew. He read quickly then, as though he had every intention of starting the article over as soon as he skimmed it fast enough to find whatever it was he was looking for, to figure out what was stealing his attention from the very words on the page.

Finnegan skimmed over the name of every new kid coming up. How many college kids and minor league kids, and hot-shit players around the world looked great when they were seventeen and then never made a sound again. Give him the players you could count on, the hitters who flirted with .400 averages, and forty homeruns every season, give him the Hall of Fame names who were there plugging away year after year.

This kid, though, he's drafted in the sixty-second round behind nearly three hundred other players no one will ever remember, drops out of college before his first class, goes 4-0 for his Single-A club, 3-0 for the Double-A Cubs in Daytona, shoots up to the Triple-A club in Iowa where he finishes the season 3-0 with them, and gets an invite to pitch in the Arizona Fall League where he goes 5-1.

Finnegan continued reading. Decent size. Six-two, 195-pounder, listed as LHP/RHP. He had a pretty good stick from both sides and hit just over .300 in nine games as a pinch hitter. And less than a year after his draft, the 'Enemy Lines Scouting Report' at the top of the page encouraged little leaguers to spend their offseason studying Danny Granville.

Granville.

The kid was nineteen. A shy, clean-living, lifelong fan of the Chicago White Sox is drafted by the Chicago Cubs. Still lived at home, still drove the Ford Focus his father passed down to him, still dated the girl upstairs. If he hadn't started in the minors so late, the article read, he would certainly have been voted the Minor League Player of the Year.

Finnegan added up Granville's minor league wins.

"Fifteen wins as a pro," Finnegan said outloud. "Seven on the left side, eight on the right—in a quarter of a summer."

This is what he brings to the game, Finnegan read. *Finesse and velocity on both sides, an expertly located fastball in the high 90s, and with movement when he wants it, a low 90s curve with a sharp downward break that starts at the letters and breaks out of the strike zone, and two variations of mid 90s slider, one that dips and one that cuts. He has a change-up, he likes to sandwich between two pieces of fastball bread that could make your heart stop. And as soon as you think you got him figured out, he comes at you with something else.*

Finnegan shifted in his seat as he skimmed the remaining paragraphs of the article. He flipped back a page to find the kid's name again. Danny Granville.

Of his fifteen minor league wins, two were no-hitters, six were complete games, and he had never thrown more than ninety pitches in a game. Six complete games and he never topped ninety pitches!

Three more games would have been perfect were it not for first inning singles by the leadoff man.

The switch-pitcher had a daily workout regimen he designed with the help of his father, a high school science teacher from Chicago.

"Granville." Finnegan said out loud. Mr. Granville from U-High. It had to be. Goddamn. He was Mr. Granville's kid. A switch-fucking-pitcher.

The kid must've been nine or ten years old when Finnegan was sitting in Mr. Granville's class. And the old man was a baseball nut. He was talking about baseball in class all the time. The Social Life of Animals. And he hardly could speak about the development of animals and their response to the environment without saying something about his kid.

The final paragraph of the article noted Granville's 149 strikeouts in 117 innings. Now, in his first year in the majors, he would be reunited with the young Chicago Cubs catcher, Mickey Wells, Danny played travel ball with as a kid.

"Danny Granville could've played up here when he was in high school," the Midwest scout, Lenny Porter, was quoted as saying. "Don't blink your eyes, baby. This kid's gonna be good."

Finnegan read the article again. The history. Until then, switch-pitchers had been little more than a novelty in sports. Every once in a while maybe you read an article about a ten-year-old kid who started both games of double-header, but nothing serious.

A sidebar article quoted beat writers across the country who speculated how their own team would put Danny Granville to work if they'd had the foresight to draft him.

Toronto needed a lefty pitcher so they were capable of having him focus on the left side, and forgetting he was a switch-pitcher at all. The Brewers had him starting every two days and the Giants had him pitching middle relief. Oakland would have made him their number one closer; throwing him righty and lefty where they needed him most.

Rob DeVaney, a baseball writer from the *Mesa Sentinel* was at a pre-season meeting in Mesa when Danny sat down with the Cubs' front office staff, the GM, the manager, and the pitching coach to discuss the team's plans for Danny.

"*I've started games my whole life,*" Danny said. "*You want me to pitch from the bullpen, let me know. I'll put another plan together. But if want me to start six-seven ball games a month for the team, though, let me go with this plan here.*"

"*I'm telling you,*" DeVaney said, "*Kidder, Bennett, and Sharp were drooling at the table while he laid out his plan for spring training.*

"*In a perfect world I pitch one game righty, one game lefty. I throw no more than eighty pitches unless it's absolutely necessary. Give me four days rest until my fourth game and then three days rest for the remainder of the season. By April I'll be ready to go every three days for the rest of the season, and maybe I'll be up to eighty-five pitches by mid April.*"

"Unfuckingbelievable," Finnegan said.

He looked up from the magazine as the train stopped at UIC/Halsted. If this kid was the real deal he'd be able to break baseball records left and right. He could win thirty games a year. Maybe more. The Cubs got a two-for-one deal with Granville, and they could stock up on another slugger, or another ace. The possibilities were mind-blowing. In a seven-game playoff, or World Series battle, opponents might face this guy four times.

Finnegan leaned against a pole and read the headline of the Granville article once more as he waited for the doors of the Blue Line train to open at Congress Parkway. *Danny Granville: Two, Two, Two Pros in One.*

Maybe this was Finnegan's lucky break. A national story that would get him some attention. Enough attention to maybe quit this fucking job and start writing for crying out loud. Start doing what he was meant to do. Then he could get to the story of the Commodities Exchange that was churning within him.

He shook his head at the *Sports Illustrated* article and whispered to the opening doors of the train.

"How the *hell* did you pull this one off, Doc?"

He would find out. No one could make it to the pros without a story, and no one made it to the pros the way Danny Granville made it without one hell of a story, and Danny was going to do it. Finnegan would find Doc Granville and he would get the story. He would follow and observe and write, and he would wait. If it took a year to write, Finnegan would take his time. And if Danny turned out to be as good in the majors as he was in the minors, Finnegan would have his breakthrough story. He would sell it to *Harpers* or *Vanity Fair* or *Atlantic Monthly* and his phone would ring off the wall for evermore.

On the subway platform a street musician was butchering Nat King Cole's "Mona Lisa." Finnegan rolled the magazine and put it in his back pocket. He put a five-dollar bill in the musician's empty guitar case, making sure the musician saw it for what it was, a five-dollar bill, and as he climbed the stairs to the street, Finnegan repeated the *Sports Illustrated* headline.

"Two, Two, Two Pros in One."

Today, at least, Finnegan was glad for the last three blocks to work. There was something hopeful about the streets of downtown Chicago this morning. With the sun rising over Lake Michigan and splaying its long westbound fingers on the city, the downtown thousands—with their suits and skirts and hurried strides—didn't seem so hopeless; this morning they moved as though playing some essential part in the operation of the world.

Finnegan stopped at the corner of LaSalle and Wacker and sat on the edge of a flower planter on the median strip that separated the north and southbound traffic and paused—for only a minute—as a hundred or so smartly shod human beings passed him on their brisk and hopeful walks to the offices where they performed their roles in the human gain.

Was any one of them thinking of *him* just then? Thinking that Michael Finnegan was a player as well? As he walked into the pits of the Chicago Commodities Exchange—where acne-scarred bullies ruled like lions at the waterhole, where whores were hired for company parties, and where men made more money on the day terrorists attacked the World Trade Center than other men made in their entire lives—was any one of them thinking that Michael Finnegan was a player as well? Or was their indifference as staggering as it always seemed?

Well, they would have no choice but to notice him one day. One day, this would be Finnegan's story—"Animals at the Water Hole: The Darwinian Universe of the Commodities Exchange." One day. And Danny Granville's story would help him get there.

So pass him today all you downtown thousands, with your skirts and suits, your smart shoes and purses and wallets, your purpose. Pass him today you bully brokers and traders with your pastel jackets and your paper-stuffed pockets.

But know this: among you is an observer, a watcher of people and a taker of notes. And he has seen through your suits and skirts, seen through your false hope and into your hopelessness. He has peered into the ugly and dark places where you have made your beds. He has read your nametags, badges, and laminated access cards. He has taken names. Pass him today dressed in your staggering and fashionable indifferences. Do not raise your eyes today to the man who rests on the edge of the flower planter on the corner of LaSalle and Wacker, for he wears neither skirt nor suit, you downtown thousands, but he most certainly is watching you today. Today. And hope—in the shape of a rolled-up magazine—pokes from his back pocket.

When Henry sat at his stool, Kevil slapped the baseball preview on the bar and pulled a glass from a shelf behind the bar and started to pour a beer for a customer at the end of the counter.

"I thought your days at Kevil's were over," he said. "Figured you'd be drinking at a fancier place once your this came out."

Henry picked up the magazine and looked at Kevil.

"Page thirty-eight," Kevil said. He tilted a glass under the Killian's tap while Henry opened the magazine to the two-page spread on the Cubs.

"You look like you're reading the obits," Kevil said, setting a pint before Henry. "What's up?"

Henry shook his head. "Nothing," he said. "I'd just be happier if I never had to read a word about him."

"You have any idea how many folks in this town alone would like to be reading an article like that about their kid?" Kevil said.

"I know," Henry said. "It's just that the season hasn't even begun."

"I wouldn't worry about it," Kevil said. "Nobody reads this shit anymore."

It seemed to Henry as though Kevil was on the verge of some greater bit of wisdom on a topic of which he knew nothing, when behind him a caprice of the March wind caught a waitress, coming in for her shift, by surprise. It whipped the brass handle from the woman's fingers and slammed the glass door against the extent of its hinges. The waitress cowered at the sudden explosion of sound, as though she expected it to come with pain and pieces of broken glass, but it did not. Twice more the door banged against its hinges before Henry reached it to pull it shut, before Kevil asked his waitress if it was she who ordered the wind.

"I had nothing to do with the wind, Mr. Young," she said, and she looked up at Henry Granville.

"Hi, Mr. Granville," she said, and held out her hand. "Erin Molloy. I went to middle school with Danny."

"Hi, Erin," Henry said.

"I just read that article about Danny in *Sports Illustrated*," she said.

"Did you?" Henry said, and he looked at Kevil, who stood at the threshold of the entrance rubbing his thumb against the high hinge of the door and shrugging his shoulders at what his waitress had said.

Before his first pre-season game against the San Francisco Giants, Danny stood on the mound absorbing the certain and specific sound of the crowd. It seemed from his vantage on that mound— the highest point on the field—as though he would never hear that sound, that exact and cumulative roar pouring at him from every-where, ever again. It took these exact twelve thousand people, in the stands and bleachers and on the lawn, to make this sound. It was the sound that followed twelve thousand baseball-less winters, the sound of promise and pure joy, perhaps—finally released after a terrible caging. It was the sound of summer. Danny Granville stood there on the mound and closed his eyes so that he might recall something of that sound in the future. If the dream ever ended, he would want to have this to recall.

When he opened his eyes, he looked in the first row of seats above the Cubs dugout to look at two of the 12,600 people in the fixed seats of Hohokam Park. His father sat off the aisle in the netted section behind home plate, his mother sat next to him. Henry, on the verge of something bigger than happiness, waved his gloved hand at Danny. Lori was as close to a laugh as a crying mother could be.

On the top step of the aluminum bleachers behind the third base fence, a man wearing a vintage Cubs jacket sat alone taking notes. He squinted and pursed his lips as he sipped from a tall cup of something hot. He tipped his Irish cap.

Danny pitched lefty against the Giants, throwing nine pitches in the first inning and the only batter to reach base was the leadoff hitter who lined a single to right field. The next pitch resulted in a double play and five pitches later the inning was over. Danny threw eleven balls in the second inning and no one reached base. The same result occurred in the third inning at the cost of eleven pitches. When Danny reached his self-imposed limit of sixty pitches, the Cubs had a 4-0 lead in the bottom of the sixth. Danny had knocked in two of the runs with a bases loaded single in the fourth inning.

Four days later Danny had his second professional win against the Seattle Mariners, and the first in which he pitched into the glove of his old friend, Mickey Wells, the Cubs' back-up catcher. He pitched six and one-third innings and left the game with a 6-1 lead. When Danny faced Seattle for the second time, his seventy-pitch limit earned him his fourth win.

On March 25th, Danny entered a game against the Los Angeles Angels of Anaheim with a 7-0 pre-season record. He threw seventy-five pitches and left the game with no one on base at the end of the eighth inning. Hucker Norton entered the game in the ninth, though, and after saving the previous three pre-season games, served up a single and a homerun and the Angels won.

On the 28th of March, Danny threw an eighty-pitch, complete game one-hitter against the Colorado Rockies. The only hit to leave the infield was a hard grounder a right-handed batter poked through the right side. Danny threw two straight three-pitch innings.

He headed into the Cubs' final pre-season game, his third right-handed start against the Mariners, with an 8-0 record. The Cubs had a 1-0 lead after eight innings, but when Danny faced Seattle's leadoff hitter in the ninth inning he had already thrown seventy-four pitches, six shy of his highest pitch limit. It cost Danny seven pitches to induce the batter to hit an easy grounder to shortstop, and when the Mariner's number two hitter came to the plate, Danny had surpassed his pitch limit by one.

In the dugout, the manager, Trey Bennett, and the pitching coach, Phil Sharp, both eyed Danny. Sharp held his hand up toward the umpire and jogged to the mound.

"How you feel, Danny?" he said. "You want to give it a couple more?"

Danny looked at the batter, John Parmer, a rosy-cheeked veteran he had faced several times during spring training games.

"Let me see if I can finish this guy off," Danny said.

Sharp nodded and headed toward the dugout.

Danny stood on the mound with the ball and glove at his left shoulder. Another sell-out crowd at Hohokam Park had come to see Danny in his last pre-season game. How many new Cubs jerseys with Granville's name on the back were already out there in the world?

Danny shook his right arm to loosen it. He eyed the batter, and as he prepared to step from the mound into his windup a new sound replaced the din of the stadium crowd: a silent scream that deadened sound. A scream, felt more than heard, and felt by only one man among twelve thousand, and with it came an involuntary closure of Danny's eyes, against the backdrop of which flashed the unmistakable image of the batter, John Parmer, falling to the ground with his hands pressed against his neck, his eyes opened wide and his mouth in the shape, perhaps, of the same silent scream that ruptured Danny's head. Danny shook his glove from his hand, dropping it to the ground. He pressed his hands to his ears and from the dugout came running the trainer, Kidder, and Bennett. Mickey came running from behind the plate, his lips moving in the shape of *What the fuck, Danny! What the fuck just happened!*

The crowd was silent as Danny walked, the scream within diminishing with each step toward the dugout. Parmer, red-cheeked, stood still at the plate.

From the dugout, the scream gone, Danny watched Hucker Norton give Parmer a free ride to first base on five pitches. From the dugout, Danny watched Hucker serve up a first-pitch fastball that the next batter sent deep into the left field lawn seats, ending the game.

In the dugout Danny did not tell the trainer or his coaches what happened on the field. Neither did he tell Mickey, who saw to it that the reporters kept their distance from Danny in the clubhouse after the game. At the reporters' insistence for even some paltry information to offer their readers, Mickey gave them this: "Tell them he got a fucking headache, all right? You could fucking quote me."

The papers reported the headache without Mickey's colorful assistance. They weren't completely unsatisfied, as Danny Granville had helped the team to the best pre-season in Cubs history. A rookie pitcher was about to lead the Chicago Cubs into opening day with a 8-0 pre-season record. A man capable of that should be forgiven a headache now and then.

The sign worried Danny, though. Since his drive home from Kettle, a drive in which he had committed himself to paying attention to the universe, he had forgotten about the signs. Inside the swirling energy of profession baseball—from his first day of single-A ball with the Peoria Chiefs—Danny had focused so intently on symmetry and preparation for the major leagues, he had forgotten about the signs.

Or was it a sign at all? Was it urged on by the universe? Or was it prompted by Danny's pushing himself past his pitch limit? Which, though not arbitrary, was at least self-imposed. How was it that his flirtation with a self-imposed parameter could be responsible for a vision?

One thing was clear, though. If it was a sign—if it was evidence, somehow, of the burdengift—if the vision-sound that came to him on that final pre-season game was an indication of things to come, it was certain that Danny Granville would no longer have to worry about *looking* for a sign in the future. If there were visions out there still to be had, they would now find Danny.

Twenty-second

ON OPENING DAY IN CHICAGO THE APRIL SUN WAS A COLD AND rimless white ball in the center of a milky sky. The blue of it was more figment than anything—a trick of the eye. Some wizarded reflection. The visual echo of forty thousand blue-coated Cubs fans onto an April sky that was rarely more than gray.

Mickey Wells, on the verge of animal gladness, sprang from his crouch in the bullpen.

"How you feeling, Danny Boy?"

"I'm good," Danny said.

Mickey scuttled to Ty Wilhelm, who would be resting his knees for most of April. The old catcher, leaning in a chair against what passed for a bullpen wall, settled the four legs of the chair and thumbed the sign of the cross on Mickey's forehead like an Ash Wednesday priest.

"Go, my son," Wilhelm said, "And win us a fucking ballgame."

The field was a sea of green within the brown and ivyless arc that swept Wrigley. As they crossed the left field foul line, the hinged throat guard of Mickey's helmet clicked against his shin pads. Cheers exploded as the doors opened and they stepped onto the infield grass.

Danny glanced at his father's seats in section 104. He spotted Bridget first and then his parents. Lori was wrapped thickly in a hooded parka. She spread her blanket over Bridget to her left and when she caught Danny's eye, his mother snuggled closer to Bridget, as if to say, *Look who else we brought, Danny*. Henry waved and Bridget seemed to try, but her arm was blanketed at her side.

Henry looked at the fans in the section behind him. He would have silenced the crowd like students in his classroom if he could have,

Danny thought. *A little respect for the moment,* he would have said. *That's my son out there.* And at the sight of the smiling pride in the man who had done so much to make it possible for Danny to be walking across that historic grass in what felt like slow motion, Danny wished his father could feel that same grass under his own feet in that same moment. Henry had told him once that his dream was to feel it under his shoes one day, and his dream of dreams was to feel it under his bare feet. His father had laughed as he said that, as though, even as the dream spilled from his lips, he could feel the certain tickle of its truth.

On the walkway behind his father, a dot of kelly green in the arc of Cubby blue. A man in an old Cubs jacket wearing a flat green cap, seemed to look at Henry and nod.

A sudden explosion of music filled the stadium then—like the raging music of some epic film, and the Jumbotron began to play the pre-game montage of Cubs history. The first time Danny had seen that film in a pre-season team meeting, he had turned to Mickey and said, "We stole that idea from the White Sox."

Mickey had nodded and shrugged his shoulders. "It was a good idea," he said.

No one could say for certain why the first forty thousand fans to sit in the experience of the brand-new Jumbotron sat in staggered silence. It was possible that some of those thousands were witnessing technology they never thought would reach this storied place. Others, perhaps, were overwhelmed by the explosion of sight and sound, the aggregate glory of history and image and sound—full, orchestral sound—that raged, heroic and beautiful, beneath the flashing footage of what seemed to Danny like more than just the history of the Cubs, more than just the history of baseball, the footage seemed like the history of the world itself. It seemed possible, in fact, that all of history had led to this moment.

When Danny ascended the mound at Wrigley Field it seemed as though he had stepped into the music, had planted his feet inside the giant and pounding thrum of song.

Danny had viewed Patrick Decker's footage of every hitter he would face that day. He had listened to the scouting report on every

Reds player in the starting line-up and on the bench, and had listened closely to the pitching coach's report on the left-handed second baseman that stood at the plate. But when Danny looked into Terry Southworth's eyes, he did not try to recall any of this information, all of it was gone—the lefty who could pull the ball or beat the shift, the righty who never saw a pitch he couldn't go yard on, the curveball hitter, the gamer, the stealer, the contact hitter, the peeker, the guesser, the bunter, the free swinger, and the protector who Coop said would drive Danny crazy with foul balls—all of them were gone. There was only Southworth standing in the box. The umpire waiting for the first pitch. There was only Mickey, smiling behind his mask at the plate, signaling a fastball high and tight.

Mickey was thinking *book*. Pitch Southworth by the book. The hitter in the one-hole had two responsibilities. First, get on base; second; look at as many pitches as he could. Give the team a few pitches to see.

Throwing right handed, Danny gave him a fastball high and inside, and from the look on Mickey's face it was closer to the plate than he wanted it; a hittable pitch for Southworth at any other time in the game, but he took it for strike one.

Next, Wells signaled a fastball low and away, and Danny shook him until he called for another high and in, and Danny gave it to him. It whistled in just below the first location and caught Southworth looking for something else. By the time he finally swung, the ball seemed to have already slapped into Mickey's glove, and Southworth was looking at an oh-and-two count.

Danny thought Mickey might call for a change-up or a breaking ball, but he called for another fastball, low and away. Danny didn't shake him this time, but he signaled a change in location, and threw another fastball high and in, off the plate this time and still lower than the first two. Southworth flailed away too late and shook his head. When Mickey had the ball in his glove he waved it at Danny, a pat on the back from sixty feet away.

If Mickey hadn't figured out what Danny was doing by the time Southworth was in the dugout, by the time the next batter was looking at an oh-and-two count after two fastballs inside, Mickey's smile seemed to indicate that he had figured out what Danny was doing: pitch by pitch, he was establishing the strike zone, finding the perimeter.

The strike zone was seven balls wide and ten balls high, and without regard for batter and tendency Danny was giving shape to the rectangle, each pitch informing the umpire that Danny could hit the edges whenever he wanted.

Two pitches later and the number-two hitter was watching his pop fly fall into the third baseman's glove.

After thirteen pitches and three straight outs, Mickey waited for Danny on the third base line and put the ball, which had yet be hit into fair territory by a Cincinnati bat, into Danny's hand.

"You still got balls," he said, and Danny laughed.

Danny found the low corners with his curve ball and change-up, setting them up with fastballs, high and in, through eight innings. He had batters looking at balls that bulleted into the middle of the box and batters whiffing at balls that dropped a full foot out of the strike zone.

Three Reds made hard contact with Granville fastballs in the top of the eighth: a hard grounder to second, a blast to the warning track, and a line shot to short. At the end of the inning Bennett put his hand on Danny's shoulder when he entered the dugout.

"Listen, Danny," he said. "I'm gonna throw Hucker at 'em for the last inning. Nothing personal, kid. That's a handsome outing," Bennett said. "Eight strong. Better than I hoped for. But they're starting to hit you hard, and I'm not gonna let you take a loss here. Norton will get you the win."

Coach Sharp picked up the dugout phone and sent a call to the bullpen. Jack Ryan sat on the riser of the bench and chewed a sunflower seed. Shook his head.

"Fuck," Mickey said. He threw his glove against the wall and knocked three bats to the ground.

No one booed when Hucker Norton started warming up in the bullpen. Not yet. The Cubs still had a 2-1 lead, and Danny had a one-hitter going. The heart of the order was batting in the top of the ninth. Perhaps the most optimistic fans in the stadium hoped that Norton was throwing just to throw. Just to stay in shape.

No one booed until the third out of the Reds' half of that quiet inning when Hucker Norton threw his last bullpen pitch and began his trot to the pitcher's mound.

Then came the boos. They came with the memory of Hucker's struggles through the last two weeks of the preseason. They came with the memory of Hucker blowing save opportunities in two of their Danny's pre-season games. And once again Bennett was sending out Hucker Norton, thief of hope, breaker of hearts, who, in the cynic's eyes, had done his best to dash hope at the end of the pre-season, and would do his best to take a win away from their two-armed hero in his major league debut.

When the boos came they came with thunder and bass. They fell like violence, like cannon blasts in an echoing place. Danny put his hands to his ears, and walked into the clubhouse hallway to get away from the sound, but he could not. In the clubhouse, the boos thundered like the rumble of beer kegs on the concourse above him.

There was nowhere for Danny Granville to go to escape the hateful sound, not until eight warm-up throws and two pitches later, when the final violent boo was drowned out by the summative sigh of the city, by the collective fracture of forty thousand hearts.

In the clubhouse after the game, Mickey Wells kept the press from Danny. Bennett held his conference in the press room and said all the right things. He could not have asked for anything more from Granville. Yes, it was exciting. Yes, he was aware that the fans felt Granville was the most exciting thing to come to the Cubs in God knows how long. But let's not get ahead of ourselves, yet, he said. And let's not throw in the towel on Hucker Norton yet, either, folks. He's only two years removed from a twenty-win season. He threw two pitches today, people, and we ain't ready to send him to Iowa because of two lousy pitches. Let's focus today on an nineteen-year-old kid who had one helluva major league baseball game.

Just then, a nineteen-year-old kid, freshly showered and ready to pick up his girlfriend from her lakeside condo on Division Street and drive her to Forest Park for a steak dinner with his mother and father at the Golden Steer, walked back into the dugout where one man remained, sitting on the riser of the dugout bench amid the gloom and spit, amid the shells and crushed Gatorade cups.

Danny walked the narrow dugout to Hucker and sat on the bench next to him, allowing minutes to pass in silence.

Danny picked Hucker's glove up from the dugout cement, and handed it to him.

"Let's get out of here," Danny said, and Hucker looked up at Danny without taking the glove.

"Why did you come out here?" he said.

"Just to tell you it's April," Danny said. "It's only April."

Behind Danny, fourteen others remained in the stadium. One man sat in the right field stands wearing a retro Cubs jacket, binoculars strung at his neck, a kelly green cap on his head; one cleared the shells of sunflower seeds from the dugout cement on the visitor's side; and twelve others spread out along the concourse like hours of time, sweeping away the detritus of a city with conditions to its love.

At the Oak Park station, Michael Finnegan bought a *Sun-Times* and skimmed the headline accounts of Danny's debut as the train pulled up to swallow the earliest of Oak Park commuters and carry them on its rail-screeching back into the city.

NORTON BLOWS GRANVILLE DEBUT

HUCKER NORTON, ALMOST A CURSE

TIME TO GO, NORTON (TAKE BENNETT WITH YOU)

Every article was an opportunity to trash Hucker Norton. Nothing more. No writer had taken a shot at anything but the easy story: how Hucker had single-handedly diminished the hopes of a city.

The Cubs had given him a shot—a two-year deal after a bad year with the Mets—had crossed their fingers on the chance that there was something left in that long body. But after four straight bad starts for the Cubs the year before, after he consistently fell apart after two or three innings, they transitioned him into the bullpen. The shorter outings allowed him to return to a version of his former self; through the rest of the year he converted thirty-five of thirty-six save opportunities, so they signed him for three more.

And now, every writer was a mouthpiece for the fickle fans of the Cubs: it was time for Hucker to go. The angle had even crossed Finnegan's mind. He might have gone with it, too, if he were less sensible; but clearly the story—the *stories*—belonged to Danny Granville.

The story, first, of his nearly brilliant debut, which every other writer glossed over or neglected it completely. They had ignored the *music* of the story. Had they even watched the game? Had they witnessed what Finnegan had witnessed? What about the energy in that crowd? What about the wave? Fifteen revolutions around the stadium. Michael Finnegan had championed the fight against the wave for as long as he could remember, disparaging wavers, calling them mindless drones in his fight against idiocy. And there he stood after its seventh lap around the stadium, tentative at first, and then yielding to the fullness of it, yielding to the pull of it.

Finnegan was *there*. Instead of sitting in the press seats he had convinced his editor at the *Oak Leaves* to secure, he sat in the stands where he could see Doc Granville without being detected. He had seen the pride in Doc's face when Danny had looked his way, had seen Danny walk across the field under the arm of Mickey Wells, had seen Mickey Wells, busting Danny's balls by making him look at himself on the Jumbotron, had watched Danny stand like a soldier with his cap at his heart, had seen his lips move to the words of the "Star-Spangled Banner," had even seen Granville's eyes go soft at the song. Michael Finnegan *was fucking there*.

He had tracked every pitch, had joined in with the crowd at their cheers for "Da-*nee*! Da-*nee*! Da-*nee*!" Had come together with the cast of thousands as they booed Trey Bennett's decision to replace Granville with Hucker Norton. Hucker, big as a fucking barn—and now that Danny Granville was here—the only thing standing between the Cubs and a World fucking Series.

Finnegan *was there*. He had watched Hucker walk to the mound that day to save Danny's major league debut, a one-hit shut-out in the top of the eighth. He'd seen Hucker walk to the mound and pick up the ball and look around at the crowd and he watched him bury his face in his glove as though he were screaming *fuck you* to the booing stadium. He watched Hucker climb the mound with his leggy fuck-you swagger.

When Hucker started warming up on the mound Finnegan circled the stadium to get a better view into the Cubs dugout. Through his binocular sights he had seen Danny Granville sitting on the bench with his hands over his ears, as though the terrible arrows of sound that had been targeted at Norton had pierced Granville instead.

And though it killed him to do it Finnegan recorded every nerve-wracking warm-up pitch of Hucker Norton's, too. He made dramatic note of every significant detail and the touches of a writer's flourish as well: the thousands of fingernail bits that fell to the stadium concrete in and among the peanut shells and cardboard trays and Cracker Jacks and hotdog wrappers as Hucker Norton, with his tongue stuck out at the whole fucking city, threw his eight warm-up pitches into Mickey Wells' glove like *let's get this thing over with*.

Finnegan recorded Hucker's game-time pitches as well. Not so tall an order as there were only two of them. Two fucking pitches it took Norton to screw up a near-perfect debut; one roped into left for a pinch-hit double and one crushed onto Waveland Avenue by the unlikeliest of heroes: five-foot-seven-inch Cash Rogan who had hit only two other homeruns in his first six years in the majors.

And that was merely the story of the game. Beneath it was another. Finnegan stayed in his seat at the end of the game. There was a stillness to Hucker as he left the mound after his second pitch. He did not throw his glove against the wall and stomp into the clubhouse as Finnegan expected he might. As his teammates' shoulders dropped in their gloomy parade back to the locker room, Hucker walked into the dugout and sat on the bench as the remaining players passed him without a word.

Finnegan stayed in his seat and watched Hucker until every other ticket holder in attendance had long been gone. Finnegan stayed long enough to watch Danny Granville enter the dugout from the shadowy frame of the clubhouse hallway. Finnegan watched Danny Granville sit next to Hucker on the bench. Through his binocular sights it seemed as though Granville sat in his presence like a father. No, like a grandfather.

No one else had the sense of story that Finnegan had. What the fans wanted to know were the stories underneath that story. How long had Danny held his hands to his ears to block sound? What did Hucker think about all those cheers for a rookie? For a fucking *rookie?* A boy, for chrissakes, who hadn't proved a fucking thing. And what was going on in the dugout?

And still, there was more to the story. The real story—the one beneath them all—was how Danny Granville got to the big leagues in the first place. In the hundreds of articles Finnegan had read about Danny, no writer had gone to the source for that story. That would be Finnegan's story.

Finnegan would write his articles. That's what he would do. He would write of Danny walking across left field, and he would wonder with the rest of the world what it felt like to walk across that field. He would wonder with the rest of the world if Danny Granville felt the spirit of the ghosts of baseball, the Ruths and Robinsons and Gehrigs and DiMaggios who had walked those very steps.

He would write other articles, too. One for every game. There was another debut in his left arm. There was another story. He would publish them in the *Oak Leaves* and he would submit them to other papers as well. He would submit them to magazines, to *The Sporting News*, to the *Sun-Times*, and the *Daily Herald,* to the *Tribune Magazine*, and if they didn't get published he would continue to write them just the same. He would record every pitch of Danny's rookie year. Every ball, every strike, every pitch-out move to first, every leg kick and release, every ball and strike. He would note each grimace or smile Danny grimaced or smiled. He would watch every minute of Danny's appearances this year. He would go to every home game he could. He would write off everything as a business expense. He would tape the televised away games.

He would watch Danny like the mother of young child—closer, even; for a mother sometimes turned away from a child and in a moment a boy could go for miles. He would watch Danny as closely as the mother of a newborn—closer, for even a mother could tire, a mother could close her eyes a moment, and in a moment a newborn child could fall. He would watch Danny closer than that.

Twenty-third

HENRY HAD PLANNED TO WATCH DANNY'S NEXT GAME, A LEFT-handed start against the Milwaukee Brewers, from his usual stool at the bend of Kevil's bar on Circle and Marengo; Kevil had promised to reserve it for Henry whenever the Cubs played away. But when Henry came home after the school day at U-High, Bridget and Lori had homemade pizza baking in the oven and were waiting in the living room for the game to begin.

When Danny came to bat in the top of the third, Henry looked at Bridget to his left and Lori to his right and each of them reached for his hand and smiled nervously. He looked at the TV screen and closed his eyes, until a wash of blue cheers filtered through the speaker and into the living room. Henry opened his eyes and smiled while Danny rounded first base and reached second on a stand-up double. Lori jumped from the couch and screamed. She pulled Bridget to her feet and they danced around the couch, laughing.

At the start of the fourth inning, Bridget tapped Henry's shoulder and pointed at the lower left corner of the giant screen.

"That's da Vinci's *Vitruvian Man*," she said.

Fox Sports had created an animated graphic of da Vinci's sketch. They had replaced da Vinci's classic overlapping figures with two mirror images of Danny wearing baseball gloves on opposite hands. Simultaneously, the left-hander, in a pin-striped jersey and the right-hander wearing Cubby blue, stepped out of da Vinci's famous circled square, jogged to opposite ends of the television screen and threw fastballs to each other.

"Smart graphic," Bridget said as the two Danny Granvilles returned to da Vinci's sketch and the image vanished with the poof of a bursting cartoon cloud. "When I come over to paint with Lori on Sunday," she continued, "I'll have to remember to show you some sketches."

Henry smiled at Kevil after seeing the index card reserving his seat near the waitresses' station. Kevil, on the telephone at the other end of the bar, winked and gestured for Henry to help himself to a beer. Henry took off his jacket and spread it over his stool. He might have forgotten the envelope were it not for the muffled sound of rustling paper in his jacket. He pulled it from the inside pocket and set it on the bar. Henry selected a glass from a shelf behind the bar with exaggerated care, all for the sake of entertaining Kevil, whom Henry felt watching and smiling. He lifted it to the light in a dramatic gesture of inspection while Kevil laughed silently into the telephone. Henry poured Killian's Red into his pint glass from the still parade of knobbed options on tap, filled it to the lip of the mug and walked as though the floor were a tightrope beneath him.

When he returned to his stool, Henry flinched at the sight of the envelope, still waiting, like a surprise. A spill of ale edged over his glass and onto his finger.

The envelope. Henry clicked the edge of it against the bar and sipped his beer. The clock over his shoulder. Ten minutes fast. Seven-twelve. Henry leaned toward the counter to check for wetness in the glare of light off the bar. He set the envelope down. Brushed his fingers over it, unfolded its contents: two sheets of paper, and turned them face down on the bar, absently flattening the creases.

Bridget had handed him the sketches the day before. She told him she had forgotten about them until the game against the Brewers when the graphic of the *Vitruvian Man* reminded her.

The first sheet was sketched from the front and the second from behind. Measurements were scattered at dozens of points above, below, and along the sides of each sketch, with lines connecting points along Danny's body to their corresponding measurements.

"I thought you'd be interested in these," she had said to Henry. "Not the sketches so much, but the measurements."

She let Henry look at them for a moment before she spoke again. "They're exactly the same."

"Isn't that something?" he said.

"I think it's more than *something*," Bridget said. "Don't you think?"

Henry shrugged.

"I mean, my method wasn't scientific or anything," Bridget said. "I only used a tailor's tape, but you can see there isn't the slightest deviation from one side to the other."

Henry's heart raced, but he only nodded.

"I've seen a lot of bodies as an art student, Henry. Hundreds probably. We're lopsided messes," she said. "All of us."

She raised her eyebrows and held her hand before her, fingers spread and curled as though she were expecting Henry to hand her something for the discovery she made. As though she were expecting something more from him than a sound from his throat and a slow nod of his head.

"May I keep these?"

"They're copies," Bridget said. "I made them for you."

On his barstool at Kevil's, Henry shook his head and quick-breathed through his nostrils. He felt a pinch of guilt as he recalled his display of indifference when Bridget revealed the sketches to him. In a weaker moment he might have giggled with the pure pleasure at the sketches, at the perfect symmetry she had recorded.

Henry had considered measuring Danny countless times in this exact way, though he would never have done it himself. The thought of it alone—the mathematics of it, impersonal and scientific—struck him as a kind of infidelity, a breach of parental trust. He felt, in fact, that if he were ever capable of measuring the limbs of his own son, there might be nothing to keep him from countless and greater infidelities.

So when Bridget showed him the sketches he felt at once the push and pull of them, felt the scientific delight that came with the proximity of proof, and felt the guilt of that delight as well. And as much as he liked Bridget and was certain of her goodness in all of their lives, he had never shared the details of the symmetry crusade with anyone, and now, barely one week into Danny's major league career, Bridget had put numbers to his campaign, and in those numbers Henry felt ill equipped to keep the watery secret from slipping through his hands.

And even now, some eighteen years after the idea of the campaign had first occurred to him, he protected the secret. Even now, for as Kevil returned the telephone to its cradle and began to walk toward him, Henry felt the pinprick breach of the sketches. He refolded the sheets of paper, returned them to the envelope and slipped them under his thigh.

Two days later, pitching right-handed against the Houston Astros, Danny won his second game at Wrigley Field. His eighty-pitch limit took him into the ninth inning, which allowed Hucker Norton a reprieve from being booed into the game. Shin Taguchi pitched to two batters to earn the save.

Danny was not so lucky in the game that opened the series against Cincinnati. Though he had a 6-2 lead going into the sixth inning against the Reds, he had already thrown seventy-five pitches and couldn't protect Hucker from the fickle heart of the fans. Taguchi held the Reds for two more innings, but Hucker entered the game in the top of the ninth and had nothing in his arm with which to argue against the disapproving crowd. He loaded the bases and walked in two runs before giving up a three-run triple and blowing the save that would have earned Danny his third win.

In the opening game of the home series against San Diego, three days later, Hucker failed to earn another save for Danny, and the boos of the crowd carried over into the sports pages of the newspapers and across the airwaves of sports radio.

Columnists and radio personalities argued infinitely about how Trey Bennett should manage the Cubs.

He should let Danny pinch-hit at least once a game; his batting average was better than any of the position players.

He should play Danny at second or short field when he wasn't pitching.

The *Sporting News* said that Danny should be the designated hitter in interleague games. Other writers said he should be pitching every two days instead of three.

They questioned Danny's self-imposed pitch limit. A caller on the Score Sports Radio called him a *wuss*.

"He's just like the rest of the organization," the caller said. "He's soft. Eighty pitches? My kid throws more than that in Little League games."

Another caller said he thought the pitch limit was a good idea, but speculated that if Danny limited himself to fifty pitches, maybe he would be able to start every game of the year.

Another said they should start shaping Danny for middle relief.

They all said to get rid of Hucker.

On the off day that followed the San Diego series Danny spent the morning watching video of Hucker Norton's delivery. In the afternoon at her lakeside condo, Danny took Polaroid snapshots of Bridget to take with him on the road. In one, she stood on a chair at the kitchen window looking out at a square of blue lake the size of a sugar cube. In another, she sat at her kitchen table in the soft light from the periphery of the sun. In several others she lay on the sofa in the main room— three of them looking away from the camera, at the wall, or at the ceiling fan above her. When Danny asked her to look at him, she looked at him, it seemed, as though no one else mattered in the world. He finished the film on this look, and after he pulled the spent package from the camera and spread the developing images on her kitchen table, he returned to Bridget at the couch. She was lying on her stomach naked from the waist up, waiting for Danny to show her that it was true: that there was no else in the world.

In Atlanta, before the first game of the Braves series, Danny sat in a padded folding chair in the visitor's bullpen next to Phil Sharp, the

Cubs pitching coach. They leaned the backs of the chair against the wall and watched Hucker warm up. A sound lodged in Sharp's throat as he watched Hucker throw a wild pitch over the bullpen catcher's head and into the stands. Three boys with gloved hands chased the errant throw.

"Fuck," Sharp mumbled.

Hucker kicked the padded wall behind him.

"I think it's his grip," Danny said to Sharp.

"It ain't his grip," Sharp said. "His grip is fine."

"His fingers are fine," Danny said. "But his grip might be too tight."

Sharp settled the legs of his chair in the dirt against the wall and looked back at Danny.

"He's trying too hard," Danny said. "His knuckles are white before his release point," Danny added. "I was looking at some video pretty close."

"Did you tell him?" Sharp said.

"He doesn't want to hear it from me," Danny said, and Sharp nodded as Danny walked to the cages to take batting practice.

Over the stretch of games that took the Cubs through their next four series, Hucker began to return to the form he had known in better days, helping Danny to a 6-0 record by April's end, and renewing the hopes of Chicago by helping the Cubs to a 17-9 record and the top spot in the National League Central.

In a game against San Diego, Danny went three for three with a walk-off homerun, and in a single game against St. Louis, he hit two homeruns and shut out the Cardinals in his third complete game.

Before the first game of May, against the Pirates in Pittsburgh, Ty Wilhelm began a game of long toss with Danny. Next to them, Black Jack Daley and Mickey Wells began a game of long toss as well. Wilhelm pointed to a section of fans behind Danny.

"Check it out," Wilhelm said.

When Danny turned around to look behind him, the group of fans turned their backs to show him his last name on each of their jerseys. A dozen *Granvilles* arcing over the number twenty-two.

"Everything changes now," Wilhelm said.

"Brace yourself, Danny Boy," Daley said. "No more quiet dinners with your girl."

"No more movies," Wilhelm said.

"No more running to the grocery store for eggs and milk," Daley said.

"No more nothing," Wilhelm said. "Maybe at an away game you'll go out for a beer and no one will recognize you, but don't count on it."

Mickey laughed.

"Don't laugh, Mick," Daley said. "It goes for you, too."

Mickey winked at Danny. "Bring it on," Mickey said. "Bring it on."

It began slowly. For a while it seemed there was hardly a soul who recognized Danny when he was out of his uniform. On his way to Bridget's lakeside condo after a game in May, a group of women on Division Street squinted and pointed and wondered before waving at him. There were double takes in restaurants and bookstores, and while he was with Bridget at the art store once, an elderly man shopping for a portfolio with his granddaughter asked him for his autograph.

At games, he sometimes signed two at the same time, one with his left hand and one with his right. He watched how other players handled the celebrity. Ty Wilhelm signed a few autographs before games, never after. During that first week in May, while Danny and Mickey Wells sat in a booth across from Wilhelm and Molina at Rosebud on Taylor Street, a boy and his father came to their table during dinner and asked for autographs.

"I'm sorry," Wilhelm said to the father, "I don't let these guys sign while we're eating."

Wilhelm never looked at the boy. He shrugged his shoulders and looked at the father. "My policy," he said.

At a game in Atlanta, Jack Daley told Danny he only signed one autograph per game when the team was visiting another field.

"I pick out a hot chick wearing Cubs shit," he said. "If she ain't hot and she ain't wearing Cubs shit I don't sign nothing."

When Danny and Chick Molina signed autographs next to each other on Kids' Day at Wrigley, Chick never looked up at a fan. Danny asked him afterward why he didn't look at the fans.

Molina shook his head. "I never look 'em in the eye. You can't," he said. "If you look them in the eye you'll never stop signing." He told Granville about a game during his first spring training in the majors. He signed autographs for forty-five minutes while he talked with a reporter from the *Sporting News* and he had to rejoin the team while there was still a line of people waiting for autographs.

"Some dad grabs my arm and says, 'What? You can't sign one more autograph for my kid?' And behind that kid there's a whole line of kids with their dads, so I tell the guy I'm sorry, I gotta go, and the guy, right in front of his kid and this whole line, calls me a fucking jagoff."

Molina shook his head. "Forty-five minutes I stood there. Now I'm a fucking jagoff."

The articles began in May: speculations about a World Series for the Cubs. Nothing seemed to be missing, they said. The Cubs had starting pitching, a bullpen, five position players with batting averages hovering at .300, and possibly the best hitter on the team was a switch-pitching starter who had just won his ninth straight game.

At home, in Forest Park, nothing seemed to have changed. They had always known him there. Before the rest of the world had ever heard of Danny Granville, they had known him there. In Forest Park it felt as though he belonged, that his wins were nice, were something to talk about, but they weren't everything. At home they would wave hello and come to his booth at Louie's Grill and sit for a moment whether he'd won or lost a game. Nothing had changed at home. On off days, and even after home games now and then, he filled in for

Patrick Decker who still umpired Little League games. Bridget would order pizzas for the teams afterward, and sometimes Danny would get on the mound and throw batting practice to the boys after the games. Nothing had changed at home.

But everywhere else—in Chicago, on Division Street outside Bridget's condo, and even in the other cities the Cubs played— celebrity was an unreal fog; it felt as though he were breathing through a blanket in the summertime. Outside the ballparks, when the fans came up to him for autographs, it still felt as though they had mistaken him for someone else, as though they had no idea who they were approaching. When he signed his name he signed it with the fraudulence of a guilt-ridden forger.

No one else seemed to wrestle as much with it, with the irrational and overblown interest of others. Most other players seemed to thrive on it. Expect it. At every game Wilhelm and Molina looked for attractive women in the stands and then sent the bullpen security personnel to request phone numbers from them. Wilhelm ignored his policy against signing at restaurants if a pretty woman were involved.

And on the nights when the player curfew was lifted, nearly everyone seemed to dive into their celebrity as though it was this for which they had been working all along.

It was easier, Danny felt, on those days when the Cubs lost, or on those days Danny left the mound without getting the win. He could deal with those days. He could look into the eyes of his fans on those days, because less seemed to separate him from them. Any man on the street could lose a major league ball game, he thought.

But the easier it was for the Cubs to overcome their obstacles on the field, the tougher it was for Danny deal with his celebrity off the field.

On his twentieth birthday he threw a seventy-eight-pitch no-hitter against the New York Mets. On the mound, it felt like he hadn't wasted a single pitch, hadn't thrown a single baseball outside of its precise and intended path, and even the fans at Shea Stadium seemed to pull for Danny once he made it to the seventh inning without giving up a hit.

After the game, Danny wished he could stay in the clubhouse with the team. He was aware of the lock of his eyes on the ground as he left the stadium. It was more than not wanting to lift his eyes. He wasn't certain it was even possible.

He stayed in his hotel room after the game. He didn't want another night of looking up in any direction and finding their eyes on him. The women who stared at him from across a room, and smiled when he looked up. Thirty minutes later when he looked up again, they would be there still. And the men, too, who looked at him with envy or hatred or whatever it was. It didn't matter.

It was after that no-hitter that Danny felt things begin to change. He stopped going out with his teammates after away games; he had food delivered to his room. After day games he spent the evenings drawing and painting. Before night games he did the same, sending his artwork ahead to meet him in the next town. Wherever he was, he called his mother at eleven o'clock every Sunday night.

Three days later, after winning his eleventh game in a row without a loss, Danny drove to Bridget's condo on Division Street to take her out to Forest Park for dinner at Caffe de Lucca. He called her from the lobby on his cell phone and by the time she appeared in the lobby elevator, they had to fight through a crowd of fans to reach Division Street. In the car, Bridget rested her elbow at the base of the window and sighed heavily into her hand.

"I'm sorry," Danny said.

"It's not your fault," Bridget said. "It's just—"

"What?" Danny said.

"Nothing," Bridget said, and Danny pulled onto Cannon Drive.

"Sometimes it feels like I'm living someone else's life," she said.

Danny said nothing until he merged into traffic on Lake Shore Drive.

"I know," Danny said.

"I'm not even sure what I mean," Bridget said. "But that's how it feels."

"I'm sorry," Danny said.

Bridget reached toward Danny and traced her fingernails in circles across his shoulders.

Danny was 13-0 at the end of May, and by June 11th, the first off day for the Cubs after seventeen straight games, he was 16-0. That morning, after Bridget left for a summer class she was teaching at the Art Institute, Danny pulled his car into a parking garage on Waubansia Street in Bucktown and drove in a descending spiral two floors below the sidewalk before parking next to a red Mercedes. A tiny woman stepped out of the Mercedes as Danny opened his own door to meet her.

"Hello, Mr. Granville," she said. "Missy Skyler."

"Danny," Danny said.

"Missy," she said. "I should tell you that my son is never going to believe this."

The woman clicked the stiletto heels of her tiny shoes onto the elevator floor and keyed open the door. Inside, she inserted another key in the locked button at the top of a brass panel. She turned it to the left and the button lit up. She looked at Danny.

"Private entrance through a parking garage," the woman said. "Is it private enough?"

"So far so good." Danny said.

The elevator door opened up into the penthouse loft, which seemed as long as a city block.

Through seven windows along the eastern wall the sun painted quadrangles of light on the hardwood slats of the floor. On the western wall, seven more windows stood like soldiers waiting to fulfill their own promise of sun.

Missy Skyler's voice, trebled and insistent, was spilling numbers —lengths, widths, and heights—into the empty air of the loft entrance. As Danny walked to the afternoon windows, the woman's tinkling words faded into the great expanse.

Danny thought of Bridget. He saw her silhouette in the morning sun on the east wall, saw her standing at an easel in the afternoon, saw her sundressed and smiling, saw her laughing and singing and floating, dancing to Tony Bennett CDs in the muted evening light of the Damen Avenue street lamps. He could see her filling the space of the giant loft with life.

In the kitchen, Danny followed Missy Skyler from the refrigerator to the oven to the sink. From the north wall Danny could not hear her voice as she gestured at the appliances, the ceiling fan, the cabinets. When Missy Skyler pulled out of the garage in her red Mercedes, she had his earnest money in her shiny black purse.

All along, his intention was to tell Bridget about the loft. He would buy a bed first, and linens. A washer and dryer. Then he would tell her. During the Seattle series he would have Patrick make a call to Steppenwolf—or Victory Gardens, or the Looking Glass—to see if they would sell him some old theatre flats to partition the bedroom from the rest of the loft, and then he would tell her. He would set a studio up along the west windows for Bridget. And then he would tell her. During the San Diego series he would paint that portrait of her standing on her kitchen chair at the lakeside condo, would hang it in the studio between two of the afternoon windows, and then he would tell her. While the Cubs were in Texas he would have Patrick fill the pantry, buy a broom and dustpan, a mop and bucket. When they came back to Chicago for that series against the White Sox, he would go to Marshall Field's—Macy's now—for kitchen things, would hang excellent pots and pans from the wrought iron rectangle suspended from the kitchen ceiling, and then he would tell her. On the day off after the Rockies' series he would buy a sofa and a rug and set them right in the middle of the loft, plug a television—nothing too big—into the outlet on the center pillar. He would finish the painting of her sitting in the lakeside kitchen and then he would tell her. He would buy a dining room table and chairs; he would make spaghetti with meat sauce after the set against the Brewers; he would call his mother and get her recipe for bread, buy candles and wine, he would give Bridget the address, would meet her on the corner downstairs, and then he would tell her.

But there was nowhere else to be alone as the winning continued. With the onset of June, the *Chicago Tribune* had begun reserving its front-page headlines after Danny's starts on the mound, to print nothing other than 14-0 or 15-0 or 16-0, to note his improving record in bold font, as though in the wide world of news there was nothing of greater import than the Cubs and Danny Granville. After every game the streets of Wrigleyville were packed as thick as parades until the bars closed.

And as the winning continued, as the din of the crowds spiraled toward deafening heights, and as the vortex of his celebrity began to worry at the edges of Bridget's life, too, Danny pulled slowly away from the lakeside condo. He met Bridget at his parents' house in Forest Park when the Cubs were in town for a series, or they met at a Little League game in the park and spent the night together in her old apartment above the Granvilles' flat, and soon the secret of the Damen loft was a harder thing to give away than to keep.

And so he kept it. He kept it from Bridget, and from his parents, too. He kept it from Mickey Wells. Kept it from everyone but Patrick, who stocked it with food and supplies. The loft was Danny's haven. His Chicago sanctuary. He felt its comforting stillness the moment his front tires turned into the parking garage. He painted portraits of Bridget and hung them in the spaces between windows. He drew sketches of her in poses she had never held for him. And soon his walls were filled with images of her.

Twenty-fourth

BY THE TIME THE LATEST CROP OF SENIORS HAD GRADUATED FROM U-High, life had begun to change for Henry as well. When he climbed the stage of the assembly hall to distribute the science awards and to say farewell to a retiring colleague, two thousand people attending the graduation gave him a standing ovation for having a son named Danny Granville.

Even Kevil's Bar felt the pull of Danny's fame. As the news spread that Henry Granville watched road games from the stool next to the waitress station, fans from Oak Park, River Forest, and Forest Park packed Kevil's whether Danny was on the mound or not. And when he was, they looked to Henry when Danny baffled hitters, one after another. They looked to Henry to see him smile, to the see the gentle and subtle pump of his fist after a curveball buckled a grown man's knees. They looked to Henry after Danny dished a batter the last pitch he'd expected to see. They looked to Henry to get as close as they could to whatever it was a man felt when his son was Danny Granville.

Between commercials they shook Henry's hand. They told him their uncles played baseball with him back in the seventies. They told him he taught their cousins at U-High and went to college with their aunts. They told him they saw Danny hit four homeruns in a Little League game. They told him they saw Danny hitting balls in the cages at Stella's once and they bought him slugs just to see him hit. They told him they would have paid a hundred bucks to see him play a tee ball game when he was four years old.

On weekends, Lori went with Henry to Kevil's to watch the away games. They sat in a booth then and ate dinner like local celebrities. It was enough for Lori to eat and drink among friends, and to see her son on the television in every corner of the bar.

Lori was not with Henry, though, on a Monday in June, where from his seat at the bend of Kevil's bar he watched Danny win his twenty-second straight start, a fifty-seven-pitch complete-game one hitter against the Washington Nationals. The first pitch was thrown at 1:05 P.M. and by 2:15 the game was over.

Kevil's wasn't crowded to begin with, for the afternoon game, and by 2:45 the bar was nearly empty. And it was then that Kevil brought Henry a pint of Killian's Red.

"What are you doing to me?" Henry said. "I've had my two."

"The man insisted," Kevil said, nodding his head toward the booth against the wall. "And he tipped me generously."

Henry looked in the booth at a man in a Kelly-green cap.

"Says his name's Finnegan," Kevil said. "Italian kid," he joked.

Henry smiled, and raising his glass to the man, bowed his head.

Finnegan walked to the bar.

Henry thought it might have been one of Danny's old friends at first—something familiar in his face. But this guy was older. Mid-thirties maybe.

Henry nodded.

"Your son is having quite a year, Doc."

Henry might not have turned his head to engage the stranger more completely, but it was the "Doc" that threw him, turned his eyes toward the man again. Something familiar.

"Do I know you?" Henry said.

"Michael Finnegan," the man said. "Alumnus of University High. I took your class my senior year. The Social Lives of Animals."

"Ah," Henry said.

"Mind if I join you?" Finnegan said.

Henry opened his hands away from his fresh pint of beer as if to say it didn't matter one way or the other, and Finnegan sat at the bar.

"What are you doing in town, Mr. Finnegan?"

"Been out here for a couple of years now, Doc. I'm working in the city and watching baseball whenever I can."

They drank in silence for a while, as the lips of ESPN commentators moved silently on the television that hung from the corner of the room.

"Are you still at U-High, Doc?"

"Still there," Henry said.

"I think about that class of yours quite a bit," Finnegan said.

"Why?"

"Mostly this idea you covered about sexual selection," Finnegan said. "The whole notion of what females of a species look for in the male. I still find that remarkable."

"Not married, yet, huh?" Henry asked.

Finnegan laughed.

"No, Doc. Not yet."

Henry nodded. For an instant, he had Finnegan placed solidly in a classroom. In the cast of thousands of former students there were alums he ran into now and then who could trigger exact seating arrangements, and Henry would point to them and say, "Nineteen ninety-two," and they would nod their heads, and for an instant he placed Finnegan in a certain classroom, but then it was gone.

"Anyway, I loved your class. I actually considered going into science for a while there, but ended up an English lit and journalism major. After school I bounced around a bunch of jobs for a while before I started working at the Commodities Exchange downtown. And I'm sure it sounds crazy but I've been there like six years now—longer than I care to remember—and not a day goes by without me thinking about all this animal behavior stuff from your class, and how animals evolve and sometimes it seems like it's all related in a way."

Henry nodded his head while Finnegan spoke. He sipped from his Killian's. Rolled the U-High alumnus's name in his head—*Finnegan, Finnegan*—until the flash of familiarity returned.

"Anyway, I knew you were living in Forest Park and a million times I thought how great it would be to pop in a bar and find you sitting at a stool with a space open next to you."

Henry lifted his glass for Finnegan to clink.

"Here's to animals," Henry said.

"Here's to animals," Finnegan said, and in a swallow, they each finished their beers. Henry ordered another round.

"This one's mine," he said.

Kevil knocked two pints on the polished wood in front of the men.

"Here's a little something for you that we probably didn't go over in class," Henry said. "Only because it wasn't out yet. We've known for some time that testosterone promotes aggression, right? Nobody would argue against that. That's the old view—cause and effect; higher levels of testosterone induce higher rates of aggression."

Henry looked at Finnegan.

"You with me, Finnegan?"

"I'm with you, Doc."

"Well, what you may not have known is that *successful* aggression appears to produce higher levels of testosterone. Researchers have gone to sports bars and have taken saliva samples from males watching big games," he said, "like the Superbowl or a Division Series. And lo and behold the males whose teams were winning had raging levels of testosterone compared to males whose teams were losing."

Finnegan shifted in his seat giddily.

"If you're wondering what kind of idiots allowed men in white coats to poke Q-tips in their mouths in the middle of Superbowl, I got nothing for you, Michael."

Finnegan laughed.

"But the point is this," Henry continued. "*Successful* aggression augments the testosterone secretion.

"So the old view of cause and effect is all well and good, right? You can draw an arrow pointing from A to B, but more and more, we're finding that you should draw an arrowhead on both ends of that line. A causes B, but a modulation in B will affect A. So this is an example of how vicarious winning and losing affects testosterone. The individual, responding reciprocally to signals from its own behavioral initiative, is inspired, bootstrapping its way to unusual success."

Henry looked at Finnegan here, certain that his interpretation of the reciprocal relationship between testosterone and successful aggression would be mind-blowing to anyone whose favorite class was the Social Life of Animals.

"Pretty sweet, huh, Finnegan?"

"Pretty sweet, Doc," Finnegan said, holding his glass up for another clink.

Henry obliged.

"It's nice to see you, Mr. Granville," Finnegan said.

"Please," Henry said. "You're like thirty years old. Call me Henry."

"I might just stick with Doc if that's okay," he said.

"Fair enough," Henry said.

And so it was not a surprise the next road game when Finnegan sat next to Henry at Kevil's. And even less so, the next. Finnegan often thought about the lioness of the Serengeti plains as he slowly and carefully came closer to the topic from which he never completely roamed. It was after several Killians into a fourteen-inning game, a nail-biter in which Danny would not figure as a pitcher that Finnegan finally approached the issue of Danny's ambidexterity.

"You know," Finnegan said, "I have a vague memory of you talking about your son that year I took your class—he must have been five years old or something back then, but I didn't think about it again until I read the *Sports Illustrated* baseball preview last spring."

Henry tilted his head toward the dozens of black and white wedding photographs from the forties and fifties that decorated the wall at the end of the bar. He nodded his head in bouncing smallnesses as though his former student was guiding him on a tour of the places he'd been. A baseball diamond. His backyard.

"Sometimes I find myself brushing my teeth or combing my hair lefty," Finnegan said, "and it's like impossible to will myself to do it for more than a few seconds."

Henry locked his eye, as he often did, on a smiling bride with a gap between her front teeth.

"Up against the difficulty of that, I guess I can't help but wonder at how incredible it is that Danny can throw like Tom Seaver with one arm and Sandy Koufax with the other."

Henry laughed, maintained his slight nod as though he were putting shape to some future certainty, and when Finnegan paused here, Henry looked at his former student. He wanted to see the kid's eyes. He'd studied animals all of his life, but the eyes of men and women were something different.

If this conversation had been happening in the classroom—if a student had approached him with a question in a tone as pure and sincere as Finnegan's—Henry would have suspected immediately that the kid had to be blowing smoke up his ass. Henry Granville had taken pride, even as a young teacher, in his ability to detect bullshit.

But who in the history of academia ever *returned*—ever came back to the teacher—but the student who was ready to learn? Was it so hard to believe that a former student had been attentive enough to see the human implications of evolution and development among animals? Henry had heard the stories of the trading pits at the Board of Trade or Options or wherever it was that Finnegan worked. Was it so hard to believe that a former student, even a punk, would have made some connection between the animals in question?

Kevil slid another pint of Killian's in front of Henry.

Henry had designed the course at the directive of his department chair at the time, in order to give left-brained students an accessible option for fulfilling a science credit requirement. Students laughed at the title as they filled out their course selection forms, as though they were working the system. Even Granville's colleagues in the science department thought it sounded like a blow-off course.

But maybe there had been students listening all along. Was it so hard to believe now—more than a dozen years later—that someone actually wanted to discuss what remained the single academic passion of his adult life: animal behavior?

Developmental biology was his thing. No matter what course he was teaching, he turned the subject to the beautiful mysteries of development. How much more there was yet to learn about what a genome was and what sorts of principles regulated its self-expression, and the countless critical issues of life on this planet and the point of all it. It was a lonely profession, really. Even his peers didn't seem to give a damn about the questions to which Henry had devoted his working life. What was he but a member of a very small club of widely dispersed humans who really got it?

And as he felt his head bobble slightly in a way that a former student might interpret as suggesting reflection, Henry thought that maybe Finnegan got it, too. Or that Finnegan was finally ready to get it. That he was making himself available to get it. Maybe this was Finnegan's window. Maybe Finnegan was the kid who came back five, ten, fifteen years down the road, to say thank you to the teacher who finally had a thing to say; to have a beer with his former teacher, who was really just a man after all these years.

And it was that rare teacher's joy—along with five Killian's Reds, the look in Finnegan's eyes, the certain beauty of developmental biology, and the life-giving pleasure of a secret's release, tumbled together in such a way that Henry was urged to share with Michael Finnegan —a man he had not seen since before he had become a man—what he felt was his greatest contribution to animal behavior: his own and only son. Danny Granville.

Without hesitation or apology, Granville began to unfold the history of the boy with two arms before Finnegan's nodding and smiling head.

He connected, for Finnegan, the identical histories of human dexterity and the history of hemispheric brain separation. He called it a psychological insult in the human brain, which caused a similar split in right and left sidedness.

"We," Henry say, "which is to say, we men of the western world, are stuck in the mud of the left hemisphere." Henry wiped the sweat of his pint glass with his thumb from bottom to top to let those words sink in.

"And here we flail, mostly with our right hands, to get out. It prevents us from being the fully human, creative thinkers that we can be."

He told Finnegan of the family trip to the Brown Cow when Danny surprised him with a perfect left-handed throw. They ordered two more pints of Killian's while Henry detailed the symmetry campaign for Finnegan.

"The driving question of my life, Finnegan," he said, "became the question of the possible intellectual and social outcomes of a lifelong crusade toward absolute bilateral dexterity."

And soon Danny was alternating left and right on his own, Henry told Finnegan. Excelling at every sport, even ones to which he had never been introduced.

Henry told Finnegan all he could recall of the symmetry crusade: the thousands of catches in the alley behind Lathrop, the hundreds of outings at the batting cages, their trip to the Rawlings factory, the six-fingered glove, the art lessons with Bridget in the apartment upstairs.

When Henry voiced her name, when the word *Bridget* reached the air between him and Finnegan, Henry remembered the sketches still pocketed in the jacket draped over his stool. He removed the envelope and handed it to Finnegan.

"Take a look at these, Finnegan," Henry said.

"Danny's girlfriend made these sketches," Henry said. "She's an art teacher; she measured him with a tailor's tape and do you know from one side to the other she couldn't find a single instance of asymmetry?"

Finnegan looked up again at Henry. Raised his eyebrows.

"Not a single one," Henry said. "Identical."

"How long has he known Bridget?" Finnegan said.

"He met her his freshman year," Henry said. "First day of school."

And it was then that Henry was reminded of the bus accident at Madison and Desplaines, and it was only then that Henry paused in his chronicle of Danny's perfect ambidexterity, that Henry felt the guilt, the betrayal, the infidelity, of having said too much.

"Excuse me, Mr. Finnegan," he said, and stood at his stool, taking a second to steady himself. He stepped carefully and deliberately to the bathroom then, under the weight of a beer-swelled bladder and a cheater's guilt.

At the urinal he looked at his wristwatch. He had spent three hours with Finnegan. Five thirty-three.

Through the entirety of the telling, Henry Granville ignored his gift for detecting bullshit. After his fifth Killian's he seemed to notice nothing—neither the appropriateness of Finnegan's gestures, nor his nods of agreement.

Too late now to reconsider his gift for detecting bullshit. Too late now to look at the bubbles of deceit which stuck in a lying man's throat. Too late to see that Finnegan's beer barely diminished in volume. Too late to see either the giddiness in Finnegan's eyes or the wild rush of adrenaline pumping behind the slim tape recorder in the pocket of Finnegan's shirt.

Too late even to notice that when he returned from the bathroom to say farewell to Finnegan, the envelope of sketches had been removed from the pocket of his jacket.

Twenty-fifth

IT WAS NOT SILENCE THAT FILLED THE VISITOR'S DUGOUT IN Pittsburgh; there was the click-clack of cleats, the spit and tap of sunflower seeds, there was the tap of Mickey Wells' baseball bat on the dugout cement, and there was the constant hum of the crowd muffled in the dugout like the endless and incoherent sounds of a midsummer forest. And there were voices, too: Phil Sharp was talking about a fishing hole, not more than twice as big as an on-deck circle, right next to a beaver dam in Missouri somewhere, and he couldn't wait until the all-star break so he could fill a cooler with beer and fish there for three days. Trey Bennett was laughing over something the batboy said. There were definitely voices. None of them were meant for Danny Granville, though. No one was speaking to him.

It was the eve of the all-star break, and five innings deep into a left-handed start against Pittsburgh, not a single Pirate had reached first base. His teammates, it was clear to Danny, were honoring the long-established custom of saying nothing about a perfect game as long as the potential for it existed.

When the Cubs took the bench in the top of the sixth in the still perfect game, every player took the same spot in the dugout as he had for the previous two innings. The trainer sat in the seat closest to the dugout with his right leg crossed over his left. Trey Bennett had his right leg raised on the top stair of the dugout. No one said a word to Danny for fear that his concentration would be lost.

When Mickey Wells selected his bat, though, and headed for the batter's box, Danny pulled him back in the dugout and addressed the players. Not one of them raised his eyes to Danny.

"There's no such thing as a perfect game," he said, and the

players looked at one another in disbelief. He said it again.

"There's no such thing as a perfect game," he said again.

"Shut up," Molina said, and everyone looked at Chick. "What the fuck are you doing, Danny?" he said.

"I'm trying to win a ball game," Danny said. "And everybody thinks they're doing me a favor by not talking to me, and all I'm saying is that as long as there's an umpire behind the plate, as long as there's a human being back there deciding what's a ball and what's a strike, there is no such thing as a perfect game."

"I gotta go hit," Mickey said, and he walked to the batter's box.

"Say it with me," Danny said to the players who remained on the bench, but there was silence.

"Say it with me," he said again. "There's no such thing as a perfect game."

"You a crazy fucker," Molina said, and he said it again. "You a crazy fucker."

Despite these words, though, Molina was the first of his teammates to say what seemed like the wrong thing to say in the midst of a perfect game.

"There no such thing as a perfect game, you crazy fucker," he said, and like a reluctant choir director he raised his arms to the huddled mass of blue uniforms behind him, and together they repeated the phrase as Molina had rearranged it.

"There no such thing as a perfect game, you crazy fucker," they said.

When Danny took the mound in the bottom of the seventh he threw only six pitches before the Cubs returned to the dugout to explode for five more runs. After seven additional pitches in the bottom of the eighth, the Cubs' bats were stilled in the top of the ninth, and Danny returned to the mound seven throws away from his eighty-pitch limit, and three outs away from a complete game, perfect in every mind but his own. But when he reached his eightieth pitch, one out short of a perfect game, he called Sharp to the mound.

"What's up?" his coach asked.

"I'm done," Danny said.

"You can't handle one more?"

"That's eighty," Danny said. "That's my limit."

"Okay," Sharp said. "You're twenty-three and oh, Danny, and we're barely half way into the season. You've earned the right to make that call."

Danny smiled and handed the ball to Sharp.

"Do me a favor," Danny said. "Give the ball to Hucker."

Sharp pointed to the visitors' bullpen where Hucker and Taguchi were warming up. Sharp placed the palm of his hand on his own head, raised it, and lowered it again, calling Hucker, the tall one, to the mound.

"Thanks," Danny said, and Sharp patted his ass.

Somewhere along the way, the crowd, it seemed, had turned its allegiance to the Cubs. There seemed a greater blue in the Pirate's stadium.

Danny stood at the dugout rail and waved the players to join him. He wished the crowd to Hucker's side, and then turned around and faced the fans along third base and lifted his hands to wish them to their feet. And they stood. They stood in the first row of the section behind the Cubs' dugout, and then the second. They ascended then like rising dominoes, and in a slow wave the fans began standing in the sections to the right and left of the dugout and then left and right the sections rose to their feet—a slow and silent, sacred wave—and by the time Hucker had settled his eyes on Mickey's glove, the crowd had come into Hucker's hands by way of Danny's.

From the rail, Danny signaled the pitches to Mickey Wells, and six throws later Danny was the first to run to the mound, the first to run into Hucker Norton's arms. He screamed over the cheering tens of thousands.

"That thing I said in the dugout today," Danny said, "about there being no such thing as a perfect game. Remember that?"

"Yeah," Hucker said.

"I didn't know what I was talking about," Danny said. "That was perfect, Huck."

Four days later, Danny was in Houston preparing for his role as the starting pitcher for the National League All-Stars at Minute Maid Park. Though the three days of events gathered more reporters and photographers in one place than Danny had ever thought possible, they spread themselves among the long roster of superstars so that Danny felt more at ease than he was even when the Cubs played on the road. There was a lightness in Houston.

In the clubhouse, he was a kid again. He brought a bag filled with Cubs gear: warm-up jerseys and tee shirts, baseball caps and wristbands to trade with his National League teammates. He brought his camera and took pictures of the players in the clubhouse.

Before the homerun derby, he asked Rube Lovstad, American League's batting practice pitcher, if Danny could throw a few pitches in his place. When Lovstad shrugged and stepped aside, Danny stood behind a pitching net and asked Andy Bower, the American League catcher from Minnesota, to take two practice swings. Danny studied the paths of Bower's left-handed swings and nodded. He held up his right hand to let the hitter know where the ball was coming from, and Bower smiled. Danny eased in a batting practice pitch and Andy met it at the apex of his powerful swing, blasting it into the right field bleachers. Danny laughed. He raised a baseball in his left hand then, and threw another pitch to Bower in the precise and definite path of his swing and Bower roped that one into the stands as well. Bower hit two more pitches into the stands before the next batter came to the plate.

When Carmen Dye, a former World Series MVP from the Chicago White Sox, took Bower's place, Danny led him through two practice swings and fed him four homerun pitches as well. He did the same for three more batters. He moved like a tai-chi master taking balls from the basket in front of him and releasing them right and left in a constant and lyrical swirl for the American League All-Stars, who pounded every one into the stands. The crowd roared with every pitch.

And when Danny finished, the crowd stood to its feet. It whistled and screamed and clapped until Danny disappeared into the American League dugout where the American League players urged him to take a curtain call.

When he walked back into the dugout after his wave to the crowed, Carmen Dye shook his head at Danny.

"Batting practice," he said. "You got a friggin' curtain call for throwing batting practice."

Danny smiled, shrugged his shoulders, and asked Dye if he had a baseball cap he wanted to trade. Dye took off his cap and gave it to Danny.

Danny wasn't certain until he threw batting practice prior to the homerun derby, which arm he would pitch with in the All-Star game. It was only while he tossed batting practice balls to the American League sluggers—when he felt the ease and precision, the perfection of that rhythmic swirl—that he decided to use both arms. He would switch from his left to his right arm, batter to batter, without regard for where the batter stood. When he walked to the mound after the pre-game ceremonies that lasted most of the day, he was certain of nothing else.

This was the order of the nine consecutive putouts that Danny effected in the three innings he pitched for the National League All-Stars:

Top of the first:
1: Roble Pierre: grounder back to the pitcher (1-3)
2: Eduardo Lopez: pop-out to catcher (FO-2)
3: Clifton Mallik: foul-out to first base (FO-3)

Top of the second:
4: Carmen Dye: line drive to second base (L-4)
5: Sou Tokohama: line drive to third (L-5)
6: Bobby Lifka: grounder to shortstop (6-3)

Top of the third:
7: Demetrius Mobley: flyout to left field (F-7)
8: Andy Bower: flyout to center field (F-8)
9: Cecil Walker: flyout to right field (F-9)

This is how the official scorer noted the putouts for the official record of the game:

1: (1-3)
2: (FO-2)
3: (FO-3)

4: (L-4)
5: (L-5)
6: (6-3)

7: (F-7)
8: (F-8)
9: (F-9)

Of the millions of baseball fans who witnessed this three-inning event, perhaps a thousand understood its significance. Among that latter group, these two people most certainly did: Joe Brayden, the announcer for Fox Sports, and Henry Granville.

When Danny walked into the dugout to ice his arm in the bottom of the third inning, after retiring Cecil Walker with that long fly ball to the right field warning track, Brayden sighed deeply on national television.

"Oh, my," he said. "You must forgive my reticence regarding a spectacular occurrence that has developed over these past two-and-one-half innings, fans. In the interest of holding a jinx at bay I've kept the details of a remarkable feat from you. Please be patient with me as I attempt to explain.

"Danny Granville," he continued. "has just offered us a new definition for the word *perfect*. This extraordinary young rookie from Illinois, barely nineteen years old, has already participated in one flawless game this year, and now, before a national audience, seems to have extended, for us, once again, the boundaries of that word.

"For those of you who are less familiar with the finer points of the game," Brayden continued. "A diagram may be of some assistance." And on national television, then, Joe Brayden quickly rough-sketched a baseball diamond on the back of a player bio sheet, drawing stick figure players and explaining the assignment of numbers to the nine defensive positions on the field.

"More important than the fact that Danny Granville has set a perfect game into motion for the National League," Brayden said, "he has somehow managed to retire the first nine batters of the game in a way that allowed for each of the position players to participate in their numerical putout.

"I apologize," Brayden said, "If I am less than articulate in my description of this brilliant outing. In my defense, though, I dare say it has never been done in the history of baseball. Words have not yet been prepared for this.

"And even as I sit here in the booth, staring at my scorecard and at the fact of this oddity, I cannot believe that a man could perform such a feat by design.

"It's enough," Brayden continued, "that Granville retired nine of the world's best hitters. Is there *anything* this kid cannot accomplish on the mound?

"After an outing like that, the least that John Love, the manager of the National League team, could do now is allow Danny Granville to bat for himself before he leaves the game.

"That's a star out there, folks," Brayden said.

Despite the fact that Bridget, Henry, and Lori most certainly could have attended the all-star game in Houston, they watched the event together on Bridget's television at the lakeside condo. It was Bridget's idea to put the tickets up for auction on eBay and donate the money to the Uptown Baptist soup kitchen.

She grilled burgers on what Danny called the world's smallest barbeque grill on the world's smallest balcony, serving Henry and Lori on her living room couch.

Nothing seemed out of the ordinary to Henry during the first inning, but as he made notations in the same scorebook he kept for Danny's home games, he noticed, in the top of the second, what Joe Brayden must have noticed at about the same time: that Danny was retiring the American League in an order that bordered on freaky, whether Danny intended it or not. By the top of the third, Henry voiced his predictions for the outcome of each at bat.

When Demetrius Mobley walked to the plate, Henry said this to Lori and Bridget:

"This guy's gonna fly out to left."

When he did, Bridget asked how he knew.

"Lucky guess," Lori said. "He talks to the television at home, too, and he's always wrong."

When Andy Bower stepped in the batter's box, Henry said, "This guy's gonna fly out to center."

Bridget and Lori were silent when the batter flied out to center.

When Cecil Walker came to the plate, Bridget said, "Is this guy going to right field now?"

Henry looked at Bridget and smiled. "Very good, Bridget," he said. "You're beginning to catch on to this game."

"Yes, my boyfriend plays the sport," she said, and Lori smiled, placing her arm across Bridget's shoulder.

And when Walker's long fly ball fell into the glove of the right fielder at the warning track, Henry shook his head.

"Son of a gun," he said. "Son of a gun."

And as though the National League manager had heard Joe Brayden's request that Danny Granville stay in the All-Star game long enough to bat for himself, John Love pointed to Danny at the end of the dugout bench.

"Get a stick," Love said. "And get your ass at the plate."

Danny smiled. "Nice," he said.

As Danny walked to the batter's box to face Joe Lucero, the twin brother of Chuy, the American League starter, a roar exploded into the opened dome of the stadium; the hands of men, women, and children went to their ears even as they participated in the collective scream.

If Danny had never seen Lucero's slider, he might have thought it was heading straight for his helmet, but Danny had seen the pitch before. It wasn't the best one Lucero had thrown. It started breaking early and seemed to be heading further away than Lucero had probably intended. From its great breaking path Danny determined it would cross the middle-outside of the plate about knee-high. Danny swung his bat, and felt, but did not hear, the crack of the ball against it.

Through most of the flight of Danny's blast, Tuck Wilson, the American League right fielder, just sent in to replace Dye, approached the ball as though he thought he had a legitimate shot at gloving it, but as he leaped into the air something seemed to happen to the sphere as it closed in on the end of its journey: it seemed to have eyes, so deftly did it elude Wilson's glove as it sailed into the right field bleachers.

It seemed cocky to smile as Danny rounded the bases after his homerun, but he could not help it. His teammates greeted him at the plate and buried him in a swarm of National League color. When they finally returned to the dugout, Love caught Danny's eye and nodded his starting pitcher toward the field to make a curtain call. Danny walked up the dugout steps and with his right hand doffed his cap to the fans on the left side of home plate, and with his left hand, doffed his cap to the fans on the right.

Danny took a red-eye flight to Chicago from Houston and then a shuttle to his car in the O'Hare parking lot. He spent the night at his loft on Damen, and in the morning, he wore the Twins warm-up jersey from Andy Bower and pulled the White Sox cap he got from Carmen Day, low over his eyes. It was eleven A.M. when he pulled up in front of Bridget's condo on Diversey and called her from his cell phone.

"Hey," he said.

"Hey," she said, sleepy still.

"Come downstairs," he said, and Bridget quicklaughed into the phone.

"I'm not dressed, yet," she said.

"Perfect," Danny said. "I'm coming up, then."

"Is there a crowd down there?" she asked.

"No" Danny said. "I'm incognito."

"Good," she said, and five minutes later Danny tapped his knuckles softly at her condo door.

When Bridget unlocked the door, Danny opened it, flashed inside, and closed it with exaggerated quickness. He picked Bridget up into his arms and twirled her around inside her foyer.

Bridget tried to speak, tried to catch her breath through her laughter, tried to tell Danny to put her down, but even when he put her down and she tried to steady herself from the morning spin, he did not let her speak.

"Do you have any idea how much I love you?" he said, and before she could answer he said, "I don't think you do, Bridget."

He held her at her hips and leaned back as though to consider what he missed since he had seen her last, twelve days before. Memorizing her for some future portrait.

Bridget smiled. Her eyes glistened. She stood in silhouetted relief against the morning light from the kitchen window. She smiled so completely she nearly slipped over the edge of her smile and laughed.

"Look who's having a dig-me day," she said.

"That would be me," Danny said.

They had lunch on the private balcony at Caffe de Lucca, where only Artie, the owner, recognized Danny under the brilliant and deep-shadowed disguise of a White Sox cap.

Bridget laughed when the waitress, a girl named Becket, recognized her from the summer class Bridget had taught the year before. Bridget and Becket spoke about classes at the Art Institute as though Danny were not even present. He sat up with exaggerated height and flipped the bill of his cap backwards to tease Bridget into introducing him to Becket, and Bridget nearly laughed.

"Oh, I'm sorry," she said. "Danny, this is Becket. I used to teach her at the Art Institute."

"Hi," Becket said, and without another word to Danny, turned back to her former teacher and their talk of art, while Bridget smiled at Danny crossing his arms and pretending umbrage.

They drove to the house on Lathrop. Danny parked his car at the end of the block and they walked through the alley and tiptoed up the backstairs of the building and into Bridget's old apartment where they made love, where Bridget stood at her easel, wearing only Denny's warm-up jersey, and made quick sketches of Danny on the bed in his boxers.

They made love again before evening. Afterward, they tiptoed downstairs and walked around to the front of the house and knocked at the front door of the Granvilles' flat.

Lori opened the door, and Henry stood over her shoulder.

"Hey," Danny said, "What's cooking, Mom?"

Lori crossed her arms and tapped her foot on the ground.

"We were just wondering when you were going to come downstairs," she said, and Bridget slapped Danny's arm.

At dinner, Henry said only this about the All-Star game: that it was a fine game, and that only one other All-Star game ended up with 1-0 score.

"What year?" Danny asked.

"I don't know. Sixty-eight or something," Henry said.

In the morning, Danny and the Cubs flew back to Houston for a three-game set against the Astros. There, the Cubs improved their record to a league-leading 63-27. In the third game of the series, Danny threw a seventy-eight-pitch, complete and perfect game.

On the airplane ride to San Francisco that night, it seemed to Danny as though there could be no end to happiness. It seemed as though the world had been made for him—that when God, or whomever, had first come upon the excellent idea of a world, he had done so with the image of Danny Granville in his head; he had done so, laughing and smiling at the possibility of Danny Granville. It was possible, even, that God had waited this long billions of years in anticipation for that to happen.

In the dark of that morning, while the Cubs slept in their king-sized beds at the Prospect Hotel in San Francisco—while they slept the sleep of a division-leading team thirty-five games above five hundred, the sleep of a team who had a rookie switch pitcher on their team with two perfect games already on his resume—hotel employees were sliding *USA Today* newspapers across the carpet in front of their hotel doors. They would wake in the morning to an article written by a man named Michael Finnegan. They would wake to Bridget's studio sketches of Danny Granville. They would wake to a headline that read:

THE MAKING OF DANNY GRANVILLE: BEAUTIFUL FREAK

In the room next to Danny's, Mickey Wells would awaken before anyone. He would kiss a girl in the open doorway to his room, and watch her walk down the corridor away from him. He would watch her turn around for one more look and flit her fingers at him. Mickey would look at the newspaper at his feet, would see the headline, and leaning against the frame of his hotel room door, he would read Finnegan's article about a man obsessed with science and baseball, a man who had set his son on a bizarre and regimented, lifelong course of perfect symmetry. A man who had sacrificed all else for his son's switch-pitching superstardom, had channeled every ounce of energy into the development of a perfectly symmetrical world-class athlete.

Sketches of Danny were on the bottom of the front page; the measurements handwritten on one side identical to the measurements on the other. Plastered across the newspapers on a million doorsteps across the country.

Mickey would walk back in the room to his bedside table for his plastic key and gather every newspaper on the Cubs' side of the hotel, but even as he piled them in his thick arms, dumped them in the garbage can at the end of the hall, and went back for more, he knew he could not protect Danny Granville from this.

Twenty-sixth

ON A SATURDAY IN 1976, HENRY AND HIS FATHER WENT TO THE only morning White Sox game ever held at Comiskey Park. Charles Granville parked the car on 33rd and Wallace in front of Dressel's Bakery where they bought four doughnuts. On the Wallace side of the building a brown-haired boy sat on the stairs that led to the bakery apartments and stared emptily at the base of a metal trashcan at the curb in front of him. Henry and Charles sat on the ledge between the bakery entrance and the boy, and when they finished their doughnuts and cartons of milk, Henry took his father's garbage and his own and walked toward the trash can. It was there, on the sidewalk at the base of the garbage can, that Henry read the message at which the brown-haired boy had been staring.

Fuck you Mary Nelson, 1970.

Henry was barely into his teens that summer and yet his first thought, upon reading the words, was of Mr. Nelson—whom he did not know—the father of the girl whose name had been etched on the other side of a curse.

Henry looked at the boy and when their eyes met Henry managed an expression that was closer to an apology than anything, and the boy's eyes seemed to want to return something to Henry for his apology: a smile, perhaps. Or forgiveness. But nothing changed in the shape of the boy's lips. Henry nodded to the boy and shifted the trash can so that it covered all but the year of the message.

The Granvilles walked quietly to Comiskey Park that morning, Charles with his arm across Henry's shoulder part of the way and Henry wondering if Mr. Nelson bought bread and doughnuts from Dressel's, wondering if he bought a cake for Mary's First Holy

Communion there, wondering what a father might think upon seeing such a thing written about his daughter as he walked into a bakery.

And when Henry heard the report of Finnegan's article on ESPN, he thought again of the words that had been written to Mary Nelson. And when he read the headlines above Michael Finnegan's article, reprinted in the *Chicago Sun-Times* the next morning—when he saw Bridget's sketches at the bottom of the page—he thought he might finally have known what Mr. Nelson felt when he first saw that message written to his daughter.

For nearly a year, Henry had read every article about Danny that the *Sun-Times*, *The Tribune*, the *Sporting News*, and *Sports Illustrated* published. Most days it wasn't so bad. Most days the city seemed to have a crush on Danny, pumped its fist in support of him and wore his jersey on its back. But on those days when every man, woman, child, and drunken idiot on the street had a better idea than Danny of how to win a ball game—Henry wished he could just pass by the newspaper stand and not see or even care what they had written about his son that day.

But like the other days, Henry could not pass the article by. He read every word, clenched his fist into a white-knuckled weapon at Finnegan's betrayal—at Henry's own words twisted into a nightmarish story of Frankenstein and his monster. And even as he read his former student's words, Henry knew the betrayal was as much his as Finnegan's. Three times, as he read the article, Henry flipped back to the front page to torment himself at the sight of Bridget's sketches. He had even taken Bridget down with him.

Henry said nothing to Lori about the story. Between countless phone calls to reach Danny, he hoped that Lori would never hear about the article. But before the day had ended, Lori had entered into a hateful silence around the house on Lathrop, straightening conspicuously, cleaning loudly, banging the vacuum cleaner into the legs of chairs, seeing to numerous annual household projects in the course of one day, shutting windows and slamming doors, moving furniture and appliances to get at the deeper dirt of the house; cleansing their home, Henry thought, of him.

❖

After all of his work to keep Danny from seeing the newspaper—after removing every copy from the Prospect Hotel in San Francisco, it was Mickey Wells himself who knocked on Danny's door and handed him the *USA Today*.

"I threw away like fifty newspapers this morning," Mickey said, setting a cup of coffee for Danny on the desk behind him. "And then I said 'fuck it.'"

Danny took the article from Mickey and read the headline. He flipped the paper open and saw Bridget's sketches.

Danny looked up at Mickey standing at the foot of Danny's bed. "These are Bridget's drawings."

Mickey shrugged and shook his head.

Danny began to read, but stopped less than a minute into the article.

"This guy interviewed my father," Danny said. He lifted his eyes to Mickey again. "And how the hell did he get Bridget's sketches?"

Danny tossed the newspaper on the second bed in the room and finished tying his shoes. Mickey said nothing. He stood there and closed the hinged doors of the television console.

"Why can't I just play baseball?" Danny said.

Mickey said nothing.

"I can't just fucking play baseball, Mick?"

Mickey sat on the bed while Danny walked to the door and then to the window, rubbing his temples.

"Is this my life now, Mick?"

Wells said nothing.

"Is there anything about my mother in that article?" Danny said.

"No," Mickey said.

"Don't lie to me, Mickey," Danny said.

"I ain't lying," Mickey said. "I wouldn't lie about that."

On the desk next to the console Danny's cell phone rang. Mickey picked up the phone and turned to Danny.

"I don't want it," Danny said. It rang again.

"Who is it?" Danny said.

Mickey flipped open the phone.

"It's your old man."

"I don't want it," Danny said.

"Fuck it," Mickey said. "Let's get something to eat."

"Go ahead," Danny said. "I'm not hungry."

The players were quiet on the bus ride to the stadium. After Danny's off-day workout he took batting practice with the team. He considered leaving the park after taking his swings. The easy thing would have been to take a cab back to The Prospect. Or to watch the game from the clubhouse. But when he walked into the dugout after the national anthem, and felt the pre-game energy of his teammates, felt it in the sound of tightening Velcro straps and the click of metal on the dugout cement, it felt as though the game of baseball had been returned to the men who played it.

The game, Danny thought. *The game.*

At the start of the game Danny charted Jerome Saint, the opposing pitcher. He told his hitters about Saint's tendencies when he was pitching ahead of the count, and what to look for when he was pitching behind.

By the time Mickey Wells came to the plate, with one out and the bases loaded, the crowd seemed lulled into an early silence, but when Mickey hit Saint's first pitch, a middle-in fastball, into an inning-ending double play, the fans were pulled back into the game. The stadium trembled with a collective scream of delight at the quick turn from danger to safety.

Danny started at the surge of sound. Every swell in the volume of the crowd had the same effect. Every push of sound a reminder to him of the world outside: the press, the article, his father, his mother, Bridget. He wished he could fight against every distraction with silence, but every wave of sound seemed to push him with greater strength to his room at The Prospect, to his paintings of Bridget, to some greater depth within.

At every threat of the world outside, Danny reminded himself to stay inside the game. "The game," he said again. "Keep the game."

When he returned to the hotel room after a Cubs victory, there were thirty-one voice mail messages on his cell phone. He scrolled down the list of missed calls to see Bridget's name repeated a dozen times. He turned the phone off and set it on the bed. He emptied the coffee Mickey had brought him that morning and put his cell phone in the empty cup. He crumpled the cup around the cell phone and tied the plastic bag from the wastepaper basket around the cup and threw it in the bathroom trash.

On his easel, which faced the windows at the end of the room, the bones of a painting. Bridget sitting on the cement steps of the house on Lathrop resting her elbows on her knees. A cup of coffee on the step between her feet. Smiling. In the space left empty next to her, another cup: his.

Danny sat at his traveling stool before the canvas. He did not plan to work on the painting. The newspapered image of Bridget's sketches was etched so clearly into his thoughts he feared he would not be able to focus on that moment with Bridget on the porch.

It had taken less than a year for Bridget to be drawn into the vortex that Danny's life had become. And even before the article she had complained of living someone else's life.

The image of Bridget. Her fingers locked oddly: pinky at thumb. In her eyes, the suggestion of morning.

Danny worried he would not be able to paint that morning in Bridget's eyes, nor all the other things she could say with a single look:

—that the space next to her that was empty was meant for Danny;

—that just because he could sip from the same cup of coffee through all the hours of a day, she liked hers when it was too hot to drink;

—that she wanted company with her coffee: his company;

—that it was too early to be photographed in the morning; that no one should think to have a camera in his hands in the morning;

—that it was annoying to be photographed when there was a morning to be had.

But that it felt good, too. It felt good to be wanted as a photograph. At the start of a day, in the middle of living, it was nice to be wanted. To be thought of as a painting while your hair smelled of daybreak.

Danny had not planned to begin painting her. He meant only to paint the coffee cup in the space next to her. He meant only to paint his cup of coffee, minus the steam. Later, he thought, he would give the steam of his cup to hers. He would give her double steam. A double-steam latté, he would give her. But he lost himself in the painting, as he was certain he would not. He lost himself in his cup of coffee first, and then in hers, and he lost himself in her corduroyed pants—the color of sand—and he lost himself in her sweater—the color of a September sky in the morning—and he lost himself in her eyes.

Danny spent the night painting Bridget in the changing light of his hotel room, and it was only in the minutes before sleep that he remembered the article in the *USA Today*, the photo of his father on the clubhouse television.

To his right, the easeled painting of Bridget was a vague shape in the unlit night. A darkened triangle the world would never see. Bridget would not even see the painting. She was living someone else's life because Danny had made it so. And now her sketches of him had been sent into the world somehow, had become front-page news.

He would complete the painting after tomorrow night's game and send it home. He would not wake to see it in the papers one day, or on the cover of the *Sporting News*. When the team returned to Chicago he would hang it somewhere in the Damen loft where it would be safe. In the kitchen: it was a painting of the morning and it belonged to the kitchen.

He would no longer subject Bridget to the foreign life she had worried over. He would return Bridget to her own life.

As though they were still riding the crest of some greater wave than the one that menaced Danny from within, the Cubs won the second game of the series as well. In the clubhouse after the game, Mickey

Wells, Chick Molina, and Hucker Norton stood in a half-circle around Danny to keep the press from him while he dressed. Jack Daley blasted his stereo to ward off any reporters interested in talking their way through the arc of Danny's teammates to get through to him.

Trey Bennett had forbidden Daley to blast music in the clubhouse after hearing a song during spring training that he said sounded like "open mic night in hell," but when he walked into the clubhouse to find the wall of players around Danny, he ignored the explosion of heavy metal. He ignored the music, the reporters, and the players and he left the room.

When Danny returned to the Prospect Hotel he ordered room service from the hotel menu and finished his painting.

By the time the Cubs took batting practice before game three of the Giants' series, the ballpark was filled to capacity. Danny wished he had thought of earplugs. The stadium seemed louder. Not louder. It seemed *specific*. The crowd had now developed a sort of specificity. He felt as though he could look up into the stands in any direction and see a familiar face or find everyone in that section staring at him, ready to speak to him personally. He cut his warm-up short and stretched in the visitor's clubhouse.

On his way to the mound for his lefty start he looked at no one. He was afraid he would see into somebody's eyes, and that the one look would be enough to give shape to the words in that single fan's heart. Whether of sympathy or disdain or anything else, it did not matter. Danny wanted something between himself and them: a shield; a way to silence them.

As he threw his eight warm-up pitches on the mound he imagined a stadium with a sound-proofed capacity—something built into the shape of the arena to turn the voices of the fans back in so that they could hear themselves. Perhaps they would be shocked at the sound. Perhaps their voices, coming back at themselves in that way, would deafen them into silence. Maybe they would become like fans at a golf or tennis tournament—cheering between points and then sitting silently until the next moment because they realized their words had some effect on the human beings on the field.

Between innings he was reminded of the fans, but through the war of uncountable battles between pitches, their tens of thousands of voices merged into the indecipherable din of a single sound; like a dome over the stadium, he told himself. Their voices were a thing between the grass and the sky.

The score was tied at two in the seventh when Danny reached his pitch limit. Shin Taguchi relieved him, but gave up a two-run homer in the bottom of the ninth to earn the loss for the Cubs.

They went on to lose the final match-up of the four-game series against the Giants, and two days later Danny had a right-handed start against the Arizona Diamondbacks. He left the game in the bottom of the seventh with the score tied at three, but when the Cubs returned to their hotel they did so under the weight of their fourth loss in a row.

For three days that followed the article, Henry met Bridget for lunch at Freddy's Place in Cicero, where if anyone recognized him, no one would say so. On the first day Henry told Bridget what must have happened: that Finnegan had fooled Henry into spilling everything months before, and then glommed the sketches from Henry's jacket and taken everything to the papers. They commiserated over coffee and lunch like the remnant kin of a kidnapped child, Bridget counting out for Henry the times she had called Danny's cell phone, the times she had tried to get to him through Mickey Wells. Three days she cried. Three days Henry apologized to her. On the fourth day they both stopped calling Danny and Bridget told Henry to stop saying he was sorry.

"Knock it off, Henry," she said. "Don't apologize for Danny any more. He could grow up and answer his goddamn phone."

Henry waited by the phone on Sunday night after the Cubs fifth-straight loss, hoping Danny would call. Lori might have waited up with Henry in the living room if he could have torn himself away from ESPN. She had seen and heard enough of Henry and his interview with Finnegan. Neither could she stand to hear another announcer or broad-caster tell the world what he would do if he were Danny's manager.

"If I fall asleep before Danny calls," she said, "make sure you wake me up." And so Henry waited alone in the living room. He listened to a lengthy report on *Baseball Tonight* that connected pieces from the Finnegan article with Danny's self-imposed pitch limits. The analyst wondered whether Henry Granville was still exerting his influence over Danny's game, if he was still maniacal in his attempt to control every move his son made. Henry did not turn the channel. As though to accept the punishment for whatever sin the world believed he had committed, Henry listened to every word, mortifying himself like a penitent without argument.

When the telephone rang at eleven o'clock, Henry waited with his hand hovering over the phone to see if Lori would pick up first. It did not ring a second time. Henry walked to the bedroom where Lori was reading a novel with her knees raised. Lori looked up at Henry in her doorway. He shaped his mouth and eyes to the question of their son.

Danny?

Lori nodded and looked away. When Henry returned to the doorway during the next commercial Lori was speaking quietly into the phone, twirling her reading glasses in her hand. Smiling. He waited for her to look up at him and when she did he held one hand to his ear in the shape of a phone and pointed to himself with the other.

Lori turned away from the door.

On an otherwise purposeless walk to the kitchen, Henry walked past the doorway once more, looking in as he passed, and by the time he returned again the bedroom door was closed.

In the morning, Henry drank three cups of coffee and read both papers and waited for Lori to wake up.

There was an interview on page three with an animal behaviorist from Bucknell University, an expert on gene manipulation from the University of Chicago, an ethicist from Harvard, and psychologists from Penn. There was an editorial by a woman from Naperville comparing her husband to Henry Granville. A sportswriter from the *Tribune* wrote an article rebuking Finnegan, revealing him as an opportunistic and ambitious young writer willing to get his break at any cost.

Between the lines of what is right in sports journalism and what is wrong, there is room for great debate, the sportswriter wrote. *But regardless of the rules that dictate ethics in journalism, Danny Granville's fans will determine whether Michael Finnegan's articles are ever read with genuine interest again.*

Neither did the sportswriter excuse Henry for his part. He questioned Henry's reasons for revealing himself to the reporter. "Henry Granville should know better," the reporter wrote.

While a pot of decaffeinated coffee was brewing, Lori woke up and joined Henry at the kitchen table. Henry poured her a cup of coffee and spooned a teaspoon of sugar into her cup.

"Thanks," Lori said.

"Did you tell Danny I wanted to speak to him last night?" Henry said.

"He didn't want to talk to you," she said. "We didn't talk about baseball or you or Finnegan."

"Well, how is he doing?" Henry said.

"He's fine."

"He's fine?" Henry said. "That's it? He's fine?"

"He asked how Bridget was doing, and I told him she's worried about him. All we talked about was Bridget."

Lori stirred her coffee and looked at Henry.

"He'll call you when he's ready to talk," she said.

"Did he say that?" Henry said.

Lori lifted her spoon from the cup and watched the slow swirl of coffee in the wake of the spoon.

"No," she said. "He didn't say that."

Henry poured a fourth cup of coffee and began to walk toward the living room, but he changed his mind when he looked at his keys on the dining room table. He set his cup down, picked up his keys, slipped on his shoes and walked to his car at the bend of Lathrop.

He turned the key in the ignition to *accessories* and clicked on the radio. Analysts from the sports station were doing the speed opinion segment. Callers had ten seconds to make their point before one of the analysts clicked them into oblivion.

"I don't care how the Cubs win," a caller said. "As long as they win."

"Poor Danny Granville," the next caller said. "We should all be so lucky to have a monster like Henry Granville for a father."

"I had that same idea," the next caller said. "I meant to do the same thing with my son. Turn him into a switch-pitcher. It was my idea."

Henry set the windows down and leaned back in the driver's seat. If Danny didn't have it in his heart to forgive him, Henry would have that to add to his regrets in life. If Danny did have forgiveness in his heart he would come around on his own. Until then, there was nowhere to go.

On July 25th, ten days after Danny's last win, a perfect game, the Chicago Cubs flew to St. Louis, Missouri, for a three-game series against the Cardinals.

When Danny took the mound to start the series he did his best to shut his ears against the world, but the high pitch of a young boy's voice pulled away from the collective roar of the rest. A single voice pierced the air. Danny did not look toward the voice, but in the seated sea of red in the stands behind home plate, a white-jerseyed blur stood apart and yelled, "Freak!"

The boy waved his hands and yelled again.

Danny spun the ball loosely in his hand. Now there was this. He was a freak. In the eyes of at least one boy, he was a freak. And how many others in the world felt the same way? Felt his father was a mad scientist—a freakmaker—and felt his girlfriend was in collusion as well? Danny had been in the public eye long enough to know how these things worked with fans. It was not anger he felt toward his father, or Bridget—he was certain there was a simple explanation for all of it. It wasn't even anger he felt for Finnegan. It was the incapacity of the world to care enough about him to see him for what he was, to know him. And was there any way the world would ever know him for more than what he did on the diamond?

"Freak!"

When he heard the word *freak* a third time, the boy's image came to Danny. He could no sooner disremember the face of the boy than he could his voice. He could not not lose that voice among the throng of red and blue.

Though the boy was silenced after his third utterance of the word, the echo played in Danny's head long after. He could not separate his memory of the word from the word itself. He spent nineteen pitches in the first inning, and seventeen more in the second. In the third inning he walked the first batter, and retired the next two hitters before throwing a first-pitch fastball that was roped into deep left field for a run-scoring double. By the end of the third inning Danny had already thrown fifty-three pitches—every one of them accompanied by the freaksong of the boy in white.

The Cardinals were still ahead 1-0 with two outs in the fifth when Danny closed in on his eighty-pitch limit. He walked the third batter of the inning and before Danny threw his first pitch to the next man at the plate, Phil Sharp signaled time-out to the plate umpire and jogged to the mound.

"You're at seventy-eight," Sharp said,

"I know," Danny said.

"I got support for you in the pen," Sharp said.

"I know," Danny said.

"You want I should call one of them in?" Sharp said.

"Not yet," Danny said.

"You want to pitch to this guy?" Sharp said, nodding at the plate.

"Yeah," Danny said. "I'm good."

"Just say the word," Sharp said.

Danny nodded and showed his glove to Mickey Wells behind the plate.

His next four pitches were balls. There were two men on with two outs and Danny had thrown eighty-two pitches.

The Cardinals' Ty Bail stood in the box while Danny waved off Phil Sharp at the dugout steps. Bail took two slow practice swings with his eyes locked on Danny's left hand. It was then that something stronger than sound—a violent and deafening silent scream beneath and beyond the roar of tens of thousands in Busch Stadium—a usurper of sound, raged inside Danny's head. The sound of a freight train, perhaps, just inches beneath the mix of clay and dirt into which his cleats had purchase. Sound enough to kill all other sound but the freaksong of a boy.

In the batter's box Ty Bail crowding the plate.

In Danny's head the silent scream, a gray and inarticulate mass of some screaming thing.

In Danny's head the piercing *FREAK!* of the boy in white, now a sound only in memory.

In Danny's head the image of a fallen man. Ty Bail's bat falling over his shoulder and his hands flying to his throat.

The game, Danny said, his words reaching no one.

Keep the game.

He shook off the image of the fallen man and looked at Mickey Wells crouching at the plate and calling for a fastball high and tight to push Bail away from the plate.

The game.

In his head, though, the scream.

In his head the *FREAK!* of the boy in white.

In his head the image of Ty Bail on the ground.

Against the scream, against the vision, against the crowd, and against the voice of the boy, Danny reeled back and loosened his fingers from a grip he could not explain. In the less than half-second of time between the frictive and certain release of the ball from his fingers and thumb and its violent concussive end at the neck of Ty Bail ticked thousands of conspicuous calibrations of time.

Danny had meant to author a two-seam fastball but his fingers were not his own. His right foot had not yet touched the dirt in front of the mound when he felt, or heard, he wasn't certain—what seemed then like the absolute erasure of sound. There was either a hellish suction of sound, or else its opposite: the complete amalgamation of all of sound—like the deafening *whoompf* of some great and terrible winged creature amplified to an unbearable din.

His right foot stuttered above the ground as though it couldn't wait to land, as though it sought midair purchase to more quickly propel him toward the baseball just missiled from his fingers so that he might recall the baseball before it hammered against the side of Ty Bail's neck, before it knocked the batter to the ground in the chalked rectangle of dirt just sixty feet away.

Danny did not hear the gasp of sound that filled the stadium as Ty Bail fell to the ground, his hands at the side of his neck, his legs writhing violently from one side of home plate to the other; neither did he hear the booing thousands as he removed his glove and dropped it on the mound, as one foot impelled him toward the dugout and the other toward Bail.

Danny heard nothing. His ears felt submerged beneath water, below an invisible surface line, above which he could make out only the muddled and flooded enormous hum throated by forty-thousand red and blue humans.

Mickey stepped around the kneeling crowd gathering around the fallen man and walked toward the staggering figure of Danny Granville, urging him toward the visitor's dugout but to no other certainty.

Twenty-seventh

DANNY COULD NOT SAY HOW HE KNEW IT WAS TREY BENNETT knocking at his door that night just after ten, but he was less surprised at this certainty than at the sound of the knock; for it was then that he realized his ears had finally unpopped. Before answering the door, he turned on the television and raised the remote volume until he was confident in the truth of his returned hearing. When he tossed the remote on the bed and it bounced toward the edge, Danny caught sight of his painting. A sketch still. The ghost of a figure. She would soon be standing over a pot of oatmeal he had not yet drawn, with her hand at her hip. A dishtowel on her shoulder.

He took the canvas off the easel and leaned it against the wall. Folded the easel and set it on the floor at the foot of the bed.

At the next knock Danny opened the door for Bennett without looking up. He walked to the bed without looking back.

Bennett sat on the second bed and watched the television, a long point played out on the blue surface of an indoor tennis court. The point that followed ended after two hits.

"Long point, short point," Bennett said.

"I'm sorry?" Danny said.

"That's what they say at the club when that happens," Bennett said. "Long point, short point."

"I didn't know you played," Danny said.

"When I can," Bennett said.

Danny nodded. "Long point, short point. It's kind of true," he said.

Bennett worried a piece of skin at the edge of a fingernail, and Danny lay back with his fingers locked between his head and the pillow.

"Bail's gonna be all right," Bennett said.

Danny stared at the television and said nothing.

Bennett stood and turned the volume down on the television.

"I want you to go back to Chicago tomorrow," Bennett said.

"I'm fine," Danny said.

"I want you to sit out the series against the Reds, too," Bennett said.

"I'm not going to do that," Danny said. "I'm fine."

"Maybe so," Bennett said. "But I'm not about to take a chance on you. Stay in shape and join us again for Philadelphia on the thirtieth. I'll have you come in for an inning or two in that series against the Phillies if you're ready to go."

"I'm fine, Skip," Danny said. "I'm gonna be fine."

"There'll be a car for you downstairs at ten," Bennett said. "I called up Wishnick from Iowa and we'll do what we can to stay in this race until you're ready to come back. By the time we get to New York that first weekend in August, I'll need you to be ready to go with both arms."

When Bennett returned to his own room Danny considered calling Bridget. Maybe he'd see her in Chicago. Maybe he'd tell her about the loft and apologize for not calling.

He called Decker instead and left a message for him on his cell phone, asking him if he wouldn't mind getting groceries for a few days and bringing them to the Damen loft. He told him to bring his glove and his catcher's equipment, too.

Then Danny returned his easel to the space at the window, and his canvas to the easel, and he painted. With nothing more than a flight home expected of him on the day that followed he painted through the night. And when a shard of the first light of the Missouri morning appeared at the weighted hem of the hotel drapes he was still standing at his easel, bringing Bridget to life in the kitchen of his painting. He opened the curtains and the light to Bridget then, and painted until the image was complete.

After breakfast in his room he took the painting to the front desk with instructions to have it sent to Chicago, he bought a Cardinals baseball cap at the hotel gift shop, shaped an arc into the bill and slept in the cab. He awoke at the airport and fell asleep seconds after buckling himself into his seat on the plane.

He had not slept more than thirty minutes when he flinched awake at the immense and propulsive thrust of the accelerating airplane, the sound too similar to the silent scream to ignore. He wondered if the sound had returned once again to warn him.

When the elevator door opened up to Danny's loft, Decker was putting away the groceries. He had a loaf of Italian bread in one hand and a half-gallon of ice cream in the other. He had a pretzel rod in the easy bite of his teeth, like a gangster with a cigar, and one above each ear like carpenter's pencils.

The sight of his old friend in the light of Danny's open refrigerator, and Decker's look of feigned embarrassment, as though he'd been discovered in a moment he had hoped would be kept secret from the world, made Danny smile and then laugh. And before Patrick altered his frozen expression or had even breathed, without a warning of any kind, or any observable transition from one emotion to another, Danny stepped out of the elevator and into his apartment, set his equipment bag on the floor of the loft, and cried. Pressed his hand against his brow and let forth a weeping such as he had never known.

Patrick opened the freezer and set the ice cream on the lowest rack inside the door. He put the loaf of bread on the table and untoothed the pretzel cigar. And with the pretzels over his ears he walked to Danny at the loft elevator and hugged his old friend, held the shuddering and weeping body of his friend in his arms and told him it was going to be all right.

"Hey, hey, hey," he said. "It's gonna be okay, Danny Boy. It's gonna be okay."

❖

Henry went to each game of the Cincinnati series when the Cubs returned to Chicago. He had heard, of course, in several of the dozens of articles he had read, or on sports radio, or ESPN, that Danny was sitting out the Reds' series, but he thought he might catch him in the bullpen at one of the games, or charting pitchers from the dugout. He did not know that Bennett had told him to stay home for the series. If he had known Danny was not at the park, he would have wondered where he was. Henry was still unaware that Danny even had a home. But even as Henry strained his neck over heads in section 104, Danny was working out with Patrick in the voluminous space of the Damen loft.

Henry did not keep a scorecard through the series. Listening to the announcers speak through the earphones of his portable radio, he watched the game with perhaps half of his heart. On the Score radio's *Baseball Hour* before the opening game of the Reds' series, Steve Jordan, the program's baseball expert, took calls from listeners. The first caller said the Cubs had no chance without Danny, and they couldn't risk falling behind anymore before starting him.

"He should start the second game like he was supposed to do before that stupid article came out," the caller said.

Jordan thanked the caller from Canaryville and addressed his listeners.

"Look," he said. "I know you Cub fans out there have been waiting a hundred years for the baseball to come along—I have, too."

Jordan paused for what seemed to Henry like ten long seconds of radio time.

"I've talked to more than a few pretty good baseball people out there who are looking at this situation a little bit different than you Cub fans out there," he continued.

"Look," he said. "This guy shares a perfect game with Hucker Norton less than two weeks ago, right? Then he goes out and throws three miracle innings at the All-Star game against the American League's best hitters—against the best hitters in the world, right? And then he follows that up with another perfect game, this time *solo*.

"You don't do that without having impeccable control," Jordan said.

"Then the guy gets a little bad press, it pulls his family in, pulls his girlfriend in, and all of a sudden he's a freak and he's under an enormous amount of stress. *Celebrity stress.* And he breaks down, and before you know it, this kid with unimpeachable control, hits Ty Bail in the neck.

"An inch higher," Jordan said, "and Bail ain't getting up.

"That ball doesn't carom off his shoulder first, and then the low arc of the ear protection on his helmet, and Danny Granville's a killer.

"There's more than a handful of baseball people saying that right now he might be a danger to himself and he might be a danger to every batter who faces him.

"Look," he continued. "He's the best player the Cubs have had for a million years. Maybe the best player in baseball. But he's nineteen years old. He's as big a celebrity as a nineteen-year-old kid could be.

"The Cubs are one-and-eight in their last nine games," Jordan said. "I'm gonna say this to you again, Cub fans. If you're waiting for baseball Jesus, don't hold your breath. Maybe this guy is the one, but right now he's a nineteen-year-old with two cannons for arms. Right now he's a young man with a lot on his mind. He ain't your Messiah."

Danny and Decker watched the second game of the Cincinnati series from a hotel in St. Louis after visiting with Ty Bail on his last afternoon at the hospital. Danny brought him a Cubs cap and Bail gave him a Cardinals cap and they traded jerseys, too. They wore them at the hospital and promised to keep the event secret. Before they left, the men shook hands and warned each other they would be wearing the proper uniforms when they saw each other next.

On July 30th, Danny met up with the Cubs in Philadelphia. He took Patrick with him and they stayed at a hotel across town from the team to avoid the press. Through the three-game series they went to the ballpark two hours before the team arrived to help Danny prepare for a left-handed start against the Mets on August 1st, in the first of a four-game series.

In the bullpen at Shea, Danny told Phil Sharp he felt great, told him he hadn't felt that good in a long time.

In the dugout he thanked Bennett for forcing him to rest those few days in Chicago, and just before the game he told Mickey he felt good.

"My skin is tingling," Danny said. "I think I'm back, Mick."

"Welcome back," Mickey said, and he embraced Danny.

But with Danny's first step onto the grass infield, his ears plugged again. He forced a yawn to pop it back to life, but still the stadium sounded as though he listened to it from below water.

He walked to the rubber anyway, not certain what would happen once he ascended the mound. Was it a protective measure? he wondered. Was the silence meant to protect him from the crowd? To numb him to the barbed scream of some idiot fan? But if there were a reason for the silent scream, if it came to warn him of some coming thing, would the warning penetrate the hearing shield that had returned? Or had the vision shifted its shape? Was this the new warning?

And on the mound at Shea Stadium—with Mickey Wells crouched behind the plate, punching his fist into his glove, the masked umpire with his hands behind his back leaning toward Danny, and Brian Kamin at the plate, the barrel of his bat swaying like a metronome above his head, Danny Granville froze. He stood on the mound like a frozen child until Phil Sharp and Trey Bennett walked to the mound and urged him back to the dugout, in a silent and senseless confusion, deaf to the boos of New York.

By the time he returned to his room at the Stanford Hotel on 32nd Street his hearing had returned. And when the elevator opened on the twelfth floor he turned into his hallway to find Bridget sitting outside his room in a folding chair.

She stood in the dimly lit hallway and Danny stopped before reaching her.

"I didn't expect you so soon," she said.

"I didn't expect you at all," he said.

"Patrick finally told me where to find you," she said. "He keeps a pretty good secret."

"He's a good friend," Danny said.

"You have others," Bridget said, and Danny might have nodded.

He let her in the room. He set his bag on the floor and sat on the bed. Bridget stood looking down at him.

"You don't have to say a thing," she said. "You don't have to say another word to me for the rest of your life. But you're going to listen to me. Your father is a wreck back home, Danny. He's like the walking dead."

Danny sat on the bed looking at a spot on the wine-colored carpet.

"So, if you're pissed at me and never want to see me again, fine, Danny. But if you're going to cry about how you're a victim, get a grip, Danny. And if you want to lump me in with the rest of the world and ignore me, and what we have together, that's fine. But your mother and father are walking around like shells back home, and you can bitch all you want, but look at your life a little bit at least and tell me how rotten you really think it is.

"Look at you, Danny," she said. "There's a fucking world going on out there and there are other people in it. If you can't handle the spotlight, Danny, then get out of it.

"You're not doing anybody a favor by playing baseball. Really."

Bridget stood with her hand on the doorknob and looked at Danny. In the silent and yellow light of the room she allowed minutes to pass without speaking.

She opened the door then, and Danny braced himself at the thought of it banging shut, but Bridget did not slam the door. She closed it quietly behind her.

When Danny walked out into the hallway seconds later, Bridget had already turned toward the elevator. Danny found her standing with her finger at the lighted down button of the elevator.

"Could you stay here tonight?" Danny said to her silhouette. Bridget did not turn around.

"No," she said. "I can't."

"I miss you," Danny said, and still, Bridget did not turn around.

"I have proof," Danny said, and Bridget turned her head to the side to look at him. In his hand he held a piece of hotel stationery on which was written the address of the Damen Avenue loft. The paper was folded around a key.

Bridget looked in his hand and then into his eyes. The elevator doors opened.

"Just take it," Danny said. "Please."

Bridget took the packet and entered the elevator. She did not look up at him until the doors were just about to meet in the middle of the elevator space.

In the morning, Danny showered but did not shave. While he was in the bathroom the phone rang. He toweled himself dry as he listened to the message from Trey Bennett.

"Hang in there, Danny," he said. "We'll give it another shot tonight."

Danny dressed in shorts and an Old Navy tee shirt and pulled a Cubs cap out of his bag, staring at it before putting it on. He rode the service elevator to the lobby, and walked out the door to 32nd Street, into a gray and shadowy, indifferent city. Its businessmen and smokers, its vegetarians and pickpockets, its artists and panhandlers. Its ignorers.

He bought a Mets cap at a sports store two blocks away from the Stanford. He put his Cubs hat in his back pocket and pulled the Mets cap low over his eyes.

In front of a turquoise and pink diner a grease-colored man who might have been black or white pulled a cup from a garbage can. He removed the plastic lid and straw and looked inside. He swirled the liquid inside the cup and sniffed it. He threw the lid and straw on the ground and lifted the cup to his mouth. The lump of his throat rose and fell as he drank from the cup. He flinched at the taste of it and wiped his mouth with the sleeve of his greasy coat.

On his way into a coffee shop on Broadway, Danny apologized to a panhandler for having no money. Inside, he got cash from an ATM machine and bought an iced espresso. When he returned to Broadway the panhandler was gone.

· An aproned man in a deli called Danny *pal* when he ordered a sandwich.

"What can I get for you, pal?" he said.

A boy with his father did a doubletake in Danny's direction, and Danny pulled his cap lower and ate his sandwich facing the wall at the counter.

At the corner of 34th and Seventh an old woman stood facing the long sidewalk away from the intersection. When she looked Danny's way he could see she had blood in her eyes.

"What the fuck you looking?" she said, and Danny looked away. When he turned back to her she was no longer looking at him.

The woman was holding a cantaloupe as though it were a bowling ball. She varied between holding it at her side and resting it at her chest in the palms of both hands as though she were preparing to bowl it along seventh Avenue.

When she held it at her chest she swore at it.

"Asshole!" she screamed. "Fucking whore!"

When he walked past the 34th Street entrance to Macy's between seventh and Broadway, the world went silent again. But it was not the plugged silence that had come upon at the Mets game the day before. Below the sound of the New York streets, below the sound of panhandling and swearing women, below the taxis and cars and horns and whistles and the black steps of a million shoes, the world went silent and Danny put his hands to his ears at the deafening press of the silent scream.

Prepared for the silent scream for the first time in his life, Danny looked in every direction. He pulled his hands from his ears and braced himself against the internal torment. He looked around in an attempt to find its source, to learn what warning was to come, but there was only New York.

The scream grew louder as Danny approached the revolving doors of Macy's. The unending swivel—a constant turning of accept and release, accept and release. Inside the revolving chamber the scream seemed to grow, and an image flashed behind his closed eyes. An explosion from inside the store. He stayed within the moving doors through another revolution to be certain of the pull of the scream. When he stepped out again out onto 34th Street, he felt an easing away from the pain. He could just keep walking, he told himself. He could just keep walking. The further he removed himself from the scream, the further he removed himself from the pain.

Danny entered the revolving doors once more to return the image of the explosion to the scream inside his head.

He re-entered the store to the growing sound of the silent scream, the din of imminent chaos. The flash of an exploding vision when he closed his eyes. No. Not this time. His eyes were open for this explosion. It was real this time. A fire. Smoke. But why had no one else seen it?

Pulled by the vision and the scream into the store once again, Danny approached a woman he passed with a child strapped to her back. He knew nothing as he passed the woman except that he had to tell her to leave the building.

"Leave the store, now," he said to the woman. But she was not convinced. "Men with guns have entered the store," he said. "Leave the store, now," he said, and the woman took her child by the arm as though Danny were the man with the gun and she hurried toward the exit.

Deafeningly louder then, the scream.

"There's going to be trouble," he said to three women he passed. "Leave the store immediately."

Instinctively they gripped their purses tightly to their bodies, and backed away from Danny but did not move toward the exit.

The silent scream beneath everything.

"Get the fuck out of the building," Danny said to them. "Now."

He felt the scream now. Felt the scream in his chest. Felt its heat inflaming him from within. It was expanding in his chest. The sound filling his head. He fought back the impulse to put his hands to his ears.

"Get the fuck out of the store!" Danny shouted to two teenage boys.

Another explosion on the screen inside his screaming head. There was another explosion coming. He ran to the boys and pushed them toward the exit.

Afraid he would not be able to clear the store completely, and worried that the scream would intensify to some unhearable degree, Danny ran to a young woman behind the register in men's wear.

"Two men with guns have entered the store," Danny said. "Clear this place, now!"

The young woman stood and said nothing.

Danny lifted the bill of his cap. "I'm not lying to you," he said. Even as he began to speak he felt the idiocy of the only thing he felt he had to convince the woman of his sanity.

"My name is Danny Granville," he said, "and I play professional baseball. I am not lying to you."

He held out his hat and his name to her, like an idiot, but he had nothing else.

"There are terrorists in the store," he said. "They have guns and bombs."

The woman stood there speechless and did nothing.

"Now!" Danny growled. "Get a fucking security security guard on the phone, now! And if you've got an alarm back there, press it or pull it or whatever the fuck you have to do, and do it now!"

When Danny thought the first level was cleared, he ran up the escalator to the second level and jumped around when a security guard, a man in his mid-twenties, tapped Danny's upper arm.

Danny took off his cap.

"Listen," he said. "Do you know who I am?"

"Holy shit," the guard said. "It is you!"

"I know this sounds crazy," Danny said. "But I know something bad is about to happen here. There are two guys with guns and bombs in the building. I saw them walk in. We gotta get these people out of here fast," Danny said.

"I can't tell you anything else now," Danny said. "But we gotta move."

"Let's go," the guard said, and he pressed a button on his radio. As Danny continued warning shoppers on the second level a piercing alarm bleated through the building. Shoppers—screaming—ran from the store. Seconds later, what had once existed only as a vision of terrible sound in Danny's head burst its violent and definite way into the real world, quaking the building somewhere below the second floor of the Macy's.

Danny carried a boy out into the street, his mother screaming at Danny's side, the boy staring at Danny the whole time. Danny put his Mets cap on the kid's head after setting him on the curb. The wail of fire engines in the distance. The screams of women. Panic. The deafening scream within still pressing against him like a weighted thing.

The boy removed the cap Danny had given him and looked at the "NY" on its riser. Danny took his Cubs cap from his back pocket and when he handed it to the boy, the boy took it without smiling and returned the Mets hat.

Danny ran back to Macy's and pulled a fat man in a business suit bleeding from his ears from under a rack of autumn jackets. He brought the fat man to the curb next to the boy. On his way back into Macy's he heard the boy speak to the man.

"That was Danny Granville who saved you, mister," he said.

Inside Macy's, a woman with her sons, two young boys.

A girl, crying, alone. Calling her mother.

An old woman in Danny's arms.

Soot, fire, and smoke filled the store. Dozens of shoppers running in panic from Macy's as the fire department arrived.

Another explosion inside the store. A circular rack of men's shirts spinning near the ceiling, its shirts flying out in the centrifugal spin.

Danny returned to the building countless times, growing less recognizable in each trip through the soot churning forth from the building.

The earth shifted beneath New York, and a new scream. The back end of the building collapsing further into itself.

Another vision, a woman trapped. Danny, covered in soot, entered the building one last time. Smoke, fire. A rack of clothes aflame to his left, the weight of a fallen shelf at a woman's waist. Danny freed her and carried her to the door.

Seconds later, behind the last wave of rescued civilians leaving the building in a final fog of smoke and dust, the ground trembled one last time and the building collapsed.

News of the Macy's tragedy covered the world instantly. The baseball commissioner conferenced with major league owners to consider canceling the game at Shea Stadium. To the mixed reactions of the world, the commissioner decided the games would go on as scheduled.

What the commissioner would not know for some time was that Danny Granville would not show up for his scheduled start at Shea.

During the pre-game, the Jumbotron aired news of the tragedy. A cashier, a rescued boy, a fat man, a mother and a child were swearing to reporters that Danny Granville was at Macy's that afternoon; that he had saved them from certain death.

"I thought he was crazy," the cashier said. "I think he swore at me." She began to cry. "He saved my life," she said.

"He gave me a Mets cap," the boy said. "I was like, what was he doing with a Mets cap on? And then he smiled and gave me a Cubs cap from his pocket." The boy went silent then. His lips clenched into muscles and his eyes tightened and he put his hands to his eyes and shook his head. His mother waved the camera away.

When the Jumbotron turned off there was no sound at Shea then. No sound. In a stadium filled with tens of thousands of men and women and children there was no sound. And not a man, woman, or child among them seemed to know what to do until the Irish tenor scheduled to sing the National Anthem stepped solemnly and silently onto the field and began to sing.

It would not be the National Anthem that filled the stadium that evening, but "America the Beautiful." And there would be no complaint among the tens of thousands. No one among them would be compelled to set the tenor straight that night. When the tenor completed his song there would be thousands who wished another verse had been added. And afterward, there would be no need for someone in charge to request a moment of silence. The tenor stayed on the field long after the unrequested silence was granted.

Along the foul lines the players of the Cubs and Mets remained on the field.

Stood silent on the infield grass of Shea Stadium.

Stood silent in the direction of the American flag.

Stood silent.

They lifted no bat.

They tossed no ball.

Silently they stood.

And behind them, some fifty thousand others stood silently as well.

Stood silently with the uniformed men on the diamond below them.

A silence, not unlike the silence at Shea Stadium, not unlike the silence over all of New York, happened upon Chicago as well. At the coffee shop in Forest Park the mayor blew softly on his lidless and steaming cup of coffee. On the table before him, the Saturday morning paper. He did not read the stories below the headlines.

TERROR AT MACY'S: TWENTY-THREE DEAD

SEARCH FOR BODIES CONTINUES

A CITY DEEP IN SORROW. AGAIN.

PLAYERS DEFY COMMISSIONER, METS/CUBS GAME NOT PLAYED

GRANVILLE FEARED DEAD

RESCUED TELL HEROIC TALES OF PLAYER WHO SAVED THEM

In Forest Park on Saturday, Lori and Henry Granville sat silently on the couch, Lori's head resting on Henry's shoulder, her folded hands held in the praying shape of his own.

When the elevator doors opened up to the loft on Sunday afternoon, they opened up to Bridget Pentecoff lying on the couch with her cheek against a tear-dampened pillow. Later that night, long after the joy that spilled from her throat and her eyes, and the heart she thought had been stolen, she would tell Danny how she had entered the loft and had stumbled back into the doors closing silently behind her to find the proof he had mentioned in New York. Countless images of her visage stared back at her. Were there hundreds of them? A cache of paintings and sketches of her held to every wall, leaning in the spaces between every window, hanging from every squared pillar. Bridget sleeping, Bridget at windows, sitting cross-legged here, sipping coffee there, napping on couches, posing on steps, sticking her tongue out in a tease to the loft.

She stood there, it seemed, for hours. Until the morning sun shifted across the loft and had become the afternoon, until the afternoon sun dipped behind the building across the street and had become the evening, until she could stand without gasping beneath a wash of tears, until she could take her hand slowly away from her heart with some measure of confidence that it would not burst through what seemed all day like the skimpy certainty of bone and skin.

She would tell Danny how she had spent all of Friday and all of

Saturday on that couch in the Damen loft. Two days she had spent considering what world she might still have lived in if only she had spent Thursday night with Danny as he had asked her. She had been considering it still when the elevator doors opened up behind her and spilled forth Danny Granville like a miracle.

Later still, Bridget would recall what emotion filled her. Chest first, it filled her. A surge of something up through her chest and flooding through her throat and into her eyes. She felt it in the back of her head as well. She would tell Danny she suspected that great and profound sadness came from the same place in the human soul as great and untroubled joy, for at some level there seemed no difference in the burst of tears that exploded from her when she saw Danny at the elevator doors and the bursts that came with her fear that he was dead.

Only two people in the world knew Danny was still alive at that moment, and yet they held that secret in the space between them on the couch in the Damen loft while Danny told her what he could recall of Friday.

There had been witnesses. A cashier. A security guard. A boy and his mother. The fat man. And others. He could leave this life if he wanted to. He could go to some other place and begin again. He could do that.

And he walked backwards then. Away from the building. He watched the smoldering ruins in a city still smoldering from other fires. A city behind him and around him. A world.

"I remember saying this to myself," he said to Bridget. But he could not put words to things he had said.

"What?" Bridget said. "What did you say?"

Danny only shook his head and pressed his teeth against themselves.

He could tell her nothing else of Friday night, nothing of Saturday.

After hours in Bridget's arms, Danny sat on the edge of the couch and brushed his hand against her tear-dried face.

"I'm going to take a shower," he said. "Please don't go away, Bridget."

"Oh, Danny," she said.

And Bridget lifted her hand to Danny's face.

"I'm not going anywhere," she said.

"Will you call my mother and father?" Danny said. "Give them the address and tell them I'm okay."

"Okay," Bridget said.

"Tell them I'm still here," Danny said. "I'm still here."